Even Sinners Have Souls

EVEN SINNERS HAVE SOULS TOO

darrell king

tysha

victor l. martin

michel moore

Introduction by k'wan

Edited by e.n. joy

Published by End of the Rainbow Projects
P.O. Box 298238
Columbus, OH 43229

Big Homie©Copyright 2009 by Darrell King
Ghetto Luv©Copyright 2009 by Tysha
Shana's Smile©Copyright 2009 by Victor L. Martin
Ya Reap©Copyright 2009 by Michel Moore

Typsetting by Kevin J. Calloway
kraycool2002@yahoo.com

ISBN: 0-9706726-5-9

First Printing September 2009
Printed in the United States of America

10 9 8 7 6 5 4 3 2 1

Submit Orders to:
End of the Rainbow Projects
P.O. Box 298238
Columbus, OH 43229
614-806-6204

Library of Congress Catalog Number 2009925011

ACKNOWLEDGMENTS

Giving all Honor and Glory to God for putting a story in each author's spirit that may touch someone's life, change someone's life, or save someone's life. Not only save their life, but more importantly, save their soul.

Amen

DEDICATIONS

This project is dedicated to Anthony Jamal Morgan of Columbus, Ohio December 6, 1988 – Mother's Day 2007. Rest In Heaven.

Big Homie is dedicated to all the lives of black men, women and children senselessly lost in the seemingly never ending street wars of South Central Los Angeles and abroad. I also dedicate this short story to documentary filmmaker Stacy Peralta, NBA star Baron Davis, as well as Stephen Luczo, who together have produced perhaps, in my opinion, the most poignant documentary film about the undisclosed world of two powerful and deadly gangs...*Crips and Bloods: Made in America.* An excellent, must see film!

-DARRELL KING

Ya Reap is dedicated to those always struggling to do 'what is considered right'. I want to thank the Almighty Creator for His hand in guiding me time and time again in the correct direction. He and He alone knows my true heart. Pray 4 Detroit.

-MICHEL MOORE

Ghetto Luv is dedicated to the memory of my cousin, Dwayne (Twin) Smith, who was my biggest fan. I also dedicate this project to my two sons, Je'Vohn M. Hill & Je'Ronn M. (Reese) Hill. You both encourage me to improve, have faith and to never settle for less in life.

-TYSHA

Shana's Smile is dedicated to my mother, Sandra J. Martin, sisters Angela R. Martin and Tremika Smith, niece Jizzy Martin, nephew Dominique Covington, future brother-in-law Alexander A.K.A. Duke, and my future wife... you know who you are. I love you all. Revelation 2:10.

-VICTOR L. MARTIN

Good and upright is the LORD: therefore will He teach sinners in the way.

-Psalm 25:8

"Oh, Sinner Man"

By K'Wan

"Oh, sinner man, where you gonna run to all on that day?...Run to the Lord...Lord, won't you hide me all on that day?" -Nina Simone

Every time I heard that song I always felt like Nina was speaking to me, and when I got old enough, and wise enough, to reflect on my life and see the kinks in my armor, I realized that she was.

Liar, thief, sinner, animal...I've been all of these things at one time or another; while growing up and even now. Sometimes it's an accurate assessment, but in most cases it's just folks being bitter because I'm trying to make the most out of the time we're allowed here on earth. For those of you who aren't familiar with me, my name is K'Wan. I'm blessed enough to say that I'm the author of almost a dozen novels, most of them bestsellers, and a contributing author to three anthologies at the time of this writing. But I'm not here to talk about me. You can figure out who I am on your own time.

When Joy reached out to me about contributing to this project I thought she had fell and bumped her head. With as much dirt as I've done, what could I possibly have to contribute? I turned down a spot in the anthology, but I've known Joy as well as some of the authors featured for a long time, and I wanted to help out, so I agreed to do the foreword. The funny thing is that after I signed on to do it, I found myself at a loss for words. Can you believe it; the so-called master of the pen couldn't lay his game down? It was the first time since I've been writing that I couldn't muster a thought.

So I found myself staring at a blank page for the next few days. Then the days turned into weeks, and the weeks into months. It got to the point where I started to think that I had sold these people a dream, and I wouldn't be able to deliver. But as with all my work, failure is never an option. See, with street books, it's second nature. The animal is never too far removed from the jungle, so I could draw on it for inspiration, but this was different. The theme of this project wasn't really about the game and hard luck; it was about the human soul; something that still to this day confuses me to no end. To truly bless this project, as I was so entrusted to do, I had to not only analyze my relationship with Him, but my relationship with *me*.

For as long as I can remember, I've rebelled against religion, or anything else that represented order for that matter. My father taught me and put me on the path of Islam when I was born, and my grandmother quoted the Bible between his frequent trips to prison. I was twisted from the beginning, so it's little wonder that I managed to slip through the cracks. I've always believed in a higher power, but to keep it 100 with you, the only thing I worshiped back in those days was a dollar. The sun shined out of the butts (of course, this wasn't the term K'Wan used) of the cats with bread, while the broke folks were forever destined to sit in the shade. As a shorty, I wanted to get rich quick and I didn't too much care about the tab I was running up in the process...until the devil came to collect.

Most of my friends sold drugs, but I didn't have the patience to stand around and deal with all of the drama that came along with that, so I jacked for mine. I'd rather have ganked it than earned it, not like slinging poison is the equivalent of a nine-to-five, but you know what I mean. I got into so much foolishness as a teenager and young adult that I could fill this whole book up talking about it, not because I was such a brilliant criminal, but because I was too stupid to understand that I wasn't! God and I both know that if physics ruled over divine intervention, there'd never have been a *Gangsta* to launch my career, because I'd have gone on to my reward a long time ago, but I'm here. I lived life leaning on my rabbit's foot, sleeping on what was going on around me. But with the turn of the century, I got my wake up call.

Some say that one life leaves the world for another, and it played out similarly with my mother and daughter. One left in pain so that the other could come in joy; exchanging faces with the transfer of souls. With my mother being diagnosed with cancer, and the impending birth of my first daughter, I fell into a deep depression. During this time, I welcomed the harsh burn of alcohol more than anything else. Those were hard times for me, and more often than not, the long sleep looked more appealing than the long walk into manhood.

The problems in my life were so overwhelming that I felt like I couldn't breathe, and the more I drank, the lower I sank. I needed to dump this load that I was carrying or it would surely consume me, so I turned to one of my mother's favorite past times-writing. I had toyed with it a time or two prior, but writing never motivated me like it did my mother. But as my mother got weaker, the voice in my head begging to be heard became louder. I didn't know it at the time, but this would be a defining moment in my life.

At the start, it was little more than ramblings scribbled on torn paper bags...then a spiral notebook. Eventually, these ramblings turned into coherent thoughts on a computer screen. All I did was drink, write and make trips to the hospital. Between my writing and my drinking, I had found a place where I wasn't hurting and where I could express what I was going through without fear of judgment. This was my memoir, the story of my life, my grief and my dreams. This was *Gangsta.*

I won't bore y'all with how it went down and how I ended up being the first author signed to TCP (Triple Crown Publications), because it's a story that's been told a million times. What I will address is the change that getting my work published caused. I was still doing dirt when *Gangsta* was on the best sellers list, but my heart was no longer in it. Seeing my work in print caused me to finally dream bigger than I had been. I hadn't intended to write more than one book, but my head began to fill with more stories. I was addicted to my craft, and I still am to this day.

As a published author, I now had something that I hadn't in the past; purpose. I looked around my hood and saw the ugliness that I hadn't really paid attention to before. Living conditions were becoming worse, the killers and the Mommies were getting younger and no one really seemed to care. So, I took it upon myself to be an advocate for the streets and a voice for what was going on.

This genre that had been dead for over twenty years was getting its second wind, and I breathed deeply. With each book I was becoming stronger and my name was becoming more recognized. I was thrilled with all the new found attention, but it wasn't all positive. As with anything alien to the general public, the media was trying to knock Urban Fiction. They were, and are, saying that it was little more than a glorification of sex, guns and drugs. That's the biggest crock I've ever heard. Granted, the things we write about are very graphic, but it's a reflection of life in the inner city. So if you think reading about it is offensive, then can you imagine what it's like to live in it?

Speaking from a personal stand point, my novels are as raw as they come. The reason for this is because I want to paint a very clear picture for urban youth and adults as to what's waiting for us behind door number two. There is no glory or rewards in the fast life, only heartache and death. Take it from someone who knows. In my books I take you through every dimension of the underworld so you won't have to experience it first hand to know it's all bull crap at the end of the day.

To me, this is my way of paying forward my blessing and letting my life and struggles serve as inspiration to others in similar situations. Nothing, no matter how easy it seems, is without a price, and sometimes the price is way too heavy. These stories are more than just ink on paper; they are a warning to the curious or ignorant.

People read my stories and think that they know me, or my character, based on what I've laid down between the pages. They have no idea how wrong they are. I was once no different than the lost souls you scoff at, but my craft and my blessing have provided me with a purpose. That purpose is to continue to entertain and enlighten people about the ills of everyday life. My intentions are to use these stories to bridge the ever widening gap between parents and children, so that the parents who are too far removed from what's going on in their children's everyday lives can really know what's going on. Can you say for sure that your kid isn't in a gang? Do you really know what it's like to grow up as part of this generation? So before you judge me because of the things I write about, get to know my soul. I think you'll be thoroughly surprised by what you'll find. These stories within this anthology are not just words; they are legacies, legacies that will be here long after you and I are dust.

K'Wan

YA REAP
by
Michel Moore

Chapter One

"Quick, bring him into trauma room four!" The emergency unit nurse motioned to the paramedics as she ran beside the stretcher. "The doctor is already waiting!"

"His pulse is dropping rapidly and we can't get a heartbeat!" one of the paramedics responded with urgency as his rubber gloves shook, full of clotting blood, knowing their gunshot victim was clinging to life. "Y'all better hurry! It ain't looking good!"

"Oh no!" Arnita screamed out in painful denial, watching her teenage son appearing to lose his battle to see another sunrise. "Please help him! Please, please! He's my baby!"

The nurse, sympathetic in tone, held up one hand. "I'm sorry, Miss, but you can't go back there." She stopped the anguished mother dead in her tracks at the swinging metal double doors that led to the operating room. "Don't worry. He's in good hands. And just as soon as we know something, the doctor will be right out to speak with you," she assured her.

"Why did this happen?" sobs echoed loudly throughout the walls of the crowded building as she collapsed into her aunt's arms who solemnly led her down the hall into a dimly lit room. "Oh, my God! Why? Why is this happening to my baby?" she cried out, hoping that sooner than later, God would answer her cry.

Auntie Bell sat in the drably decorated hospital chapel, clutching her Bible while wiping away Arnita's tears with an old tattered handkerchief. After somewhat calming her down, she suggested to her niece to take her pleas to God Himself, or the closest thing to Him for the moment, the hospital chapel.

"Even at my age," Auntie Bell reflected, "it's simply amazing to me how things can go plum berserk so quickly. I mean one minute you're riding sky high on top of your game, and then within a momentary blink of the eye, your soul is practically scraping the ungodly rock bottom of this wretched earth."

"Why? Why? Why?" the weeping Arnita continued as she anxiously awaited any news about her only son who was merely yards away with two gunshot holes in his chest the size of golf balls. "Oh, God, why?"

"Stop all that crying! Just stop it." Auntie Bell hated that she was getting so frustrated with her niece's weeping, but surely Arnita didn't need God to reveal to her all the reasons behind her query. "You reap what you sow!" Auntie Bell snapped. "And you best trust that the <u>good man upstairs will make you a believer in that.</u>" Auntie Bell preached, testifying with certainty as she wrapped her arms around her sister's child. "Now tell me, Sweetie, was all that rotten blood soiled drug money your first born showered you with worth it?... Was it?"

Arnita sniffed and didn't hesitate to respond, "No, of course not, but why in the world is God doing this to my baby? Making him suffer?" Arnita questioned, looking up toward the ceiling, arms folded as she rocked back and forth. "He could stop all this and just save my son's life if He wanted to. After all, He is God, right? He can do anything, at least that's what you're always quoting from that Bible of yours." Doubt and sarcasm laced Arnita's tone.

"Arnita, you best hush up that mouth of yours, questioning the Good Lord! Don't you dare blame Him for this tragedy." Auntie Bell jumped to her feet, shaking her finger at her niece. "This is entirely your fault, not God's! Now what you need to do is think back to the role you done played in Little Ro turning out the way he is," she proclaimed. "Truth be told, you might as well have pulled the trigger of that gun yourself!"

Arnita sat speechless at her aunt's hurtful words.

But as her mind reflected back over the years, she couldn't help but question whether or not her aunt's words might have held some truth.

Chapter Two
Five years earlier

"Little Ro, call your father and tell him dinner will be ready in twenty minutes," Arnita ordered her son. "Oh, and tell him I cooked his favorite. Fried chicken, sweet corn, biscuits and gravy."

"Okay, Ma, I will," the eldest of Arnita Mills' two children sighed, answering back as he stood over his little sister, Patrice, making sure she washed her face and hands before sitting at the table.

"Oh, and please tell him to try and not be too late either."

Roland Dean Mills Jr. was only twelve years old, but shouldered a great deal of responsibility for a boy of his age. Being the namesake of a stern but fair father was sometimes more than the rambunctious youngster could handle, yet he never wanted to disappoint the man he deemed as his time to time hero. Although, truth be told, making the usual shameful call night after night, summoning his dad home from his *boy's house*, was fast becoming a habit that was growing old with Little Ro. Each evening before he went to sleep, he'd pray his mother would get the courage to stand up for herself and stop being his father's doormat.

God, please give Momma strength to stop Daddy from going over to that nasty, stank looking lady's house all the time. I hate her and her dumb-dumb son. Amen.

The man of the house, Roland Sr., a carpenter by trade, was a tall muscular man in stature that everyone on this closely knit block on the west side of Detroit knew. Highly regarded wherever he went, whether it was out of fear of his quick fire temper or just plain respect, he was a force to be reckoned with. Migrating from Alabama, Roland Sr. had a swagger and southern charm that made him the perfect gentleman.

For those strangers who didn't know any better, Arnita was blessed with a perfect man. Omitting the common knowledge to those near him that he was involved in an ongoing affair with Salena Jackson, a single mother of one, who'd recently moved into the area and was known as the neighborhood *good time girl* who slept with just about anything that hopped, skipped or jumped as long as they paid her.

Removing that one negative and outrageous factor from the equation, the head of household rarely missed a meal with his own family. He was a good paymaster; never late on one bill that crossed the modest threshold of their brick framed bungalow. Not causing his wife to worry about the high mortgage, food in the cabinets or clothes on the kid's backs, Roland Sr. thought his blatant indiscretions, along with the sideway glances of pity his wife endured from neighbors, were somehow allowable.

"Did you call him?" Arnita asked her son a few minutes later. "Yes, Ma, I called." Little Ro secretly rolled his eyes at her stupidity of dealing with his daddy and all his madness.

"And is he on his way?" Arnita wondered as she set the table. "I don't want his dinner to get cold."

"Do you want me to go and get him from around the corner? I can." Receiving a cold, hard stare from his mother, Little Ro instantly regretted asking her that million dollar question, but couldn't help himself as he headed toward the door. "I know what house she stays in."

"What did you just say to me?" Arnita slowly approached her son with a look of venom in her eyes as Patrice watched, scared that her brother was seconds away from getting popped.

"Nothing, Ma." He wisely backed down, treading on dangerous ground, wanting to avoid trouble. "I didn't say nothing."

"I thought not." She angrily wiped her hands down her apron. In just those few seconds, her blood had boiled just enough to form a sweat. "You ain't so big that you can't get a whooping. Now go sit your wanna-be-grown-behind on that front porch and let me know the minute your father pulls up. You understand me?"

"Yes, Ma. I understand." He twisted his lip up as he thought about how his father was disrespecting his mom.

Arnita, five foot three with paper bag brown skin tone and shoulder length hair, took pride in being a devout, born again Christian. The thirty-eight year old mother stayed immersed in the Word, hiding from the reality that faced her daily as the busy bodied women in her church congregation made it their personal vendetta to give Arnita their opinion on her husband's extra marital dealings. Although most claimed they were just trying to minister to her, or share what God was revealing to them, Arnita knew they were just trying to meddle.

"For better or worse, richer or poorer," was Arnita's constant response to the women, trying to hold her head up and keep her dignity.

Unfortunately, Arnita Mills wasn't the only one who suffered the shame from her spouse's infidelity. Little Ro would catch it going to the corner store, at the playground and even in the lunchroom line. Ridiculed by his classmates for having a *play step brother* who was in the slow class, he tried his best to ignore the taunts, but stayed in detention as a result of physical retaliation, disappointing his parents.

Little Ro did as he was told by his mother. He sat silently on the wooden steps of their house looking back and forth up the block for more than twenty minutes. He grew impatient awaiting any sign of his father, but just when he thought he'd die from hunger, Roland Sr.'s two toned pick up truck turned the corner, roaring into the driveway.

"Hey, Pops. You're late," Little Ro pointed out to his father as he hopped out of the truck and made his way to the porch.

"Yeah I know, so come on and let's eat," Roland Sr. stated nonchalantly as he rested his hand on his son's shoulder and they entered the house.

They both walked into the dining room at the same time. "I could eat a horse." Roland Sr. smiled as the smell of the delicious foods assaulted his nose.

"I thought I told you to tell me when he pulled up?" Arnita tugged her son's earlobe.

"Sorry, Ma. I forgot." Little Ro sadly found his spot at the table.

"What's the big deal, Arnita?" Roland Sr. stated after witnessing his son's demeanor slope.

"He's always forgetting something lately." Arnita judgmentally raised her eyebrow. It was obvious that Arnita was more disappointed in her husband's tardiness versus her son's forgetfulness. Her eyes dared her husband to call her on it as she turned to retrieve the pan of biscuits from the oven.

"Listen here, Arnita. I'm not in the mood to hear all that nerve wrecking complaining you doing," Roland Sr. scolded his wife as if she was a child. "That's why I stay away most of the time. That mouth of yours."

"Roland." She turned with a platter of hot biscuits in her hands. "Don't say that."

"I know you not telling me what to say in my own house are you?"

"No, but I-"

"But nothing!" he insisted as he sat down at the head of the table. "Just bring me my plate so I can eat and go take a hot shower."

Arnita, always the one to submit to her husband as her Bible instructed her to, prepared her family's plates and sat down, joining her husband, son and daughter at the dinner table. As the family lowered their heads, Roland Sr., who was the biggest hypocrite in the room, led them in a prayer before the family dug in, devouring almost every dish Arnita had lovingly prepared.

Inhaling the aroma of a homemade hot apple pie warming in the oven, the troubled husband and wife went through the normal ritual of idle chit chat.

"So, how was your day?" Arnita asked Roland Sr.

"Same as it always is," he huffed while pouring honey on the last piece of bread. "Long and drawn out. I swear if I didn't have you and these kids, I'd quit and let some other fool have that headache job."

"Just be blessed you have steady work as bad as the economy is."

"What you know about the economy? You ain't got no worries!" He barely looked over to acknowledge her.

"That's not true. It's getting harder by the day to stretch the food budget on these kids," she stated, watching her son and daughter drink their glasses of Kool-Aid. "And they say times are about to get much harder."

Roland Sr., with sticky fingers and crumbs around his mouth, glanced up. "Are you saying I don't give you enough to provide for my children? Are you saying I don't work hard enough?" Roland Sr. was now on the defensive side.

"No, I was just saying the prices at the grocery store are going up." She backed down, fearing her man's harsh verbal tongue lashing would increase. "That's all."

Little Ro and Patrice were used to the mental abuse their mother was forced to undergo and knew to just be quiet and stay out of grown folks' business as they were reminded constantly.

"Why do you always find something to get on my back about?" Roland Sr. asked his wife with a slight pound on the table. "I'm out there every day busting my butt and all you do is constantly complain."

"Humph! I guess that sleazy Salena is perfect, huh?" Arnita stated in an almost inaudible tone, as if she was second guessing even making the comment in the first place.

You could've heard a pin drop around the table as

Roland Sr. dropped his fork onto the plate, giving Arnita a wicked grin. "What did you just say?"

Arnita took a deep breath before speaking. "You heard me, Roland!" she raised her usually timid voice, getting up out of her chair. She didn't know where this sudden burst of courage, or holy boldness as the women in the church would have called it, came from, but she was going to use it up while it lasted. "I do my best to make you and this family happy, and all I get in return is grief! I'm tired of being second best!"

Roland Sr. sat dumbfounded at a loss for words. His wife had never called him on his behavior before. And now, after seeing the hurt in her eyes and hearing the pain in her voice, he almost felt bad. He finally conjured up some words to speak, but before he could respond or reassure his wife of his half time devotion to her, his cell phone rang, interrupting the argument.

Taking the cell off his thick leather belt, Roland Sr. looked at the screen and saw Salena's number flash repeatedly. Confused on the reason she was calling him at this time, knowing good and well he was having dinner with Arnita and the kids, Roland Sr. disrespectfully pushed the talk button as his family listened in on the one sided conversation.

"Yeah...What? He did what? Why is he even over there? Is he touching you? I'm on my way!" Roland Sr. leaped to his feet, grabbing his keys and almost knocking his small daughter out of her seat.

"Have you lost your mind? Where do you think you're going right in the middle of dinner?" Arnita couldn't believe her eyes and ears as she and her two children followed her irate husband onto the front porch, watching him jump in his truck. "Roland!" Arnita called out. "You get back in here with your family right now! This is ridiculous! Enough is enough!"

"Arnita, y'all go back inside the house and tend to your business!" Roland Sr. yelled out as the nosy neighbors watched. "This doesn't concern you or the kids." He quickly backed out the driveway and was on his way back down the street in the same direction he had come from less than a half hour ago.

Having no choice but to do as they were instructed, Arnita ushered Little Ro and her young daughter off the porch and back into their home. Hours seemed to pass as the evening sunlight disappeared, making way for the glow of the moon. The kids had long since gone to bed as Arnita, who sat on the couch furiously awaiting Roland Sr.'s return, simmered.

I'm done! If he wants to be with that hussy so bad, he can have her, Arnita told herself, knowing in her heart that she didn't want to lose her family that easily. She closed her weary eyes for a few seconds, but was suddenly startled by the loud sounds of the telephone. *Oh, I guess he wants to call with some sort of an excuse.* Arnita recognized her husband's number on the caller I.D. and answered dryly.

"Yes, Roland," she responded angrily.

"Hello, Arnita?" A puzzled look came across Arnita's face. Although she was certain it was her husband's phone number that appeared on the caller ID, the voice speaking on the other end of the line was clearly not that of Roland's.

"Yes, this is Arnita." She paused, momentarily shocked at not hearing her husband's voice on the other end. "Who is this?"

"This is Salena." The woman's voice sounded grim.

"Salena? Salena Jackson? You have some nerve," Arnita started before she was cut off."

"Arnita, it's an emergency," Salena started.

"Oh, I bet. Well you can take your emergency to 911, sweetheart, but don't call my house-"

Once again, Salena cut her off. "Arnita, listen please. Don't hang up."

"How dare you. You've got some sort of nerve calling my house. Haven't you disrespected me and my children enough over the years?"

"Please, Arnita, just listen to me!" This time Salena yelled with authority and Arnita could tell something serious was going on. "There's been an accident."

"Why are you calling me on my husband's phone? Where is he? Put him on the line." As she became nervous by the seriousness of the female caller's voice, Arnita fired question after question out to her husband's long time mistress.

"That's what I'm trying to tell you." Salena started crying uncontrollably. "Roland's been hurt and the paramedics are putting him in the ambulance as we speak. He's on his way to the hospital."

"What?" Arnita's yells woke Little Ro from out of a deep sleep. "What kind of accident was my husband in? Where are they taking him? To what hospital?"

"I don't know. I don't know! But it looks really bad!" Salena's tears increased. "It's so much blood!" She made the last statement as if she was looking at the blood as she spoke.

The fact that Arnita hadn't appreciated Salena calling her one little bit now had to be put on the back burner as she dropped the phone to the floor and ran to get her purse. Little Ro, now out of the bed, stood in the doorway and wiped the sleep out of his eyes. At the same time, he watched his mother leave, rushing off to the hospital, somehow feeling like he'd never see his father alive again, and knowing that his young life would be forever changed.

Chapter Three

The funeral was long and grueling for the grieving relatives. Person after person got up to praise the deceased Roland Sr. for his past various deeds and work throughout the community. Finding no comfort in becoming a widow with two children to bring up in the wicked streets of Detroit, Arnita hid her face in her hands as the service concluded and they rolled her man's casket out the same church they exchanged vows at years earlier.

Climbing into the family car, dressed in a dark blue suit, Little Ro couldn't help but take notice of Ms. Jackson and her son, Deon, a.k.a. his *play step brother*, standing in the multitude of tearful mourners. It was rumored that Deon, unfortunately had witnessed the entire murder of Roland, Sr. who, during a jealous rage, had been cold bloodedly shot four times, thanks to one of Salena Jackson's numerous boyfriends.

When Arnita became aware of their presence, she wiped her red, puffy eyes, took a deep breath and confidently marched over to Salena while holding her Bible close to her breasts. As the stunned crowd looked on, the young widow gave the little boy a faint smile then directed her full attention to his mother, landing a well place smack across her face.

Arnita, furious, trembled with every word she began to speak to the woman through her teeth. "Not even on this one day can you respect the union of our marriage. The Bible speaks of Jezebels like you in the book of Proverbs. I never thought I'd have to come face to face with one, and especially under these circumstances."

Salena just stood there holding her stinging face as Arnita continued to spit her venom.

"You don't belong here. I don't care how you felt about *my* husband. You need to know that he never loved you. Never," she screamed. "I was his wife, not you. Turn around and look!" Arnita pointed to Little Ro and a crying Patrice. "Do you see my kids over there?" she angrily waved her finger. "Thanks to you they don't have a father anymore. You're nothing but a home wrecking harlot and I hope all the wives standing around here condemn you and what you stand for." Arnita shot Salena one last, long glare before saying, "May God have mercy on your soul."

With that being said, Arnita's family members ushered her to the long, dark colored sedan so they could start the lengthy procession to the cemetery, which was located across town. Each of the women in attendance, thinking that they could have easily been in the poor young widow's shoes, tightly held on to their husband's arms as they snarled, walking pass an embarrassed Salena who was still subconsciously holding the side of her face and her young son's hand.

Jezebel, tramp, and whore were some of the choice hatred filled words that the wives used to describe her as she dropped her head in disgrace.

After Roland Sr. was buried and all was said and done, and the reality of the living set in, Arnita came to find out exactly where she and her children stood. Roland Sr. had left her with several high credit card balances, one high water bill and of course the mortgage. His seventy-five hundred dollar insurance policy went mostly to burial expenses, forcing Arnita to get a job at a small factory.

"Little Ro, help me fix the eggs while I get your sister dressed to go to Auntie Bell's. I'm running late," Arnita ordered her son, who was now the man of the house.

"Not a problem, Ma."

"Oh yeah, I left that seven dollars you needed for a new gas can on the table."

"Okay, I'll get it as soon as I get finished with the eggs," Little Ro said as he began to prepare a pan of scrambled, cheese eggs. After putting plenty of eggs on two plates for his sister and mother, Little Ro scraped the last bit of scrambled eggs out the black cast iron skillet onto his plate. "I've got three yards to do today," he yelled out to his mom as he walked over to the kitchen table and sat down.

"That's good, baby!" Arnita yelled back into the kitchen to her hard working son. For the past four years since her husband's untimely death, Little Ro had assumed the role of the man of the house by taking on odd jobs in order to be able to contribute to the household. The last four years had been harder than Arnita could have imagined. At some points, she grew so weary that she would lose hope. She even stopped attending Sunday Church Services altogether. But after being encouraged by her Auntie Bell, she would attend here and there, but she was far from being dedicated like she had been prior to her husband's death. Each day in the single mother's life caused her to change for the worse.

As the days drug by, Arnita, who'd easily gained thirty pounds over the course of the last four years and began sipping on more than just a small glass of wine with dinner, seemed to get spiteful and judgmental, blaming God for taking away her husband and not yet blessing her with a new one. As the years went by, her faith weakened. Her once good life was gone and besides Salena, God was the next in line to take the blame. Arnita needed a crutch to lean on so it was second nature for her to depend on the only man in her life, Roland Jr., whether he was ready for that responsibility or not.

In between Little Ro cutting grass, staying on the honor roll at high school and taking care of his younger sister, he was faced with obstacle after obstacle. Things with his family's financial situation were looking more than dismal the afternoon he walked up to Lamont's house.

Anytime he would cut Lamont's lawn or trim the

hedges, he never needed to bring his own equipment. Lamont, a local drug dealer, had everything Little Ro required in a shed in the rear of the huge backyard. He wasn't like the average dope dealer in the movies, callous and demented with no use for anyone other than himself. Lamont used to sit on the back deck reading books to his small son as Little Ro cut the grass. Lamont also even coached football for the Children's League. Even though Little Ro didn't necessarily condone Lamont's lifestyle and the way he made his living, he still understood the hustle and the grind.

This day was different from most as Little Ro neared the front porch like he did every two weeks. Outside of all the strange cars parked in the driveway, something else seemed out of the ordinary to Little Ro. Even though Lamont knew a lot of people in and around Detroit, he never had this much company at his house at one time. The few occasions that he did see any of Lamont's cronies, they were all pushing hotter whips than the ones that were now parked on the premises.

"Yes, can I help you?"

Little Ro was rudely met by a middle aged woman with a pile of clothes gathered in her hands.

"What do you want?" the woman asked as if she was getting very impatient with him.

"I'm here to do the yard work. Is Lamont home?"

"Naw, he ain't here, so don't be expecting no money for nothing!"

"Oh, he already paid me." Lamont always paid him for the entire month up front. Little Ro tried to inconspicuously look over the woman's shoulder. He was curious as to what all the noise and commotion coming from the inside of Lamont's usually quiet home was about. "I come every two weeks," Little Ro added.

Looking down at the grass then back over her shoulder at the people inside who were getting more boisterous as the seconds passed, the woman told Little Ro to go ahead, cut the grass and leave her alone. "This is my house now anyway and I don't want it looking a hot mess. So hurry up."

"Your house? Over my dead body!" one man yelled out the doorway.

"Mine too," a female added. "He would've wanted me to have this house and that flat screen."

Heading to the rear of the house, a confused Little Ro saw Lamont's baby momma, Tanika, and six year old son pull up. Jumping out the car, Tanika appeared to be infuriated.

"How y'all gonna be all up in the house like it belongs to y'all?" Tanika huffed as she made her way up to the door, dragging her son by the hand the entire way.

"Girl, bye." The woman who had been so rude to Little Ro was being just as rude to Tanika. "This here is family business and don't concern you at all! You acting like you were his wife."

"This is his son, his blood, so that makes it my business," Tanika screamed back at the woman as she held onto her son. By now several people came out of the house and began to congregate in the front yard, loading contents from Lamont's home into their cars.

"Listen here, Ms. Thang, with ya uppity behind," one other person spoke up. "Real Talk; unless you got papers to this or that", she pointed around, "then you need to step. Lamont was our relative, so that gives us first grabs at everything in and around here."

"Y'all so disrespectful it don't make no sense." Tanika shook her head in disgust. "He hasn't been dead twenty-four hours and y'all over here behaving like a pack of wild vultures." Lamont's son started to cry as his mother shouted at his cousins, aunts and uncles. "He couldn't stand none of y'all when he was alive, so what makes y'all think he'd want y'all to have anything of his?"

"Oh, well! He ain't here to answer that himself now is he?" a cousin replied as she carried three leather jackets in tow even though it was the beginning of summer. She placed them inside of her popped trunk.

"Yeah!" another cosigned. "And anyway, what in the heck is you doing here anyway? You and that baby of yours live clean across town. Obviously you just mad we beat you to the punch."

There was laughter among several of Lamont's family members.

"Unlike all of you vultures," Tanika said with puffy and red eyes, "I've got keys to this house and the property inside that belongs to me! Y'all scrubs over here stealing from a dead man instead of mourning his loss!"

Frozen in his tracks, Little Ro realized that Lamont was just not home for the time being, but that he was deceased. Getting a hard knot in the pit of his stomach, Little Ro leaned against the concrete wall in denial. Since his father's death, Lamont had been the closest person to Little Ro that had passed away. Even though they weren't homeboys or running partners, Little Ro and Lamont had a mutual respect for one another and he would definitely miss their bi-weekly chats.

Ah, naw. Little Ro let his emotions take over as he closed his eyes thinking about why people had to die. *Life ain't fair.*

Finally, after regaining his composure, Little Ro went to the medium size shed and pulled out the lawn mower. Lamont had paid him to do a job, and even though he wasn't gonna be there on the back porch, he still knew that he wanted to cut the grass one more time to fulfill his obligation. As the loud sounds of the mower ripped through the yard, Little Ro couldn't help but overhear the shouts, screams and obvious smashing up of items from inside the house.

While trimming the hedges, Little Ro sadly noticed Lamont's small son who'd wondered out the house and was standing near the curb.

"What's going on, li'l man?" he questioned the child after turning off the lawnmower.

"Nuttin'," the boy shrugged.

"Tired of all the big people making noise, huh?"

"Yes." He covered his ears, which were big just like his now deceased father's. "And I want my daddy!"

Before Little Ro could console the small child any further, remembering exactly how he felt the day his own father passed, the child's mom barreled out the front door with an arm full of her belongings that thankfully weren't gangstered by Lamont's kin folk. Tossing the stuff in the rear of the car, Tanika looked over at her son who stared down toward the pavement to keep from crying.

"Come on, baby, let's go before Mommy messes around and catches a case!" She snatched her son up by the arm, practically throwing him into the passenger seat, not even bothering to safely strap him in.

"You best get on," one cousin yelled from the porch, watching Tanika roar off the block, which was now crowded with onlookers.

Little Ro was pissed off to the eighth degree as he marched in the back yard, grabbing a broom to clean up before he left the premises for the last time. When he was almost ready to leave, the same woman he'd first encountered when he'd arrived came out onto the back deck and walked out into the middle of the freshly cut grass. After seeming to survey his work she called him over.

"Listen here," she frowned. "I want you to take that lawnmower and all the rest of that stuff out that shed and off my property!"

"Excuse me, Miss?" Little Ro wanted to honestly smack the cow mess outta the rude woman, but was always taught to respect his elders, so he held his composure. "I don't understand what you mean."

"Everything ain't always meant for you to understand!" She placed her hands firmly on her wide oversized hips. "That shed is blocking the place where my new gazebo gonna go! Now is you gonna clean it out and take all that stuff with you, or do you want me to flag down one of these guys out here scraping?"

With a brief moment of hesitation, Little Ro happily headed over to the shed gathering as much of his newly acquired lawn equipment he could onto a steel push cart. Snatching a royal blue tarp off the floor that was thrown in the corner, he noticed something strange. Leaning over to inspect what seemed to be hidden in a cardboard box, Little Ro couldn't believe his eyes as he crotched down. Even though he was raised growing up in the church by a God fearing mother and avoided the street life that tempted him on a daily basis, he recognized what most would call a gift from the good man upstairs.

What in the...? Little Ro puzzled to himself as he glanced over his shoulder to see if the woman had returned outside to see if he was gone. *I must be dreaming.*

As he peeked into the small sized duffle bag which had a broken zipper, he pulled out a manila colored envelope with twenty dollar bills neatly arranged with all the faces to the front and several thick plastic sacks with huge amounts of pills in each. Digging deeper, Little Ro discovered another bag with a couple of baggies of weed and a digital scale. Not knowing what to do next, instinctively he tucked the bag under one of the hedge trimmers, tossed the tarp on the cart and used a few bungee cords to secure the items down.

Slowly pushing the cart out the driveway with one hand and the lawn mower with the other, sweat started to pour down his face. Turning back only once to see if anyone from Lamont's house would change their minds about the belongings, Little Ro nervously took the side streets to get to his house, totally forgetting about the other yards he was scheduled to cut.

Rushing the cart into the garage, he unfastened the cords to retrieve the duffle bag and ran in the side door to his bedroom. Turning the lock with the skeleton key, he closed his blinds and took the envelope out.

"Twenty, forty, sixty, eighty, a hundred," he repeated

seventeen times.

To many, $1,700 dollars wasn't a lot, but in Little Ro's household, that was way over the total amount his weary mother, Arnita, who often volunteered to work double shifts and overtime, made in a month. Amazed with his sudden cash windfall, he didn't pay any attention to the bags of multi-shaded pills.

"I'm gonna give half of this money to Ma," he proclaimed out loud. "Then buy me a new pair of sneakers and another lock and chain for the garage."

After spending all afternoon with pen and paper stretching out $1,700, Little Ro heard his mother come in with his sister in tow. Before he could inform her about his blessing, not to mention the tragedy of Lamont's untimely death, he saw the look of despair on her face.

"What's wrong, Ma?" He took a bag of groceries out of her hands and sat them on the table.

"My job just issued layoffs, and as you can see, your mother was one of the lucky ones."

Watching her ball up the pink slip and throw it into the trash, Little Ro knew that it was his cue to save the day, so to speak. Dashing back in his room he lifted his mattress, grabbing the money.

"Hey, Ma. Guess what?" he asked, returning to the kitchen.

"Not now, Roland," she sighed. "I forgot the sauce for the spaghetti. Can you run down to the store and get a jar?"

"Yes, Ma but-"

"Please, baby. Tell me when you get back. Your sister has to eat and I have a major headache."

Tucking the wad of cash in his front pocket, Little Ro headed out the door and up the block to the store. As soon as he bent the corner, he ran smack into a smoked out Salena Jackson, who was now the proud owner of a new title: the neighborhood crack whore. Her son, Deon, who detested the embarrassment of being birthed by such a female, was there as usual trying relentlessly to get his mother off the street tricking and to go home, but as fate would have it, she was not the slight bit interested in him or any of his bright life altering ideas. Every since Roland Sr.'s murder in her home and the neighborhood following Arnita's warning, Salena was ostracized and now ridiculed.

"Hey now, baby boy." She sluggishly slurred her words, not immediately recognizing Little Ro. "You want some of this?" She put her hands on her hips and shook her hips.

"Naw, I'm good," Little Ro replied.

"You sure?" Salena squinted while trying to comb her boney fingers through her tangled hair.

"Ma, what's wrong with you?" Deon snatched her up by the elbow. "Is you all the way crazy, or what?"

"Get ya hands off me!" she yelled at her son as Little Ro disappeared into the store. "I could've got me a few dollars since you ain't giving me nothing to work with. And I know you got it!"

"Shut up! Dang!" Deon shook Salena while slamming her against the store's concrete wall. "Do you even know who that was you were trying to push up on? Do you?"

"What difference do it make to you if he got some money to give me? You always running behind me trying to act like you my daddy or something!" Salena rubbed her shoulder. "I'm ya Momma."

Deon shook his head with contempt. "Why are you always embarrassing me?"

"What's the big deal, Deon? Why you all up in my face about some trick?"

"Well, that was Roland!"

"Huh?" Salena said in a surprised tone.

"Oh, now you wanna pay attention." Deon, head lowered, turned around, walking off before his former classmate had the chance to come out the store and clown him. "You make me sick! I wish you was dead sometimes. At least I'd be free!"

"Little Roland?" Salena said under her breath as she stared off down at the concrete. She felt a bit of shame cloud her cracked out brain and dropped her head. "Are you sure?" she called out to her son. Deon put his hand up, dismissing his mother, without even turning around as he walked out of sight.

Standing to the side of the store's door, a jumpy Salena waited as patiently as she could for the son of her murdered ex-lover to come out so she could apologize for her behavior. Even though she had a monkey on her back the size of Texas and was craving to get high, Salena let potential Tricks pass by feeling that she at least owed the young teenager an explanation as to why she'd came onto him the way she did.

Eventually, Little Ro appeared from behind the store's doors.

"Hello, Roland." Salena tried unsuccessfully to rub her matted hair into a ponytail and straighten out her oil stained blue jean skirt. "Can I talk to you about something?"

"About what?" Little Ro twisted his upper lip, shrugging his shoulder to the side in attempt to avoid Salena's filthy hands from touching him. "I already told ya nasty behind I'm tight!"

"I just wanted to let you know I'm sorry for asking you what I did. If I would've known you was my Roland's little son, I wouldn't-"

"Your Roland? Are you serious?" He stopped in his tracks, looked her up and down, judgmentally laughing loudly. "Those drugs you on must really have your mind messed up or something; stepping to me like that."

"All I meant was that I was wrong and I ain't mean to disrespect you." She followed him down the block, still trying to plead her case. Deon watched from the steps of his friend's porch. "Your father was a good man and I really loved him."

Little Ro was infuriated, trying his best to remain calm as Salena continued to painstakingly trail behind him. Carrying the several plastic bags packed with his mother's items as well as chips, pop and a few candy bars he'd bought for his little sister, he finally lost control of his emotions and let his deceased father's ex-lover have it.

"Stop talking about my father, okay! Everybody knows if it wasn't for you being such a selfish minded tramp, he'd still be alive!" Not in his usual character, Little Ro had no problem screaming at an adult. "So for real, stop bringing up the past talking about how much you loved him! Go somewhere and do what you've been doing for years; smoke crack and leave me and my family alone!"

Momentarily standing on the corner taking stock of what was said as Little Ro angrily marched away, Salena was interrupted by the sounds of an old grey Ford Tempo blowing its horn. She looked over and the occupant signaled for her to come and ride with him around the block in the alley for a few minutes before he had to go home, undoubtedly to his wife and kids.

I don't know who she thinks she is, talking to me like I care what she has to say. Little Ro contemplated with each passing step he took. *I would tell Ma what she had the nerve to say, but things are already bad enough for her.*

"What up, Dude?" Deon, with pants sagging, ran off the stairs catching up with his former classmate who didn't even slow down his pace. "Let me holler at you for a minute."

"Listen up-" Rattled with emotions, Little Ro barely acknowledged Deon's presence. "If this is about what I just said to your mother, she had it coming."

"Naw, Dude, I know she be bugging out. That's what I wanted to say." Deon pulled up his pants to keep them from falling to his ankles as he walked.

Little Ro was relieved since he didn't want or need any sort of trouble from Deon, especially because of his rumored affiliation with a local gang. "Oh, okay."

"Yeah, it's all that dope that got her acting the way she do; out here tricking with all these so called men." Feeling a small bit of sympathy for Deon, Little Ro slowed the pace of his walk back home to his hard working mother, who would never think of doing the despicable things that Salena did. "Dang, gee man, I'm sorry things are so messed up for you."

"It ain't nothing." Deon tried down playing his pain, but unfortunately wore the grave appearance of sorrow written all across his face. "That's how it goes sometimes."

"Hey, not to get into your business," Little Ro continued this strange unexpected conversation. "But how come you don't attend classes any more?"

"Come on now, Dude, you know it ain't no secret that them busters at school was trying to hold me back another year. And a cat like me wasn't going for that. School just ain't for me," he reasoned. "Besides, with a moms like mine, a brother gotta get out here and grind if I wanna eat."

Before the unlikely pair knew it, they were standing in front of Little Ro's house, met by Arnita standing on the porch. "Boy, bring your behind in this house with that sauce. You know Patrice gotta eat before she starts practicing for that recital of hers," Arnita fussed.

"Okay, Ma." Little Ro got an epiphany as he glanced downward at the bags in his hands that were stuffed with items he'd purchased with the extra dough that lined his pockets.

"Alright, dawg, I see ya moms is calling you, so I'm gonna bounce."

If he'd been any other friend from school, Little Ro would've invited him in to have dinner with his family, but considering who Deon and his mother was, Little Ro knew that definitely wasn't happening. So instead, Little Ro had an alternative idea.

"Hey, Deon, I'm not trying to step outta line, but are you busy tomorrow about noon? I've got a business proposition for you that might make us both some money."

Hearing the word money was all Deon, who was always tangled up in some get rich or die trying scheme, needed to hear. He confirmed that he'd meet up with Little Ro in front of the store at twelve o'clock sharp before heading off into the 'something dangerous darkness' that was Detroit. Little Ro then ran up the steps, and disappeared into the loving security of his home.

Chapter Four

Little Ro looked at the clock that was hung on an old rusty nail over the kitchen sink, realizing that it was close to twelve. Rushing his mother and sister out the house to spend the two hundred dollar bills he'd blessed them with last night after lying about it being an advance on some yard work at a local charter school, he paced the floor with anticipation as well as hesitation as to whether he was about to do the right thing. Looking at the wastepaper basket that still had his mother's balled up pink slip on the top, and judging from the way her face lit up when he handed her that money, he quickly decided he was definitely about to embark upon the right thing. Before he could second guess himself, he bolted out the door and up toward the corner store.

At exactly twelve fifteen, Deon turned the corner wearing the same clothes he'd had on the night before.

"What up?" Deon greeted Little Ro.

"Nothing much," Little Ro replied, suspiciously looking around the store's parking lot. "I need to show you something. Hold tight."

"Well, I sure in the heck hope it's money."

Deon had greed in his eyes as he watched Little Ro dig deep into the pocket of his neatly ironed beige Dockers.

Little Ro pulled out what appeared to be a piece of paper towel folded up.

"Dang, dawg, you killing me acting all secret, squirrel!" Deon teased.

Little Ro paid no attention to Deon's jokes while he un-wrapped the paper towel, scoping out his surroundings the entire time. "Do you know what this is?"

Deon was confused as he took one of the tablets out the napkin Little Ro held, flipping it over at the symbol that was embedded on it. "I don't get it," he laughed, moving out the way of some customers that were pulling up into the lot. "What fool don't know what these is? The question should be what your *Dudley Do Right* self doing with some Ecstasy pills?"

"I thought that's what they might've been, but I really wasn't too sure."

"Okay, but where did you get them and do you got some more?" Deon's eyes were still filled with greed as well as the sound of his voice.

"Do you feel like coming over my house?" At this point, Little Ro decided it would be better to just show Deon the deal than to tell him.

"Yeah alright, just let me grab a juice and a bag of chips for breakfast first," Deon insisted before they made their way to Arnita's house, where Little Ro could show him the plastic bags of pills and work out some sort of deal.

Within minutes of arriving at the house and Deon seeing the super size baggies full of different colored ecstasy pills, he reassured his new best friend that no doubt at twenty dollars a pop they were about to be rich, even if they split the proceeds straight down the middle. After carefully counting each pill one by one, the newly formed partners in crime determined they had over $75,000 in clear 100% profit on Little Ro's desk that was staring them dead in their faces.

Now the only thing the two had to do was to organize their game plan and get to work on moving the pills as soon as possible. Knowing absolutely nothing about drugs or the world which they came from, Little Ro relied solely on Deon and his street expertise to figure out the pros, cons and the logistics of them successfully converting bags of tiny pills into cold, hard revenue without getting shot, robbed, arrested, or even worse, killed.

Over the next passing month and a half, life for both teenagers transformed at a rapid pace. They had quickly established a long and loyal customer base, which was enabling a sudden heavy cash flow to come into their possession and make their once common *low key hood life* jump to almost being neighborhood overnight *ghetto superstars.*

From day one when Deon received a 911 call on his cell and set out to sling the first four pills of his share of the product to a dude named Tim-Tim and his boy who were having a party with a couple of females, Little Ro and Deon proved how differently they were raised and what was most important to them in their small corner of God's earth.

Trips to the mall for expensive outfits for his little sister were at the top of the list for Little Ro as well as a Blackberry and a solid gold chain with a huge diamond encrusted cross. Never before imagining he could own a pair of the latest Jordan's, especially since he knew full well his mother could never afford such an extravagance on her salary, Little Ro purchased two pairs and a track suit to go with each pair. He, of course, hooked his mother up with lavish gifts. The once wise minded kid was spending money like it was going out of style. Even though the way their product was moving they'd be out soon and with no available connection or any leads on getting any more, Little Ro still felt he owed his mother some temporary happiness. Though she'd not once questioned him on his windfall of finances, Little Ro knew that she had to know that doing yard work wasn't the result of his new gained wealth.

With the burden of being a grown man before he was truly ready, Little Ro missed out on being a young boy, watching television, climbing trees and hanging out with kids his own age. No sooner than his father's corpse was lowered into the ground and the first pile of dirt was thrown on top, Arnita pressured him to fill the painful void in her life. Every penny he'd make, every dime he found, and every waking free minute that was available, Little Ro would spend in an effort to make his often depressed mother happy once again. For that he would give almost anything.

Arnita had managed to get another job after being laid off, but she unluckily lost it after barely receiving her first pay check. She didn't fret as much as she did the first time she lost her job, because she knew her son would certainly look out for the family. Little Ro figured that this was why she naively chose to disregard his obvious change in behavior and personal appearance. Any one who paid attention knew that his change could only point to one conclusion; Little Ro was now a bonafide hustler.

As an unemployed, single mother, Arnita needed the money to pay past due bills, not to mention she could now sit back and kick her feet up. Growing up in a huge family that was packed full of criminals, backsliders, alcoholics, fast women, heathens and other folk that committed all types of atrocities against the Word of God as she used to interpret it, Arnita purposely turned away from that lifestyle knowing the street life nine outta ten ended in one of two ways; dead or in jail. She'd seen the ugly side of the so called game by attending several family members' funerals as well as made her fair share of trips to visit her kin in prisons scattered all across Michigan, Indiana and Ohio. Yet, sometimes no matter how strong one's faith is, the devil will surely devise a test, and at your weakest, most vulnerable moment he might win. Arnita herself, fell prey and got caught up with enjoying fast money and ignoring the tangled strings that were always attached to it. It was true what was always said; money does change people. Arnita became quite content allowing her son to take a chance with his life and freedom.

Deon, however, was a horse of a much different color. While most would think he'd out shine Little Ro when it came to letting go of the almighty dollar, he held onto it tightly as if he'd lived through the Great Depression. Despite being labeled street savvy and surrounding himself with plenty of females, Deon honestly didn't mind playing the background. Wearing the same three pair of pants he owned, day in and day out, was like second nature to the only child of a crack addicted whore. Deon grew up having nothing to call his own, not even his mother's love, which ultimately belonged to the streets of Detroit and whatever trick would pay for her cheap services.

Even if a stranger showed pity on Deon as a small child, giving him something as insignificant to most as a pair of new pajamas, Salena would steal them, getting whatever few pennies she could scrounge up for a hit. Now that he was older, Deon tried relentlessly to get his mother off the streets and into some sort of rehabilitation treatment, but no dice. The heavily addicted Salena would have no part of it. Secretly, at night, when he was sure no one was watching, wherever he was lucky enough to lay his head, Deon would drop to his knees, lower his head and pray to the Good Lord to deliver his mother from the evil clutches of addiction and back to her right state of mind.

Sure, prior to the death of Roland Sr. she was considered the neighborhood tramp, but in Deon's eyes, that title was miles behind the one she held claim to now. If there was one good thing that came out of Deon's ongoing ordeal, it was that the life he lived had made him stronger, and in his opinion, everything was about to start paying off.

Chapter Five

"Hey, guy, everything seems like it's moving good, don't it?" Deon counted out his share of the day's profit, putting it deep down in his pocket for safe keeping until he got home to put it in his ever growing stash.

"Yeah, you're right." Little Ro rubbed the side of his face in the mirror over his dresser, checking to see if the beard he had started growing was getting any thicker.

Deon handed him his share of the cash and the two made their way toward the front door.

"I'm about to grab something to eat, hit the mall and then go to the show with my girl," Little Ro bragged.

"Not me. I'm on my way in for the night." Deon shook his head as he walked outside and onto the front porch of Little Ro's house where he was now regularly welcomed with open arms. Greed was now the head of Arnita's household and if her dead husband's mistress's bastard son had anything to do with her new carefree lifestyle, then so be it. Avoiding as much contact with him as possible, she'd roll with the punches letting bygones be bygones. Arnita felt she'd paid her debt off in full to the world in the way of her husband being suddenly and cruelly snatched out of her and her children's lives.

"Dang, you don't ever go out and have a good time, do you?"

"Yeah, man, but right about now I'm on a serious mission."

"I understand all that, Deon, but honestly; we making nice money now." Little Ro pulled out the knot of money he intended on blowing on clothes and females. "So why won't you buy yourself a couple of outfits and maybe some new sneakers?"

"All that high priced crap just ain't for me right now. Besides, every well runs dry and you know we're running low."

"That's all good, but you don't even go out to the restaurant with me and eat good. In the past six weeks, when I think about it, all I've ever seen you eat outside of the meals my mother might cook is soup, Vienna sausage and spam. Now what's up on that? I know you got dough!"

"Listen, dude," Deon reassured him. "Let me do me and you do you, okay. I already told you I'm on a mission, so let's just leave it like that."

Little Ro followed him out the door and on to the porch, letting his curiosity get the best of him. Every since the day they'd decided to go into the *pill selling venture*, he avoided the painful link they shared from years ago. But something came over Little Ro and he couldn't resist the temptation of not bringing up the issue any longer.

"Dawg, before you go, let me talk to you about something else." He placed his hand on Deon's shoulder. "I've been meaning to ask you this, but I don't really know if I want to hear the answer."

Both sitting down on the wooden steps, Deon braced himself back in for the inevitable conversation about how Roland Sr. was shot in cold blood in Salena's living room.

"I think I already know what it is, Dude." Deon lowered his head, hesitating to speak out of turn and hoping to just let sleeping dogs lie. "But go ahead and ask just so I'll know we're on the same page."

"Well, it's about my father." Little Ro confirmed exactly what Deon speculated the topic would be. "I know it's been years, but what exactly happened that night? You know, the night my pops got killed. My mother cries almost every time somebody brings up that evening, so it ain't no way I can go and ask her. She wouldn't even let me miss school to go to the murder trial so I could hear first hand for myself what had gone down."

Although the last thing Deon wanted to talk about was that night, he obliged Little Ro and did just that. Thirty minutes or so deep off into the *back down memory lane* conversation, Little Ro felt himself grow more and more agitated at what he was hearing.

The story Deon told of the dreadful nightmare unfolded. He started at the precise moment Salena placed that ill fated distress call to Roland, Sr. That was a phone call that led to the confrontation between Salena's other man and Roland Sr. that ended with the ambulance rushing Roland Sr. off to the hospital where he took his final breath. Salena had been right there clinging to his side, much to the unliking of a hysterical Arnita who arrived at the hospital, bursting through the doors and past security just in time to see them pronounce the time of her husband's death.

Just listening to the details of how Salena's other man had been whooping on her and she had called his father over to the rescue made Little Ro's adrenaline rise. *Why didn't she call the police? Why did she have to call his father?* The more he thought about it, the angrier Little Ro got.

"You can stop," Little Ro ordered Deon. He held his head down, buried in his hands. "I don't even wanna hear no more."

"Dude, I apologize for the role my mother played in that tragic incident," Deon tried consoling his friend. "That scandalous mess she did that night is what got her so jacked up now and out her mind. God don't like ugly, so now she getting paid back everyday out in these streets."

Little Ro lifted his head slightly enough so Deon could see the redness of his eyes and the complete look of disappointment on his face. Deon then took that as his cue to get up and head to the crib.

"In case you wanna know," Deon added with compassion, "I heard ya old man pleading with my mother to call your moms and tell her he loved her and his kids."

"Oh, yeah?" Little Ro, at that point, really didn't know how to take that, so he just nodded, lowering his face back down in his hands as Deon left.

Chapter Six

Little Ro reflected on what he'd just heard, leaving himself numb to any type of respect for Roland Sr. or his legacy. *I can't believe that! Why did I even let him tell me that garbage? Then he gonna lie and say my no good cheating father said he loved us. Yeah right! That's a joke. If he loved me, my sister and my momma so much, he wouldn't have been cheating in the first place.*

His plans for having a good time later were halted as he sat on the porch infuriated, not knowing what to do next. As he simmered, he suddenly had the strange desire to not remember what Deon had put on his mind. It was only one way he could do that and it was to buy something to drink, after all, it seemed to work for his mother all the time. When she was depressed, which was often, facing the troubles of the world, that closet hidden bottle took the edge off and often seemed to put his mother in a much better and mellower mood. So slowly getting up brushing off his designer blue jeans, Little Ro headed down the block toward the corner liquor store where he was stopped by, of all people, Salena, who darted out the alley way after tricking with some old man in a red Ford F-150.

"Hey now, Little Man," Salena smiled, showing her rotten teeth as she squinted, taking notice of all the similarities and characteristics her once upon a time lover and his son had in common.

"Oh, hey, Ms. Jackson." Little Ro tried giving her a small amount of respect since he and Deon were now in business together. "How you doing?"

"I'd be doing a whole lot better if you could just spare me a little bit of change so I can get something to eat."

"Come on now, Ms. Jackson, I know your son got your pockets straight enough to get a sandwich, so go pull that hungry routine with the next mark buster."

"Listen, baby." Salena, now feeling like she and Little Ro were on good terms, placed her hand onto his shoulder. "Deon don't be giving me no money. He think I'm gonna blow it on getting high."

"And is he wrong?"

"Naw, but I'm a grown woman." Salena, already buzzed, clutched the five dollar bill she'd just worked for in the alley. "He can't stop me from doing what I do no matter how much he tries. He ain't nothing but a hypocrite. I mean, look at him running around here playing big bad dope man all week, then trying to drag my black behind to church with him on Sunday."

"What?" Little Ro was shocked as they continued to walk into the store's crowded parking lot. "Did you just say Deon be going to church?"

"Yeah, I said church. Every Sunday now for a month or so he waking me up thinking I'm going with him. He even claims he's getting baptized this week."

"Wow, that's deep," he replied. "But right about now I need for you to do me a small favor."

"Anything for you." Salena was elated he was coming to her for assistance. She knew that when anybody wanted anything from her, they paid for it. But of course, she would do anything to help out Little Ro anyway. "What you need, Angel Face?"

Little Ro reached into his pocket and pulled out a crisp fifty dollar bill and handed it to Salena. "Go in the store and buy me a drink."

"You want a drink?" she couldn't believe what the once goody two shoes had said.

"Spare me all the judgmental stares and do what I asked you! And, oh yeah, you can keep the change."

"Good looking, sweetheart. Momma got you." Salena happily went into the store so that she could cop Little Ro's poison for comfort, and soon after, with the change he so graciously was allowing her to keep, she would cop the poison of her choice.

What seemed like hours slipped by as Little Ro, who admittedly was not a drinker, attempted to drown his sorrows by nursing the fifth of Hennessy Salena had purchased on his behalf. Throwing rocks at his mother's empty flower pots, which served as perfect targets, the young man sat posted on the third step from the top yelling out at times obscenities and cursing the name of God, and yet Deon had been racing off every Sunday to go be in this so-called God's house.

Little Ro was confused and his emotions were running wild. *I hate my father! I hate him and everything about him,* echoed throughout his mind, consuming him with an intense fury and rage he had never felt before. *I'm glad that disrespectful bastard is dead! Good riddance! I hope he's burning in hell.*

Several of Arnita's long time neighbors came onto their porches to see what all the commotion was about at the house that was normally quiet, up until lately. They'd all taken notice of Little Ro's increasingly blatant and sometimes rude behavior but dared not bring the unexpected change up to Arnita pertaining her precious baby boy's demeanor since she seemed to be suffering from the same un-Christian like transformation in her own lifestyle. They were both keeping late hours, had strange cars stopping by at all times of the night, and not to mention Little Ro hadn't volunteered to cut any yards in weeks.

Seeing the young man acting distraught, Mr. Martin, seventy-one year old neighbor, former friend and lodge brother of Roland Sr., held on tightly to the black steel handrail making his way off his porch and across the street to console Little Ro.

"Hey now," he smiled reassuringly. "Do you need to talk to someone?"

"Naw, Mr. Martin. I'm good." His breath reeked of liquor as he stood to his feet, almost losing his balance.

"Well you don't look good, Son. Why don't you come on over to my house, put that bottle down, and let my wife fix you a plate of food?"

"Naw, I done told you, I'm okay." Little Ro tried stashing the half drunken bottle of Hennessy behind one of the flower pots as he wildly waved his arms, dismissing Mr. Martin. "You can go on and just leave me alone. I don't need nobody's help."

"All right, all right, all right." Mr. Martin reached in his back overall pocket and got out a small travel size Bible. "I'm gonna do just that, son, because I see that you are intent on going down the road of self destruction and defiance to the word of the Lord Our God. But while you taking that hard, bumpy and unfortunately often traveled journey to damnation, take this along with you for comfort, 'cause it ain't never too late to turn back on that road."

The last thing Little Ro wanted to hear about was God. "Mr. Martin, leave me alone! And stop calling me son. I ain't got no Daddy. He ain't care about me, my sista or my momma! He left us."

"Yes, son, that's true, I'm not your father, but remember this," he preached with a tone of certainty in his voice. "If you trust in the Lord, He'll never abandon you. And as for Roland Sr., I bet my last dollar he's up in heaven missing you every passing day. So try to be the best you can be and make him proud." With his quick, fiery filled sermon concluded, Mr. Martin while humming one of his favorite hymns, "Onward Christian Soldiers," headed back to the security of his front porch praising the name of Jesus.

Little Ro licked his lips and leaned back, reaching for his bottle, defiant in the advice he was just given. Raising it to his lips, he glanced down at the Bible Mr. Martin left on the bottom step as he took another long swig.

Mr. Martin watched the young Roland and shook his head, saying under his breath, "That child needs to take his self back to church and submerge his soul into the teachings of the Savior instead of drinking that sinful juice the Devil uses to trick folks to join his Army of the Wicked." Mr. Martin shook his head again, wondering what was gonna become of Little Ro if he kept on the path he was traveling.

Chapter Seven

On his second trip to the liquor store, a totally inebriated Little Ro tried and tried, but couldn't find Salena
to do him the same solid she'd done earlier. Barely
standing against the brick wall of the store , he attempted coaxing person after person, no matter who they
were, in hopes that one of them would be dishonest and
dumb enough to break the law and risk getting ticketed
to buy his underage self another bottle.

"Hey, you," he belched out loud as his eyes darted
around and he waved another fifty dollar bill. "Can you
grab something out the store for me?"

"Naw, Young Playa," one guy responded.

"Ain't that Arnita's son?" another one commented to
her friend as they walked pass. "It's a shame how these
kids behave. Look at him. Drunk as I don't know what.
He ain't nothing like his daddy."

Hearing people ignore his demands and then talk
about him like he wasn't there, and on top of that, com-
paring him to his two timing, cheating, womanizing
father, Little Ro grew more enraged than he was when
he'd first walked down the block.

"Y'all don't know me or nothing about me," Little Ro
screamed out like the entire world could hear him. "I'm
sick and tired of y'all hypocrites trying to judge me! I'm
my own man! I make my own rules!"

As Little Ro stood in the middle of the parking lot
proclaiming his independence and manhood, two plain
clothes police officers pulled up after receiving a call
from the store's owner who'd gotten complaints from
several older customers about a teenager outside disrespecting them. Trying his best to refrain from any more

outbursts as they cautiously approached him with their guns drawn, Little Ro let the liquor take back over his system, resulting in him cursing them out without any regard whatsoever for their authority.

As if matters couldn't get any worse, one last sign that he shouldn't be drinking jumped off as he violently vomited all the contents of his stomach on one of the officer's shoes as they slammed him down against the concrete pavement, checking him for any weapons or drugs.

Struggling with the officers for a good five minutes or so, Little Ro, outnumbered and oversized by the two officers, finally stopped resisting and was thrown, hand-cuffed head first, in back of their black unmarked vehicle and quickly whisked off to the local precinct. No sooner than they arrived at the station, still defiant, drunk and pissed off, the rebellious youth used his feet to repeatedly kick the police car's window until it cracked. Fortunately for him, as luck would have it, the Desk Sergeant on duty recognized Little Ro from cutting his yard in the past and stopped the officers from any rough house retaliation that was sure to follow.

After logging in most of Little Ro's property that was on his person, the Sergeant took notice of one particular item he wasn't used to seeing in a young man's possessions. It was a small Bible. Apparently Little Ro, intoxicated and rambling, still had the mind set that God and his word was something too strong and powerful to be left on the stairs of his porch when he left to get his second bottle.

Making his one phone call, which was of course, to his mother since he was legally still underage, a dizzy Little Ro could hardly get the words out that he was arrested before Arnita started screaming at the top of her lungs. Holding the telephone receiver as far away from his ear as he could, Little Ro closed his eyes, wondering how his life had gotten so far out of control in such a short time.

It seemed to him that in between now being totally responsible for paying all the various household expenses and giving his Great Auntie Bell money to take care of his younger sister while his mom ran the streets trying hopelessly to recapture her youth, he was losing his mind.

Less than an hour later, Arnita, designer purse on her arm, neck full of gold jewelry and nails perfectly manicured, stormed through the doors of the police station yelling out obscenities and cursing in the name of the Lord. Approaching the main desk with a serious attitude, she boldly demanded to see her son and the officers that arrested him, causing her to leave the Casino earlier than she'd planned.

It was obvious to the officers that Arnita was the young boy's mother because that apple definitely didn't fall far from the tree. How they saw it, her and the boy both needed Jesus in their lives.

The desk sergeant shook his head, still amazed after all his years on the job how some so-called parents acted when their children broke the law. It was as if they were mad at the system for catching the little heathens rather than being mad at their child for being a heathen.

"Yes, are you Roland Mills, Jr.'s mother?" the Sergeant knowingly asked.

"Yes, I am," she loudly stated. "Where's my son at and what did you pick him up for?"

"There are several charges; Public Intoxication, Disorderly Conduct, Resisting Arrest and Destruction of Police Property."

"Oh, heck naw. All of that?" Arnita frowned.

"Sorry, Miss, but he's facing serious charges and his bond is rather high. Do you allow him to drink?"

"A bond?" she quizzed, planting her hands firmly on her hips. "Can't you just release him to me and stay out of the way I raise mines?"

"I wish it was that easy, but it's not."

"Yeah, well let's get on with it. How much is it?" Arnita fumed as she opened her purse, ready to get out of there as soon as possible and back to the Casino where she had been on a winning streak.

When it was all said and done, Arnita counted out $3,500. Two thousand of which she had in her purse, one thousand in small bills Little Ro had on his person, and lastly five hundred she withdrew out the ATM. Waiting forty-five minutes for the paperwork to be completed, Little Ro, still sick to his stomach, was finally freed. Before his mother yanked him out the door, the Desk Sergeant made sure to personally hand him back his Bible along with a card to his church, telling Little Ro he'd love to see him at Sunday Services.

Settling into the passenger seat, sympathy was not on his side as Arnita read him the riot act. She informed him that by the time she got home, she wanted every single penny of the bond money she'd put up on her dresser or it was gonna be hell to pay.

She's acting like I didn't give her that money in the first place. But I can't take hearing her mouth, Little Ro said to himself. He felt like throwing up again with each pothole Arnita seemed to purposely ride over.

"How much was the bond?" Little Ro asked his mother.

"You owe me twenty-five hundred," she spat matter of factly.

Little Ro didn't even think he had that much money in his stash with the way he always blew his money pretty much just as soon as he got it.

I knew I shouldn't have bought that dag on chain two days ago, he fussed at himself. Little Ro had to think quick about how he was gonna get his moms her money back and fast. Most of Little Ro's clients were young kids from his high school, but he didn't have time to wait around for them to come to him. Although it wasn't something he particular cared to do, he knew that tomorrow he would have to go up to the high school and push all the pills he could.

Chapter Eight

Little Ro paced the floor persistently in hopes of coming up with an immediate solution to ensure Arnita wouldn't be on his back about her money. His plan to go up to the school and push some pills failed miserably. The high school was on lock. There were a couple suited up security guards that had everybody noid, including Little Ro. The last thing he wanted to do was end up in jail again and owe his moms even more money.

As soon as he returned home, Little Ro was craving another drink to fight the demons that filled his head, so he retrieved a bottle of Absolut his mother kept on the top shelf of the kitchen cabinet. Twisting the top off, taking it to the head for a quick swig, he was stopped by a series of hard knocks at his front door.

Bam, bam, bam, bam. The loud barrage of bangs increased. *Bam, bam, bam.*

"Yeah, who is it?" Little Ro grabbed a pistol he kept tucked underneath the cushion of the sofa. He took a deep breath, gripping up on a gun that he'd traded a few pills for to a white boy from the suburbs "Yeah! Who that?"

"It's me, Dude." Deon pounded his fist against the door once more, causing the frame to shake. "Open up!"

Laying the gun, that made him feel tough, on the mantle above the fireplace, Little Ro turned the knob, letting his homeboy into the house. "What up, doe?" he slurred slightly, nodding his head upward.

"Dude, did you give my Ole Girl some money before you bugged out, getting yourself arrested?"

"Naw, why you say that?"

"Because she got enough bread from somewhere to get as high as three kites, and she keeps mumbling something about you and her and some secret."

"Ah, Dawg, maybe before when she copped me a bottle and I let her keep the change." Little Ro said it as though it wasn't a big deal.

"Why you do that?" Deon, out of nowhere, lunged at Little Ro, collaring him up. "That was foul!"

"Get off me. Is you crazy or what?" Little Ro shoved him back then straightened out his shirt.

"I'm sorry, guy, but I've been trying to wean her off that stuff and convince her to get some help. So when she said *secret*, I knew she must've hit you up for some loot."

Little Ro leaned over, picking the bottle off the floor then taking another sip. "You want some?" He extended the Absolut to Deon as sort of a peace offering.

"Naw, I gotta get back to the crib and make some phone calls about this house I'm trying to get. Besides, you need to put that mess down. You already jacked up enough!"

"Yeah, but I just been through hell on earth!" Little Ro smiled, realizing a solution to his money woes. "But you can help ya boy out until next week."

"What is it?"

"I'm gonna need to borrow some cash real quick to repay my Moms for that bond she had to post."

Deon, who'd been on a mission of stacking dough since the day he and Little Ro linked up, didn't waste any amount of time stopping that notion from growing. "Look, I wanna work with you, but I ain't gonna be able to do it. Now I gotta bounce and make them calls. I'm out!"

"Whoa, it's like that?" Little Ro took a huge gulp, giving him more courage than usual as he tossed the still open bottle across the room, spilling it on the new plush carpet. "Dawg, if it wasn't for me, you'd probably be still up there on the corner with that tramp mother of yours, broke!"

Deon knew after what he'd told his friend about his

Pop's death, he was in a bad way. That's probably why he had all of a sudden found a new friend in the form of alcohol. So he tried to overlook his rants.

"Look, Ro," Deon explained, "I'm saving all my money so I can buy a crib out in the suburbs and get my mother out this neighborhood, along with all the horrible memories that haunt her and me everyday. It's been hard for both of us over the years living around here, and now..." Deon continued to try to explain why he couldn't afford to loan Little Ro any money, especially the way Little Ro let money slip through his fingers like water. "I almost have enough money saved."

"It's been hard for y'all?" Little Ro stepped back. "If it wasn't for your mother being so hot in the pants seducing my dad back in the day, he'd still be alive and things wouldn't have been so hard on me. I've been the man around here since the night my ole girl came home from the hospital with my father's belongings covered in blood. And P.S., no matter where you take your momma, she always gonna be nothing more than a slime ball crack head."

"You know what? I'm gonna pray for you." Deon flipped the script. "Going to church helped me not be so angry and it can help you too. It can help you change."

"Look; been there done that. The only thing that's gonna help me is that money I need to give back to my mother, not God. So run that!" Little Ro yanked forcefully on Deon's arm then swung on him, hitting his friend dead in his jaw.

Having no choice but to defend himself, Deon fired back, delivering a strong blow to Little Ro's midsection. The harsh blow caused him to get weak in the knees. Deon then followed it up by a fist in his left eye. As chaos and pandemonium broke out inside the house, neighbors heard the noise spill out into the street and called the police.

Consumed with not disappointing his mother, whom he'd die for, Little Ro gathered his composure. He charged at his friend once more, not wanting to take *no* for an answer. Enduring three additional swift socks in his face and landing on the floor near the fireplace, Arnita's worn out, beat down son saw no other alternative as he reached up and grabbed his pistol, putting one up top.

"I said run that money," Little Ro repeated. "My momma needs it."

"Dawg, your mother ain't no better than mine despite what you think or say. And my moms needs the money too." Deon took his chances bum rushing Little Ro, which resulted in both crashing on the oak framed coffee table then rolling around in the sharp pieces of the shattered glass top.

Bang, Bang.

The loud ear deafening sounds of the nine millimeter being fired twice echoed throughout the house as Deon and Little Ro both lay motionless on the floor; one in shock of shooting his friend and one in shock of being shot. As the police sirens roared in the distance, getting closer, neither moved a muscle. Three minutes later the house was swarming with officers, including the same cops who'd arrested Little Ro earlier. Paramedics brought him out on a gurney barely clinging to life.

Mr. Martin, watching from his porch across the street, prayed quietly for Little Ro's recovery. As Deon, distraught and in a zombie like trance, was being handcuffed and led toward the squad car, Mr. Martin faithfully promised the young man that the church would stand behind him and pray for him too. Deon had recently become a member of the same church as Mr. Martin. Surely he'd be able to get off pleading self defense. After all, that was the truth, and all good Christians are led to believe that the truth shall set you free!

With Bible in hand, Mr. Martin went inside his house, and placed a call to Arnita, informing her there had been an altercation at her home and that Little Ro had been taken to the hospital.

Chapter Nine
The Here And Now

"Don't say that, Auntie Bell," Arnita shrieked, her voice echoing throughout the hospital chapel. "I'm a good mother! I'd never do anything to harm either one of my kids."

"You say that now, but you did harm him. Maybe not on purpose, but you still did. Forcing that boy to take his daddy's place and work everyday after school. Pressuring him all those times to keep his sister every Saturday instead of letting him be a child! Thank God I stepped in and took her when I did. Although now it looks like it might have been too late. But still, it was plain wrong, Arnita. There was no way that boy could fill a man's shoes!"

Arnita thought for a moment, taking in her aunt's words as she thought back on how she handled things after the death of her husband. "I never thought about it like that. I love my baby and just want him to be all right." She continued to sob.

Auntie Bell opened her Bible and started reading different verses, encouraging her niece to get on her knees and pray to God. "Tell the man upstairs you're sorry, honey, not me. He'll listen. Repent and tell Him what ails you and ask the Almighty Creator for His divine forgiveness. He'll decide in all His greatness what comes next."

Overcome with emotion and ready to submit to the will of the Holy Father, Arnita fell from the chapel's pew and onto the ground with nothing but humbleness in her thoughts as she asked for the Lord to please show mercy on her first born child who'd temporary lost his way. She also prayed for God to please not punish him for her unspeakable sins.

Our Father which art in Heaven, Hallowed be thy name. Thy kingdom come. Thy will be done in earth, as it is in Heaven. Arnita was overcome with grief. With each word that rolled off her quivering lips, she hoped for redemption as she prayed barely above a whisper. *Give us this day our daily bread. And forgive us our debts, as we forgive our debtors. And lead us not into temptation, but deliver us from evil: For thine is the kingdom, and the power, and the glory, for ever. Amen.*

Down in ER, lying on the stretcher, drifting in and out of consciousness while the doctor assessed his situation, Little Ro started to hyperventilate, realizing how serious his gunshot wounds were.

"Oh God! Oh God!" The numbness to reality caused by all the liquor he'd drank was fast wearing off and replaced by excruciating pain, almost unbearable to the teenager. "Somebody get my Momma! Get my Momma! Call her!" He squirmed from side to side as the nurses tried restraining him to put an I.V. in his arm.

"She's already here, son, so try to relax and let us help you," the doctor bargained with Little Ro, who was just about his own child's age. "Just close your eyes and calm down while we do our job."

How did things turn out like this? God, please help me make it. Little Ro prayed, feeling the pinch of a needle in his arm. *I don't wanna die like my father. Please Lord.*

For some strange reason, his thoughts turned to Lamont and the day he found out he'd died and the nonchalant manner his family behaved liked his life hadn't counted for anything but that of the materialistic things he'd owned. He didn't want to end up like that.

Powerless, turning back to his roots of being raised in the church, Little Ro reflected on the words of his Pastor preaching that it was never too late to ask the Lord for salvation and to have pity on his wretched soul. He also remembered the words of Mr. Martin about making his father proud. Little Ro knew that for the past month or so he'd been living foul, and if death was indeed God's will, then so be it.

Yea, thou I walk through the valley of the shadow of death, I will fear no evil; for thou art with me; Thy rod and thy staff, they comfort me, he said over and over in his mind, hearing the doctor announce that if he survived , it would be nothing short of a miracle. Three grueling hours of surgery passed when the doctor emerged out of the double doors and into the hospital's chapel where his young patient's mother and Great Aunt were still in there praising the name of the Lord. As he held a chart in his hands, Arnita bravely stood up, preparing herself for whatever she'd have to face. She knew that God was on her side and wouldn't give her more than she could possibly bare.

"Hello, Mrs. Mills." The doctor took a deep breath. Arnita braced herself, holding on to her elderly Aunt's arm. "It was touch and go for a good while, but fortunately we removed both bullets with a minimal amount of damage. It must've been divine intervention to say the least, because the bullets missed every one of his vital organs. It might take a week or two of hospitalization for him to fully recover, but he's young and strong willed. He'll make it."

Arnita dropped back down to her knees and cried out, "Thank you, God for giving me a second chance with my son and to make things right." Arnita raised her arms to the ceiling. "I don't know what I was thinking about, helping the devil play with my son's life."

"Praise the Lord! Praise the Lord!" Auntie Bell waved her Bible jubilantly in celebration of the strength of prayer. "I told you with God all things are possible!"

"I know you did, Auntie Bell. I know. And thank you for once again forcing me to see that God's Word is sovereign."

"That it is, indeed, Arnita. So just remember as you embrace this second chance at life with your son and mothering your children. Be careful, because you reap what you sow."

THE END

Big Homie
By
Darrell King

Chapter One

My older brother came back home during the spring of 1999. He'd just done a ten year bid for first degree murder at California's infamous Pelican Bay Penitentiary. It was something like maybe mid April, around a week or so after my fourteenth birthday, when I saw him hop off a city bus with an army green duffle bag slung across his shoulder.

As the light of the late evening sun slowly faded into dusk across the palm tree lined southern California skyline, I noticed right away that he'd definitely picked up a great deal of weight since he'd been away. Several guys from around the way stopped to greet him with embraces and small talk before he continued on toward our house. Neighborhood hoochies turned, eyeing him with a curiosity and lust, while more than one slowly moving vehicle came to a complete stop while the bandana wearing occupants within yelled out a hearty greeting to one of their own who had returned to the hood.

As he neared the front of the house, I noticed the various prison hewed tattoos that adorned his bare arms. Skull and cross bones, hour glasses and an intricately designed illustration of the Grim Reaper; a testament to his affiliation with the Reapers, South Central's most lethal gang rivaled in ferocity only by the Crips and Bloods.

He rocked a simple white cotton wife beater and baggy khaki pants with a pair of black and white Chuck Taylor sneakers on his feet. He had a bald shaved head and a silver hoop earring dangling from his left ear lobe. A healthy trimmed goatee made him look older and more distinguished than his mere 28 years suggested. At around six feet tall, my brother had always been rather lean and wiry; lanky even, but doing a dime in the Bay had forced him to pack on more than forty-five pounds of solid muscle, making him appear menacing and formidable with his assortment of homemade tats covering his upper body.

"W'sup, li'l homie? Ain't you gonna give ya big brother some love?" he said to me as he entered the front yard to our house, placing his duffle bag down on the walkway.

I jumped up off the stoop and went over to him, hugging him as tight as I could for a few seconds before my preteen machismo got the better of me, causing me to back away just in case some of the my neighborhood homies were out and about and caught a glimpse of my soft side.

It didn't take Mama long to race out of the house, yelling and screaming with tears of joy streaming from her eyes as she ran into her oldest child's open arms. Racing from the interior of the house right behind her was Mama's best friend, Shante Towson, a.k.a. Miss Shante. She was a 33 year old single mother who worked in Inglewood at Randy's Donuts. Miss Shante was a pretty lady with a bright, ready smile, beautiful hazel eyes with long thick lashes and a soft brown cocoa complexion. She was full figured, but in a sexy sort of way, which made her look even more appealing in her form fitting outfits she often wore to and from work. Miss Shante always referred to herself as a born again Christian and often read the Bible, highlighting various passages and scriptures from the Holy tome. Unfortunately though, she struggled mightily with a weakness for men and shopping.

"Shante," Mama said, wiping the tears away from her smiling face, "this is my oldest son, Montel. Ain't he handsome?"

"Oh, yes he is," Miss Shante agreed with a flirtatious

tone as she approached Montel and extended her hand to him. "How are you, Montel? I'm Shante, your mom's neighbor. It's a pleasure to meet you."

"Nice meeting you too," Montel said, taking Miss Shante's well manicured hand into his own and then planting a soft kiss on the back side.

Both Mama and Miss Shante looked at each other in surprise in regard to Montel's suave display of cultured manner. Smiling broadly, Miss Shante, playfully fanned herself with her free hand while her other hand still rested in Montel's.

"Boy, don't be doing that," Miss Shante said before Montel released her hand. She then turned toward Mama. "Angela, girl, get ya child. Got me all hot and bothered out here."

Both Mama and Miss Shante laughed it off as we all started off toward the front door. I noticed how Miss Shante turned around to stare at Montel, not once, but twice. She was sprung, and I knew it wouldn't take long before she'd make a move on my brother.

Later on that night, Mama prepared a hearty meal of fried fish, baked potatoes and collard greens, after which both Montel and I gladly helped ourselves to size-able seconds. Before we could fully digest our supper, Mama placed two large slices of hot apple pie before us, topped with a heavy scoop of French vanilla ice cream, which we both managed to somehow add to our already stuffed bellies.

After downing all that food, it didn't take long for me to start dozing off on the couch. My sleep was induced by the soft melody of smooth jazz flowing from the living room speakers intermingling with the monotonous electrical hum of the old refrigerator on the back wall of the kitchen. Yet, even in the sound of a song, snore filled snooze, I heard Miss Shante come through the front door. I could overhear her and Mama chattering non-stop with my brother about his time spent in Pelican Bay with a sense of piqued interest.

From what I was able to gather, Miss Shante was asking most of the questions, some of which were kind of embarrassing as I overheard Mama playfully chastising her friend once or twice afterwards. Obviously no question was too personal for Montel to answer, because whenever I awakened briefly to change sleeping positions, there he was holding the two women enthralled by his hardcore tales of prison life.

He left no stone unturned. His tales were filled with memories of brutal violence behind bars, which was both carried out against him as well as being initiated against so called rivals, at his request. However, he also seemed to reflect that during those long, lonely times spent locked away in solitary confinement for behavioral issues, he'd often mediate and pray each day, seeking a closer walk with the Divine as a supplement to his daily exercise routine.

Then there were the books. He said that his first read ever was the Bible. He studied it, highlighting the pages, and even committed many scriptures to memory. Much to the delight of the prison chaplain who had him lead the prison ministry for a brief period before Montel gave it up to apply himself in prison ran trade courses in which he opted to study heating and refrigeration. Montel must have talked well past one in the morning before Miss Shante said she needed to leave.

Mama saw her girlfriend to the front door after prying her away from giggling and last minute small talk with Montel. Mama shook her head, chuckling softly as she shut the door behind her.

"Child, that Shante is something else. You hear me?" she said to Montel as they made their way into the living room and took a seat. "It sure don't take that girl long to set her eyes on a man she thinks is cute and try and charm him for all it's worth. God bless her soul." Mama chuckled. "She's a nice, God-fearing girl and all, but men are definitely her sin of choice."

"Is that so?" Montel replied.

I stretched and cracked my eyes only to see Montel staring off toward the door as if he could see Miss Shante through it.

"Now don't get me wrong," Mama continued. "She ain't no tramp or nothing. She just falls in love far too deep and far too fast for her own good. You know what I mean, Montel?"

"Okay, Ma, if you say so. But why are you telling me all this?" Montel asked. "I just met the woman today. I can clearly see that she was feeling me and everything, but hey, I'm not trippin' off females like I used to. Now don't get me wrong," Montel turned the tables. "I didn't turn funny while locked up, but I'm just about handling my business in a much more mature manner. Feel me, Ma?"

"Well, excuse me, Mr. Man. I'm just letting you know how Shante rolls, that's all; not that you haven't seen it for yourself already. Heck, even a blind man can see Shante coming a mile away. I can't tell you what to do or who to do it with, 'cause you're a grown man. But I can tell you to be careful, 'cause you're still my son and I love you and care about you. On top of that, Shante is my best friend, so I don't think I need to go any further with this discussion, 'cause you know where I'm going with this, don't you?"

"Yeah, Ma, I know, but what for? Because like I said, I just met this woman. I don't know her and she sure as heck don't know me. I'm not the same li'l skirt chasin', gang bangin', Montel I was when I got locked up. I'm totally different now, Ma. You'll see. And believe me, it'll take a whole lot more than a big butt and a smile to get me interested in a sistah out here. She's gonna have to be mentally, spiritually and socially conscious for me to be interested in her. I've been a player, a mack, a lady killer. I've moved past that foolishness, 'cause I ain't got time for games from folks; male or female. My woman is gonna have to reflect those very same qualities in order to ride with me, 'cause I'm not looking for cheap thrills.

I'm looking for a soul mate, and for that you gotta have patience. So quit your worrying, Mama. It's all gravy with me, aiight?" Montel got up and gave Mama a goodnight kiss.

"Okay, son, okay. I believe you. Anyway, I'd appreciate it if you could help me tidy up just a tad, because if Leon comes over after he gets off work, I want him to come to a clean house," Mama said, referring to her boyfriend. "I sure as heck don't want no static from him when he gets here."

On that note, I decided to get out of Mama's and Montel's way. I yawned, stretched, and slowly made my way upstairs to the bathroom to shower and brush my teeth before hitting the sack to get a little rest for school the next day. It was well past the time I usually turned in for the night, however, my brother's return from prison after ten years had given me just the reprieve I needed to steal a few extra waking hours.

After I'd showered and dressed for bed, I bumped into my mama changing the sheets on my bed. Earlier she'd changed the sheets on the bed in the guest room for Montel as well.

"Ain't it nice to have Montel back home?" Mama asked me, smiling brightly. "He's put on so much weight. It looks really good on him, though, don't you think?"

"Yeah, he's pretty much cock diesel right now, but he still ain't got guns like these though," I said, rolling up my sleeves and making a muscle for Mama.

"All right , Mr. Olympus, keep ya' shirt on." Mama chuckled lightly as she hoisted a medium sized plastic laundry basket from off the top of my bed.

"I do know that Montel sure don't act the same. I mean, it ain't nothing wrong with that, but he just seems like a whole different person, that's all."

"Yes, he is different, and I for one thank the good Lord for that, because at the rate he was going before he got arrested, I just knew that I was gonna have to hurt that boy before his time. But the Lord knew better than I did and spared my baby's life. Yeah, he had to do some time in prison, but he's still alive and well. And it seems like whatever changes he underwent in there, it was definitely for the better."

"Yeah, I guess you're right, but I kinda miss having the old Montel around. He was a "G" and he had big respect from the homies out here in the hood. I dunno how cats are gonna take to him now since he's all righteous and what not."

"Cedrick, do you hear yourself?" my mother said to me in a scolding manner. "Don't nobody care nothin' 'bout what them l'il trouble makin' punks think, c'ept you. All they care about is crime. All your l'il buddies are constantly up to is no good. I really wish that you'd find some new friends, 'cause, baby, Fatz and Redrum all got issues; the kind of issues that are gonna land them in prison or the cemetery. So I'm overjoyed with your brother's maturity, and I'm sure that he doesn't give a darn what anyone around here thinks about him."

With those final comments, Mama took the load of clothes, kissed my forehead and proceeded out my room and downstairs. It quickly dawned on me that though my mother might be right in her assessments about my brother, I still kind of wished that he was the same old thug he'd once been before his arrest and conviction. But then again, perhaps all this righteous stuff was just a show for Mama. But time soon would tell.

Chapter Two

The next day, I made it home around six forty-five p.m. I'd made a beeline directly after school for Redrum's crib out in Crenshaw where I kicked it with the homies for a while. We played video games, smoked weed and clowned one another, as was routine for most of our adolescent get-togethers.

As I stepped off the city bus, up the street from our Inglewood digs, I saw Montel tinkering under the hood of Miss Shante's beat up Toyota Camry. She stood nearby chatting with both Montel and Mama while Montel moved effortlessly from his toolbox to the auto engine, tightening this and unscrewing that before getting the engine to rev up with relative ease.

"She's purring like a kitten now, don't ya think?" he said to Miss Shante, wiping his sweaty brow with a beefy forearm. "But ya gotta make sure you get regular oil changes and a tune up every few months or so, aiight? That way you'll avoid a whole lotta problems." Montel ran his hand on the hood of the car. "Caring for a whip is like caring for a kid. It requires a lotta TLC and attention. Some folks think that all a vehicle needs is gas and that's it, but no-you gotta put some work into your car if you want it to run well and last a while. You feel me?"

"Did you say something, Montel?" Miss Shante asked, not hearing a word Montel had spoken as she was too busy focusing on his biceps, glistening with sweat. "I'm so sorry. I just enjoy watchin' you. You look so-whew. Lord, help me." Miss Shante exclaimed, barely able to conceal her inner thoughts.

Mama glanced over at Montel with an, 'I-told-you-so'

look on her face, to which he simply shrugged his wide shoulders and returned several items to his toolbox before noticing and then greeting me.

"S'up, Cee-lovah? How was school today?" he asked, catching me up in a sweaty, axle grease embrace.

I wriggled free of his musty hug, and we squared off, throwing a few playful punches at one another before making it onto the front porch and settling down onto the wicker chairs.

"Class was aiight," I replied. "Just the same ole stuff, ya know."

Montel leaned forward, slightly cracking the knuckles on his massive fists as he hung his head down briefly before raising his eyes to meet mine. I didn't know what to make of my brother's sudden serious demeanor, I, however, didn't budge, but stared right back at him, awaiting words that surprisingly never came. Instead, he just smiled weakly, reached over and brushed through my long, silky braids and stood. He then leaned across the wooden banister.

"Whatcha been puffin' on, Cee? Ganja or that home-grown smoke?" he straight out asked.

It surprised me that Montel was asking me this, but it made me feel good, because it brought back memories of the original gangsta he'd been before. Smiling, I zipped open my backpack, slowly removing a small, clear sandwich bag filled to the top with a potent strain of Cali weed.

"You musta smelled the scent of that purple haze lingerin' on me, huh?" I asked, grinning while I waved the bag of bud before him. "I copped this green kickin' it at my homeboy Redrum's spot out on Crenshaw. Dawg, you shoulda been there, 'cause we got high as a kite," I said in a voice ringing with excitement.

Montel turned away from me in order to look out at Mama, Miss Shante and her daughter, Nadia, who had just walked up to them. The three of them stood catching up on the latest neighborhood gossip, not paying myself or Montel one lick of attention.

"You need to put that away before Mama gets up here," Montel said in a whisper. "And you gotta be more careful. I could smell the stink of weed on you a mile away." He shook his head. "Cee, c'mon now, you know you gotta respect Mama's house better than that, bruh. If you smoke bud, hey it is what it is. But just be a l'il more discreet, aiight?"

"What?" I said, sucking my teeth. "Look, Black, you got it twisted. See, you been gone a long time so I gotta get you up to speed on some thangs. For one, Mama, don't trip off me smoking weed. As long as I don't spark it up in her crib, she's straight."

"So you telling me Mama is cool with you smoking weed?" Montel asked, in a tone of disbelief.

"At first, when she found my stash under my mattress while changing my bedding, she had a fit. But, hey, I get good grades and basically do everything she asks me to do, so she just quit naggin' me bout it, ya know."

"Okay, if Mama's cool with it, then so be it, but I will say this; I want you to be careful hanging out with your homies out on Crenshaw, aiight? 'Cause you know that I know what the l'il homies be doing on the Boulevard. Right?"

"Yeah, yeah," I nodded, not in the mood for him to preach away the rest of the little bit of high I had left. I stuck the bag of marijuana back down into the dark recesses of my backpack, snuggly in between textbooks and a pair of gym shorts before zipping it back up again.

"You referred to me as Black." Montel's eyebrows furrowed. "That means that you've somehow been influenced by the 'Reapers'; perhaps them Crenshaw Crazy Bonez, huh? Or maybe them li'l 'Inglewood Bone Thugz'? You haven't forgotten I was set leader of the Reapers before I got busted. Me, Skippie Dee, and my man Pretty T basically started the Reapers. We orchestrated the set rules, colors, gang signs and tattoos.

Black is our greeting 'cause that's our color; basically black and white or silver." Montel took a seat again in the empty wicker, keeping a watchful eye out for Mama as he spoke gang talk to me.

"I know that you're growing up, Cee, and I know how much you like hanging wit Redrum, Fatz, Baby and all the rest of the homies, and hey, that in and of itself is all good. But I know and you know that either you're already part of the gang, or you're soon gonna be...and, Cee, lemme tell ya something, l'il bruh, you don't wanna mess around with all that set trippin' stuff, dawg. Believe me. I know first hand."

I leaned back in the chair, taking in everything that Montel was saying to me, not fully knowing how exactly to take this sudden preachy rhetoric of his. I felt that he too seemed a little bit awkward coming at me with the scared straight spiel. After all, he'd just gotten home from doing a ten year murder bid, so he was the very last person to try and get righteous all of a sudden.

It was beginning to get dark outside now and Mama finally began walking up the walkway to the porch. Both Montel and I rose up out of our seats to meet her with hugs and kisses. As the three of us made our way into the house, Montel immediately went into the kitchen, washed his hands and began removing food from the freezer and the cabinet, placing them neatly into the countertop. He announced that he would prepare the meal this time and it would be one of his specialties.

Montel had used the latter years of his prison sentence to his advantage and had become skilled in a wide variety of activities, one of which was cooking. He relayed to us that he was taught by a former chef who supervised the kitchen facilities at Pelican Bay. This man took Montel under his wing and painstakingly educated him on every culinary secret he knew. So now it brought him great pride to finally show off his skills to his family.

Mama offered to help Montel, but was told instead to

relax and enjoy television.

"Cee-lovah," he blurted out. "Help me do a li'l bit of changing and rearranging and I'm good. Trust me, it ain't gonna take long at all, pimpin'."

I reluctantly looked around the kitchen like it was a war zone or something. "Dawg, this is gonna take a long time, man. Just look around."

Montel smiled as he moved around the kitchen, rearranging pots and pans, plates and bowls from top to bottom and right to left. That's when a pair of jingling keys opened the front door. Montel turned toward the sound of the front door, as did I. We saw a pair of dusty work boots step onto the deep brown carpet of the living room. Montel went back to doing his thing in the kitchen. "That must be Mr. Leon, huh?" he asked.

"Yeah, that's him," I answered.

"I don't know why, because I don't even know this cat, but for some odd reason or another I'm not feelin' him."

I looked at my brother for a second then directed my eyes back toward the living room, snickering with a bit of anger. I'm sure that Montel had to have picked up on my sudden hostility toward our Mama's boyfriend, but I didn't care. I wanted him to know that his feelings for the man were felt by me as well, and for good reason.

Leon Guye was a tall, strapping man of around forty-two who worked for the Los Angeles County Sanitation Department. Mama had met him two and a half years ago at her church, Blesses Redeemer Baptist Temple, out in Inglewood. Originally he'd dated Miss Shante, but as fate would have it, he took a liking to Mama after his brief two week fling with Shante proved to be unsuccessful. Leon was a hard working man who made good money and an honest living as a senior sanitation worker. He was quite the handy man around the house too, attending to all of Mama's maintenance concerns whenever anything needed to be fixed. Although he was hardworking, honest and reliable on the one hand, the reserved blue collar Joe ordinary had a drinking problem. This problem brought out a mean streak in him that produced an egotistical boor at best and a hothead brute with a penchant for violence at worse.

Tonight it was clearly evident that he'd been hitting the bottle rather hard as he was hugging and groping our mother in a drunken attempt to show affection, much to Mama's disgust. She'd always been a light drinker herself, barely finishing even a single wine cooler.

"C'mon, Angie, girl. Gimme some suga, baby," Leon said, slurring badly. "I been working hard all week long. The least my woman can do for me is to gimme a kiss from them sexy lips. Can a brotha at least get that?"

Mama shoved Leon's grimy hands away from her and backed away from him. She stared at him angrily with her hands folded. "Leon, you are pissy drunk. Haven't we had enough talks about this? I told you that I didn't want you coming up into my home reeking of alcohol. You're too wasted right now for your own good. I don't find it appealing in no kind of way. So I think it's best if you just go on home, sober up, and we'll try again tomorrow.

Leon huffed, simultaneously stomping his foot in frustration. "Woman, ain't nobody drunk," Leon retaliated. "Me and the fellas just had a couple of beers downtown after work. It was just a few rounds. Now, quit all of that fussin', girl, and come on here."

"Look here, Leon, don't make me have to tell you twice to take your drunken behind home," Mama said bluntly. "You've got a drinking problem that needs to be taken care of ASAP. I care a lot about you, but I'm not going to let you keep disrespecting my home by stepping up in here drunk all the time. Now please, go home."

Leon had fully reached his boiling point now and rage had twisted his calm features with hateful ugliness. "I ain't going nowhere. I done so much work in this house that I practically co-own it," he growled, moving up closer to Mama as she instinctively backed away.

"Leon, now I'm not going to say it again; get outta my house now before I call the police on you," she insisted. "I don't want to do that, but if you think you're gonna bring your drunken self up in here, you got another thing coming." Mama yelled back at her worked up boyfriend.

Leon's thick hands clenched into massive fists as he drew even closer to Mama in the dimly lit living room. "Go ahead, Angie, call the police. I ain't scared of no pigs, woman."

I'd seen and heard enough, so I headed out into the living room to go have my mother's back. Upon making my way to Mama, Montel blocked my path with his arm, turning to me simultaneously to assure me that he'd take care of the situation.

Strolling slowly into the living room, Montel gently took Mama by the hand and moved her behind him as he stepped directly in front of the menacing garbage man. "Listen, Leon, I know we haven't met yet, but I don't want no trouble and neither does my Mama. So I'll tell ya what; go home, sober up, and come by tomorrow, man, 'cause you don't wanna do nothing stupid that'll get you in trouble. And trust me, I don't either."

"Oh, you must be Angie's oldest boy, Montel." Leon squinted his beady little eyes and squared his wide shoulders as he stared at Montel from top to bottom, sneering wickedly as he did so. "You ain't got a thing to do with this, boy. You need to learn some respect and stay in your place before you get ya self knocked out!" he barked at Montel with breath tart with the stench of cheap booze.

Montel stood his ground, calmly staring at the raging Leon without so much as blinking an eye. "Look, man, I don't wanna fight you, but you will leave this house tonight fa sho." Montel stood in between Mama and Leon with his arms folded across his chest.

"Angela!" Leon looked past Montel and shouted. "You

gonna stand there and let this ill-mannered punk talk crap to me?"

"Well, for starters, neither one of my kids are punks and they never will be," Mama told him matter of factly. "Now for the last time, Leon, leave my home."

Leon gritted his teeth angrily, with his gaze shifting back and forth from Montel to Mama. Leon was now worked up, resulting in a shouting match between him and Mama.

Without saying a word, Montel puffed out his chest and stood toe to toe, and nose to nose with the older man. It was as if the Montel of old had suddenly reappeared. For several tense seconds, the two men stood staring each other down with fists clenched, nostrils flaring, and jaws taut. Each one daring the other to react.

Mama moved around the tense face off between her eldest child and her man, quickly throwing the front door wide open while standing against it. "You've been standing here long enough, Leon...goodnight." Mama stood in the open doorway impatiently tapping her foot as she closed her eyes in mounting frustration.

Leon looked at her in disbelief. "Aiight. You got it, baby. If it's like that, I'm outta here." Leon slowly backed away from Montel and turned toward the open door. He shot my brother one last sinister glare before exiting.

I joined Montel and Mama on the porch where together we watched an inebriated Leon stagger slightly in route to his van. He mumbled angrily and kicked a can or two along the sidewalk as he went. We watched Leon get in his car. The twinkle of his rear lights grew dimmer and dimmer until they disappeared altogether, enveloped by the cool California night. Before long, Mama and I were back in the living room listening to the sound of sizzling pans accompanied by the mouth watering aroma of slow cooked seafood being prepared by Montel.

Tonight had proven to me that although Montel no longer considered himself an active gang banger, he still could go there if he needed to. I liked to see him like that, because in our neighborhood, a person had to prove that they were hard. I was glad to see my brother stand up like a true "G" and not let Leon punk him. I knew that Mama felt good about that too. She would never admit to it, but she liked the fact that Montel had come to her aid when she most needed it. She knew that I would've mashed on that fool a long time ago or either my homies would've given him a beat down for me, but Mama was hard on me about fighting and hooking up with any of my homies because she knew that almost all of them were a part of the local Reaper or Crip sets. For that reason, I had to grin and bear it. Most times Leon acted stupid around Mama. But I guess even though Montel had changed for the better, she still felt a sense of safety having him around, and so did I.

Chapter Three

The very next morning I awoke to the aroma of a wonderful breakfast being served down stairs. I quickly showered and joined Mama and Montel at the dining room table to enjoy the hearty meal before brushing my teeth and preparing to leave for school.

As I gathered my textbooks, Miss Shante sauntered in through the front door. She had her toddler daughter in tow, who immediately broke free from her mother's hand, racing headlong into my waiting arms. She laughed with glee as she tugged at my Raiders' fitted cap and playfully pinched my cheeks. Her mother paid only scant attention to either me or Mama with the exception of saying good morning. After that, Miss Shante had made a bee line to the couch where Montel sat reading.

Miss Shante wore a form fitting denim dress with a long split down the right side, revealing way too much leg. She had on a pair of black high-heeled pumps, which gave her lower legs, particularly her caves, a sexy curvature. Her hair, nails and toes were neatly mani- cured while her make up was flawless in its application. As she shimmied past me toward the seated Montel, the sweet, seductive fragrance of Versace's 'Blue Jean'5' waffled through the air. She eased onto the couch close to Montel, who didn't seem to even notice her presence.

After staring affectionately at him for several sec- onds, she roughly bumped into him with her wider hips to jar his attention from the book to her.

"Montel, don't play with me. You saw me sitting here. You could've at least said, good morning."

Smiling, Montel placed the book down beside him

after dog-earing the page he wanted to return to. He then directed his attention to her. "My bad. Good morning, Miss Shante. How are you doing this fine day? You sure look beautiful this morning"

"That's better," Miss Shante smiled. "I'm doing just fine, even better now that I've laid eyes on you," she said, showing a mouthful of pearly whites. "So w'atcha reading? Must be really good if it took away your attention from all of this." She stood and posed in several super model inspired stances.

"You are something else, aren't you?" Montel chuckled. "Well, anyway, this is called *The Art of War*. It was written by an ancient Chinese philosopher/warrior named Sun Tzu. It helps you cope with certain challenges in life and teaches you self-discipline. When I was in the pen I studied this book religiously. It gave me the ability to deal with all of the madness that goes on inside the joint. It allowed me to rely on my own innate gifts rather than that of a gang. I owe who I am today to God and The Art of War...oh yeah, and of course my mama," he said, winking in Mama's direction as she cleared the table of dirty dishes.

"If you'll excuse me," Montel said, picking up the book, "I'm gonna get back into my studies."

Miss Shante stood for a few seconds in front of Montel with her arms held akimbo and her feet tapping frantically on the living room carpet for emphasis. Miss Shante was the type of woman who hated being ignored and it clearly showed. I could tell that Montel could sense this and was purposely agitating his admirer.

"So all you do all day long is sit around reading about some China Man?" Miss Shante spat, not willing to give up so easily.

Montel shrugged. "Pretty much. That and help Mama with household chores and what not. I've also been working on my resume in order to get a job."

"My God, look at you two." Mama shook her head. "Y'all acting like a married couple already and ya practically just met each other." Mama looked to Miss Shante. "Girl, we gotta get going. I ain't trying to get caught up in that downtown L.A traffic this morning. Besides, the weather man is saying the smog is gonna be thick for a few hours early on until around noon. I don't know about you, but I don't wanna be out in that stuff." Mama tossed a bulky, leather purse on one shoulder.

Miss Shante dragged herself away from in front of Montel, but not before sticking her pierced tongue out at him in a mischievous, silly, school girl sort of way. "Come on, Nadia," she ordered her daughter who left my side and went heading over to her mommy.

The three of them, as well as myself, left the house. We waved goodbye to each other as they went their way and I went mine.

Throughout the school day at Compton High, I was bombarded with questions about Montel by my homies, especially my Reaper homies. I thought they'd heard enough the day before. But I guess not.

We had a substitute during my last class, Social Studies. We were just completing a pop quiz when I was struck from behind with a spitball. I instantly turned around, peering over the bowed head of my fellow classmates who were still busy writing the final answers to the quiz questions they'd been given.

Redrum, sporting a fresh, intricate braided hairstyle acknowledged that it was he who'd pelted me with the miniature projectile with a slight bob of his head and a broad smile to which I responded with a middle finger salute. The mean looking substitute raised her head from the book she'd been reading while we took our quizzes. However, she saw nothing unusual so she returned to her book.

Once it was certain that she was well back into her book, Redrum quietly convinced the kid sitting next to me to switch seats with him. "What up, Black?" Redrum whispered to me. "Man, I heard since Widow Maker, been back home, he been reppin' Reaper. It's good to hear that my man been putting it down."

I didn't quite understand why Redrum thought that Montel, whose street name was Widow Maker back before he got locked up, was somehow still gangbanging. That certainly wasn't the case. But not wanting to make Redrum, a rising star on the mean streets of Compton, think poorly of my brother, I told him about the confrontation between Montel and my mom's boyfriend. I exaggerated the whole thing by stating that Montel had beaten Leon to within an inch of his life as well as drawing a loaded handgun on him afterwards.

Redrum smiled wickedly, nodding his head slowly in appreciation as he listened intently to my fabricated tale of thuggish violence. "That's what I'm talking 'bout, Black." He'd said it louder than he meant to, causing the substitute to once again look up from her book. We both buried our heads down with pencils in hand until the sub resumed reading.

"It's all about Santana Black Skull, 'N' Bones Reapers for life, Pahtna," Redrum continued in a low whisper. "Widow Maker should have blasted on that punk. I know I woulda."

"Yeah, he woulda peeled his cap back, but you know our Mama was right there, so he didn't want to do her man in front of her. You feel me?" I said, quickly finding a reason for Montel's reluctance to murder his enemy. "Plus, Mama was getting all scared and whatnot, so Widow Maker just let him go with a straight up butt whippin'."

Redrum smiled with proudness. "Ya brother's a true 'O.G', Cee-love, you do know that right?" he whispered. "He's a legend out here on these streets, homie, and there ain't nothing that the homies in the hood wouldn't do for him-ever."

Just then, a known Reaper entered the room and went and sat at his desk several rows to my rear. He looked up at the clock and then at the substitute. "Sorry

I'm late," he said, knowing there was only fifteen minutes of class left. The sub just shook her head and returned to her reading.

About a minute went by before a piece of scrap paper was handed to me. It read, "Now that your brother Montel, A.K.A. Widow Maker, is back home, it's about time for you to get with some real cats who put in work and get money. Blood in, blood out. Santana Block SNB Reapers 4 ever!"

I looked back at the dude who had just entered the classroom late and he flashed the infamous gang sign of the feared Reapers.

As April came to an end and May began, Montel was home less often, as he'd begun working whatever odd jobs came his way. And came they did. Almost every week he was repairing or detailing someone's car, or carrying out minor carpentry, flooring or drywall duties for Mr. Larry, a long time Santana Block resident with a small carpentry business. I also found myself hanging out much more with my homeboys out on Crenshaw Boulevard. Though I ran the street with my Reaper homies as often as possible, I always made sure I completed all of my household chores as well as any homework, work which I knew Mama would check. And if either of those two responsibilities weren't met, I'd be in for a long, unpleasant night to say the least.

I made it a point to be sure to walk across the street to my man Fatz's crib where we'd make a beeline out back to his tool shed. Inside we were growing three marijuana plants that we called Sally, Sue and Jane. We'd been growing the plants since September of the previous year and all three had yielded us a fine crop of high grade Cali weed that we both smoked as well as sold.

Fatz was a seventeen-year-old high school dropout who lived with his aunt Reba. His mother had died shortly after giving birth to him and he never knew the identity of his father, neither did anyone else. His aunt Reba was a long time welfare recipient who did little more than sit around the house eating cheap carryout food, gossiping on the phone, and surfing cable channels. She was also a major pothead whose appetite for indo rivaled even that of Snoop Dogg's. So therefore, we never had a problem doing business out of her place. As a matter of fact, Aunt Reba helped us to plant and cultivate the illegal crop as well as weighing, packaging and selling the resulting chronic harvest.

After a particularly tedious evening of harvesting, weighing and bagging the weed for distribution, I bid farewell to my fellow hemp farmers and took off for home. I'd lost track of time and didn't want to arrive too late, because Mama would most definitely let me have it. She knew all about what most of my peers were into as did everyone else living in the city of Compton. She feared for my well being whenever I was away for long periods of time, but always prayed that God would protect me. Thus far He hadn't let her down.

No sooner than my keys entered the front door did Mama snatch it open, nearly dislocating my shoulder in the process. "It's dang near eight o'clock at night. Where were you, Cedrick?" she said seething. "If I've told you once, I've told you a thousand times to stay away from those hoodlums you call friends. They ain't nothing but a bunch of criminal thugs that I don't know why you insist on being around. I be worried sick about you."

"But, Mama, you always say, 'Why pray if you just gon' worry?'" I responded.

She had her hands on her hips and her eyes narrowed with ire as she berated me further. "Don't get smart with me, boy. I've got a good mind to take a belt to your narrow li'l hind parts, or better yet, punch you in your doggoned chest for being so disobedient!" She made a sudden move, which made me flinch, wincing in anticipation of the smack across the face I was sure to receive.

Fortunately for me, that blow never came. Instead, she simply said, "Boy, get outta my sight before I lose my Christianity."

I hung my head shamefully and walked away as my

mother leaned her head back against the couch, sighing with both exhaustion and relief. Once I reached my room I pushed through the door angrily before sitting on the edge of my bed, staring across the room at the wall covered with posters of curvy swimsuit models and Tupac. I picked up a football from the floor and flipped it around while lying on my back. I began reflecting on the recent events of the day and wrestling with the truth of my mother's heartfelt, albeit harsh, warning about my peers against my own burning desire to fit in with Redrum and the rest of my Reaper homeboys.

It was but a matter of time before I would be given a final ultimatum to join the neighborhood Reaper set, but would I be ready? What would happen if I turned down the offer? I already knew the answer though, and it wasn't like I'd have a choice once I was given the invitation. Street gangs never take no for an answer, and the Santana Block Skull 'N' Bones Reapers were no different. My only question was when I'd be officially presented with the inevitable.

Chapter Four

The next day, I arrived home from school earlier than usual, only to find a slew of yellow stickies attached to the door of the fridge. They each detailed various chores I was to complete before Mama got in. I grumbled angrily to myself as I went about dumping the garbage, washing the dirty dishes, and vacuuming the carpet. It seemed as fast as I completed one chore, there were three or four others that needed to be done. It would be dusk by the time I finally finished up.

When Mama arrived later that evening, the house was spic and span. I had worked my butt off cleaning it from top to bottom just as she'd instructed me to on refrigerator notes.

I was upstairs in my room, when I heard Montel's husky voice, mingled along with Miss Shante's girlish giggling, following Mama into the living room down stairs. I went down stairs to greet them. Mama had been grocery shopping and my brother and Miss Shante had brought in the majority of the bags already, so I went to work helping Mama unpack them and stock them into the fridge and cabinets.

Montel and Miss Shante joined us in the kitchen, playfully bantering each other as they removed and stocked groceries from the plastic bags. Giggling and laughter filled the room as Mama joined them in the humorous cross talk. Through the joking and laughter, I silently went about my work not saying a word to anyone nor reacting to the humor one bit.

"What's the matter with you, Cedrick? You being anti-social tonight. Did you break up with a girlfriend or something?" Miss Shante asked me.

"Naw, I'm aiight, just kinda tired that's all," I answered, hardly looking her way as I placed a box of Frosted Flakes into the cabinet. "Besides, I ain't got time for no girlfriends. I'm too busy to be tied down to one chick."

Miss Shante snickered loudly. "Well excuse me, Bishop Magick Don Juan."

"Cee-love ain't no playa. He's just saying that he's too young right now for a serious relationship, right Cee?" Montel playfully grabbed me up in a headlock, which caused us to tussle about the room for a bit before Mama lightly scolded us about horseplay in her kitchen.

"My bad, Mama," Montel apologized. "Tell ya what, y'all wanna have something different for dinner tonight? Like say, Mexican maybe? Or how about a really exotic Moroccan dish? I'm telling you, I can do it all now."

"Let's just have some regular old soul food like every other black family in America. Is that alright with you, Chef Montel?" Mama chimed in while placing several carton of eggs into the fridge. "I'm in the mood for chicken and dumplings myself. How 'bout y'all?"

Miss Shante and I nodded in agreement with Mama as we put away the final grocery items.

"Well, in that case, I'll just run over to Inglewood to Roscoe's Chicken and Waffles and pick something up," Montel said, grabbing a set of car keys off of the kitchen countertop.

"I thought you wanted to cook something, not go get carryout," Mama said, turning around to face Montel.

We all stared at Montel, expecting an answer. Montel stopped just short of the doorway and slowly turned back around to reenter the kitchen area. Mama placed a checkered apron around her waist as she stood up against the stove.

"Hey, if you got something else to do, then go ahead, baby," Mama told Montel. "It's all right. I'll fix a li'l something for us. Your plate will be ready for you when you get back."

Montel smiled his usual easy going smile as he stood in the entrance way of the kitchen. He walked over and planted an affectionate kiss on Mama's cheek. "Naw, Mama, I ain't gotta go nowhere. I just thought that maybe y'all wanted something different for a change, that's all. But, hey, if y'all want chicken and dumplings and not chicken and waffles, then so be it."

"That's what I'm talking 'bout," Mama said, draping her arms around Montel in a warm hug. "I would've loved to cook, but I just got back from Leon's house, dropping off a plate of left over pot roast for him 'cause the poor man's been working overtime each and every day this past week. I figured that was the least that I could do for him." Mama removed her apron.

Both Montel and I stared at each other for a quick second. Each of us recognized the disgust in the other's eyes behind hearing that Mama had taken that lowlife boyfriend of hers back after all that had recently went down.

"Some things just never change, boy, I'll tell ya," I grumbled under my breath, turning to leave out of the kitchen and into the living room.

"Mama, I don't mean no harm nor any disrespect," I heard Montel say, "but I just don't like dude, ya know? But you're an adult and you're my mother, so I'm gonna have your back no matter what."

Mama smirked while sucking her teeth. "I'm a big girl, Montel, and you know good and well that I can take care of myself."

"Aiight, Ma. I just want you to be happy, that's all." Montel slowly eased up against the kitchen counter next to his mama.

"Well, are you gonna cook dinner or what?" Miss Shante finally interrupted the family moment.

"All right, already. I got you. But if y'all want me to hook something up real quick, y'all gonna have to vacate the kitchen."

Everyone, except me, hugged Montel for his decision to prepare dinner. I, instead, dapped him up as he went toward the upper cabinets for ingredients.

"That's right, get it together, Mister. You've kept us waiting long enough to eat, don't you think?" Miss Shante rolled her eyes mischievously.

Montel shook his head, grinning all the while staring at Miss Shante as she sashayed out of the kitchen.

Mama, Miss Shante and I enjoyed the hilarious antics of Chris Tucker and Ice Cube in the movie *Friday*, while the delectable aroma of Montel's cooking wafted from the kitchen. Within the hour we all enjoyed a mouth watering chicken and dumpling meal, compliments of Montel. As we ate and laughed together, I was thinking deeply about what Montel had said to Mama concerning Leon. I knew that it was but a matter of time before the two of us kicked Leon's drunken tail once and for all. The thought made me smile a truly wicked smile.

Chapter Five

On the afternoon of May 22, 1999, I had just finished helping Montel out with one of the various neighborhood clunkers sitting in Mr. Larry's cluttered backyard. It took us both the better half of two hours to overhaul the transmission of a 92 Plymouth Sundance. Mr. Larry, who was also something of a part-time grease monkey himself, offered Montel the lion's share of his auto repair gigs whenever possible, which was nearly all of the time. Montel had proved to be an invaluable asset to Mr. Larry's carpentry company, so as a favor, Mr. Larry allowed Montel to use his property to repair the cars, which originally were to be his projects. Mr. Larry also allowed Montel to keep the money he earned from the auto repair jobs he completed each week.

"Hey, Montel, I'm gonna need some more drywall, paint and plywood from Home Depot for that job out in the Valley tomorrow morning," Mr. Larry told him. "We're looking at one of our biggest paying jobs yet, so there's no way I'm gonna let something as simple as a lack of supplies sabotage that." Mr. Larry went into his pocket and pulled out a set of keys. "Here," he said. Mr. Larry handed over a ring of jingling keys to Montel. "Take the pickup downtown and do that for me, okay? I would do it myself, but I gotta make a couple of calls and round up a few more workers for tomorrow's job."

Montel slathered his grease-blackened hands with a citrus scented cleaning solution before wiping them free of engine scum. "I got ya," he replied, placing the keys in his pocket.

Mr. Larry patted Montel on his back, smiling at me as I wiped my dirty hands on the soiled towel given to me by my brother. "Oh yeah, just charge the supplies to my credit card, aiight?" He reached over to Montel and placed a platinum Visa card into his palm. "See you two in a few."

"C'mon, Cee, let's dip," Montel ordered.

We made our way to Mr. Larry's big, red Ford F150 that was parked beneath a long, slender palm tree at the corner. Montel pressed down on the key chain's button, releasing the locks. We both stepped up into the plush leather seats of the truck, then shut the doors behind us. Montel revved her up and we started on our way.

"I'm getting kinda hungry, Cee. How 'bout grabbing a fat burger after we pick this stuff up?" Montel asked me.

Of course, I agreed, being that I hadn't eaten since breakfast.

We spent nearly forty-five minutes at a downtown L.A. Home Depot gathering up, buying, and finally loading up the truck with the building supplies. Shortly afterwards we drove back uptown toward south central in order to get a quick bite to eat. We went through the drive-thru of a local greasy spoon and ordered us thick, juicy, double-cheese fat burgers. I dug into the sloppy, succulent sandwich with gusto, hardly paying attention to my brother as he parked the truck and then stepped out.

"What's up?" I asked with a mouthful of food.

"I need to go exchange this sandwich. It's only a single cheese burger."

As Montel headed toward the carry-out window, the pavement rattling tunes of D.J. Quick blared from the loud bass heavy speakers of a midnight blue '64 Impala. It bounced from side to side on switches. Its rowdy occupants whooped it up to the explicit gangsta lyrics before pulling into the restaurant's parking lot. I recognized the driver right away as Terrell Bush, A.K.A, "Baby," who was no more than maybe seventeen or eighteen years old.

Baby was Redrum's first cousin and a newly initiated member of the Santana Block 'SNB' Reapers. He had dropped out of high school two years ago and was now constantly running from the law for one thing or another. Armed robbery and car theft were his specialties, and it was these criminal skills that had gained him membership into the Reapers' evil fold.

Once the car came to a halt, an older cat exited the car from the passenger's side. He was a tall, lanky, dark-skinned hoodlum with a wicked looking scar etched across his narrow right cheek. He appeared to be between twenty-three to twenty-five years old. He, too, wore the typical black and white of the Reapers. A thick, shiny silver necklace with a diamond-encrusted skull and cross hung from his neck. His various tattoos, particularly the half empty hourglass and the symbol #13 tarot card which stood for death was tatted on his forearm. This suggested that he was not only a high ranking member, but also an accomplished murderer.

The booming bass of the Impala suddenly went silent as did the engine. Baby got out of the car and the two gang members crossed the parking lot in route to the carry-out window. The two thugs chatted and laughed loudly among themselves as they both approached the open window and stood behind my brother.

Both individuals ceased their chatter as they observed my brother slowly counting a wad of money before peeling off a bill. I assumed he was buying something extra, or they had only charged him for a single burger and he had to pay the difference for the double. Nonetheless, Baby's eyes narrowed and he pulled the older hoodlum over toward him, whispering into his ear.

The long, lean dude listened for several seconds, but seemed to be disagreeing with his homeboy as to what it was that was being told to him. Almost as quickly as they had arrived, the two Reapers were once again snaking their way back across the partially empty parking lot toward their vehicle, fussing with one another each step of the way.

Our pick-up was parked not far from where the Impala sat, so I heard the entirety of their conversation once they'd distanced themselves a ways from the carry-out window.

"C'mon, Black! We can do this!" Baby spat. "So what, he's a little bit swoll; the two of us can take him. Plus, don't forget I got the sawed-off right here in the trunk if you just wanna bleed him before we roll."

"Naw, that ain't gon' happen. I'm tellin' you, dude is one of us...Skull and Bones Reaper black!" Baby's partner stated. "I seen my man before. You gotta read them tatz he got on them guns of his. That '86 on the hourglass tat, it means that he got jumped in the year 1986. And the barbed wire tats around his forearms means that he did time behind bars. That man is an original gangsta, Baby, and you don't mess with them; you show respect."

Baby defiantly threw caution to the wind, despite his partner's warning. "I don't care who he might be. I don't know him and I've never seen him before. As far as I know, he could be some ole busta perpetratin' a fraud."

Shaking his head with disbelief, the older hoodlum entered the car and leaned back against the cool vinyl of the passenger seat. He pulled out a partially smoked blunt from the glove compartment and sparked it up.

Baby frowned and busted his partner off with a quick sweep of his hand as the other thug offered him the smoldering blunt, but Baby refused it. His mind was set on something else as he decided against getting in the car, but headed back toward the fast food window instead.

I just couldn't sit there and let that creep rob my brother, so I hopped out of the truck and walked toward the window, all the while checking my rear to avoid a sneak attack from his homie. I slowed to a shuffle as I observed the surprisingly long line that had just recently formed outside the carry-out window.

Montel patiently waited until the cute, smiling girl on the other side of the window brought him his correct order. He stepped aside, peering into the green and gold paper bag, making sure that his order was indeed right this time around. He paid little, if any, attention to the silent black clothed figure skulling up next to him.

Baby lit a cigarette, taking two or three drags off of the cancer stick before moving toward Montel. Brushing rudely through the line of customers in pursuit of his mark, I too followed Baby as he pursued my brother. Realizing that he was being followed, Montel stopped just short of the pick-up truck, turning to face his pursuer.

"S'up, Big Homie? What set you claim, Cuz?" Baby asked Montel.

Montel saw me walking up behind the gang banger and calmly waved me over to his side where he handed me the fast food bag and car keys, bidding me to return to the pickup.

"I don't claim no set, young brotha," I heard Montel say. "I used to, but not anymore."

"You don't claim no set, huh? Well, yo' tats say otherwise, my man. S'up, you tryin' to perpetrate somethin' you ain't, homie? I hope not, 'cause that's dangerous, dawg." Baby flashed the gang sign of the Reapers toward Montel.

My brother stared stoically at his young, brash counterpart, nodding silently before answering with his own gang sign hand movement.

"S'up, Black. This here is Baby reppin' Santana Block Skull and Bones Reapers 4 ever, Cuz. Speak on it."

Montel adopted the aggressive stand of the infamous Compton Street gang. "S'up, Black. This here is Widow Maker, blood in 1986, dime piece duf in the BAY, boss playa O.G," he said in a solemn tone. "But now it's all over. I'm done, retired from the game forever. That's it."

Baby wrinkled his youthful face in confusion as he took in the words of a Reaper superior. "Say what? Retired? Naw, naw, see...you got it twisted, Black. Once you get in, you can't get out. It's Reapers 4 ever. Ya feel me?"

"Is that what you think? It ain't no way out? If so, then I feel sorry for you, young brotha." Montel shook his head. "Listen up, Baby, I'm not your enemy. I'm just another black man out here tryin' to make it just like you. When I was your age I didn't have a father figure because he ran out on my mama when I was just a little boy. The Reapers were my family; Pretty "T", Skippie Dee, DiAngelo, Paco Lovett and all the rest of the old school street legends of the past. Yeah, I slang rocks, pulled drive-bys, pimped hoes and robbed cats at gunpoint. All of that so-called gangsta stuff. And ya know what? I still ended up in prison. And inside the pen it was every man for himself."

Baby stood there listening intently, while I stood a couple feet away, disobeying my brother's initial orders.

"There was no kinda 'brotherhood'," Montel continued. "I saw betrayal on a regular between fellow Reapers. I even knew of homies who were marked for death by Reaper homies. I'm tellin' you, you have your own mind, brotha. Do you, and forget about pulling' the trigger of a gun for some warped idea, or insane sort of gang loyalty. You're just being brain washed to kill your brotha, another black man who may look just like you or me. There's no honor in that, Baby. You know it and so do I."

Montel turned away briefly from Baby and turned toward me. "Go on and crank up the ride, Cee. I'm coming in a second."

I gave Baby an evil stare before doing exactly what Montel had told me to do. Baby never once glanced over at me. His attention was totally consumed by Montel's words of wisdom. For a minute he even seemed to be considering the truthfulness of what he was being educated on, but then he returned to his street savvy persona.

"Man, forget all that crap you talkin'," he snapped. "You ain't nothin' but an ole busta! A sell out! You don't deserve them tattoos you got, fool! Matter o' fact, you don't deserve to live, dawg!" Baby raised his tank top, revealing the rubber grip handle of a semi-automatic pistol tucked into the front of his creased khaki pants. "I bet you scared now, ain't you, homie?"

Montel didn't reply. Baby chuckled, as if proud he'd instilled fear in an old G.

"Yeah, you ain't nothin' but a busta!"

Montel's eyes narrowed into slits as he eyed the gun bearing youth before him. He cracked his knuckles on each huge hand. He flexed the bulging pecks in his chest. He moved his head from side to side, cracking the bones in his thick, bull like neck like a heavy weight prize fighter preparing for a bout. It quickly became apparent that Montel's prison hardened aggression and bravery had now taken full control as he faced down his adversary with the courage of a lion.

For almost a full two minutes, Montel stared Baby down before he finally turned his back to him and walked toward the truck. A large crowd had gathered in the distance and mumbled amongst themselves as the tense parking lot show down ended in a bloodless truce.

Baby flashed Montel and me his middle finger and spewed a torrent of choice words our way before the crotch grabbing thug strolled triumphantly toward his '64 Impala. He threw up gang signs before entering the driver's side of the classic vehicle. Baby put the big car into drive after cranking up the engine and squealed out of the parking lot, bouncing along on hydraulic shocks as, once again, gangsta rap music blared from the interior before he disappeared down the distant South Los Angeles freeway.

"I hate that fool," I growled angrily, referring to Baby. "And tell me, Montel, why didn't you just beat him down? If I had known you'd just stand there, I would have whooped his punk butt for you." I stared with angry frustration at my big brother who simply stared forward at the highway up ahead.

For a split second, I thought of my brother as somewhat of a coward. But then I knew better. Montel Philips was never one to back down from any individual or situation regardless of how dire it might appear. He had, after all, survived a notoriously ruthless prison. It was now clearly evident that Montel, in deed, was a changed man. That was all good for Montel's sake, but Baby was another story, and something told me that our interaction with Baby would not be the last and any future run-ins might just result in bloodshed-or worse.

Chapter Six

By Memorial Day weekend, the summer of '99 kicked off with urban tales of Baby's recent run-in with a seemingly invincible foe. Word on the street was that Baby had emerged triumphantly, easily trumping his adversary in a show of gangsta bravado that caused the man he faced down to cower before him like the punk that he was. This blatant exaggeration of the incident, spread throughout the hood like a wildfire generated by the Santana winds.

The Reapers began harassing me with a renewed sense of urgency to join up with them. Redrum, being the set leader, seemed to take great pleasure in singing the praises of his suddenly popular cousin and went as far as warning me of the fact that Baby was still in pursuit of my brother.

After school Redrum did what he and the rest of the teenaged Reaper thugs always did; gather at the bus stop on Santana Street, which was down the street from Mr. Lee's corner store. I had decided to ride home with Fatima Smith, an upperclassman at Compton High who had a big time crush on me. I never really felt the same way about her because she wasn't really my type. She was far from ugly, just not my type. But she pushed a clean ride; a plum colored Buick Enclave that she let me drive on several occasions.

As we entered my neighborhood, Fatima begged me to stop at Mr. Lee's so that she could get a slushie and a bag of cheese puffs. Reluctantly, I agreed. I felt it was the least I could do for a lovelorn girl whose advances I'd spurned so many times each passing week. Upon arriving at the store, we exited the car and went inside. We were both walking through the cheap goods stacked aisles when three wise cracking ruffians dressed in the typical black Skull and Bones print garb brushed past us. While Fatima and I moved through the aisles in search of cheese puffs, we were followed closely by the thugged out trio.

"Pick up a couple bags of chips, some cookies, doughnuts and two or three liters of soda aiight?" the oldest looking dude of the three said loudly to his boys. "'Cause homie right there and his broad is gonna buy our stuff. Y'all feelin' me?"

"Naw, Black, we aiight for today, but we'll catch up with him again. Then we'll go up in his pockets," another said.

I ignored them and just kept it moving.

"Hey, homeboy, your time's runnin' out," the oldest said. "You either gonna rep Skull 'N' Bones Reapers, or get dealt with. So if you know what's good for you, you'll make the right decision."

The three flashed me and Fatima evil looks before walking out of the store, nonchalantly cracking jokes with each other as if nothing ever happened. I would have to endure several more incidents similar to that one as the school year came to a close. Though I took more than my share of verbal insults, putdowns and direct threats of bodily harm, no one had resorted to any physical violence. Not yet anyway.

I, on the other hand, surprised myself with the amount of quiet patience I exhibited during those trying times. I guess a lot of what Montel had been teaching me had began to sink in somewhat because I truly began to realize just how childish and pathetic the whole 'bash Cee-Love' thing was. And even more importantly, I realized that as long as no one dared touch me, I could care less about their rude comments or childish behavior.

When it became clear that I wouldn't be moved by their actions or comments, the angry gang affiliated students began spreading vicious rumors around school that I was afraid to speak up for myself, much less fight back. Soon a large part of the student body in and around Compton High began to believe the hype, with even a few of my so-called close friends shunning me. On the home front, situations were hardly better with Mama's hard drinking boyfriend Leon back in her life and acting a fool as usual. Even Leon himself, who'd learned of the incident from fellow co-workers down at the sanitation plant, began making little off color comments around the house in regards to me and Montel's supposed cowardice. It became increasingly evident that nearly the entire neighborhood felt compelled to ridicule and make fun of us.

Montel had grown up quite a bit mentally and spiritually during his time spent behind bars. He'd battled some of Pelican Bay's most violent inmates, winning some scraps while losing others. He'd been shanked and had shanked, other prisoners. In short, he'd gone through hell and high water during his ten-year sentence. So there was nothing outside those prison walls that could possibly bother him out on the streets. Besides, most of the gossip was mainly from punk kids and wanna-be thugs anyway.

Most of the true riders like DiAngelo Lovett, Paco Lovett, Skippie "Dee" and Francisco were either dead or doing hard time in one of California's overcrowded penitentiaries. These cats were the founders of the Reaper Nation and would never stoop to the lowly status of being gossipmongers, unlike their contemporaries. However, when the neighborhood's growing disrespect reached out and touched Mama, it was a different story.

I had just turned the corner, headed home, after finishing a physical game of street ball early one Saturday when I observed two of the neighborhood kids sassing Mama as she confronted them near the entrance to our house. Mama sometimes slept in late on the weekends, particularly Saturdays. This happened to be one of those Saturdays. Two of my classmates, Toby Wilder and his younger brother Jeff, seemed to always manage to wash and wax their '74 Chevelle on Saturday mornings. They also blasted their car stereo for the full hour or so. Mama had grown weary over the past month awakening irritably to the thump of bass just outside of her window each Saturday morning.

"We ain't turnin' nothin' down, lady!" Jeff spat, eyeing Mama angrily. "You always complaining 'bout something. What you need to be doing is keepin' ya punk sons in check."

Mama nearly lost it after that snide remark. I thought that she was going to slap his face. "You're much too disrespectful for your own good, so I'm going to have to call the cops."

Jeff glanced over toward Toby who shrugged his shoulders before he went back to waxing down the whip.

"I know you're familiar with the term 'snitches get stitches', aren't you?" Jeff asked. "Well, I'd say you'd just better leave well enough alone, if you know what's good."

By the time I walked up on them, Toby had decided to add his two cents and now both he and Jeff were yelling at my mama angrily.

"Back up off of my mama or you two are gonna need the Reapers and every other gang in L.A to get me off of y'all!" I was breathing heavily, more from building anger than the basketball games I'd just finished. I quickly stepped in between Mama and the two frowning Wilder brothers. I calmly asked Mama to go back into the house while I took care of the situation.

Mama left only after I promised her that there'd be no fist fighting between myself and the Wilders, and even then she went reluctantly, keeping a watchful eye on us from the living room window.

"Listen Jeff...Toby, I don't care what y'all think about me or my brother, but none of y'all bet not ever talk to my mama like you just did, feel me? The only reason we ain't going to knuckle up right now is 'cause I promised her not to. Now I'm going inside."

The two Wilder brothers said nothing as they slowly backed away across the street toward their car, mumbling audibly as they went. As I turned to walk toward my house, three neighborhood kids came swiftly up the adjoining sidewalk, yelling out to me at the top of their lungs.

"Cee-love, you gotta come down to Mr. Lee's," they yelled.

"Why? What's happening?" I asked.

"It's your brother. He's down there getting ready to do somethin'," one of them said. "I dunno, he looks pissed!"

"A'ight, let's go!" I bailed down the street swiftly behind my peers. I could see other kids from around the way racing at breakneck speed also in the direction of Mr. Lee's convenience store.

When we arrived, winded and sweaty from running, we all saw Montel sitting calmly on the hood of Mr. Larry's Ford pickup. Seemingly carefree and relaxed he sat clad in a white cotton tank top, and meticulously creased khakis with the bottoms cuffed up over his black and white Chuck Taylor's. The morning sun kissed the deeply bronzed skin of his brawny frame as he quietly munched on salted sunflower seeds, spitting the shell out indiscriminately on the cracked sidewalk.

"Hey, Cee-Love. S'up witcha? You mind getting me some more sunflower seeds?" Montel asked me. "These things are good. Boy, I'm tellin' you. Get ya self somethin' too if you'd like," he said to me as I approached him. He scanned the faces of teens who'd gathered by the dozens along the sidewalk. They were staring back at him and mumbling softly amongst themselves.

The next thing I knew, he was handing me some money. Not knowing what else to do, I went into the store and did as he'd asked. I came out of the store with his seeds and change and leaned up against the truck next to him, waiting for something, anything to pop off. Then a sharp gasp went from the assembled crowd as Baby and several other Black clothed Reapers emerged from around the corner of the store advancing with slow, yet determined steps toward my brother and I.

"Well, well, well...I see ya li'l cats are serious about reppin' yo' set, huh?" Montel stated. "A'ight then, you leave me no choice than to show you how real G's get down."

Everyone gathered along the sidewalk watched with bated breath as the baby faced thugs approached the muscle bound O.G. As the Reapers came closer, a pair of chromed out low riders screeched to a halt along the sidewalk next to the pickup truck. Immediately, ten black and blue bandanna wearing, machine gun toting thugs hopped from the insides. They surrounded the seated Montel as they faced Baby's startled set with drawn weapons at the ready.

Montel hopped down from the hood of the truck onto the sidewalk below. Slowly, he walked over to the teens who stood staring with uneasy silence at the cold, hollow barrels of the assault rifles pointed their way. "This here's gonna be a fair fight today," he started. "A whole lotta you kids been talkin' about me and my li'l brotha, Cedrick, behind our backs. Well, I'm here to tell you that today all that is gonna cease."

Baby and his crew just stood there in shock as Montel continued.

"See, my homies right here behind me rep Avalon Gangster Crip and Four Deuce Reaper gang. They're gonna make sure for an ole O.G like me that there'll be a fair fight, and afterwards, the winner will lay down the law to which everybody in the hood will adhere to...no questions asked. This is the way we did it back in the day and it's the way were gonna do it now."

I was sort of nervous, yet anxious to blow off so much needed steam, which had built up to the boiling point ever since the initial incident with Baby. So, I rolled up my shirtsleeves and trotted out onto the sidewalk to face Baby. The large group of teens gathered around the both of us, becoming loud and boisterous as they egged us on in anticipation of the inevitable fight to come.

Baby was relieved of his pistol and switchblade before he was allowed to step to me. We circled each other, each one of us looking for an opening to strike as we bounced around upon the concrete, throwing punches while bobbing and weaving amidst the frenzied yells of the ghetto crowd. Seeing an opportunity, I struck with cat like quickness, landing a solidly thrown punch on the right side of Baby's bandanna wrapped head. The blow caused his knees to buckle instantly as he simultaneously slumped forward to the pavement below. Baby broke his fall with his outstretched hands, but as he crouched on all fours trying to shake his head free of the cobwebs into unconsciousness, I again struck him forcefully with yet another blow to the head and two or three sharp kicks into his ribs.

The cheering kids had now reached a fever pitch as I continued to pummel the Reaper into the pavement with no mercy. Still Baby was no punk, and although he'd taken a sound beating, he arose battered and bloodied to land several brutal shots of his own, one of which opened up a nasty gash above my left eye, temporarily stunning me.

I saw an opening, a bare patch of earth along the cracked sidewalk, that provided me with what was needed to turn the fight in my favor. Without hesitation, I grabbed a handful of dirt, tossing it forcefully into Baby's face as he stood above me swinging wildly amid the pandemonium spectators. Baby shrieked, as the flying soil entered his eyes, nostrils and mouth, allowing me just enough time to cold cock him with a hard blow from my clenched fist to his jaw. As he tumbled to the pavement below, it was now my turn to unleash a barrage of fearsome punches to his head and face area as I straddled him.

By the time my brother dragged me off of him, Baby's entire face was a bloodied, mangled mess. Even a few of the gun wielding gangstas who were present winced at the sight of his injuries. Baby himself was pretty much unconscious except for an occasional blood sputtering cough or two.

Montel hoisted the battered teenager in his muscular arms, slowly carrying him through the human pathway given to him by the now silent mob. The adult Crips and Reapers followed him closely. Montel placed Baby carefully along the plush leather back seat of the brown El Dorado Low-rider parked nearest to his truck. As if on cue, the ten bandanna wearing thugs gathered around the ex-con whom they all held in reverence, awaiting instructions.

"Take this li'l homie to Cedars-Sinai, 'cause I want him to get the best care he can get. He might have a broken nose and a few loose teeth. I know he's gonna need some stitches to close up these gashes along his scalp and cheek area, but other than that, he's awright."

Suddenly, Baby stirred, mumbling something sounding like gibberish as he attempted to sit up in the backseat of the low-rider.

"Relax, li'l homie, we got you," Montel assured him. "You gonna go see a doctor right quick awright? So, just chill for now." Montel quickly flashed the gang sign of the Reapers before placing his hand gently on Baby's curly head. "I'll be there a little bit later on to pay for his medical expenses and to bring his Mama up there to see him, if necessary."

He then backed out of the vehicle, shut the rear door and waved the older gang members on as they all piled into the low-riders and headed toward L.A.'s famous Cedars-Sinai hospital. Montel then came over to me, carefully assessing my wounds. The cut above my left eye had swollen considerably into an ugly black and blue shiner, which though painful, helped stop the blood flow that had seeped down my forehead and into my eye during the fist fight.

After checking me out all over, Montel was pretty much satisfied that other than a couple bruises to my knuckles and face, I was okay and not in need of medical attention. He then turned to gaze upon the silent multitude of Compton teens who stood around looking back motionless and silent.

"Listen up," Montel called out. "What you kids saw here today was a fair fight between my brother and Baby. They fought with their bare hands...like men. There was no need for guns except to make sure that nobody in this crowd would dare use 'em." He focused his intense stare on Baby's group, who seemed to huddle together nervously as the O.G made eye contact with them." Things are gonna change here in this neighborhood," Montel barked with authority.

The teens all seemed petrified to even move as they listened to Montel's husky booming voice preaching a reformed gangsta's sermon of change. "Yeah, I used to bang back in the day, but I've changed my life for the better. I still got Reaper homies and I got Crip homies. I even got a few Blood homies, but they just can't let it be known that we're tight with each other, that's all. And for what? Some stupid colors? Don't get caught up, li'l homies."

With that said, Montel commanded the kids to leave, to which they obediently dispersed. As the both of us sat up against the truck, Mr. Lee came outside along with Mrs. Lee and carefully applied dressings to my wounds from the contents of a small, tin first-aid kit.

Mr. Lee bowed, as did his wife, before Mr. Lee spoke. "So, so glad to have you back, Montel, only better now. Please don't take that the wrong way. It's a compliment."

While applying a liberal amount of Neosporin ointment to my bruised knuckles, Mrs. Lee smiled happily and agreed in kind with her husband. "Yes! No one has ever taken a stand against these hoodlums before, until now. We thank you for doing what you did today."

"No disrespect, Mrs. Lee, but those kids ain't no hoodlums," Montel stated. "They're just misunderstood, that's all. And please don't thank me for anything. All I did was kick them some knowledge." Montel looked up to the heavens. "Now it's up to the man upstairs to put it in their hearts to take heed."

I know that I, for one, hoped things would change for the better. Because if the cats in the hood decide not to take heed to Montel's words, with my getting the best of Baby, I know he wouldn't just let that go. I'd have to sleep with one eye open at all times in wait of his method of revenge.

Chapter Seven

Eventually June strolled around and I along with the rest of Compton High's class of '99, proudly walked across the auditorium stage amidst the raucous cheers and flashing cameras to receive our diplomas. All seemed to be well with the hood since Baby and I fought on that Saturday morning in May. The neighborhood kids showed me a new found level of respect, which they extended toward my mother as well. No longer did the Wilder brothers disturb the quiet of the neighborhood on Saturday mornings with their booming gangsta rap. As a matter of fact, they never again waxed or washed their car outside on the streets of the neighborhood period.

Local boys who were once known to be rude, foul-mouthed bullies, now greeted my mother and other elders of the hood with respect. Gang graffiti throughout our neighborhood was painted over on the strict orders of Montel himself who saw to it that the painstaking task was carried out by the local youths over the course of an entire weekend. Montel's former street creed was now paying off in a much different way. Soon miscreants such as drug dealers, pimps and prostitutes began leaving our neighborhood, realizing that their presence was no longer wanted.

Montel himself at times seemed to be wrestling with his own inner demons, unlike when he'd first arrived from prison. He felt a need to mediate and pour over the pages of the Bible and Sun Tzu's *Art of the War*, in addition to working out four times a week. The events of the last few weeks had pushed the limits of his composure to the breaking point. He knew better than anyone how easily it would be to re-enter the turbulent world, which he'd worked so hard to distance himself.

More often were the times that he was away than when he was at home amongst his family. And when he was at home, he was mostly there in body alone, because mentally he'd be consumed by his auto repair duties, which could easily take up most of the day. And finally, when he would finish his work with the cars, he'd simply dine, shower and retire to bed for the night, being far too tired for much else. His burning desire for self perfection was amazing to watch as he effortlessly bench pressed the heavily weighed bar several dozen times under the cool shade trees in our backyard. He'd stop for a moment's breather, take a sip of Gatorade and then direct me to add yet fifty more pound plates to the already impressive stack encircling both ends of the iron bar. He'd then hoist the weights once more.

"Man, Montel," I stated. "You've already knocked out five sets of ten repetitions. I'm gonna start training like you, so the next time when I get into a fight I can knock a fool out with just one punch."

Montel sweated through his final three reps before sitting up to face me with a sweat drenched, frowning face. "You don't train your body or your mind just to whup up on people, Cee. You do it because the body is God's temple, feel me?" Montel paused briefly to wipe the perspiration from his face and body. "These kids don't know nothing about being a gangsta. They have no idea what they're getting themselves into. So what I did was let you take on Baby who'd basically set himself up as the ring leader of his li'l weak crew. By kickin' his butt, you pretty much let everybody around here know that not only are you to be respected, but not to give any ear to any of that flack Baby and his boys be spittin'."

I simply nodded my head in silence. I had to admit that I was a little confused by my brother's conflicting rhetoric of passive aggression; however, in time I would eventually come to realize the truth of his words.

Mama and Miss Shante acted as if everything was everything whether Montel was around or not. But over the passing weeks, Miss Shante seemed to be making it a point to try and find time to be alone with my brother. He knew it also, but unlike before, he didn't try to brush her off. He even seemed to enjoy the attention that he was receiving from our flirtatious next-door neighbor.

The day after Father's day, I'd just slipped into the house through the back door so as not to alert anyone to my presence. Fatz had run out of twenty dollar sized zip lock bags to package the bud with, so I had to go into my shoebox down in our basement to supply him with a dozen or so bags to work with. That's when I overheard Montel and Miss Shante talking upstairs.

Mama had gone out to dinner with Leon an hour earlier, according to Miss Shante, whose high-pitched nasal-like voice chimed through the vents along the basement wall. Curiosity overcame me and I weaseled my way up the steps ever so slowly so that I might stare at them through the small crack in the basement door near the knob.

They were both sitting arm in arm on the couch facing each other while watching television.

"I want you, Montel. Can't you see that? I've wanted you ever since I laid eyes on you, baby. Why don't you want me?" Miss Shante asked, moving in so close to him that her lips were literally mere inches from his own.

"Shante, you make it real hard for me, or any man for that matter, to show an interest because you come on too strong, too soon, that's all," Montel answered. "You're a very attractive woman. Any man would love to have you, but just slow your roll a bit. Let the men come to you for a change."

"I don't want any other man, I want you, Montel Phillips. Let me be your lady. I'll be the perfect woman for you, if you'll just give me a chance."

"You're sure about all that?"

"Positive." Miss Shante ran her dainty fingers with long pink colored nails across his smooth bald head, staring into his eyes with the infatuated look of a lovesick teenager.

"Girl, you know better than to wanna be down with somebody like me, don't you? You're on some ole good girl likes bad boy type stuff. I'm here to tell you that, that ain't cool."

Before he could say another word, Miss Shante slowly and seductively pressed her thick, pouting lips against his in a sensuous kiss while draping her arms around his shoulders. The tender embrace was immediately reciprocated by Montel. When they at last broke free of their steamy lip lock, they held each other close while Montel gently caressed Miss Shante's cheek with his left hand.

"Whatever happens, Montel; don't ever leave. And I don't mean me; I mean don't ever leave period. Cee needs you, Angie needs you and God knows I need you. As a matter of fact, this whole neighborhood needs you!"

Montel stared into Miss Shante's moist eyes. I thought that I might have detected a teardrop form and slide down his ruggedly handsome face as well. Miss Shante leaned her head against Montel's chest while he ran his fingers through her long, silky hair.

"I'm glad that you're here with your family, Montel, because something's gotta be done about Leon. Leon, as you know, is a very difficult man to deal with to say the least. I'm sure that your mama didn't tell you he puts his hands on her, not to mention the numerous times he's been caught cheating on her with the neighborhood hoochies. I know that Cedrick wanted to kill him more than once. I even stepped to Leon once or twice myself about hitting on Angie because I love ya mama like a sister and I wouldn't dare let anything happen to her. I know I'm a thick woman and all, but I'm no match for that big jerk but you are."

Montel slowly raised Miss Shante's chin with his

right hand so that she might look him in the eyes. He appeared to whisper something to her, which made her giggle lightly. "You're a special lady, Shante. Who knows? You might just bag me after all. But as for Leon; he ain't ever gonna disrespect my mama, Cee, or you, for that matter ever again. You can quote me on that one."

Miss Shante sighed softly as she snuggled up against Montel's chest. "Baby, I don't want you to get into any more trouble, so please be careful about how you approach Leon."

Montel kissed her on top of her head. "Quit your worry'n, 'cause ain't nothing bad gonna go down. I'm just going to talk to dude, man-to-man, awright?"

I'd seen and heard enough, besides, I didn't want to keep Fatz waiting any longer than I already had, so I eased back down the stairs and left out through the basement door. As I walked away from the house, I could only feel a sense of anxiety about the coming confrontation.

Chapter Eight

For the entire month of June, the hood was pretty much quiet and drama free. Montel's old gangsta homebody kept the young, trigger-happy riders out of the neighborhood, so the usual gang beefs that caused so much trouble on the streets now became a thing of the past. I wasn't aware of whether Montel had confronted him yet, but even Leon visited our home less, to my satisfaction. Montel paid much more attention to home and to Mama, making sure that she had a newly refurbished '81 Monte Carlo, which eliminated the need for Leon to chauffeur her around.

By the time the Fourth of July came around, Mama, along with Miss Shante and a few of the other neighborhood mothers, prepared a cookout at a local park. Mr. Larry gathered some of his workers to set up all of the fancy firework kits, which would bring a spectacular ending to the annual midsummer's holiday. Still, everyone knew that summertimc in Compton was a peak season for gang violence, so no one was taking the peaceful period for granted, especially Montel.

Crenshaw Boulevard was hopping with activity on the holiday. It was the number one hangout spot for teens and young adults from all across South Central. My homies and I loved hanging out on Crenshaw, especially on the Fourth of July, because we knew that all of the sexiest hoochies would be posted up there by the dozens.

I prided myself on my macking skills as I hopped out of a whip with my boys at the entrance of Crenshaw, while making a beeline for the first group of giggling hood rats we'd lay eyes on. I set my sights on Fatima's cousin, LaToya. It was just my luck, though, that Miss Shante happened to be cruising past Crenshaw when she spotted me and my friends gathered together along with the girls. I tried my best to play it off as if I didn't see her, but unfortunately she'd already seen me long before pulling up to the curb. I knew that Mama had to have sent her out looking for me because I was supposed to be at Compton Community Park for the cookout. Few teens, if any, ever went there for the celebration, because to us it was boring, with only old folks, little kids and parents in attendance. This meant restrictions on everything and anything us teenagers deemed fun.

Miss Shante parked her Toyota and exited with Mama and Montel in tow. I had been so focused on spotting Miss Shante's car that I didn't even think about the passengers.

"Cedric, don't act like you don't know we're here, boy! Don't play with me!" Mama barked out.

Reluctantly, I stepped out from among the suddenly silent crowd. Montel stepped forward, wrapping his arm around my shoulder all the while convincing our infuriated mother that everything was under control and that she and Miss Shante could wait back in the car while he talked to me. Several of the girls eyed Montel with the wanton look of hormonal craving. Montel stood among the blunt smoking teens laughing and talking without giving much attention to his young, flirtatious admirers. He was offered the smoldering blunt by a youngster beside me, but he declined it with a smile. He simply seemed to enjoy being in the presence of his brother's peers, in a place, which he'd frequented with his own homies long ago.

Mama and Miss Shante waited back at the car for a short time before Montel waved them on. Hesitantly, they both drove off back to the park, but not before Mama berated me a bit more to the amusement of my peers as well as Montel himself. A few short minutes later, a '58 Plymouth Fury low rider came roaring up on the curb, bouncing like crazy from the driver's manipulation of the switches. Once parked, the hopping, swaying chromed out whip settled down onto its sparkling Dayton rimmed tires. A group of seven bandanna wearing thugs, grasping forty ounce bottles of old English malt liquor and smelling heavily of marijuana smoke, stepped out onto the sidewalk. Among the hard looking gangstas was Redrum, decked out in full Reapers' regalia. His sinewy arms were covered with grinning skull tattoos, while a thick platinum chain bearing a diamond and X encrusted Grim Reaper pendent swung loosely from his neck. His black jean shorts hung way below his skull print boxers in which the handle of a nine millimeter protruded near the small of his back.

Another young Reaper initiated named 'Petey', whose mother was a math teacher at Compton High, walked with a confident, thou rough stride next to Redrum. He belched loudly after downing a mouthful of malt liquor. Petey was Baby's best friend who seemed to share his homeboy's love of armed robbery and had done four years in the Los Angeles county Juvenile detention center after dropping out of school in the ninth grade for just such a crime.

The other five cats weren't recognizable to me from either school or the hood, but it was my guess that they had to be from either another part of Compton or Inglewood. All of my friends, along with the chicks at our sides, suddenly went silent as the seven Reapers approached us from the opposite side of the boulevard. I stood my ground while my homies, who were mostly high school jocks, faced the oncoming thugs with unspoken courage. I could feel an uneasy sense of apprehension all around me. The girls drew closer to those of us who stood next to them, or embraced each other as they fearfully watched the gangstas step into our personal space.

Montel stepped forward to stand in between us and

the Reapers. I boldly stepped up beside him as he stood eye to eye with the scowling gang members.

"Naw, Cee. I'm gonna handle this one myself," Montel told me.

Everyone there had heard of my brother's past exploits many times over. He had become a hood legend to the young generation of Compton heads, so now to be present during a confrontation, which might very well prove or disapprove all of Montel's hype, kept everyone giddy with excitement.

"S'up, young brothas? How can I be of service to y'all today?" Montel asked them.

The seven gang members stood side by side seemingly sizing up Montel as he stood with arms folded across his chest awaiting a response. Other teens along the boulevard fell silent as they all either came over to where we were or simply climbed atop garbage bins, parked cars or whatever was available in order to catch a glimpse of the brewing conflict. Redrum stared past my brother fixedly in my direction, as his homies began to mouth off on either side of him. Montel cleared his throat loudly, which caused Redrum's evil eyes to suddenly leave me and begin focusing in on Montel.

Several voices from the crowd rose above the raucous gangsta rap music blaring from the caddy's speakers, egging us on to start fighting. Even still, Montel and Redrum were much too preoccupied with each other at the time to hear anything or anyone.

Two Rollin' 60's Crips in their mid thirties came forth through the crowd flashing their gang signs to both Montel and Redrum as they walked up on them. Both men greeted the elder and the junior Reapers with firm hand shakes and hugs before speaking up.

"My homie and me been peepin' y'all out for a minute or two, and it seems like y'all got some static goin' on between y'all," one said. "Now I know you, Montel. I remember when you used ta bang. I remember when you got locked up, and I do know that you ain't bangin' no more, which is all good, 'cause you done paid ya dues." He turned his attention to Redrum. "And you, Redrum. I know you too, li'l homie. You been putting in big work out here on these streets, slangin', bangin' mashin' on fools for their jewels and what not. You a straight up "G" on the come up, right?"

"Dang on right," Redrum replied while starring at Montel.

"It's all good, 'cause it is what it is. But peep this, li'l homie. We know that you and your partnahs is strapped, but we can't let y'all peel nobody's cap back, specially not my man Montel, 'cause he's a Reaper O.G. If ya don't know, well now ya know. Crip nation and Reaper nation is one nation, and ain't no way I'm gon' sit here and watch a rookie take out a vet befo' my eyes. It would be a violation of the G-code, pimpin'.""

Both Crips had drawn Uzi machine guns and held them down at their sides as the speaker concluded his statement. Redrum brushed off the words of his elders by responding with bold nonchalance.

"Cuz, I don't need to cap this big bubbled up fool to let him know who's boss," Redrum spat and then looked at me. "Yeah, Cee, you ain't hard without your brother, homie. You think you're gonna whup up on my cousin and not have to eventually see me?"

"You know what?" Montel replied before I could. "I'm 'bout tired of playing with you toy soldiers. Y'all ain't no real thugs, but I'm 'bout to show you and ya homies what it feels like to get rocked by a true Reaper O.G!"

In an instant, Montel was no longer Montel; he was once again the dreaded 'Widow Maker' who knew no fear and whose heartless acts of crime filled his enemies with terror. His hands quickly clutched Redrum around the neck, lifting him up with ease while simultaneously tossing him up against a garbage dumpster. Upon letting him go, his limp body flopped to the pavement, moving only slightly while he groaned out in pain. His six friends came in to engage the angry Montel with swinging fists, taking him backward onto and across the hood of a parked car.

I stepped forward to aid my brother, but he put his hand up to stop me. "No, Cee. I need to show these fools what a true gangsta is all about." So with that, I stepped back.

The six teens were able to match Montel blow for blow as they piled on top of him. Petey was viciously stomping and kicking away at Montel's upper body in a concentrated attempt to land a fatal blow to his temple while the five other hoodlums wrestled with him along the ground in a frenzied whirlwind of grunts, groans and knuckle blows. Montel seemed overwhelmed at first as the young gang bangers stood above him ostensibly crushing him underfoot. However, in reality, Montel was simply buying time in order to strike at the right moment.

Swift as lightning, Montel swung his right foot out, tripping one of his attackers who stumbled backward onto the parked car, bowling over one of his fellow gang members in the process. A loud gasp, followed by resounding laughter echoed from the ghetto spectators as they watched the two thugs topple over one another up against the car and onto the street below.

Redrum dragged himself up from the pavement and was shaking his head free of the cobwebs which still clung to his senses like a wet blanket. Through the fog of his hazy awareness, he made out the blurry images of his remaining homies locked in a brutal fist fight with the legendary ex-con.

Montel's energy never wavered though he was several years older than the youths that he fought. He took their best shots in stride, wobbling slightly once or twice, but delivered more than a few blows of his own, which caused considerable damage to the recipients themselves.

Petey, who proved to be the hardest of Redrum's gang, was also the first to be dropped by one of Montel's power punches. The remaining two hoods quickly glanced at each other, then back at the heavily breathing, sweat drenched Montel as they slowly backed away from the fight toward the edges of the crowd.

Somewhere within the crowd of onlookers, the crash of shattered glass sounded and a partially broken bottle of gin was tossed to one of the youths from an unidentified spectator. The youngster caught the make shift weapon in midair and lunged headlong toward Montel, swinging the jagged edge of the broken bottle with deadly intent. Miraculously, Montel swayed backward just as the razor sharp points of glass cut through thin air, missing his chest by mere inches. The very momentum of the swing itself left the gangsta severely unbalanced and at a major disadvantage, causing Montel to seize upon the opportunity to land a muscular elbow down with brutal force upon the dude's lower back. The thug fell hard onto the pavement, bruising himself up badly as he skidded along the gravel.

No sooner than he'd polished off that cat, did the final member of Redrum's little posse attack. This one was a heavy set, dark skinned hooligan of about eighteen or nineteen and weighing what seemed like 240 or 245 pounds. He charged into Montel with the velocity of an angry linebacker. Both of them crashed headlong into a row of metal garbage cans, all the while grappling furiously upon the weather beaten sidewalk, with each combatant desperately trying to gain leverage during the struggle. The stout kid was getting the better of Montel for a few seconds and the crowd gasped in anticipation of a knock out punch landing any minute up against Montel's square jaw.

"Knock him out, dawg!" Redrum snarled out as the two men threw punches at one another amidst the din of the noisy crowd.

After rocking Montel with one hard punch after another, the stocky boy made a crucial error when he decided to charge Montel as he stood on unsteady legs, teeter-tottering from side to side. Though dazed, Montel sidestepped the rushing opponent seconds before contact. The young thug's momentum carried him harmlessly into the throng of onlookers, who helped him to his feet only to toss him back into the fray. By that time, Montel had gotten himself together and met the strapping youngster with a quick knee to the groin, which felled the ruffian like a pine. When the black clad Reaper slumped to the ground holding his privates in agony, Montel was sucker punched from behind by a scowling Redrum.

Unbeknownst to Montel, the set leader had fitted a pair of shiny brass knuckles to his scarred right hand, and it was these, which nearly floored him. Luckily for Montel, the first blow merely grazed off of the back of his head, enough to hurt but not to K.O. him.

"Watcha go'n do now, big homie?" Redrum quipped, snickering sarcastically as he circled in on a wobbly knee Montel. He darted in swinging a sharp right hook at Montel's jaw with the brass knuckle encircled fist. The punch was accurate and solid , landing a mighty blow against Montel's jaw, knocking loose a tooth or two in the process.

At that point, I didn't care what Montel said, I couldn't stand to watch my brother being beaten like that anymore, so I sprung toward my ex-comrade with clenched fists and eyes seeing red, only to be snatched backward by a strong hand. Mr. Larry had arrived on the scene out of nowhere. He seemed out of place in his old, dingy overalls with dried splotches of paint all over it among the chick, jewel laced teens who'd gathered to watch the brawl. An unhappy frown formed along the corners of his wide mouth as he surveyed the after math of the street fight.

Mr. Larry noticed Montel down on one knee bleeding from the mouth, and trying to steady himself from falling. Then, without warning, the old man lunged forward, pimp slapping Redrum with enough force to have broken his neck. Redrum sank to the street below, holding his reddened face and wincing painfully. The other Reapers were all slowly but surely recovering somewhat from their wounds and fight inflicted vertigo.

Slowly the bruised and battered gang members backed away into the crowd as they watched Montel being helped up from his kneeling position by the old carpenter. A few of the onlookers booed and threw debris at Redrum's homies as they made their way back toward the chromed out Plymouth sitting along the sidewalk on the opposite side of the street. Montel stood wobbling about on unsteady legs before finally gaining his balance. He dabbed at the blood, which trickled from his loosened teeth, while spitting a glob of red tingled saliva to the ground. Silently, he turned to view the surrounding crowd through black and blue, swollen eyelids.

The onlookers slowly began to fall back, leaving only myself, Mr. Larry, and the two Crips standing by stoically alone in the middle of the lot. Montel grimaced slightly from the pain of his various cuts and contusions before coming over and wrapping a sweaty arm around my shoulder. As he hugged me, he began to cry. Not a weepy, sorrowful cry, just a silent, stone faced shedding of a tear or two...or perhaps three. Tears of frustration and anger at himself for losing control of what little discipline he'd taught himself to adhere to. Anger at himself for not being able to utilize his so called 'street creed' for ending violence instead of giving in to it. And finally, frustration with the state of affairs in the hood, which hadn't changed one bit since he'd been imprisoned a decade earlier.

Redrum was approached by the older gang members who ordered him to relinquish both his brass knuckles and his pistol before he limped away, bruised and battered across the street, toward his equally exhausted and beaten homies. Mr. Larry came over and embraced both Montel and I simultaneously before offering to drive us both to Cedars-Sinai in order for Montel to have his wounds properly dressed and treated. My brother kindly declined, as he was commended by the two Crips who'd acted as referees of sorts.

As a young boy, I had never really seen my brother engage in any real acts of violence against anyone, with the exception of a shoving match. And that had only been against one of his friends during a heated crap game. His love and respect for his family forced him to keep those dark tendencies of his at bay whenever he was around us. But now I, and dang near the entire city of Compton, had seen the legend himself in action.

By now Montel's mouth had pretty much stopped bleeding once he'd soaked the majority up with a bandanna that had been given to him by one of the Crip homies. As Montel, Mr. Larry and myself began walking toward Mr. Larry's pickup, we all spotted two LAPD squad cars parked a few feet away with their sun shade wearing occupants staring motionless in our direction.

Mr. Larry threw his arms up in exasperation to this newly developing issue. "Man! This is just what we need! The cops! This is not good, not good at all!"

Laughter escaped the mouths of the two Crip O.G.s as they listened to Mr. Larry rant and rave about the cops who seem to do little else but stare at us occasionally, even waving at us once. "Calm yo' nerves, Pops," one said. "Five-o ain't gonna do nothin'. They know us and we already told them 'bout what was going down. Trust me; they want these young riders off the street just as bad as y'all do."

"Yeah," the other Crip agreed. "We still rep Crip, but me and my homeboy don't rob, steal or kill folks no more." The two gang members then followed us across the street to the awaiting pickup.

Montel acknowledged the words of his Crip ally with quiet dignity. "I appreciate everything y'all did today, but as of today, I'm truly and officially out of this gang crap."

Montel opened the door to Mr. Larry's F150 and ushered me in first before he slid his aching body in afterwards. Mr. Larry got in on the driver's side, started the engine and slowly pulled away from the infamous Crenshaw Boulevard toward home.

We stopped at Mr. Larry's first, and it took over an hour for Montel to get cleaned up before he felt comfortable enough to step out. After a long, hot shower and the application of a few bandages, it still did little to hide the fact that he'd been in one heck of a fistfight. His face resembled that of a prizefighter who'd just finished a 12-rounder. His knuckles were also scarred and raw with dried blood on them and he wore dark Ray-ban shades to cover his puffy black and blue eyes.

We arrived at Compton Community Park just in time for the fireworks. Mama was understandably peeved at each one of us, including Mr. Larry himself for coming so late and missing most of the food from off the grill, not to mention news of the fight which had occurred earlier. Mama pretty much chewed both me and Montel out behind that one. Luckily for us, her vicious ten minute tongue lashing was largely drowned out by the racket of the exploding pyrotechnics above.

Montel took the entire blame for the incident. Miss Shante was feeling sorry for Montel at this point and quickly took the time to intervene. After speaking with Mama for a few minutes, she asked Montel if he would take a ride with her in order to let Mama cool off somewhat before returning. He agreed and off they went in her hooptie toward God-knows-where.

As far as Miss Shante's baby daughter, Nadia was away visiting her father in San Diego and would not return until late summer, so Miss Shante had the house all to herself and no baby-sitting issues to concern herself with, so I'm certain she intended to take full advantage of this prime opportunity to spend quality time alone with the apple of her eye.

Chapter Nine

July passed with relative ease on into August. The heat of the Southern California mid-summer evenings was humid and relentless. The gangs seemed to react with much less violence than ever before. Montel's legend grew even though he rarely, if ever, hung around his old Reaper homies. Redrum ended up in jail for the third time in five years for armed robbery, and with his arrest and conviction, most of his little bandanna wearing lackeys lost interest in gang activity and wound up pursuing more constructive activities.

I noticed that after spending time together Fourth of July, Montel and Miss Shante shared a special closeness. They now appeared to be dating seriously. In fact, Montel had moved in with her and little Nadia. Surprisingly, no "I told you so," came from Mama.

I was enjoying the summer mainly because I had somehow ended hooking up with Fatima after all, who proved to be a jewel in the rough as a gal pal for me. Mama, too, had a pretty good summer as well. She had just received a raise on her job.

Alone at the house playing Playstation, I rolled up a few blunts and called over a couple of my boys to play a few games for some money. Within twenty minutes, five of my best homies walked up in the crib carrying their own game controllers and a pocket full of cash. We began our virtual football battle against each other on the big screen. The house was filled with the loud trash talk of pubescent boys and simulated stadium crowd noise echoing from the television speakers. Buttered popcorn, colas, and friendly put-downs flowed freely while twenty dollar bills were exchanged from hand to hand as losers relinquished their controllers to the victors.

After thirteen total games, my winnings amounted to over $200. I turned off the Playstation and TV before walking my disheartened pals to the threshold of the door, thanking them for their time and money as they filed out one after the other. I recounted my quick winnings, smiling proudly from the small stack of twenties and tens that I held in my hand. As I stuffed the wad of cash down into my sagging khakis, I noticed Fatima waltzing up the sidewalk. She picked up the pace of her gait when she saw me standing on the porch. She rushed toward me, squealing with delight with her arms outstretched. We held each other tight and passionately locked our lips together in a sloppy, teen kiss.

Our raging hormones tugged at us both to take advantage of the empty house. But common sense won over adolescent lust, and fortunately so, because Montel and Miss Shante pulled up with Mama, after an afternoon of grocery shopping, as Fatima and I stood chatting on the porch.

"Y'all had better not been doing nothing nasty while I've been gone," Mama said jokingly as she exited Montel's new Thunderbird.

Both Fatima and I laughed as we rushed off the porch to embrace Mama simultaneously before helping with the groceries. An hour after we had gotten all the groceries in the house and got settled in, the sound of a familiar vehicle came rumbling up along the curb in front of the house. Irritation immediately replaced my ebullience as the powerful engine just outside the window came to a halt. Montel, as calm as always, sat back flipping slowly through the pages of the old Testament book of Judges.

"Mama, it's Leon, and I betcha he's drunk, as always," I presumed. "But I'm gonna ask you with all due respect, Mama; please for me; for us all, do not argue with him, okay?" The last thing I wanted was for

Mama and Leon to get to going at it in front of my girl. "I promise you he will not make a scene, 'cause I won't let him." Mama rolled her eyes a bit She sighed audibly before raising up from the couch to get the door just as Leon lumbered up the walkway and onto the steps leading to the entrance.

Leon stopped at the threshold of the doorway to greet Mama with a kiss and hug before proceeding inside before her. Unlike usual, Leon was dressed fairly well on this evening. He was also clean shaven and sported a nice looking, well overdue haircut, which seemed to take at least five years off his hardened and deeply furrowed face. He slowly chewed on a stout, unlit cigar, as he stood tall in the middle of the living room floor. He barely acknowledged the rest of us sitting on the couch, except with a brief nod in our direction, before immediately turning his attention to Mama.

He seemed to have put on a few more pounds to his already mammoth frame, but it looked to be more like muscle mass than fat. Even as he stood handing Mama a lovely bouquet of red roses, his peaceable look did little to put the three of us at ease. We knew all too well how unpredictable the big man's moods could be.

"I wish that for once we could have this place to ourselves," he complained. "C'mon, baby, let's go and catch a movie or somethin', all right?"

"Ya know what, Leon?" Mama said in a tone that hinted she was about to decline. "I thank you for the roses and all. I really do, but I've got to pass. I'm so wore out. I'm fixin' to go lay down. So let's just get together tomorrow," Mama suggested.

Leon's response wasn't so gentle. "See, I try to do something nice and you reject me." His tone picked up.

Mama just shook her head. She looked at me as if recalling what we'd just talked about. "Why are you always so negative when you come around here? It's just not right, Leon. You and I have a relationship, but this is my home and I can't just let you keep disrespecting my home and family like this." Mama pushed the flowers toward Leon. "So here; take your flowers back and enjoy your movie."

Leon's face frowned with displeasure. "Listen up, woman. I ain't got no time for ya foolishness tonight. I ain't come all this way up here for nothing. So get ya self together and let's bounce. Don't lemme have to tell you twice."

By now Leon was talking so loud that I'm sure all the neighbors could hear him through the screen door.

Mama spoke back sternly before taking her seat on the couch among Fatima and me. "Goodbye, Leon," she said without batting an eye.

Leon could tell she meant business; that she wanted him to go, and more than likely, to never return. "C'mon, Angie. Stop playin' with me and let's go now. I ain't got time for this tonight."

"I said, bye, Leon."

In a huff, the now infuriated Leon tossed the long stem roses forcefully against the door before snatching it open with anger. Before walking out on to the porch, he stopped in his tracks and turned to look at Mama one last time. "You gonna learn one way or another on how to treat a man with the proper respect that's due him." The burly brute turned once again after descending down the steps a ways and stormed back up them, kicking the screen door furiously, startling us all.

By now Montel was on his way to the porch. Montel stood before his glowering adversary. "Leon, look man, I've watched you cold disrespect my mother. I'm sorry, but you're getting up outta here today." Montel cracked his knuckles. "Now, we can do this the easy way and you can walk outta here on your own, or we can do it the hard way, and you can get carted up outta here on a stretcher. The choice is yours."

Leon gritted his teeth and squared his wide shoulders while sizing up the much younger man standing before him. He smirked, backed away slowly, then went to his truck and drove away.

Fatima was so shaken by the turn of events that I had to wrap my arms around her in a comforting hug in order to quell her sobbing.

Mama rose up from her seat to face Montel after he entered the house from the porch. "Look, Montel, I appreciate you taking, care of your mama, but my business is my business, and you don't have to come to my rescue every time, okay?"

"Mama, I'm sorry, but I just can't let that cat disrespect you. I'll be darned if I'm gonna let anybody hurt you."

Mama could see the hurt in Montel's eyes. She walked over to him and placed her hand on his shoulder. "Look, son, I know I've been going about dealing with Leon the wrong way, but so have you. Actually, I don't think it's either one of us who should be dealing with him at all."

Montel and I waited to see if Mama was going to tell us who the mysterious person was that should be dealing with Leon. The wait wasn't long.

"We both need to let go and let God." Silence fell over the room, a strange but peaceful silence, such as only the kind that words of wisdom can bring.

"Yeah, Mama, you're right," Montel agreed. "We both talk about God, but do our actions speak louder than words?"

Mama thought for a minute and then said solemnly, "I know that I need to rededicate my life to Christ. How 'bout you, son? Huh? What about you?"

Without verbally answering, Montel allowed his actions to speak louder than his words. He extended both his hands; one to me and one to Mama.

"Let's all join hands and seek God in prayer," Mama said.

Mama, Fatima and I stretched forth our hands until we were all linked together. As we all closed our eyes and hung our heads, Mama began to pray. This was a first for the family, and I must admit, the hush that fell over the room was so powerful, that I secretly hoped it wouldn't be the last.

Chapter Ten

We must have praised God on that humid night in August '99 for well over an hour. Even I danced a holy gig for the very first time. I felt completely care free. Carefree from all other worries or distractions, and I could tell by the shared reactions that so did everyone else.

Afterwards we embraced each other, silently recognizing how deeply we were touched by the spirit. Mama sank down into the couch, exhausted from expressing her love for Christ in such an energetic way. Montel walked out onto the front porch in the warmth of the southern California evening to be alone with his thoughts. Fatima gave each of us a warm hug before returning home for the night.

I began to reevaluate my own young life. I began to study the Bible regularly and even replaced my beloved gangsta rap CD's with those of contemporary gospel artists such as Kirk Franklin, Fred Hammond and Yolanda Adams.

Days later, I was going about my daily chores when I realized that Montel hadn't gone out back into the yard to work out as he did daily. It seemed sort of strange to me because he never neglected his exercise routine. Mama and Miss Shante were upstairs in Mama's room discussing Leon and one of his latest meltdowns. As I climbed the stairs, I couldn't help but grow angrier and angrier as I heard the details of the garbage man's physical assault of my mother.

"I am really going to leave Leon for good this time; you'll see," I heard Mama cry to Miss Shante. I felt sorry for my mother because I felt that she was finally sincere for the first time.

I heard Montel stroll through the front door, not uttering a word to any of us as he made his way upstairs and into the room which had been his before he'd moved out with Miss Shante. Only a couple seconds later did Montel walk back down the stairs. Miss Shante took off downstairs to catch up with her man. As she ran downstairs, me and Mama were close on her heels. The three of us darted across the living room floor and through the open door, and onto the porch.

The porch and the front yard were silent and empty. There was no sign of Montel anywhere. Mama looked beside her toward Miss Shante, who smiled back weakly. "Pray for Montel, Shante. Please pray for him, and for me. I know his silent treatment and attitude is because of silly ole me. Something tells me that he's gonna go after Leon for hitting me. I know my child, Shante," Mama confessed while shaking her head. "He's gonna go after Leon, and who knows what he might do?"

Miss Shante held out her arms, and she and Mama hugged each other real tight. "That boy has come too far to backslide now," Mama cried. "Lord knows I don't wanna see my baby end up back behind bars because of me."

The silence of the porch was broken by our mother's bitter sobbing, in conjunction with Miss Shante's own. The two women embraced one another for what seemed like an eternity, crying together for a man whom we all loved. As for me, I simply leaned forward over the wood railing, staring out across the street as dusk settled upon Compton.

"Mama, I think I might know where Montel is," I said. "He might be at Mr. Larry's place. Mr. Larry will be able to talk some sense into him. So, I'm gonna take a walk over there. I'll be right back."

As I walked briskly down Santana Block, I paid only scant attention to shadowy images of cats hanging out, shooting dice and loitering near the local liquor store. A couple was even pan handling for beer money. Passing

Mr. Lee's convenience store, I noticed a late model Lincoln Town car cruising slow and sinister in neutral. Immediately, my heart began pounding and I quickened my pace a bit more. The tinted window rolled down just a tad.

"Cee-Lovah! It's me. Montel, c'mon. Hop in!"

A strong sigh of relief left me as I turned and crossed Bowed Lane toward the grim looking vehicle. The back door opened wide and I stepped into the spacious inside. Two of my brother's homies sat in the back guzzling down Old English malt liquor while another of his old Reaper buddies drove the whip, puffing on a half smoked blunt that fogged up the interior with its hypnotic smoke.

Montel lounged beside the bandanna-wearing driver, listening to the mesmerizing, violent gangsta poetry of Eazy E as he took the blunt from the driver's fingers and inhaled the potent smoke deeply. When he turned to face me, I could see that he was extremely high with glassy, reddened eyes and a serene but serious bearing. A black bandanna covered his head in a Tupac style wrap and he held an ebony hued banana clip in one hand while he puffed on the blunt with the other. An A.K 47 lay silent and menacing across his broad thighs as he sat up front.

The blunt passed around the car several times, which I surprisingly refused to partake of. Talk of the bloodletting and redemption rattled throughout the darkened Lincoln as we crept slowly down the dimly lit streets of our Compton neighborhood. Assault weapons were being loaded all around as my brother and his homeboys discussed a drive-by shooting. Montel had completely returned to his psychopathic roots; the same ones that had landed him behind bars in the first place. This was now a Compton gang banger. A death-dealing rider who brought dread to all the residents of the hood. Total recall of Montel's Reaper past had now fully taken control of his very being, and it wasn't pretty to look at.

Palm trees, willowy and dark, breezed past the partially open window as we cruised down the street toward Leon's house, which was about a half mile way. Montel flicked the remainder of the blunt out of the passenger's side window into the dark void beyond before adding a handful of hollow tip shells to the banana clip he held loosely.

"I just wanted to get your attention, that's all," Montel said to me. "But I think you'd better go on back home, 'cause this ain't no place for you to be right now, feel me?" Montel filled the clip with rounds.

I was disappointed in my brother for the first time in my life, and I felt that I had to let him know how I felt. "Montel, man this ain't you, Black. You're better than this, dawg. This ain't gonna solve nothin'. It's just gonna make things worse...for you especially!"

"Do you think I care? I been to the pen before. I can survive. That ain't no problem. And I'd rather go back to prison than to let some punk, mark hit on Mama!" Montel snarled with anger. "I tried, Cee, I really did. I made a lotta positive changes in my life, and I'm proud of that. I know that what I'm about to do is wrong, but I ain't letting this ride, Cee, 'cause Mama ain't never gonna leave Leon for good on her own. And who knows what he'll do to her next?"

As I listened to Montel's response, I got even angrier with him. "Dawg, you a sucka. How you gon' come here from prison talking all of this righteous, Zen master stuff and now you gonna flip the script and go back to bangin'? Not only have you confused the heck outta me, but you should be ashamed of yourself for being such a hypocrite!"

Montel slammed the full clip into the bottom of the assault rifle angrily, then he turned in his seat to face me. "Look, boy, you'd better calm down before I calm you down!"

"Forget you, dawg. I'm gonna speak my mind, playa," I snickered. "Watcha gon' do about it? Shoot me, too?"

"Who do you think you're talking to, Cee?" Montel replied deep and guttural. "Get out, Cuz!"

Before I could utter another word, I felt the swift painful sting of my brother's opcn palm hard on the left side of my face. He then had the driver pull over abruptly to the curb and he himself yanked me from the back seat, tossing me out onto a nearby lawn before squealing off in a wake of white burning rubber. The town car was deathly silent as it moved down the street.

Chapter Eleven

Even though my body ached and I staggered about with groggy unsteadiness, I was determined to prevent my big brother from ruining his life by making this most horrible of choices. I steadied myself and began to move quickly up Myrrh and Willowbrook, pass the Heritage house, which stood out dark and forbidding amongst the shadowy cluster of palm trees surrounding it. The faint flutter of a police copter overhead mingled with the distant wail of squad car sirens brought me a slight sense of dread for several minutes before I regained enough composure to proceed. After about fifteen minutes or more, I saw the tricked out Lincoln roar past me down Willowbrook, seemingly back to our house.

I could have walked back home if I'd wanted to, but instead I hailed down a passing taxi in order to get to our place as soon as possible. By the time the taxi pulled up along the curb to our home, I could see both of Montel's homeboys' rides as well as Leon's car parked on the street, not far from each other. I hurriedly paid the driver his fare and sprinted with breakneck speed up the winding sidewalk and across the steps. When I entered the house, Montel stood alone, without his homeboys who had obviously been waiting for him in the car, in the living room area. Sitting on the couch next to Mama was Leon. Miss Shante sat in a chair across from them.

I stepped to Montel, motioning with my head for him to take a walk with me outside into the night where he could reconsider his motives. He brushed me off nonetheless.

"Cee, I got this, dawg. I know what I'm doin', all

right. You just take Mama and Shante next door to Shante's crib while I handle my business with old Leon here. After that, everything will be gravy." Montel cracked the knuckles on his thick fists loudly while glaring at Leon, who in turn glared back with equal animosity.

I shook my head defiantly after hearing Montel's words. I then reached to take hold of him but stopped just short of touching him.

"Do what I said, Cee," he reiterated.

Mama was talkative and unmovable at first, but after some heavy duty coaxing by Miss Shante, she reluctantly left with me and Miss Shante, still demanding to know what actions concerning Leon would be carried out in her absence.

As we exited the house, I just had to see for myself what was going down. Perhaps there was a chance I could still talk Montel out of doing something stupid. So I told Mama and Miss Shante to go ahead while I stayed, returning back into the house.

Montel's eyes were locked with the older, burly Leon. "Look, Leon, I really don't wanna go there with you, Cuz, but you're making it real hard for me not to. That's my mother you've been putting your hands on. I'm telling you to your face that you're never gonna hit my mother ever again."

Leon stood before Montel, moving only slightly as he slowly twirled a toothpick back and forth in between his sun chapped lips. Then he took the toothpick from his mouth and moved just a bit closer to Montel. "What goes on between ya Mama and me is our business and is of no concern to you or nobody else." Leon stood mean mugging the young, chiseled man-child in front of him. He really didn't want to tangle with the ex-con in all honesty. He even backed up a few paces as a result. Unfortunately for him, this was what his adversary was waiting for.

The two men stood their ground, watching and waiting, waiting and watching, as the chestnut encased grandfather clock ticked away loudly. Then the inevitable happened; quick, fast and in a hurry. I didn't even see it coming, leaving me no time to try to play interference.

There was the rumble of muscular bodies colliding together violently, while simultaneously crashing into furniture all across the room in the process. When the tumultuous thirty-five seconds finally ended, Montel rose up staggering briefly, but of no worse for wear except for a split bottom lip, which leaked crimson as he wiped it clear upon the back of his hand. The same, however, could not be said of Leon as he lay groaning on the floor in a beaten, bruised and bloodied heap.

I had to admit, I was somewhat relieved by the fact that Montel had decided to go man to man with Leon versus straight out shoot him.

"This didn't have to happen like this, Leon, but you left me no choice, man," Montel said gently as he collapsed down on the floor, leaning his broad back against the wall opposite the prostrate form of Leon. "Lord Jesus, have mercy on my soul! I come to you now seeking your face for forgiveness and mercy."

I couldn't believe it as I stood there listening to Montel begin to pray for forgiveness.

"And while you wash me in your blood, sweet Jesus," he continued, "please remember poor Leon here for he's your child, too. Give him a mind to praise your name, Father."

The look on Leon's face was that of a stunned man; a man who couldn't believe that his enemy was praying for him. I was stunned too as I watched Montel hang his head and close out his prayer.

Slowly he rose to his feet and walked over to Leon who was still lying there. He bent down and took the big man in his brawny arms and hoisted him like a baby, carrying him over to the couch where he placed him down onto its soft cushion. He went out onto the front porch where scores of neighbors had gathered around outside of their homes, apparently drawn by the loud arguing and fisticuffs. Eventually, after realizing nothing more was going down, the two dozen or so neighbors shuffled back inside their homes, leaving Montel alone with his thoughts.

"S'up, big homie?" I asked while taking a seat on one of the wicker chairs on the porch that was facing the street. "Looks like you gave Leon a serious beat down back up in the crib."

Montel paused before saying, "I feel like a failure, Cee. I really do."

"A failure? You ain't no failure. Now when you were riding around with your homies earlier, loading up gats, now that was dumb. But this here tonight was long overdue. When you were inside the pen I would've fought Leon a long time ago, but I was just too young, that's all. But even still I stepped to him about it."

Montel chuckled momentarily. I knew it made him proud of me to hear that even as a little boy I had heart just like he did.

"Yeah, you're my li'l brother for sure. Never let anybody disrespect Mama.

Sirens shrieked in the far distance, growing closer with each wail. It was the paramedics and the police. I felt a lump raise in my throat.

"Cee-Lovah," Montel said.

"Yeah, what up?"

"No matter what my reasons were for beating Leon down, this is strike number three for me. I've been to prison two times now; once for two years when you were very young. And no doubt the ten year sentence that I just did is gonna count against me. So you already know what time it is. So just keep ya head up and live for God like I seen you doin' thus far and everything will work out fine for you in this life. I'm glad that you've had a chance to experience a li'l bit of what not to do."

"You talkin' crazy, dawg," I said, brushing off the

reality that my brother could very well be headed back to jail. "It ain't like you just killed somebody or something. You just had a fight, that's all."

"That's all it takes in Los Angeles County for a felon like me, Cee-love. Face it, Cuz. I'm gonna be arrested on assault and battery charges most likely. I'm going down for the long haul this time for sure."

"Whatever, dawg...whatever." I refused to accept Montel's assessment of the situation.

"Just give Mama and Shante my love and be a positive role model for this old hood."

In no time, the noisy, flashing lights of the emergency vehicles were upon us. Tens of dozens of assorted paramedics and LAPD officers scurried all across our modest front lawn in an effort to get up the steps and into the front door. Quickly, the rescue workers went to work on the battered Leon before lifting him onto a white sheeted stretcher and whisking him outside the door and into the waiting ambulance.

As the ambulance sped away in a spectacle of blue and red brilliance, Montel was already handcuffed and being read his Miranda rights by a black clad LAPD cop whose partner eyeballed me warily as I watched my brother being taken into custody. Before his head was pushed forward into the back seat, Montel said to me, "Be strong, Cee. You got this."

I rushed off of the porch toward the squad car, but was blocked by a cop. "Get back up on that porch, kid, before you end up taking a little ride downtown yourself. Comprende'?"

I stopped in my tracks, staring over the short, stumpy policeman's shoulder, watching the squad car melt away in the darkness of the distant Compton street. The cop made a caustic remark before leaving, to which I paid little attention to before returning to the front porch where I plopped down onto the wicker chair in an unpleasant medley of emotions. I had once again lost my brother.

Chapter Twelve

Mama came up the stairs appearing pitiful. Miss Shante walked slowly behind her holding Nadia by the hand, sniffling and wiping her reddened eyes with a handful of tissue. No one said a word to one another. Other than the soft crying of the two women and Nadia's childish babbling periodically, the front porch of the house stood still and deathly silent.

Mr. Larry's truck pulled up against the curb in front of our house where he exited with his usual paint splotched work clothes and cap. He marched from the street to the walkway, up the steps, to the porch. He stood up against the column closest to the steps, taking in the solemn scene before him. "Angie, baby; I'm so sorry. I wish that I would've been here for Montel tonight. I...I dunno what to say."

Mama gave Mr. Larry a weak smile as she looked up toward him with sad, tear moistened eyes. "I know, Larry. It's not your fault. Montel and Leon was just a disaster waitin' to happen." Mama sighed with grief. "Ya know, Larry, I think that it was God's will, I really do, because I've lost my oldest son once again, and I've been taught a bitter lesson." Mama rocked back and forth slowly on the old rocker sitting at the far left corner of the porch. "I should have left that man a long, long time ago, but I was hard-headed, thinking only about my needs as a woman and not those of my kids. Now, I've lost one of my kids because of my selfishness-maybe forever." She looked at Mr. Larry. "Try living with that."

Mr. Larry leaned back against the banister and lit a cigarette, deeply dragging on the Salem menthol before exhaling a thick cloud of smoke into the cool, night air.

"Don't you dare blame yourself, Angie. Montel only did what any good child would wanna do, and that's protect their mother. There's no shame in that. "

"He's right," Miss Shante jumped in. "If it wasn't Montel, eventually it would've been Cedrick who would've beat his butt down. It was bound to happen."

I agreed wholeheartedly with both Mr. Larry and Miss Shante. "Yeah, Mama; I can't stand Leon! I mean, I respect you and love you, but if left up to me right now, I would've probably killed dude!"

"Cedrick Rohan Philips," Mama shouted. "You quit all that nonsense about killing folks, 'cause I don't wanna hear talk like that. You understand?" Mama's demeanor quickly switched from downcast and somber to hot-headed and fiery. She seemed to stab the thin air as she forcefully pointed her finger angrily at me. "You will not now nor ever be a statistic of this neighborhood. Do you hear me? It's happened to one of my sons and I won't allow it to happen to another!"

"I don't think Cedrick meant it like how it sounded, Angie," Mr. Larry said in my defense. "You've got a bright and promising young man here who only wants the very best for his mother, just like Montel did." Mr. Larry took one last drag on the cigarette before flicking the smoldering butt off into the dark street beyond. "I know the Lord works in mysterious ways, and I feel in my heart of hearts a lot of good is gonna come from this. Just you watch and wait on God."

"Amen...Amen. You're so right, Larry," Mama said in a more calming tone. "Please pray for my strength in the Lord, because I sure need it."

"What Satan meant for evil, the Lord is gonna change for His good. You just watch and see. I'm telling you," Mr. Larry prophesied as he took my mother's hand into his own, comforting her as best he could.

Early the following morning, as I fiddled around under the hood of Fatima's Buick, I was tapped on the shoulder by someone who'd approached me from the rear. Slowly, I backed away from the open hood and turned to see who it was. I was surprised to see my old archenemy, Baby, standing in front of me smiling. I hadn't seen him since the fight a while ago back in May. His hair was neatly trimmed as was his goatee and mustache. He'd traded in the bandanna, wife beater, khaki's and chucks for a casual, salmon colored, buttoned oxford shirt with navy blue linen slacks and a pair of spiffy looking black leather penny loafers. He also carried a leather bound copy of the King James Bible tightly in his left hand. He slowly stretched out an open palm toward me, to which I clasped after a moment of apprehension.

"That's what I'm talking 'bout...Praise the Lord! How are you doin', Cee? Man, it's really good to see you again." It looked like Baby. It sounded like Baby, but this couldn't be the Baby I knew standing in front of me talking about praising the Lord.

I was in a state of disbelief. I just stood facing Baby, looking dumbfounded for several seconds before gathering myself again. "Yeah, it's good to see you again too, Baby." Even then as I spoke those words toward my erstwhile enemy, it came out sounding hollow, with a hint of surprise thrown in.

Baby chuckled lightly at my awkward reaction to his sudden extreme makeover. For over an hour and a half, Baby and I talked, laughed and talked some more. He spoke of how he'd plotted with a few other neighborhood kids to kill me and Montel right after our fistfight, but he could never quite orchestrate the drive-by properly and how a slew of personal tragedies befell him one after the other, culminating with the shooting death of his cousin, Petey, at the hands of the fearsome Pirv Bloods. It was these unpleasant events that led him to attempt suicide.

"Yeah, Cee, I tried to take myself out, dawg. I must've drank over a fifth of Vodka, straight and then I got in my whip. The next thing I knew, I was waking up in an emergency room with tubes and stuff attached to me. My whole body was bandaged up like a mummy. I went over an embankment out near Ventura Highway. My car fell twenty feet down to the rocky bottom. Paramedics had to use the jaws of life to free me from that burning car. I was airlifted by helicopter to Cedars Sinai where I was hospitalized for what seemed like forever. I was in real bad shape, Cee."

I shook my head at the horror Baby had survived as he continued.

"I was told that I was comatose for over a week. But check it; I was visited by some type of beaming light or something. I know it sounds crazy, but this is real talk, Cuz. I'm talking about a figure of pure light. The feelings going through my body, Cee-I'd never felt anything like it in my entire life." Baby shook his head as if not only couldn't he believe what had happened himself, but he couldn't believe he was telling me about it.

"I felt every emotion; pain, pleasure-you name it, dawg, that I had given to the people around me. All I could hear was moanin', cryin' and voices of people screamin' or hollerin' out in pain. I could actually feel the presence of a whole lotta people. Then the place started to smell bad. I 'm talking 'bout real, real bad; like a whole lotta dead bodies or something. On top of all that, it started getting really hot, and then came the flames."

To my surprise, I found myself listening intensely to Baby's every word, as if I didn't doubt one bit that something like that could happen to a person; could happen to him.

"It was hell, man," Baby said.

"I bet it was," I replied.

"No, for real. I was in hell," he clarified. "I was given a choice to enter the light or come back into my broken body and receive Christ as my Lord and Savior and become a responsible soul. I wanted to go into the light at first because it was so peaceful, but after I got a glimpse of that, I didn't want to end up there for eternity. So I chose to come back and make things right with God. I've given my life over to Christ because I know now that He is the only way to salvation and ever lasting life; not bangin' and runnin' the streets with a gang."

Baby gently took the bolt ratchet from my hand and ducked down under the propped open hood of the Buick, turning and tightening, only pausing long enough to switch tools twice. After ten minutes, Baby had the big luxury car purring like a kitten.

"Wasn't nothing but a slight li'l radiator leak, Cuz," he told me. "Luckily for you, you had a bottle of engine stabilizer at the bottom of your tool box. It'll pretty much take care of your' minor engine problems for a minute."

I gave Baby a fist pump, thanking him for both his automotive assistance as well as his eye opening testimony, then we both sat on the hood of the car reminiscing about Montel. Baby said he had no grudge toward Montel for the fight outside of Mr. Lee's store and promised that he'd visit Montel at the L.A. county jail before his trial date was set. Baby opened up his Bible and recited the thirty-ninth Psalm aloud and with passionate conviction before turning to face me. He concluded by closing the sacred text.

"This Psalm was for all the boys in the hood and cats out here on the grind, in general, but it was for Montel in particular," Baby stated. "No matter what happens to Montel on his court date, the Lord is gonna have the final say. And trust me, Cee. It's God whose gonna get the glory regardless of what man decides as a final verdict. So keep ya head up, Cee. Just keep doin' you and trust in Him. You'll be fine." We bumped fists one final time and then he walked away, melting into the distant streets, praising God's holy name triumphantly as he went.

Epilogue

It's now 2008. I'm twenty-three years old and a graduate of Southern California University with a Bachelors degree in criminal psychology. I'm going back to finish my Masters this coming autumn after Fatima and I get back from our honeymoon in Morocco. Fatima's father, who happens to be Moroccan, was very pleased that his daughter chose me as a husband and has spoiled the both of us ever since our June 5th marriage. He footed the bill for the wedding and the honeymoon, which wasn't cheap by the way, especially in the recession era economy we're suffering.

Mama is a deaconess at our church home, Blesses Redeemer Baptist Temple. Mr. Larry still does painting, construction and light auto work in the neighborhood. He has since quit smoking and attends church regularly with Mama. I think those two are gonna hook up real soon, at least I pray that they will, because I really dig Mr. Larry and I know they dig each other a whole lot.

Leon moved to Orange County. Some people say he's married now to a rich Jewish lady, but I don't know how true that is. What I do know is that I haven't seen dude since that fateful night back in 1999. I wish him all the best. I don't hold anymore grudges against him because I've been changed. I once did for a long time though, but not anymore - thank God.

Miss Shante gave birth to a boy back in '99. She named him William after her favorite actor, Will Smith. He's nine now and looks remarkably like his Pops. As a matter of fact, Mama always calls him li'l Montel. I do also, and as far as Montel goes, well he was indeed found guilty of assault with intent to commit murder, which landed him back in prison for a 50 year bid with no chance of parole.

I used to go up to Pelican Bay to see him all the time with Miss Shante, Nadia and Li'l' Montel. I haven't been up there to see him in about a year, because with the wedding and all, I've had a really busy schedule. But he knows this and is very understanding.

Gang bangers and ballers around the way still remember Montel as being the tough talking, gun toting Reaper he'd once been. His exploits as a rider became the stuff of local street gang lore, amongst the various gang sets in general, and amongst the Reaper sets in particular. I, however, don't think about my brother in that way because he's so much more different now than even before. He runs the kitchen in Pelican Bay and heads the Inmate Development Program, which since 2003 returned 2300 hardened criminals back into society with fantastic results and only a three percent return rate. He's now studying criminal psychology himself and is making remarkable progress in his studies.

Today, I realize that my older brother may never see the outside of Pelican Bay's walls again, however, I know that just as Baby said awhile back, that no matter what, God would be in control of it all. You know what-He is. No matter how long Montel is imprisoned, he taught me, and all of us, in our small little Compton neighborhood a little bit about a lot. To his family, he will always be our blood, and to the hood as a whole, he will always be considered everyone's *Big Homie.*

The End

Ghetto Luv
by
Tysha

Chapter One
Friday Morning

"Shakayla! Shakayla, help your sisters get dressed. We runnin' late again."

"I am, Mommy, but Brianna still in the bathroom."

"Well, get her out, and y'all hurry up."

Kanesha couldn't understand why she had to go through the same thing every single morning. If she had to do it all over again, she would have waited to have kids, but it was too late for regrets and second guessing. Her mother had warned her about nappy headed boys in heat, but like many misguided teenagers, Kanesha ignored the advice. Now, ten years after losing her virginity to the first pretty boy to cross her path, there she was; twenty-six years old, four kids, four different baby daddies, two part-time jobs and one lazy, sorry excuse for a man.

As Kanesha laced up the shoes of her three year old son, she thought about how her life might have turned out if she would have just listened to her mother's teachings.

"Y'all, come on, now. Let's get it movin' before we miss the bus."

"All right, Mommy, we coming. Dang! I'm doin' da best I can," Shakayla said with pure frustration.

"You betta watch ya nine year old mouth, girl, if you wanna see ten. I ain't in the mood." Kanesha sighed and returned her attention to her baby boy, Jordan, when she vaguely heard Shakayla still running her mouth.

"Did you just say what I think you said?" Kanesha turned the corner and stormed into the bedroom ShaKayla and Brianna shared.

"I'm doin' da best I can, Mommy," whined Shakayla,

"but Brianna and Malisha give me a hard time, and say they don't have to listen to me."

Kanesha knew she heard the words 'these ya kids, so you come do it,' but she was not in the mood to go toe to toe with her daughter. Anyway, Shakayla was right, they were her kids. Kanesha knew she depended on her nine year old daughter too much, but she needed the help. Most days, Shakayla seemed more like the mother and Kanesha the child.

"Brianna, put ya dang shoes on and get that scarf off ya head. And make sure you have every single barrette in ya head when school is out. Just because you got long hair don't mean ya little friends got to be playin' in it."

"Okay, Mommy," whispered Brianna.

"Malisha, go brush your teeth, and the next time your sista' tell y'all to do something, do it."

Kanesha walked into her own bedroom in search of Jordan's jacket and her purse. She had to be out the door in twenty minutes, and the kids still hadn't sat down and eaten their cereal.

"Woman, you can't get dem kids up without all that yellin'? Shoot, you know I'm in here sleep," said a groggy and still drunk, Percy.

"I'm sorry, Percy, but you know how it is. They just kids and we leavin' in a few minutes."

Percy smacked his lips and drifted back off to sleep. Kanesha stood over him wondering why he never helped her out with the kids. None of them were his, but he was living in her house, using her water, heat and gas. She watched his chest rise and fall with each breath. The smell of morning breath, stale cigarettes and whiskey filled the air around him. Kanesha walked out of her bedroom, wondering why she had to ride the city bus when her man had a decent running car parked in front of the run-down duplex. As she closed the bedroom door behind her, Kanesha could hear her mother's words echoing in her head. *"If a man doesn't take care of you,*

you don't take care of him. Always remember, there's no romance without finance."

Thirty minutes later, Kanesha stormed down the street with her three daughters in tow and baby Jordan on her hip. After the girls got on the school bus, Kanesha and Jordan walked one block down and waited for the Youngstown WRTA city bus to pick them up. After dropping Jordan off at daycare, Kanesha boarded another bus and finally arrived at the dollar store where she worked as a part-time cashier.

Seven hours after leaving her duplex, Kanesha sat back in her seat as the number seven bus rode down Market Street. Kanesha's weeks were long and exhausting, but she rarely complained to anyone besides her children. It was Friday, and in a couple of hours the kids would be gone for the weekend and she could relax a little before going to her other part-time job at the bar. During the school year, Kanesha began each week day at five-thirty A.M. and ended around midnight. Her life was based around her kids and nothing else unless she happened to have a man to distract her.

Like clockwork, Kanesha and Jordan returned home at mid-afternoon to find Percy planted on the couch. Kanesha looked at the forty ounce of beer resting in front of Percy and rolled her eyes at him in disgust. For the second time that day, she heard her mother's voice again. *"If you're working one job and still struggling, then a man should be working two jobs and hustling in between."* Hearing the words so clearly made Kanesha turn around in search of her mother. It was a lesson her mother, Cynthia Brooks, had tried desperately to hammer in Kanesha's head years before.

"I see you've had a relaxin' day while I was out bustin' my tail," said Kanesha with her neck rotating and one hand on her hip.

"Don't start that mess with me today, woman," Percy responded as if it was Kanesha in the wrong and not him.

"Percy, I know you ain't been sitting here all day. You didn't go out looking for a job? How you plan on paying me back my money if you ain't looking for a job?"

"Naw, girl, don't nobody go job hunting on Fridays, and I'm tired of you on my back about that couple of dollars you gave me. I'm gon' get you dat money, just get off my back." Percy took a drag of his Newport, a swig of his beer, and resumed surfing the channels with the television remote.

"Apparently don't nobody go job hunting the other days of the week either," spat Kanesha.

"Girl, don't come strollin' in here starting nonsense," he growled.

"Whatever, man; you sitting on my couch. Let's not get this twisted, and I need my couple of dollars, as you wanna call it. The season is changing and that hundred is going toward my kid's summer clothes."

"Calm down. I'll hit the pavement hard come Monday. I promise."

Kanesha had heard it all before. Percy had been *not* looking for a job for the past four weeks. It was also the same amount of time the couple had known each other.

Kanesha and Percy met each other at the neighborhood bar where she worked part-time as a barmaid. Percy had been a regular in the bar, but until the night he introduced himself to Kanesha, the two had never held a conversation. He had set out to hook up with a woman, any woman, that would take care of him because his woman had gotten fed up with his freeloading and thrown him out on the streets. Percy was a wolf in sheep's clothing and Kanesha was the unsuspecting Little Red Riding Hood begging to be taken advantage of.

After fixing Jordan a snack and meeting her three girls at their school bus stop, it was time for Kanesha to help them get ready for their regular weekend away from home. They would all be going to spend the night with their respective fathers and grandmothers.

Shakayla was the easiest to help because she didn't

need an overnight bag. She had her own bedroom at her father's house and everything she needed was there waiting for her.

Just as five year old Malisha finished stuffing her overnight bag with her favorite doll, the doorbell rang.

"Percy, can you get the door please?" Kanesha called out from the two eldest girls' bedroom.

"You come get the darn door. Ain't nobody coming to visit me," replied Percy who was seated next to the front door.

"Come on, Percy. I got my hands full trying to get the four of them ready to go. Anyway, you're sitting right by the door."

"Whatever, I done already told you to get it ya self."

Kanesha could not believe how childish Percy acted at times. He was fourteen years older than her, but having him around made Kanesha feel like she had another child to raise. Their age difference was one of the reasons Kanesha got with him. She mistakenly thought that being involved with an older man would mean there would be no mind games played and Percy could take care of her. Had she taken the time to get to know the man she was moving into her home and the lives of her children, Kanesha may have discovered how irresponsible and manipulative Percy truly was before he could get his paws too deep in her.

Percy put his forty ounce up to his lips and took a few gulps of his warm, brown liquid when the doorbell chimed for the second time. Kanesha ran from the girls' bedroom to answer the front door.

Stephon Brown was always the first baby daddy to pick-up his child. "Hey Kanesha, how are you?"

"I'm cool, come on in," Kanesha smiled and stepped aside so that Stephon could enter the apartment.

Stephon and Kanesha met during their junior year in high school. Both were members of the French club and Stephon was the football quarterback. Their relationship moved fast, and before long, the seventeen year olds became parents. Despite the setback, Stephon went on to attend Florida A&M, leaving Kanesha behind to care for their shared responsibility.

"Is Shakayla ready to go?" Stephon tried not to sound impatient.

"She's helping Malisha put her shoes on, so have a seat for a minute."

"Naw, I'm cool," replied Stephon as he took three steps into the doorway.

"Dang, y'all can't see me tryin' to watch videos? Kanesha just get her out the dang door so this man can rise up out of here," demanded Percy.

Stephon looked at Percy then back at Kanesha, waiting for her to respond to his ignorance. To Kanesha, Stephon must have known she had no intentions of putting Percy in his place, because he turned to leave.

"Wait, Stephon; she's coming now," said Kanesha.

"I'm straight; just send her out to my car," responded Stephon.

"You don't have to leave, Stephon. Just ignore him," said Kanesha with pleading eyes. The last thing Kanesha wanted to do was antagonize Stephon in any way. Regardless of what happened between the two of them, Stephon was a wonderful father to Shakayla, and Kanesha would never do anything to alter their relationship.

"Daddy!" Shakayla ran into her father's arms and led him out of the door.

"Shakayla Patricia Brown, aren't you forgetting something?" asked Kanesha.

"I'm sorry, Mommy." Shakayla turned back to give her mother a kiss and hug before leaving.

There was another knock on the door immediately after Kanesha locked it. She answered it to find seven year old Brianna's daddy talking on his cell phone. Kanesha mouthed the word, 'Hi,' and stepped back to allow Byron Taylor to walk inside.

"Yo, Mami, I gotta hit you back," said Byron before

snapping his cell phone closed and giving Kanesha his full attention. "Yo, shorty, what it do?"

"I'm good, Byron. What's up wit' you?"

"Shoot, I'm doin' real good. Me and my Little Mami gon' chill together until Ma gets off work," explained Byron as he looked over at Percy. "You straight?" Bryon cut his eyes at Percy and gestured hello with a nod of the head.

"Yea, I'm straight," replied Kanesha.

"Why wouldn't she be straight? What you tryin' to say?" snapped Percy.

"Man, chill with all of that," warned Byron.

"Whatever, man. Just get yo' kid and keep it rollin'."

"What's his freakin' problem this week?" Byron asked Kanesha.

Unable to think of an answer, Kanesha shrugged her shoulders and held her breath. She was all too familiar with Byron's quick temper and knew the situation had to be defused before things got out of hand.

"Why you asking her about me like I ain't sittin' here?" Percy said snidely and lit up another Newport. Having never done anything with his life to be proud of, Percy was very intimidated by other men. His goal in life was to be taken care of by a woman, any woman that would have him. Percy had numerous women in his life time but sooner or later they would all grow tired of his laziness and kick him out on the street.

"Look here, old timer, all that tongue play 'bout to get you deep into something you ain't gon' be able to pull up out of," warned Byron.

The two men stared at each other for what felt like an eternity to Kanesha. All three of them knew that Byron could and would lay Percy down without hesitation. The last thing Kanesha wanted was for something to happen in front of her kids. Percy opened his mouth to say something just as Brianna ran into the room with her overnight bag.

"Hey, Daddy! Where is Big Ma at today?" Brianna

squealed, looking over her father's shoulder for her grandmother.

"Big Ma had to work late, so me and you gon' kick it for a little while. Cool?"

"Yea, just me and you?" asked the seven year old with excitement.

"Yep, Little Mami, just me and you," replied Bryon.

"All right, Kanesha, I'll holla at you later. And on the real tip, you need to check that in," Byron nodded toward Percy.

Byron may not have been a contender for any father of the year awards, but he loved his little girl with all he had.

When Kanesha and Byron met at a house party, sparks flew between them. With his hair braided straight to the back with precision, over sized T-shirt and sagging pants, Byron Taylor was truly a hood boy. Kanesha received warning from her girlfriends not to get involved with him, but she reasoned that every girl gotta have a ruff neck at some point in her life.

Their relationship was volatile and filled with break-ups and make-ups. To Byron, their relationship was only that of friends with benefits, but Kanesha thought they had a future together. When one of their make-up sessions resulted in Kanesha getting pregnant just months after giving birth to her first child, she thought Byron would marry her and fill the void that caused her to feel empty and alone.

Byron told Kanesha that he was not in the market for a wife and kids right before suggesting she run her tail right on over to the clinic. Kanesha refused and Byron had doubts the baby was even his because of the reputation Kanesha was mapping out for herself. Sleeping with any man that looked her way was not a good thing, especially in a small town where everyone knows what so-and-so did five minutes after they did it. Seven months later, Brianna Marie Taylor arrived and Byron fell instantly in love with her. He does what he can to provide for Brianna, and his mother picked up the slack.

At times, Kanesha and Byron mixed like oil and water, but he remained in Kanesha's system. Over the years, the two continued to kick it every now and then. Neither would have it any other way.

Kanesha stood in the doorway wondering why her body continued to crave a man who broke her heart too many times to count. Before getting behind the wheel of his car, Byron blew her a kiss and winked his eye at her.

"Two down and two to go," said Kanesha as she closed the door.

"Why you ain't check that fool fo' talkin' to me like that?" questioned Percy. Kanesha simply ignored his question, because she couldn't believe he honestly wanted an answer.

"Malisha and Jordan, y'all come on in here with me," ordered Kanesha. "Y'all will be leaving in a few minutes.

Malisha was the only one of Kanesha's children who had no relationship with her father. Mike Whitaker was passing through town the night Kanesha met him. She saw his chocolate, tall, athletic frame stroll through the doors of Juin's Bar & Grill and knew immediately she had to get a taste of him. Their physical attraction was automatic, but all Mike could offer was a nibble. Kanesha accepted the offer of the one night stand, believing she could change his mind after giving him the most precious thing a woman can give a man-her body. He had a wife and three kids back home in Chicago and no woman would take him away from them. Mike made his living as a sports agent and was in town looking to sign two Youngstown State University athletes. Despite his marital status, Mike opted not to wear a condom during his sexual escapade with Kanesha because they both reasoned that it took away from the natural feeling. Kanesha was on birth control pills, but she was very irresponsible with taking them as prescribed. She just convinced herself that if she got pregnant she was supposed to be, and that was that.

After sleeping with Kanesha, Mike left his business card on the bed side dresser and hit the road. One month later, Kanesha called Mike at his office to tell him she was pregnant. He accused her of trying to trap him and hung the phone up on her. Malisha Nicole Whitaker was now five years old and had never met her father, but Kanesha's mother spoiled the child to no end.

Cynthia Brooks hated the fact that her other grandchildren spent weekends and vacations with their fathers while Malisha had nowhere to go, so since the day Kanesha gave birth to Malisha, her mother made certain the child never felt rejected. Not long ago, Cynthia confessed to Kanesha that she knew it was wrong to play favorites with her four grandchildren, but she just couldn't help herself.

"When is Dea coming to get me, Mommy?" whined Malisha.

"She'll be here any minute, so come and get your jacket on," answered Kanesha. "It feels like the air is changing and cooling down."

To avoid another disagreement between Percy and her mother, Kanesha decided to wait outside for her to arrive. Malisha and Jordan chased each other in the yard while Kanesha sat on the worn porch steps enjoying the breeze from the cool spring air. Like clockwork, her mother and Jordan's father, Je'Ronn, pulled up to the curb at the same time. Kanesha hugged and kissed her two youngest kids, made small talk with Je'Ronn who always picked his son up for the weekend, but always left him to be cared for by his mother and younger sister.

After Kanesha made her usual promise to her mother that she would try to make Sunday morning church services, she turned on her heels and went back inside her cramped three bedroom ranch style duplex. As expected, Kanesha found Percy in the same spot, looking lazy.

This man has got to go, but not until I get the money he owes me, thought Kanesha. *I don't know why he asked me to help get his raggedy car fixed; he never lets me ride in it. He probably just wanted the money for his cigarettes and beer.*

Kanesha plopped down on the couch where she planned on remaining until it was time for her to go to her second job. For the first time since she had gotten home, Percy pried his eyes away from the television.

"Come here, woman, and tell me 'bout ya day."

"Not now, Percy. I'm tired. I just want to relax for a minute."

"You always tired and got something else to do besides take care of me," complained Percy.

"Whatever. Maybe if you'd help out 'round here, I'd have more time for you." Kanesha couldn't believe his nerve. Not only was he rude and ignorant toward Stephon and Byron, but he sat on his rear end all day, and now he was hinting for sex. "So, you just sat and watched music videos all day?"

"Wasn't nothing else to do."

"You should have been looking for work. That was something to do," barked Kanesha.

"Look, why I always got to repeat myself for you? I done already told you, girl, don't start that mess wit' me. I'll get a job when I get one."

Kanesha decided she was too tired to argue with Percy and focused her attention on the music video playing on *BET*.

"I should have been one of them video dancers. Maybe then I'd be living better," Kanesha unconsciously said out loud.

Percy laughed at the comment before saying, "Yea, right. Not with that saggy pot belly and all those stretch marks you got. Shoot, girl, you can forget that pipe dream."

Kanesha's feelings were hurt, and again, the voice in her head spoke to her. *'If any man can't love you, both inside and out, cut him loose,'* Cynthia often preached to her only child. With her head hung low, Kanesha sat daydreaming about meeting the right man one day. One that would love, honor and take care of her without any strings attached. Deep in Kanesha's soul, she knew that she deserved better than what she was used to getting. Her only problem was figuring out a way to get what she wanted from a man without sacrificing her self-respect in the process.

"So what you cooking fo' dinner?" Percy asked, interrupting Kanesha's thoughts.

"What?"

"You hard of hearing now? I said, what you cookin' fo' dinner?"

"Nothin, you know dog-on-well I don't cook on Fridays and Saturdays because my kids ain't here."

"Well, your man is here and you'd look good getting up off yo' lazy butt and fixin' me something to eat," demanded Percy.

"Partner, you don' lost ya darn mind." Kanesha smacked her lips and rolled her eyes at Percy. She couldn't believe he expected her to cook for him after working one part-time job, riding the city bus both ways and the other one hundred and one things she'd done that day. Kanesha had no intentions on lifting a finger until it was time for her to go to work.

Kanesha heard Percy's stomach growl from across the room, but she still refused to move.

"Look, girl, I ain't playin' with your stupid tail. Get in that kitchen, now," fumed Percy.

"You got a lot of nerve to make demands on me. You got me messed up."

"I'm not gon' say it again."

"And I ain't gon' tell you 'no' again. If you that dang hungry, you have two options. One; get up off your butt and fix your own food. Or two; get up off your butt and go buy something to eat."

Kanesha returned her attention to the music videos

and tried her best to ignore Percy's demands. What came next happened so fast that Kanesha didn't have time to brace or protect herself. Percy's fist met the left side of her face with enough force to knock her onto the bare hardwood floor.

Kanesha's hand immediately rose to her left eye and felt blood draining from her nose. Stunned and dazed, Kanesha attempted to lift herself off the floor.

"What is wrong with you?" cried Kanesha.

"I'm sick of that smart mouth of yours. No wonder you got so many kids and still by ya self. It ain't a man around who would put up with you mouthing off all the freaking time." Percy bent down and grabbed Kanesha by her hair, forcing her to her feet. "Now get your simple behind in that dang kitchen before I choke the life out of your ignorant butt."

Kanesha continued to hold her face as tears mixed with blood. She could feel her eye swelling and wondered if her nose was broken. Percy punching her like she was some man on the street, dumbfounded her.

Again, the voice in her head spoke to her, *'We teach people how to treat us, and so, you just make sure you teach them well.'* Kanesha shook her head to quiet her mother's voice as she stumbled into the small kitchen and did as she was told. Nursing her wounds would have to wait until after Percy had his meal.

Chapter Two
Baby Please, Baby Baby Please

Kanesha had never been so embarrassed in her entire life. She didn't usually wear make-up, but with a black eye and bruised cheek, there was no other option. It took her almost an hour to shade her eye before it looked half way decent. *I guess wearing sunglasses is going to be a must,* thought Kanesha. She still couldn't believe that Percy punched her as if the word *Everlast* was tattooed on her forehead. Kanesha could not figure out why all the men in her life resorted to beating her down one way or another. She felt that life had done that enough.

Growing up in Youngstown, Ohio was a struggle. As a child, Kanesha Diane Brooks was one of the fortunate souls to have stability in her life. Her parents made certain that every birthday was recognized with expensive gifts, and every holiday was celebrated with family and friends. Dale and Cynthia Brooks took Kanesha on family vacations every summer in an attempt to expose their daughter to life outside of the poverty stricken city. Dale worked on the assembly line at Packard Electric and Cynthia was the office manager for a law firm. The couple worked hard, enjoyed life, and praised the Lord as directed by His word.

The last family vacation the Brooks embarked on was to Albany, New York to visit Dale's side of the family. Kanesha was excited about the trip because she had not seen her favorite cousins, Talissa, Tammy and Tameka, in four years. The night before the trip, Dale worked a mandatory twelve hour overtime shift, but insisted that he drive the first half of the trip. Whenever they drove to their vacation destination, Dale wanted to get on the road no later than four o'clock in the morning to avoid traffic.

Two hours into the eight hour drive, Dale felt sleepy, but decided to keep on driving. He wanted to knock off the last hour of his driving shift and let Cynthia get more rest before they stopped for gas. Kanesha lay in the back seat of their new Nissan Maxima, sound asleep. Dale turned up the volume on the jazz radio station and fought to stay awake. As his eyes got heavier and heavier, Dale still refused to wake Cynthia to take the wheel. Before the family knew what happened, the car veered into the opposite lane of traffic, hitting a semi-truck, head-on. The family was rushed to the nearest Pennsylvania hospital. Cynthia suffered two broken legs and a fractured pelvis. Kanesha escaped with a broken right arm and a dislocated shoulder. The impact killed Dale instantly.

Only fourteen at the time, Kanesha was devastated by the death of her father. Cynthia was lost without her husband of twenty years and fell into a deep depression, leaving Kanesha to grieve alone. After the funeral, and weeks of physical therapy, Kanesha wanted to join her father in the afterlife. For the first time in her life, she felt alone and began looking for attention anywhere she could find it. Now twelve years later, Kanesha's search continued.

The woman in the mirror with a black eye was a stranger to Kanesha. She was a pretty woman with light brown eyes, a bronze complexion. and shoulder length dark brown hair. Kanesha felt low and worthless as she stared at her reflection. "Why do you let these men disrespect you like this?" she asked herself. A piece of her died along with her father and she had no idea how to revive it. The void left Kanesha's soul feeling hallow and she doubted it would ever be fulfilled.

Percy wasn't the first man to lay hands on her in anger; Stephon held that title. He held the bragging rights to many firsts for Kanesha. He was her first kiss, first slow dance, first sexual experience, first love, first heartbreak, first let down and first beat down. Stephon had taken the initiative and made something out of himself by going off to college and graduating at the top of his class, but he trampled on a lot of people to get there. Stephon provided for his daughter but in the beginning, it was not by choice.

He was furious when Kanesha got pregnant and acted as if he had nothing to do with the unplanned pregnancy. Kanesha couldn't believe how angry Stephon had gotten when she refused to get an abortion. She was totally caught off guard when he began beating on her like she was some man who had disrespected his mother. When Kanesha's mother saw her only child battered and bruised, all heck broke loose.

Cynthia filed a police report and had Stephon arrested for assault. She was not going to make his going off to college an easy task. Despite her efforts, Stephon left to obtained a college degree one year after his daughter was born.

After Kanesha delivered Shakayla, there was no doubt Stephon was the father. The baby girl looked just like her daddy. Stephon's mother apologized for her son, paid for the paternity test and set up a shared custody agreement between the two teenagers. Stephon was forced to cut grass in the summer and shovel snow in the winter. He collected soda bottles, worked part-time at Sparkles' Grocery Store, and cut hair on the side in an effort to help provide for his daughter. Stephon instantly fell in love with his precious baby girl the second he saw her.

He then began apologizing to Kanesha for hurting her the way he had. For Kanesha, no amount of 'I'm sorry' could heal her broken heart.

Almost ten years later, Kanesha could still feel the emotional pain of her first love. Kanesha often felt as if God was punishing her for some wrong doing in her life. She could never understand what she had done so bad that God felt it necessary to take both her father and her self-worth from her.

Kanesha had been fighting back tears since Percy knocked her on her behind, but watching her eye swell and change from blue to black, she felt no need to hold them back any longer. She cried until she heard a voice speak to her, '*My beautiful child, it doesn't matter how pretty you are on the outside if you're butt ugly on the inside.*' Kanesha immediately looked around the cramped bathroom to make sure she was still alone. The voice was so clear and loud, and for a split moment, Kanesha thought her mother had come back for something. Kanesha was remembering all the life lessons her mother had tried to instill in her. After confirming she was still alone, Kanesha allowed the tears to stream down her face until she felt she could cry no more.

If she heard Percy lie about being sorry one more time, Kanesha felt like she would throw up. Having a black eye and working as a bar-maid were two things that did not go together. Personality, mixology and presentation equaled big tips for any barmaid, and that night, Kanesha would be off her game in all three categories. Even with the thick coats of Fashion Fair foundation and sunglasses, she still felt as if there was a huge neon arrow hanging over her head.

Wilson, the bar's security, kept watch out for Kanesha while standing outside of the bar. He knew Percy would most likely have her walking to work instead of riding comfortably in his beat-up hooptie. For the life of him, Wilson could not figure out why a woman as beautiful and as delicate as Kanesha would lower herself to be with a man who did not respect her. After what seemed like hours of watching, Kanesha's figure appeared in the darkness causing Wilson's heart to skip a beat. Just one look at Kanesha's slumped shoulders and her eyes focused on the ground, and Wilson knew something was not right with her. He whispered a quick prayer, asking God to watch over his friend and protect her from the devil living under her roof.

"Good evening, Kanesha," greeted Wilson as he opened the door for her.

"Hi, Wilson, thank you."

Kanesha forced a smile but refused to meet Wilson's gaze. She could feel Wilson watching her as she stepped through the open door. As much as she appreciated the chivalry Wilson always showed her, Kanesha was in no mood to make small talk. She felt like every eye in the place was automatically drawn to her black eye when she walked into the bar to start her shift. Despite her flaws, Kanesha was in the habit of walking with her back straight and head held high, but the shame of the black eye that adorned her pretty face devastated her.

"Hey, girl," greeted Miss Yolanda. "It looks like we'll be busy tonight."

That was the last thing Kanesha wanted to hear.

Miss Yolanda Williams owned the bar and worked seven days a week to keep it turning a profit. She was living proof that the old saying, "black don't crack," originated from fact. At fifty-six, Miss Yolanda didn't look a day over thirty-five. Kanesha often told her that she hoped to look as good in twenty years. Miss Yolanda suggested Kanesha try making some better life choices so life didn't beat her down so often.

Miss Yolanda looked up from taking inventory as Kanesha walked past her without a word.

"Baby girl, what happened to your eye?" Miss Yolanda asked, with concern, although she could guess the answer. Seeing Kanesha tear up, Miss Yolanda said, "Never mind, you don't have to answer that."

She gave her friend a tight hug and rubbed her back. Kanesha returned Miss Yolanda's hug with as much love and compassion as it was given while she fought back tears she thought were already shed.

"You know I'm here for you, right?" asked Miss Yolanda.

Kanesha nodded her head and wiped away the tears from her cheeks, she was shocked that Miss Yolanda saw right through her attempt to hide behind the dark shades she wore.

"How did you know? I guess the make-up and shades are more of a neon sign than I thought," Kanesha spoke softly from embarrassment.

"Honey, my ex gave me his fair share of black eyes back in the day. It was that last black eye that landed him in the hospital with a steak knife sticking out his back," Miss Yolanda laughed.

"Let me go in the back and get myself together," said Kanesha.

"I can have my sister come help out tonight, so why don't you go on home?"

"No, Miss Yolanda, I don't want to bail out on you."

"Don't worry about anything or anyone right now, but you," said Miss Yolanda. "Are the kids gone for the weekend?"

"Yes."

"Then worry about you just this once. Go on home and put some ice on that eye and take a couple of Motrin before going to bed. Call me tomorrow and let me know how you feel."

"Thank you, Miss Yolanda. You are such a good friend to me," cried Kanesha.

"Girl, please, you'd do the same for me. Now go on and get out of here."

Kanesha was quick to respond to her boss and picked up her purse before heading home. The next morning, Kanesha was up early giving her cramped home a good cleaning.

The soothing sounds of Dave Hollister singing about taking care of home kept Kanesha company while she scrubbed the small bathroom down with Ajax and Pine Sol. After cleaning the kids' rooms, she decided to apply more ice to her eye. It was rare for Kanesha to have time for herself, but she enjoyed the quietness that surrounded her.

"What's up, baby?" said Percy as he entered and closed the door behind him.

Kanesha was relieved to find Percy gone when she got home the night before. The last thing she wanted to do was have to tend to his needs instead of focusing on her own. She regretted giving him a key and thought about having her locks changed, but she didn't have the money to purchase a new set. Kanesha slept alone that night and she enjoyed it. Kanesha was surprised that she hadn't wondered where Percy spent his night. Nonetheless, Kanesha was just happy he was not around her.

"Hi," greeted Kanesha dryly.

"You all right?" Percy paused in an effort to put some remorse to the sound of his voice, "Do you need anything?"

"No, I'm cool," replied Kanesha. "Please don't walk on the dining room floor, I just mopped it."

Percy took a couple of slow paces toward Kanesha, who was sitting on the couch. He slipped his keys inside his right pants pocket and sat down next to Kanesha on the couch. He reached over and began running his fingers through her hair, causing Kanesha to instantly tense up.

"Baby, you know I didn't mean to hurt you yesterday."

"If you didn't mean to hurt me by punching the mess out of me, I'd hate to know what you would have done if you *were* out to hurt me." Kanesha stared out of the living room window, trying to will Percy's hand off of her.

"Girl, I'm sorry and it will never happen again," pleaded Percy. He touched Kanesha's face and gently turned her around to meet his lips with a kiss.

"You hurt me, Percy," cried Kanesha.

"I know I did. It won't happen again. Just let me make it up to you."

Percy kissed Kanesha, forcing her mouth open

enough for his tongue to find hers. His right hand found its way up her nightgown and between her legs. Laying her on the couch, Percy began to kiss Kanesha with more force as he shoved his fingers inside of her. Kanesha tried to allow her body to enjoy the impending pleasure, but the pain pounding in her eye would not allow it.

Percy kissed and fondled Kanesha's body until his hands found the V between her thighs.

"Relax, let me make you feel good," whispered Percy.

Kanesha reluctantly did as she was told. Her mind kept thinking of the day before when she had trouble picking herself up off the floor. She was made to feel worthless, like a piece of old furniture that was no longer able to serve its purpose. Kanesha wanted Percy to stop touching her, for him to find another way to make her feel human again.

Kanesha was tense and the feel of Percy's hands on her body made her want to scream. She had never felt so uncomfortable with a man before. Her hands formed into a fist when Percy stood up in front of her. Kanesha thought he might hit her again but this time she would be ready for combat; even if she lost the round, there was no way she was going to forfeit the fight.

Percy stood up and planted his body between Kanesha's legs, removed his shirt and got down on his knees. Kanesha tried to search Percy's eyes for any sign of regret for the way he had treated her the day before.

"This isn't a good idea, Percy," sighed Kanesha. "Just let me get up and out of your way. I don't want a repeat of yesterday."

"Shhh," was the only reply Kanesha got.

Percy went back to kissing on Kanesha's body as his hands rested on her soft and smooth thighs. *'Men use women all the time and on more occasions than not, we use them without them realizing that's what we are doing. When that rare occasion arises, play it for all it's worth.'* It was loud and clear to Kanesha, whose voice spoke those words. Her mother had just said that to her four weeks earlier when she discovered Percy was living with her.

Kanesha found a comfortable position on her couch and allowed Percy to take care of his ugly business. As she lay back, a piece of cracked paint on the ceiling caught Kanesha's eye, and she thought, *I'm going to have to call the landlord about that first thing Monday morning.*

Chapter Three
All Work And No Play

After Percy brought Kanesha to a moderate sensual peak, he began undressing, causing her to frown. As far as Kanesha was concerned, their sexual escapade was over in record time, ten minutes. Kanesha was saved by the ringing of her doorbell. After making herself presentable, she walked to the front of the duplex to find her next door neighbor, Denise Ramsey, looking to use her phone. Kanesha invited Denise in and made small talk in an effort to avoid having any further sexual encounter with Percy. The two women talked for twenty minutes. The short visit would have lasted longer if it was left up to Kanesha, but Denise had to get back to her sleeping sons.

"All right, girl, let me get ready to take my baby to the doctor. He been teething for the longest and for some reason, he's been sick with a fever," explained Denise with a small measure of sadness in her voice.

"Whew, sweetie. I'm glad all of my kids are far past the teething stage. Motrin always worked for them, did you try it?" Kanesha asked with genuine concern. Though she was stalling to get back to Percy, she hated to hear about a baby being sick.

"Yea, girl, I had to dip into my light bill money to buy it. When it didn't give him any relief I tried Tylenol, but it was useless too. I called the kids' doctor and they told me to bring him in."

"Don't worry, Denise; he probably just has a virus or a cold."

After the two women hugged each other good-bye, Kanesha walked into the kitchen before going to the bedroom. She stood in the middle of the room and began humming Lyfe Jennings new song, *"Will I Ever"*. Just before she got to the chorus, she was interrupted by the voice in her head again. *Look inside your heart child, the foundation you need to stand tall is buried inside of your heart.* She could not figure out why her mother's words had started replaying in her head all of a sudden. The words sounded so precise and exact, Kanesha was surprised that she remembered it all. All Kanesha could do was give herself a hug as if she were giving it to her soul. Percy put a pause to the light bulb moment Kanesha was having with herself. "Dang, he always knows the wrong time to come at me," she whispered to herself.

"What did you say?" Percy frowned.

"Nothing, I was talking to myself. What do you want in here?" asked Kanesha with some attitude in her tone.

"Dang, you been talking to yourself a lot lately. I'm starting to think you going crazy." Percy walked further into the kitchen and grabbed a beer out of the bare refrigerator. Before Kanesha could reply, Percy changed the subject. "That witch couldn't wait to use da phone?" barked Percy. Kanesha ignored Percy and left him in the kitchen alone. Just the way she wanted to be, alone.

"What is going on with me?" Kanesha asked herself out loud. Before pondering the answer, she decided her soul searching would have to wait or she would be late for work. Kanesha had lost money the night before because of Percy and she'd be darned if it happened again tonight.

The warm water rolling down Kanesha's body felt so good she took a longer shower than usual. After getting dressed, primed and prepared for the night, Kanesha left the place she called home without uttering a word to Percy. If he noticed the slight, he said nothing and kept his attention on the bare behinds dancing on the television screen.

Kanesha strolled the two blocks down Cleveland Street at a steady pace, looking forward to getting to work. She liked the fact that her second job was only a couple of blocks from her place. She didn't have to worry about missing the bus or asking Percy to drive her. Kanesha found out early that Percy was a lazy man but it didn't seem to bother her during those first couple of days together. That was the length of their honeymoon stage. On the second day, Percy moved his few possessions in with Kanesha and her four children.

The only time Percy seemed to leave his spot on the couch was when Kanesha worked the bar. He had come to be a nuisance to Kanesha when he accompanied her to work. His evil attitude made for small tips from the men who would normally flirt with Kanesha whenever Percy wasn't around. There were two things Kanesha knew how to do well, one was make babies and the other was mix drinks.

"Hey, girl, you feeling better tonight?" greeted Miss Yolanda.

"Yea, I'm all right. Were you busy last night?" Kanesha inquired.

"Nothing I couldn't handle. My sister helped me out behind the bar and my nieces ran things in the kitchen for me."

Kanesha walked behind the bar and took inventory of the liquor and beer. She made a small list of empty bottles to be replaced and asked the bouncer to go get them for her. Wilson returned within five minutes and helped Miss Yolanda and Kanesha place everything in its proper place before going back to guard the door. Kanesha liked Wilson because he was a man of few words. Besides saying hello to her, he barely ever opened his mouth. Despite his huge frame and intimidating presence, he possessed a gentle soul.

"Kanesha, what is he doing here?" asked Miss Yolanda as she pointed at Percy who was seated at the opposite end of the bar.

"Probably to watch and make sure I don't replace his sorry tail with a newer, younger model. He was so wrapped up in the music videos I didn't think he was going to come in here tonight," replied Kanesha. "Don't worry; he won't be around for much longer. I just need him to pay me back before I kick him out."

"I hope you not really expecting him to give you a dime. Like I told you the night you met him, Percy Watkins is now, and forever will be, a user of women. He'll stay with a woman long enough to make empty promises and drain her dry. All he knows how to do is take from people. The word 'give' is not in that man's vocabulary."

Miss Yolanda and Percy attended the same high school and ran the same circles in their younger years. Percy had messed around with a couple of Miss Yolanda's acquaintance over the years and the movie was always the same. Percy's mode of operation was to meet a woman, sweet talk her, move into her home, spend every dime of her hard earned money and leave her pockets with nothing but lint.

Kanesha liked Miss Yolanda because she never bit her tongue. She always let a person know where they stood with her. The night Kanesha took Percy home with her, Miss Yolanda warned her he wouldn't leave until a gun was put to his head forcing him to vacate.

"Kanesha, I'm not trying to be in your business, but you already got four kids. Why would you want to raise another? Especially since he's already been raised?"

"I hear you, Miss Yolanda, but please believe it when I say, that man is on his last leg and about to be sitting on the curb."

"Just remember one thing." Miss Yolanda carefully chose her words. "Your children see everything you do. There is a fifty-fifty chance that your girls will grow up and get a man that treats her the way you have allowed men to treat you," Miss Yolanda paused briefly. "Jordan may grow up and treat women the way he sees you being treated."

Kanesha never thought about how her children saw

her. She just assumed that they were too young to understand the world she had created for them.

"I'm no Bible toting, saved, Holy Ghost filled, sanctified woman by any means. I own a bar for pete's sake, but I do know about the virtuous woman spoke of in Proverbs 31. As long as you have breath in your lungs, it's never too late to repent and change your ways."

"I promise, I'll think about what you've said. Thank you for caring," whispered Kanesha with her head hung low.

It was two-thirty in the morning when Kanesha finally got a break from pouring drinks. The crowd was making their way out the door. By the time Kanesha looked up from counting her tips, the bar was empty except for the D.J., Wilson and Percy. The small crew had just finished closing up the bar when Miss Yolanda asked Kanesha to come into her office.

"I ain't got all night, girl. You got five minutes and I'm gon' leave your wide tail to walk home alone," Percy grunted.

"That's all right, Kanesha," interjected Wilson. "I'll make sure you get home safe and sound if this man won't." He took a seat next to Percy and folded his arms across his massive chest. Kanesha waited for Percy's response, but none came.

"Thank you, Wilson, I appreciate that." Kanesha rolled her eyes at Percy, grabbed her tip jar and made her way into Miss Yolanda's office.

One could tell by Percy's body language that the look in Wilson's eyes was making Percy very nervous. Percy remained seated long enough to hear the door to the office close before he stood to leave.

"So what's up, man? You gon' unlock the door so I can bounce or what?" Percy's voice was shaky, but Wilson took no pleasure in it. In Wilson's opinion, weak men used and abused women in order to make themselves feel like a big man. The thought of Percy mistreating Kanesha made Wilson feel sick.

"You tell me what's up, man? How did Kanesha get that black eye?" Wilson stood up and Percy almost emptied his bladder.

"Ain't ya momma ever tell you that what goes on between a man and his woman is between that man and that woman? Why you all up in mine?" Percy was unable to look Wilson in his eyes, so he fixed his gaze on the wall behind him.

"I learned a lot from my mother. Number one being to never put my hands on a woman in anger." Wilson was growing more impatient with Percy with each second that passed. "It seems to me that you're the one who missed a few life lessons. Women are meant to be treasured and treated like queens. Kanesha is my friend, and I'm very protective of all my friends. So, hear what I'm about to say to you." Wilson paused to heighten the fear he saw in Percy's eyes. "The next time you want to raise your hand in anger, come see me. Just keep in mind that I hit back."

Percy wanted to run out the door, but Wilson was in no hurry to unlock it. With each word Wilson spoke, Percy thought the free drinks he swallowed might end up on the worn hardwood floor. Wilson outweighed him by at least one hundred pounds and stood a foot taller than him. Percy was not fool enough to get into a physical altercation with Wilson, especially not over some young tail with four kids.

Wilson said all he needed to say and decided it was time to let Percy out of the virtual corner he had backed him into. The last thing Wilson needed was any type of legal problems, but he would take an assault charge any day, all day, if it meant protecting Kanesha.

Dwayne Mason Wilson had spent seven years, seven months and seven days in an Ohio state prison after pleading guilty to a felonious assault and arson charge. After moving into his own apartment, Wilson's mother, May, decided it was time to start dating. While raising her son, she never married because she didn't want any man, other than his father, over him. It was her responsibility to raise her son to be a strong, independent man, and she felt strong enough to face that important task alone. A friend from church introduced May to a man she described as kind, gentle, and hard working.

May Wilson and Nelson Tritt dated for five months before her beaten and battered body was found sprawled on her kitchen floor. There had been signs before that tragic day that Nelson was physically mistreating May, but she always denied it when her son would ask about various bruises on her body. It was Wilson who found his mother beaten to death, and rage immediately took over. Wilson was unable to grieve until he made his mother's killer pay for his crime. Unfortunately for both men, Wilson tracked Nelson down before the Youngstown Police Department could, and altered their lives forever. Wilson did not beat Nelson to death, but he beat him into a three month coma and turned him into a paraplegic.

Nelson was subsequently found guilty of second degree murder and sentenced to life plus twenty years by the state of Ohio. As a result of the beating Wilson put on him, Nelson would spend his remaining years in a wheelchair, adult diapers and a feeding tube. Due to the circumstances surrounding the crime, prosecutors offered Wilson a plea deal they felt was fair and he accepted.

Wilson made good use of his time behind bars. He took advantage of the classes offered and learned a trade that would keep him fed on the outside. Wilson studied hard to become a certified mechanic. He also took small business courses and accounting classes. Having served every day of his sentence, minus earning credit for good behavior, Wilson was released from prison without the weight of parole being carried on his shoulders.

Working at the bar was only Wilson's side hustle. During the day he worked for the city of Youngstown as a mechanic at WRTA bus garage. There was nothing behind steel bars that Wilson missed, but he wasn't able to stand by and pretend not to see the obvious signs of physical abuse on a woman. Behind brick walls, Wilson attended church services and Bible study classes faithfully. He returned to the McGuffey Road Church of Christ when he was released, where he was baptized and added to the body of Christ. Wilson was on a walk with the Lord and didn't feel ready to commit to a relationship. Wilson fell in love with Kanesha the first time he saw her but he knew he wasn't able to offer her anything, at least, not just yet.

"Sit down, Kanesha. We need to talk," said Miss Yolanda.

"Sure," replied Kanesha nervously. Miss Yolanda's voice was stern and commanding which made Kanesha nervous because whenever she heard that voice, it meant something was wrong.

"Did my drawer come up short or something?" She sat down waiting for the answer. Miss Yolanda sounded too serious and Kanesha wondered if she was being let go for some reason.

"No, your drawer was fine. Our problem is the tab Percy ran up."

"What? I assumed that since he was ordering from you he was paying for all those drinks."

"No, baby, he didn't. I know that's your man and everything, but Miss Yolanda can't allow anyone to run me out of business, especially not the likes of Percy Watkins. Anyway, you know I don't pay for any man, including my own. He can't just relax, toss back an endless supply of drinks and leave me to flip the bill."

"I'm sorry about that, Miss Yolanda. Did you give him his bill?"

"Yes, I did. He said you were taking care of it."

Kanesha was at a loss for words. "Why would he do that?" Percy had stayed out all night and Kanesha figured he had at least been out grinding, making money.

"How much does he owe?" Kanesha pulled the money from her tip jar and began counting it.

"Fifty-five dollars, sweetie, fifty-five dollars. Do you want me to take it out of your pay? Maybe half from your paycheck and the other from your tips? I trust you and I'll work with you on taking care of this."

"If I don't take care of this now, I'll be busting my behind for nothing," said Kanesha.

She counted out her tips and came up ten dollars short. As she handed the money over to Miss Yolanda, Kanesha stood up to leave. Her head hung lower than it had the night before.

"Goodnight, Miss Yolanda. I'll see you Friday. I'm sorry about this. It won't happen again."

"Kanesha, don't worry about the ten dollars, just please remember what I said earlier."

"Yes, ma'am, I will."

Kanesha opened the office door and peeked out. Wilson was sitting on the same bar stool, but Percy was gone. Kanesha wondered to herself why she expected anything different. She remembered something she read by Maya Angelo. 'When someone shows you who they are, believe them.' As a tear fell down her cheek, Kanesha questioned how she had gotten to the point where it was okay to be used and abused by a man.

Unwilling to openly show her emotions, Kanesha wiped the single tear from her cheek and lowered her head. Wilson sat silent, giving Kanesha a moment to get herself together before volunteering to see her home safely.

"Kanesha, I can give you a ride to the crib," said Wilson in a comforting tone.

Kanesha raised her head and gave Wilson a forced smile to say, "Thank you."

Once outside, Wilson opened the passenger car door for Kanesha, making sure she was seated comfortably before closing it for her. The small gentlemanly gesture made Kanesha feel special, and even a little worthy.

Wilson drove slowly up the street wondering why Kanesha had allowed a man like Percy into her life. The question had been on his mind for the past month. Wilson saw how Percy was pushing Kanesha down to his level instead of her pulling him up to hers. He thought of Kanesha as a good friend, and wanted nothing but the best for her. Wilson knew that Percy was bad news. Although he was dying to ask the question, Wilson decided not to pry into Kanesha's private life. He reasoned that if she wanted to talk to him, she would open up to him when she was ready. All he could do was be a good friend and let her know he was there for her if she needed anything.

"Thank you for the ride, Wilson, I really appreciate it," Kanesha said sadly.

"No need to thank me. I'm just looking out for you the way a real man does," said Wilson before exiting the car to walk around and open the door for Kanesha. She grabbed a hold of his extended hand and lifted herself out of the car. Kanesha stood up on the curb and gave Wilson a hug before turning on her heels and walking toward her small porch. Before she got the key into the lock, Wilson called out to her.

"Kanesha, I'm here for you if you ever need anything. Cool?" quizzed Wilson.

"Cool," replied Kanesha.

Once inside, just as expected, Percy was nowhere to be found. He probably knew if he had been there, he would have had to have heard Kanesha's mouth about running up that tab and sticking her with the bill.

Kanesha dropped her purse on the couch and flopped down in her arm chair. She laid her head back and sat in the dark for over twenty minutes as one tear after another fell from her eyes. Kanesha had never felt more alone than she did at that very moment. There was no mistaking the fact that her life had taken a turn down the wrong path and with each tear, Kanesha wondered if there was a way to turn things around. Despite the fact that she held down two jobs while raising four children on her own, Kanesha didn't feel very good about herself. Something inside her made it acceptable for Kanesha to settle for less. Kanesha wondered if that was why she was always on the prowl for a man to love her. She tried to get a better understanding of why she always looked for reassurance in the arms of men who meant her no good. For hours Kanesha cried her heart out and called out to God for the answers she was searching for.

At four in the morning, Kanesha's tears dried up and her thinking became clearer with each passing moment. Kanesha used the clarity to try and figure out why she was hearing her mother's teaching in her head as if the words were just spoken to her. She thought back on her teenage years when she began allowing her grades to drop and trying to smoke weed to deal with the grief of losing her father. Kanesha gave her mother reasons to worry about her and even more reasons to throw her hands up high and give up, but her mother never did. Cynthia stood firm in her teachings and kept her daughter in prayer. Kanesha remembered overhearing her mother crying out to God for strength and guidance in search for the right way to reach her troubled child. She wondered if God could be punishing her for being a sinner. Wednesday night Bible study classes she attended assured Kanesha that she served a forgiving God; all she had to do was confess her sins and repent of those sins. Kanesha felt bad for the way she had treated her mother and she wondered if it were too late to make it up to her.

Kanesha felt as if the weight of the world were resting on her shoulders. She felt weak, lost and alone. It was the exact same feeling she had when her father died. The thought of her father was always so sad because instead of remembering his life, Kanesha dwelled on his death. For the first time in over twelve years, Kanesha had a heartwarming memory of her father.

Dale Brooks was a strong, intelligent, God-fearing man who loved his family and treasured the life they had together. Kanesha was a daddy's girl, and she could always be found tagging along right beside him. To Kanesha, the sun rose and set on her daddy. One of her favorite things to do with him was have tea parties. Dale would look so uncomfortable in the tiny chair, but he would sit for hours with Kanesha and her stuffed animals and dolls if that was what she wanted. The memory made Kanesha smile inside for the first time in a very long time. Kanesha closed her eyes trying to picture her father's face and recall his smell. Slowly, his face came into view and Kanesha got a sudden, tight, warm feeling in her chest. The feeling startled her. She didn't know how to put it into words, but her heart fluttered as she said a little prayer.

Dear Lord, I have not called out to you in a very long time, and for that I'm sorry. I'm coming to you now asking for a favor. I'm in a very difficult place right now and I need to have just one more talk with my daddy. Lord, I miss him so much. You know that his death left an emptiness inside that is indescribable. Please, tell him that I miss him, that I need him in my life right now. I know I've made some mistakes, but I'll try to do better, Lord. I promise. I just need to have a little talk with my daddy. Amen.

After praying and drying her eyes, Kanesha went to bed and slept better than she had in a very long time.

Chapter Four
R.E.S.P.E.C.T.

Kanesha often tried to sleep late on Sunday mornings, but her body was on a schedule of its own, not allowing her to get extra rest. Working two part-time jobs and taking care of four small children during the week left Kanesha feeling worn. After the good cry and prayer she said the night before, she felt renewed.

She was up at nine o'clock, fuming at herself for allowing Percy to take advantage of her. "When did I become so desperate?" Kanesha asked herself out loud. "He's not even my type, all out of shape and unattractive."

She thought back to her relationships with the four men who'd fathered her children. Each one of them left Kanesha hurt, alone and pregnant. She believed Stephon when he promised they would be together forever. Byron was real from day one by telling Kanesha straight out that it was only about sex and nothing more, but Kanesha believed things would change as they grew closer.

Mike lied and kept the fact about his wife and two sons to himself until Kanesha called him about her pregnancy. Je'Ronn only loved Je'Ronn, but again, Kanesha thought she could change him.

Had she paid attention, she would have realized that the only thing Je'Ronn loved more than himself was sex. He had three women pregnant at the same time, each giving birth to baby girls just weeks apart from one another. Even after that revelation, Kanesha thought Je'Ronn would be with her because she bore him a son.

Kanesha had taken Je'Ronn to the *Maury Show* to prove paternity. Maury said, "Je'Ronn, you are the father," and the flood gates flew open. A month after the show aired, four women had Maury saying his famous line to three of them. Even with the blood test, Kanesha never received one red penny from Je'Ronn because street pharmacists are not required to complete a W-2 form or pay into social security, but it wasn't money she was after. Her search was for protection, security and love. Kanesha could hear her mother whispering in her ear, *'Your man should be able to match or contribute to what you bring to the table. If you have a furnished house, so should he. Don't settle for less.'* Her thoughts forced a light to go off in her mind. Kanesha shook her head, trying to quiet the whisper because she knew that was exactly what she had been doing; settling.

As Kanesha put fresh sheets on her bed and sprayed the room with Febreze, she heard the front door creak open.

"Kanesha, you 'ere?" screamed Percy.

Kanesha sucked her teeth and rolled her eyes back in her head. She didn't want to deal with Percy, but knew she had to in order to get the money he owed her. Kanesha hated the fact that she even handed over her hard earned money to a man without a nine to five or a side hustle. Unfortunately, it was too late to beat herself up about it now. Instead of acknowledging his presence, Kanesha walked into the room Malisha and Jordan shared and began picking up toys.

"Kanesha, you ain't hear me callin' your name?" Percy slurred his words. The fowl order of Thunderbird filled the kid's room.

"Yea, I heard you. What do you want?"

"It's too early fo' you to have an attitude, woman."

"Whatever," dismissed Kanesha. She returned her attention to the task at hand. Percy turned around and walked into Kanesha's bathroom, slamming the door behind him. She thanked God that Percy got the hint that she was not in the mood to deal with him. After his three minute shower, he fell asleep across the freshly made full size bed.

Hours later, Kanesha had cleaned every inch of the

cramped box she called home. The rent was income based paid through HUD which made it affordable. She decided to relax on her couch and watch a movie and sip on a strawberry wine cooler. Half way into the movie, Percy interrupted her quiet time.

"You should have lain down with me. I wanted to taste you again," said Percy.

Kanesha rolled her eyes at the thought of him touching her before refocusing her attention on the movie.

Unfortunately, Percy would not be dismissed so easily, again. "Why you acting so funny, like you got an attitude?"

"I do have an attitude. You drank up my tip money last night."

"I got you," lied Percy.

"I don't work my next shift at the bar until Friday night so you have until then to get all of my money *you* owe Miss Yolanda together. And, let's not get it twisted; the only thing you got is my money. You keep yapping that you gon' pay me yet your tab keeps going up," fumed Kanesha. Though she had paid the bill, Kanesha was determined Percy would repay her for everything.

"I said, I got you. Just give me some time and-"

A knock at the door put the impending argument on hold. Kanesha opened the door for her mother and Malisha to come inside. It seemed as if the time had raced by. She looked at her watch that read six fifteen and realized it was time for the kids to start coming home.

"Hey, baby girl," Kanesha hugged her daughter. "You have fun with 'Dea?"

"Yes, she got me a bike, but I have to leave it at her house," beamed Malisha.

"Oh, did you ride it?" asked Kanesha in a sweet voice.

"Yes, it's a black Barbie bike. Dea' said it was ordered special just for me," bragged Malisha.

"You are special, Malisha Nicole. Give 'Dea a hug and

go put your bag up. Make sure you remember to throw your dirty clothes in the basket," instructed Kanesha.

Malisha hugged her grandmother, grabbed her overnight bag and ran to her room. Cynthia sat on the couch and made small talk with her only child. She tried to ignore Percy, but being in his presence irked her to no end. Cynthia knew he was no good and his only agenda was to bring Kanesha down.

"Hello, Percy. I see you're enjoying this quiet Sunday afternoon," Cynthia said in a flat tone.

"Cynthia," replied Percy while simultaneously lifting his forty ounce of beer in the air. "I see you're here to blow my high. Can't you find anything else to do with your time besides annoy me?"

Kanesha and Cynthia gasped in unison.

"Percy, you will not talk to my mother that way. What is wrong with you?" Kanesha stated.

"It's okay, baby. People like him don't care about nothing, but being miserable. Kanesha, keep in mind that misery loves company," stated Cynthia.

Cynthia grabbed her purse and headed for the door. She turned the knob and looked at Kanesha. "Kanesha, you work hard to provide for your babies and I applaud you for that. Please, hear what I say." Cynthia paused and glanced at Percy before focusing her eyes back on Kanesha. "It is much easier for somebody to drag you down than it is for you to lift them up. You may not see what level you are on but believe me when I tell you; it's much higher than a man without a pot to piss in. You'll see that once you stop thinking you need a man and stand on your own two feet. A man should *not* define who you are." With that being said, Cynthia left.

Kanesha was irritated by Percy's disrespect. For the first time, her mother's words sunk in from the start. Another knock at the door put what would have been another argument on hold.

"Hey, Kanesha. What it do, baby girl?" greeted Je'Ronn.

"Hi, Je'Ronn. How did Jordan do this weekend?"

"My l'il man was chillin'. Right, buddy?" Je'Ronn patted Jordan on his freshly cut fade.

Kanesha picked up her son and gave him a kiss on the cheek.

"Tell Daddy bye and go see what Malisha is doing," said Kanesha.

"Bye, Dad, see you," said Jordan.

"Stay up, buddy, and remember to ask Mommy to brush your hair and put on your wave cap before you go to bed every night," said Je'Ronn.

"Okay," replied Jordan as Kanesha put him down and he left the room.

Kanesha was thankful for her kid free weekends but she missed her children whenever they were away.

"All right, Kanesha, my moms said she'll pick up my son Friday night. Cool?"

Je'Ronn offered very little financial help but he made sure his presence was felt in his son's life. He and his mother spent a lot of time with Jordan and they loved him. Kanesha assumed that he loved Jordan more than his other kids because he was his only son. At last count, Je'Ronn had fathered five daughters. Some he saw and some he refused to claim. Kanesha did not concern herself with his other kids because they were not her responsibility.

"Okay, I'll have him ready at six," Kanesha smiled at him.

Je'Ronn gave a nod in Percy's direction and asked, "You straight?"

"Yes, I'm straight," replied Kanesha in frustration.

"You sure, 'cause that black eye says different," said Je'Ronn.

Kanesha was speechless but the questioning look she was giving Je'Ronn said what she couldn't. She thought the make-up and dark sunglasses masked the black eye Friday night when she went in to work.

"Girl, you know I got eyes everywhere," Je'Ronn was

talking to Kanesha but kept his eyes glued on Percy. Kanesha never could hide anything from Je'Ronn and figured that one of his friends must have noticed her on Friday. It had lightened up but Kanesha still wore two coats of foundation to hide her black eye from both Je'Ronn and her mother. *Well, I guess one for two ain't bad,* thought Kanesha.

"She said, she straight," barked Percy.

"Slow ya roll, old man," warned Je'Ronn. "I ain't a woman and I hit back. I'm a straight up menace and spending a night in the county for beating you down don't mean a thing to me. You remember that before you come at me the wrong way."

Jordan and Malisha heard the angry voices and sprinted down the small hall way to see about their mother. Kanesha scooped Jordan up in one arm and wrapped the other around Malisha's neck. Jordan tightened his grip around his mother's neck as Malisha hugged her mother's leg.

"Je'Ronn, y'all have the kids all scared. Everything is cool, I promise," said Kanesha in an effort to calm Je'Ronn. As bad as she wanted to get Percy out of her life, she had to wait until she could get the money he owed her first.

"Yea, whatever. You got my cell, so hit me up if this so called man of yours step to you the wrong way again."

Kanesha watched Je'Ronn do his pimp stride out the door. His sagging Avirex jeans were at least three sizes too big, but his size thirteen Timberland boots let all the women know what he was hiding underneath his gear. Kanesha became flush as she remembered intimate moments spent with Je'Ronn.

"Hey, shut the dang door," grunted Percy.

"Hold on, you don' got a little too comfortable up in here."

"Oh, that young boy gave you a spine? I know you ain't tryna stand up to me," taunted Percy.

Kanesha walked away from Percy to put Malisha and

Jordan in their room. She put their favorite DVD on before returning to the front room to finish her argument with Percy.

"Look, I need my money and I need it tonight," demanded Kanesha.

"No, you look," roared Percy, "don't be nagging me about no freakin' money. I'll pay you when I pay you. That's what wrong wit' witches like you. Y'all don't know when to stop running your mouth."

Kanesha had failed to lock the door after Je'Ronn left and was startled when it opened and Shakayla stood in the door frame.

"Mommy, is everything okay?" asked Shakayla.

"Yes, baby, everything is okay," Kanesha lied. "How was your weekend?"

"It was fine. My daddy said he'll talk to you in a couple of days about summer break. He said this year we're going to visit Myrtle Beach," beamed Shakayla.

"That sounds like fun. I went there with my parents when I was around your age," smiled Kanesha. She was happy that Shakayla was being exposed to life outside of Youngstown. Her biggest regret was that she was not able to give her other kids the same exposure.

"I'm going to pick out an outfit for tomorrow. I want to look pretty for my school pictures."

"Is that tomorrow?"

"Yes, it is. You didn't forget that me, Brianna and Malisha need money for our pictures and I need a pair of shoes?"

Kanesha felt backed into a corner with no way out. She had forgotten about the pictures and that Shakayla's shoes were worn over. Shakayla had a full wardrobe at her father's house, but she was never allowed to bring any of those things home with her. The clothes she wore to Stephon's house on Friday were the same ones on her back on Sunday evenings. Not once in nine years had he been late with child support payments or failed to get his daughter when he was supposed to. The problem now facing Kanesha was she had loaned her last child support payments from Stephon and Mike to Percy.

"I don't know if you and your sisters will be able to take pictures tomorrow, but I will take y'all to Wal-Mart for some family pictures," explained Kanesha. Seeing the hurt in her daughter's eyes, Kanesha felt as low as she ever had before, especially since it was her fault. Disappointing her daughter made her chest flutter again and the voice in her head spoke. This time, it was definitively the still quiet voice, but it spoke its loudest. *'I cannot provide what you do not ask for. It's time for a change, lean on me when you're at your weakest and I shall strengthen you.'*

The voice was so soothing it sent a chill down her spine. Kanesha was speechless, embarrassed and troubled as she watched Shakayla's shoulders drop and tears fell from her eyes.

"Okay, Mommy, whatever you say," replied Shakayla with a tear rolling down her cheek. Shakayla turned and walked down the hall toward her bedroom.

The ache in Kanesha's heart was strong. *How could I put a man before my children?* She asked herself. Kanesha looked at Percy with daggers in her eyes. He sat drinking his warm beer, and staring into the screen like there would be a mid-term at the end of the film. Percy, watching the movie as if he didn't have a care in the world, brought Kanesha's anger to its boiling point.

"I'm going in the back to check on my daughter. When I get back, you better have figured out how you are going to repay me all of my money, or get the heck out!"

Percy fanned a hand at Kanesha in a dismissive way and continued to study Billy Dee William's mannerisms. Kanesha wanted to cry as she slowly walked down the hall leading to the bedrooms. Shakayla had closed her bedroom door, causing Kanesha to pause before going inside to check on her. Stalling in order to collect her thoughts, Kanesha peeked in on Malisha and Jordan.

"Hey, l'il man, why you in here by yourself? Where is Malisha?" Kanesha inquired.

"In dere wit' Kay-Kay. They say I can't come in," whined Jordan. "I don't care 'cause I play wit' my truck."

"Oh, so you a big boy and don't need to have your sisters around all the time, huh?"

"Yep, I a big boy." Jordan's eyes never left his Tonka trucks.

Kanesha bent down and gave Jordan a quick kiss on his forehead and decided she had stalled enough. She left Jordan to play with his trucks and crossed the small hall to the girls' bedroom. Slowly turning the door knob, Kanesha could hear her daughters talking.

"Don't cry, Shakayla. We can take pictures later, and you can wear my shoes," said Malisha.

"I can't fit ya shoes, but thank you though," replied Shakayla. "Mommy just hurt my feelings because she promised we could take pictures. She said she was going to buy me those shoes I wanted too. They were going to be my reward for helping out with you and Jordan last week. The shoes are at her job and I need them for gym class. The ones I got now are raggedy and the kids at school are talking about me and teasing me almost every day."

"You want me to fight them for you? I'll make them leave you alone," offered Malisha.

"It's okay. I'll be okay. They just hurt my feelings when they tease me."

"It's Percy's fault we can't take school pictures," declared Malisha.

"I know it is. Why do Mommy always do stuff for her boyfriends before she do stuff for us?" cried Shakayla.

"Maybe she love 'dem more than she love us."

Kanesha stood outside the bedroom feeling low. In her desire to have a man around, she never realized that she was jeopardizing her relationship with her children. *'When you have kids, they eat before you eat; they wear cleaned and iron clothes even if you don't. They come before you and that's nonnegotiable.'* This time there was no question that the voice belonged to her mother. Cynthia had been drilling that into Kanesha's head since the day her first pregnancy test read positive.

"I hear you, Mom. I get it; I finally get it," whispered Kanesha as tears streaked her face.

Chapter Five
Hard Lesson to Learn

The words that came from her five and nine year old daughters' mouths were more than Kanesha could handle. She turned and went in her room and sat on her bed, wondering how she could have been so stupid to focus all of her attention on men who never cared anything about her. Kanesha's head began to hurt as all the lessons her mother had been trying to teach her over the years raced through her mind. She couldn't keep living like this; her daughters would end up being just like her when they grew up. Kanesha worried that they would resent her. She couldn't let that happen.

Kanesha fixed her eyes on a pair of Percy's ugly cowboy boots and heard the voice in her head again, *'Put your kid's needs before your wants.'* Kanesha began to realize that if she just focused on their needs, she would have realized Shakayla's childhood was being cut short because of the responsibilities forced upon her. Brianna was silently crying out for her attention by trying to be perfect. Malisha was forming a thick skin, and poor little Jordan didn't understand any of it, yet.

Kanesha went to lie across her bed. She cried for damaging her children. Tears flowed for the loss of her father for the first time in years. She wondered if she had been looking for a man to replace her father, but dismissed it with the logic that *they don't make 'em like her daddy anymore.* Her father was strong, hard working, God fearing and dedicated to his family. Kanesha knew she had to make things right and stop hating the life she'd made for herself. If not, she risked her kids hating her one day. "No time like the present to begin a new way of life," said Kanesha.

Kanesha dried her eyes, blew her nose and felt an amazing strength wash over her. She decided it was time to make a positive change in her way of thinking and in her life. She swung the bedroom door open and shouted Percy's name as she made her way to the living room where he was.

"What's wrong with you screaming like that?" snapped Percy.

"Get up, get your hand full of stuff and leave," instructed Kanesha.

"Leave? What you mean, leave? Don't you know who I am by now?"

"Yea, Percy, I know exactly who you are. Let's see; where should I start?"

"Start what?" Percy asked with a perplexed look plastered on his aged face.

"Telling you who you are. In the time I've known you, all you've done is take from me and my kids," shouted Kanesha angrily.

"Witch, I ain't took nothin' from you. You ain't got nothin' fo nobody to take."

"Oh, I got a roof over ya head, I got a bed fo you to lay in every night. I got a couch for you to engrave a butt groove in." Kanesha picked up the couch cushion and threw it on the floor. "I got food fo you to eat-up, gas, lights and water for ya use. Now, what ya old butt got besides arthritis in your back? You can't even please me the right way."

"Look, Kanesha, you need to calm down so we can straighten this out. I know you mad, but I'm gon' pay you back." Percy offered another empty promise in a pleading voice.

"When, partner, and with what? You been *not* lookin' for a job since I met you and ya bill is past due and got interest applied to it."

"Kanesha, baby, I got a job lined up this week. I'm just waiting for him to get at me."

"Get at you? Shoot, you forty something years old

and ain't figured out yet that you have to get at a job; a job don't get at you."

"I'ma pay you everything and some. I just need a little more time," begged Percy.

"You ain't done anything for me since you followed me home like a lost puppy. Got my stupid behind walking around with a black eye and sore jaw! Now you jeopardizing my job and keeping me from providing for my babies. I'm straight on ya sorry, butt. I finally realize that I can do bad all by myself," fired Kanesha.

She stood and glared into Percy's eyes waiting for his comeback. When none came, Kanesha figured he was done pleading and begging for another chance. Kanesha was fully prepared for what came next.

"To heck with you and all dem kids you got. Call they daddy, I mean daddies, for whatever it is they need. Oh, that's right; it's one Dad for each bastard child. Forget you and dem kids."

Bam!

Kanesha knocked Percy in the chest with a baseball bat she had been holding behind her. Percy had hit her once and gotten away with it, but Kanesha would commit herself to the nut house before she allowed it to happen again without a fight.

Percy caught himself from falling by holding on to the wall behind him. After catching his balance, Percy smacked Kanesha, causing her to stumble.

"Aw, punk, you done lost ya mind!" shouted Byron.

Kanesha and Percy had been so caught up in their argument, that neither of them heard Byron and Brianna come into the house.

Byron body slammed Percy and began punching him with as much force as he could muster.

"Sucker, I'll kill you over mine," proclaimed Byron. He continued to pummel Percy as all four kids began crying and screaming at the sight. "What, partner? Hit me da way you hit a woman! What, partner, what?"

"Daddy, Daddy stop. Please stop," cried Brianna.

"Mommy, do something, he's going to kill him," begged Shakayla.

Jordan cried because his sisters were crying. Malisha smiled at the sight because she never liked Percy. He was mean to her, and her sisters, and brother. Plus, he was always grumpy.

Percy lay on the hardwood floor with blood oozing from his mouth, nose and ears.

"Stop, please make it stop, Mommy!" Brianna screamed.

"Byron, stop! Stop, Byron, he got the message," Kanesha reluctantly said. She was grateful for Byron's arrival and thanked God that he cared enough about her to intervene.

"Get out and you betta go a different way than the one I take 'cause if I ever see you again, it will take a DNA test to identify ya sorry behind!" Byron stood just inches away from Percy as he spoke. Though he didn't want to upset the kids any further, Byron hoped Percy would make a wrong move so he would have a reason to beat his weak opponent some more.

Percy stumbled over and over before he was finally able to stand on his feet. A trail of blood followed him as he walked toward the door Kanesha proudly held open for him.

After throwing the drawer holding all of Percy's worldly possessions out on the lawn, Kanesha and Byron calmed the children down. It took two hours to convince the kids that Percy was not coming back and that they were safe. The kids only fell asleep after Byron promised to stay the night and watch out for them.

Kanesha felt like a complete and total failure after seeing the light by which her daughters saw her. For the past nine years, Kanesha made herself believe she was being a good mother. She had always fed and kept them clean, made sacrifices for them, made certain they had all of their shots and worked hard every year to give them a Christmas to be proud of. Over the years, she

colored with them, played jump rope and dribbled bas-
ketballs. In her heart, Kanesha thought she was giving
her best to them, but she had just received a complete
eye opener.

Having her children look up to her was important.
She wanted to be their hero, the back bone and the
shining light in their lives. She wanted to provide her
children with the type of life her parents had given her.
A life free of financial worries and the belief that all
blessings shower down from the heavens above. Before
the car crash and the tragic death of her father, the
Brooks family was very active in their church. Kanesha
had been a member of the youth choir and volunteered
in the church nursery during Sunday morning devotion.

Cynthia did the best she could to teach Kanesha how
to lean on God during their grieving, but Kanesha's
anger toward Him was blinding. Instead of turning
toward God for comfort and strength at her most vulnerable time, Kanesha rebelled and promised herself she
would never forgive Him for taking her father from her.
As Kanesha's heart began to lighten, so did the weight
on her shoulders. Kanesha knew her life was lacking
substance because she failed to do as God would have
her do.

The recent events in her life made Kanesha see she
had failed to put God first. Shakayla, Malisha, Brianna
and Jordan needed to know Jesus and the ultimate sac-
rifice He made for them. Kanesha knew it was her
responsibility to introduce her children to the almighty,
for she was responsible for their souls. She had to be a
living testament to the love of God. She promised herself
she would turn her life around and reconnect with her
Savior. *Jesus wept*, whispered the voice in her head.

After the drama with Percy calmed down, Byron
insisted on staying the night. Kanesha tried to convince
him to leave after the kids fell asleep, but Byron would-
n't hear of it. Deep inside, Kanesha was relieved he
stayed because his presence made her feel safe. There

was no telling where Percy's head was at, and Kanesha was afraid he might return to hurt her.

Byron and Kanesha got little sleep that night. They talked about Percy, Kanesha's revelation on the damage she had done to her children, and her determination to change. For a while, Kanesha rested her head on Byron's lap and cried tears of relief.

"Don't cry, girl. You know I can't stand to see a woman cry." Byron stroked Kanesha's back to soothe her tears.

"I'm sorry, but sometimes our souls need a good cry," sniffed Kanesha. "That's one lesson from my mom that I've recently come to understand."

"What does that mean?"

"Remember growing up, and your mom telling you things that you didn't understand at the time? Especially as a teenager, when you thought you knew it all and later discovered that you knew nothing at all."

Byron laughed and shook his head. "I wish I could go back to being taken care of by my moms," joked Byron.

"I hope you don't think I'm crazy, but while Percy was here, this voice in my head kept talking to me," explained Kanesha.

"I know you ain't going crazy on me." Byron raised his right eye brow and lowered his eye lids, waiting for Kanesha to respond.

"No, all I'm saying is that some of the things my mother tried to teach me are coming back to me. I finally understand what she was trying to say."

"That's what's up; I feel you," replied Byron.

The two went on to talk about their relationship, the kids and their future. Before long, Kanesha and Byron were entwined in each other's arms kissing passionately. Kanesha's body was warm and hungry for what she knew Byron could give her, but her heart was not into the moment. Unlike all of the other times when her body wanted one thing and her mind another, Kanesha was determined not to take the easy way out. She listened to her mind and stopped things before they went too far.

"Stop, Byron, this isn't right," sighed Kanesha, while pushing herself away from Byron to put some space between them.

"What?" asked Byron as his hands continued to roam over familiar terrain. "Why we got to stop, girl? You know I won't hurt you."

"No, Byron, we're moving too fast. I appreciate you coming to my rescue earlier, and it means the world to me that you care enough to sit with me and the kids tonight, but this isn't right." Kanesha stood up and walked across the room in an attempt to find the right words. The last thing she wanted to do was cause another scene. "For years, I've been looking for a man to take care of me. Each time I was left with a baby and a broken heart. It's time for me to grow up and make a change. The voice in my head wasn't just that of my mother's, it was also the Lord trying to get my attention." Kanesha paced the floor, searching for the right words to get Byron to understand her sudden change. Her voice sounded nervous but her heart and soul felt free and proud. "As much as my body wants to be intimate with you, my soul needs more. I'm done with the one night stands and using my body as if I never had any home training. So, if that's what you want, I can't give it to you."

Kanesha looked at Byron, trying to read his face for some type of reaction to her words. She knew Byron was surprised by her new found self-respect because so was she. Byron's face was blank, but his eyes were soft and caring.

Kanesha rejoined Byron on the couch and looked deep into his eyes. "If you want to be with me, in a relationship with me, you have to put on the brakes and slow things down. At the end of the day, if we are meant to be, we will have built a foundation on which to stand."

"Wow, that's deep," was Byron's only response as he

sat staring into Kanesha's eyes.

"I pray you understand where I'm coming from, but if you don't, there are no bad feelings. We'll always be cool, no matter what."

"I feel you, baby girl. You making it hard on a brotha, for sho', but I respect where you coming from. We did rush things when we first got together, and you don't ever stress me like those others chicks that got my babies. We can move as slow and steady as you want, just tell me what you need from me," smiled Byron.

Kanesha let out a sigh of relief and wrapped her arms around Byron's neck and held him tight. Kanesha was leery of Byron's willingness to move slow, but if she could change, who's to say he couldn't change as well.

"Thank you, Byron. We can just spend some time talking and spending time together before we get all serious. I've had my kids around enough men to last a lifetime."

"It's cool, I ain't trippin. Get out a deck of cards and let me beat you down in some Tonk right quick," requested Byron.

"You still want to stay here tonight?" asked a stunned Kanesha.

"I said we were cool, didn't I? Anyway, if that fool Percy decides to come back, I want to be the one to welcome him in. I can sleep on the couch and take the girls to grab some shoes before dropping them off to school in the morning." He reached into his pocket and pulled out some cash. "Here, take this fifty and let them take school pictures like everybody else. Don't be scared to ask for something the kids need, understand?" Byron maintained a steady and serious stance while talking, to let Kanesha know he was serious about his. Just when it looked like Kanesha was about to burst into tears, Byron cracked a smile and asked, "What's up with those cards, girl? And grab me a beer while you up."

Kanesha did as she was told with a smile on her face and gratitude in her heart.

Chapter Six
A New Day, A New Life, An Old Love

Four months had passed since the incident with
Percy, and although he never paid back the money he
owed, Kanesha was as happy as she had ever been in
her adult life. Percy stayed away from her home and her
job; that fact alone was priceless to Kanesha.

The seasons had changed from spring to summer
and a new routine had begun. Shakayla spent every
summer with her dad, Malisha with her 'Dea, and
Jordan with his dad's mother and sisters. Brianna split
her summer between being at home and spending time
with Byron's family. The fact that her parents were
working on getting back together did not alter her
schedule.

Kanesha began attending Sunday morning church
services with her mother on a regular basis. Cynthia
beamed with pride every Sunday when she walked
through the church door with her daughter by her side.
She had no idea what happened between Kanesha and
Percy, but Cynthia praised the saints when she found
out that dead weight was out of her daughter's life. Two
months after attending Sunday morning services,
Kanesha shocked her mother by asking for a ride to
evening services. Cynthia was so pleased with the tran-
sition that she cried.

Cynthia thanked God for getting through to
Kanesha. She was forever grateful for having her daughter back. Kanesha gained much strength in her Bible
studies and decided to start visiting her father's grave
site with her mother. The first Sunday of each month
following the accident, Cynthia took a fresh bouquet to
her husband's resting place. Malisha always accompa-

nied 'Dea and listened intently to the stories 'Dea told about the grandfather she would never know.

Kanesha was on a spiritual walk with Jesus. It showed in her face, her smile and her actions. She felt free, safe and proud of herself. Her life was finally worth waking up to each blessed morning. When Kanesha had a question about the Bible, she would call upon her mother for advice and God for the answer.

"Mommy, do you think it's wrong for me to keep working at the bar now that I'm trying to live right?" Kanesha stared out the passenger side window as her mother drove away from Todd Cemetery.

"No, I don't think it's wrong. Why do you ask?"

"Sister Freeman said I was undoing the good God was trying to bless me with by surrounding myself with sinners down at that drinking hole," explained Kanesha.

"Listen to me, Kanesha," began Cynthia after pulling the car to the side of the road and putting it into park. "Every Christian ain't saved and every sinner ain't lost. What I mean by that is sometimes people will tell you what they believe and not what the Word says. There are some who believe you must be dressed to impress when you enter the house of the Lord. But they forget that Jesus was a carpenter and says, *Come as you are.* Man will tell you it's a sin to drink, but Jesus turned water to wine and God's word teaches it's a sin to drink to get drunk. You are doing a wonderful job staying on track with your devotion, so don't you let no busy body Christian discourage you. We all fall because we're human, but Jesus walked this earth so that He could die for our sins. Jesus knows that being in the flesh is a battle." Cynthia spoke with such pride and joy when Jesus was the subject. She had prayed for so long to be able to talk with her daughter about the sacrifices Jesus made for her, that she often pinched herself to make sure she wasn't dreaming.

"Sister Freeman said no Christian should be surrounded by a room full of sinners like when I'm serving drinks at that bar." Kanesha spoke with an air of shame in her voice.

"Oh, did Sister Freeman offer you a job? See, baby, a true, faithful Christian does not have to tell you she's a Christian, because you will know it by the way she carries herself, and by the way she lives her life. We are supposed to win souls for Christ. How can we do that if there are no sinners around to teach the word of God? His word will always blanket you, so you keep working hard to provide for your children, and God will lead you to the right job for you," said Cynthia sternly.

"Yes, ma'am," smiled Kanesha and Malisha echoed her mother from the back seat causing them to laugh.

Against Byron's objections, Kanesha began working full-time at the bar and part-time at the dollar store. Byron was helping her take care of home, but the new Kanesha wanted to have her own money. She needed to feel as if she were trying to do something with her life. Though she loved and appreciated everything Byron was doing for her, Kanesha never wanted to be totally dependent on a man again. She had no intentions on working at the bar forever, but it was a good gig for the time being. After the talk she had with her mother, Kanesha didn't feel like a hypocrite working at the bar, but she did intend on putting in her two weeks notice soon. She was determined to find a job she could be proud of and prayed on it daily. She considered going back to school to earn a certificate or degree in the health field. She figured it would be a great first step toward providing her children with a better life.

Kanesha had been showing up for work early just to update Miss Yolanda on the way things in her life had improved since getting rid of Percy and attending church regularly.

"Girl, you been smiling for weeks now. It's good to finally see you happy."

"Miss Yolanda, I never thought my soul could feel so free. I'm taking things slow with Byron this time around, but being without a man in my bed every morning feels good," declared Kanesha. "The best part is we've become close friends and sex is not the foundation of our relationship."

"When it's right, a man can make heaven on earth seem possible, but baby ain't it good when you can have that feeling all by yourself?" Miss Yolanda hugged Kanesha and kissed her cheek like a proud parent might do on report card day. "So, is everything with you and Byron going that well?"

"Yes, ma'am, I think I can trust him this time. With the kids being gone most of the time, we've been able to spend a lot of time together. He's taken me to the movies, out to eat, shopping and even for walks through the rose garden at Mill Creek Park. The best part is I never have to ask him to spend time with me."

Kanesha was smiling from ear to ear and the sparkle in her eyes glistened brightly. Miss Yolanda and Kanesha hugged before returning their attention to the thirsty customers seated around the bar. It was Saturday night and the bar was busy. When Kanesha looked up from storing beer into the freezer, she gasped.

"What is he doing here?" This was her first time laying eyes on Percy since their violent break-up. Kanesha could have gone on with the rest of her life without laying eyes on Percy again but as small as Youngstown was, they were bound to bump into each other sooner or later.

"I hadn't noticed him come in," answered Miss Yolanda. "Do you want me to have Wilson put his sorry behind out?"

"Only if you expect me to serve him. I have nothing to say to Percy, and he has nothing to say to me." Kanesha glanced in Percy's direction and rolled her eyes at him before returning her attention to Miss Yolanda.

"Is Byron picking you up from work tonight?"

"Yes. He said he would probably be in tonight for a few drinks before closing time."

"Well, the last thing I want is for a fight to break out in here. I'll have Wilson throw Percy to the curb," laughed Miss Yolanda.

Kanesha watched Miss Yolanda walk through the crowd toward Wilson. Before the two could get back over to where Percy was seated, he had left on his own accord.

"Thank God he left before Byron got here," Kanesha whispered to herself.

Wilson didn't need to be asked to keep a watch on Percy. He had been keeping watch over Kanesha since he'd started working there. He was happy when Kanesha cut Percy from her life, but disappointment set in when it became obvious that Byron had taken his place. Wilson knew that Kanesha was selling herself short by having such low expectations.

Time flew by, and before Kanesha knew it, the D.J. announced last call for alcohol. Byron and his boy had arrived just in time to toss back a couple of drinks. Kanesha's heart smiled when Byron paid for their drinks instead of assuming they were free.

"Hey, sexy, we gon' be out in the car waiting for you, cool?" slurred Byron with a silly smile plastered to his face.

"Okay, I won't be long," promised Kanesha.

Wilson eyed the way Byron looked at Kanesha and couldn't help but feel jealous. For months Wilson had been waiting in the shadows, longing for Kanesha, watching while she settled for men he knew did not deserve her. Being a man of few words, Wilson felt the direct approach with Kanesha would be very difficult for him. He feared pouring out his heart to her, only to have the doors slammed shut in his face. Each night before closing his eyes, Wilson thanked God for the passing day and asked Him to bare watch over Kanesha and her children. Kanesha didn't seem to notice Wilson was alive, and that caused many sleepless nights for him.

"Wilson, do you hear me talking to you?" asked Miss

Yolanda.

"I'm sorry, Miss Yolanda, what did you say?" Wilson answered, embarrassed. He was so deep in thought about Kanesha, that he had failed to hear Miss Yolanda and Kanesha calling his name.

"I don't know what you were thinking about, but it must be important," laughed Kanesha.

"I apologize for that. My mind was somewhere else. Did you ladies need anything else before we call it a night?" Wilson waited for a response.

"Wilson, you are always the gentleman. Men like you are becoming an endangered species," said Miss Yolanda.

"I think so too, Miss Yolanda. You better watch out, Wilson, because I just might scoop you up and marry you one day." Kanesha smiled at Wilson, making him blush.

If Wilson didn't know any better, he would have sworn they could read his mind.

"All right, gang, the place is cleaned up, the drawers cashed out to the penny and the safe is locked up tight. Let's hit the road," said Miss Yolanda. "I don't know about the two of you, but I'm tired and my bed is calling out to me." She looked to Wilson. "Did you check both bathrooms to make sure they were empty?"

Wilson nodded in the positive.

Yolanda then looked to Kanesha. "Do you need a ride home tonight?" Miss Yolanda walked around the bar, turning off lights and turning on the alarm system.

"No, ma'am, Byron is outside waiting for me," replied Kanesha.

The three walked outside and headed toward the parking lot. Only three cars remained; Miss Yolanda's new Nissan Maxima, Wilson's old school Chevrolet Monte Carlo and Byron's souped up twenty year old Impala. Byron's car speakers were blasting the new Scarface CD. He appeared to be asleep with his head tilted back on the head rest.

"Is he asleep with the music playing that loud?" asked Miss Yolanda.

"He can sleep through a tornado if he has enough liquor inside of him," Kanesha replied. "I don't know how he does it, because my surroundings have to be as quiet as a church mouse for me to even doze off to sleep," joked Kanesha.

As usual, Wilson remained silent as the ladies talked amongst themselves. That is, until it became clear that Byron was not in the car alone.

Chapter Seven
The Beginning and the End

"Kanesha, why don't you ride with Miss Yolanda up the street and I'll wake Byron and make sure he makes it home safe," Wilson said nervously as they all stood in the parking lot outside of the bar.

"Byron and I don't live together, but if he's drunk, I can drive us up the street and he can sleep," said Kanesha. She was stopped in the middle of her sentence when she looked inside the car. It quickly became clear that Byron was not asleep and he was not alone.

"I don't believe this ignorant-" Kanesha stopped herself from cursing and calling Byron out of his name. "Byron, what are you doing?" She approached the car in a haste.

Miss Yolanda and Wilson grabbed for Kanesha as she raced toward the driver's side car door. Unfortunately, they were both too slow for Kanesha's swiftness.

"Come on, Kanesha. I'll drive you home," pleaded Miss Yolanda. She hated to see her friend hurt by another man, but she was relieved it happened before Kanesha got too deep into the relationship. "Don't give either one of them the satisfaction of knowing they got to you by acting a fool and losing that new found Christianity you've been talking about."

"Byron!" yelled Kanesha, not hearing a word Miss Yolanda had suggested. The music was playing so loud that Byron did not hear Kanesha scream his name the first time, but the second time was the charm.

Kanesha smacked the car window as hard as she could; startling Byron.

"Oh shoot," fussed Byron.

Byron was enjoying his time with the mother of another one of his kids. He was so caught up in the physical pleasure. "Stop, Mickey, stop!" Byron was so unnerved that he was having trouble zipping his pants back up.

"What? Why you trippin'," asked Mickey as she rose up to see Kanesha. "You tricking with this witch again?" Mickey spat with as much hatred as she could muster. She and Kanesha had never bumped heads, but Mickey knew who she was, and there was no way she was letting Byron go, again.

"Just get up and shut your stupid mouth," yelled Byron as he opened up the car door and got out to confront Kanesha. "Baby, don't trip. This don't mean nothing." He pointed toward Mickey. "I don't care nothing about that trick," lied Byron. He reached out to touch Kanesha, but she backed out of his reach.

"So, is that supposed to make me feel better? You talking about we can take things slow, I got cha back, I'll do whatever you want me to do so we can become a family?" mocked Kanesha. "You sitting outside of my job, waiting to give me a ride home, and you got some project hood rat with you. Are you serious?"

Byron was frozen in place because Kanesha's tone was frightening. He couldn't tell if she was angry or not. He looked into her eyes in search of some measure of emotion but found nothing.

While the two stared at each other, Mickey got herself together and jumped out of the passenger side car door. She'd heard what Kanesha said about her, and as far as Mickey was concerned, the statement earned Kanesha a smack across her face.

"I got cha project hood rat right here." Mickey rolled her neck when she spoke.

Miss Yolanda could tell that Mickey wanted to turn up the heat and get physical, but she wasn't having it on her property. "You stay just where you are," demanded Miss Yolanda. "This is between the two of them, not you. Do you understand me?"

Mickey looked Miss Yolanda up and down and smacked her lips. One look told Mickey the mature woman was not to be messed with, and besides, there would be other chances to get at Kanesha now that she knew where to find her. So, instead of causing a scene and making the current situation worse, Mickey did as she was told though with much attitude.

"Come on, baby, let me take you home so we can talk about this." Byron was not too proud to beg Kanesha for a chance to redeem himself.

"We're cool, Byron," Kanesha broke her silence.

"Sweet! Come on, baby girl, let's go," smiled Byron. He turned to open the car door for Kanesha. "Let's go to Perkins and get something to eat. We can talk everything over while we wait for our food."

"No, I'm cool. You and Mickey go to Perkins and I'm going home," replied Kanesha.

"Whaddaya mean? You just said we were cool," said a puzzled Byron.

"We are cool. I should have expected you to do something like this. All of that, take it slow talk and us not sleeping together, didn't faze you because you were doing it with one of your other baby momma's. I'm not surprised, or hurt, by catching you with your pants down. Even if I did get my feelings hurt, I would only have me to blame," said Kanesha. She was determined not to show Byron and Mickey how disappointed she was. Kanesha spoke clear and proper with her back straight and her head held high. "You've shown me exactly who you are many different times over the years, but I never believed you. That's been my bad. It won't happen again because I won't let it. You take care of yourself and make sure you continue to take care of the child we have together."

The parking lot was still. The air had a summer breeze blowing through the trees. Kanesha was proud of herself for being strong and wanting more from a relationship than sex and money. Miss Yolanda smiled at Kanesha, signaling her approval of how she handled the situation. Byron stood with his jaw hanging open in disbelief. He expected Kanesha to show out and get into a physical fight with him or Mickey. Byron wasn't sure what had just happened, but he knew for certain that the Kanesha he once knew had changed.

"Kanesha, I'll see you home safely," smiled Wilson as he extended his left hand for Kanesha to grab hold of. Wilson was proud of Kanesha and even more attracted to her than he had been. He thought it truly might be time that he let her know how he felt before the next man tried to step up. God had intervened with this one is how he saw it, but who was to say the same would be said for the next?

After confirming Kanesha was seated comfortably, Wilson shut the passenger side door and walked around the car to climb in behind the wheel. He turned over the ignition and glanced at Kanesha.

"Are you sure you're okay?" asked Wilson with great concern.

"Yes, Wilson, I'm just fine." She shifted in her seat. "I can't lie; a small part of my heart is hurting, but tomorrow is a new day that the Lord will make, right?"

"Lord willing, it sure will be," smiled Wilson as he drove off.

"I just realized that in all of the time we've been working together, we have never spoken more than three or four words to each other. Why is that?"

"I guess I'm just a man of few words," replied Wilson with a shoulder shrug.

"You seem to possess a quiet spirit; I like that about you. I may be wrong, but you appear to be very sure about yourself," Kanesha said cautiously.

"I've been through a lot in my twenty-nine years on this earth. I haven't always lived right, and it led to me giving the state free labor for a good portion of my life," confessed Wilson.

"We've all made mistakes, so don't be ashamed. Look at me. I'm twenty-six years old with four kids by four different men. I only have a high school diploma and no secure way to take care of the lives I brought into this world. My whole life so far has been a mistake." Kanesha's voice was sad. It broke Wilson's heart to hear her so down on herself.

"I don't see you in that light. You are a beautiful person, both inside and out. Any man fortunate enough to win your heart should be honored to call you his," blushed Wilson.

"Thank you for saying that. Lately I've been trying to turn my life around, and with the love of God; I believe my children and I will be fine. I haven't shared this with anyone yet, but I enrolled in school two days ago. The Career Center offers classes for adults. I chose the Surgical Technician program. I'll have a certificate in less than a year, and I'll finally have a career instead of a job," smiled Kanesha.

Wilson could tell that Kanesha was very proud of her decision to better herself. He could hear it in her voice. It was her intent to make the announcement to her mother and kids on Sunday after church services, but she just had to tell someone.

"Praise the Lord! That's great, Kanesha. You deserve to be happy. I hated seeing you with men who were beneath you. Let me correct that because it's wrong of me to judge others. You deserve to be with a man who puts you only second to God, someone who respects himself because only then will he respect you."

Kanesha looked into Wilson's eyes and noticed their color and depth. Wilson's hazel eyes, smooth almond skin and strong arms grabbed Kanesha's attention. She'd never seen Wilson swallow a drop of liquor or chase after any of the women who patronized the bar. *"And God created man in his own image,"* whispered the Lord in Kanesha's ear.

Kanesha blushed and turned her head away from

Wilson's view. After gathering her composure, she returned her attention to the man before her.

"Wilson, I don't even know your last name."

"I'll tell you everything about myself if you promise to visit my church this Sunday," responded Wilson.

"I'm sorry, but I can't do that," said Kanesha just above a whisper and with a slight grin on her lips. She got a quick glance at the disappointed look on Wilson's face before finishing her sentence. "But you can attend church services with my mother and me."

Wilson smiled as he pulled up in front of Kanesha's place. Instead of her going right in, she stayed in the car and conversed with him. The two learned more about each other in a matter of minutes than they'd learned working with each other all of the time. Minutes soon turned into hours before Kanesha decided to retire into her home, but not before placing a small peck on Wilson's cheek. Wilson watched the woman walk away. He was sure that she was the answer to his prayers.

Chapter Eight
This Is What Being Loved Feels Like

Kanesha stared into the bathroom mirror, trying to arch her eyebrows evenly. It had taken her an hour to do her hair, and not a strand of it was out of place. The scent of her Baby Phat cologne filled the air as she strolled out of the small bathroom.

"Dang, girl, I'm gon' have to sit at the bar with you all night. You lookin' as good as you wanna look," complimented Wilson.

"Thank you, Wilson," smiled Kanesha. "You ready to get to work?" Kanesha grabbed her purse and walked toward the door. Wilson followed Kanesha out the door. The two made their way down the two blocks in the direction of work. They held hands during their quick drive.

"See you inside," Kanesha said knowingly. Wilson would immediately take his post at the door.

Swaying her hips, Kanesha walked into the bar like she owned the place. A few male patrons turned their attention to Kanesha as she sauntered behind the bar to start her shift. Percy sat at the end of the bar staring a hole through Kanesha. She pretended not to notice him as she spoke to a few regular customers while preparing to start her shift. Unlike his last visit to the bar, Percy's presence didn't bother her. She was unfazed by his stares and went on about her work without missing a beat.

Life was going so well for Kanesha that even her self confidence had improved. She walked with her head up, her back straight and a smile on her face. She was amazed at how committing to serve the Lord had made such a huge difference in her life. The relationship she and Wilson were building gave Kanesha a natural high.

"Look at you, girl," smiled Miss Yolanda. "If I didn't know any better, I'd say there was a spotlight shining down on you."

"I can't remember the last time I was this happy," giggled Kanesha like a teenage girl.

"Doesn't it feel good to have a good man in your life? A God-fearing man who's comfortable in his own skin at that?"

"Yes, ma'am, it does. Wilson treats me so good and I can see how much he cares for me when I look into his eyes."

Kanesha had her back turned to Percy, but Miss Yolanda had a clear view of him. The smile on her face quickly faded, causing Kanesha to turn and see what she was looking at. Something about the glare in Percy's eyes gave Kanesha an uneasy feeling, but she dismissed it, thinking Percy was a jealous and miserable soul in search of company.

"Don't worry about him, Miss Yolanda. I'm not going to let anyone rain on my parade, especially somebody as pitiful as Percy Watkins.

Kanesha and Miss Yolanda gave each other a high-five, followed by a hug.

Outside, Wilson was focused on searching women's purses and patting men down to make sure no one was carrying a concealed weapon before entering the establishment. Just when the line disappeared and Wilson pulled the door open to step inside for a minute, Byron pulled up to the curb.

"Hey, Wilson, what's up witcha, man?" greeted Byron.

"I'm straight," responded Wilson with the black man's handshake and quick hug. He could have held some animosity against Byron for how he had played Kanesha, but looking at the big picture, he owed Byron. If it hadn't been for Byron's mess up, he might have never hooked up with Kanesha. "We ain't seen you around in a long time."

"Yea, man. That same night when Kanesha caught me with Mickey, I got popped and had to serve out my forty-five days in the county. Karma I guess." Byron and Wilson shared a quick laugh at his bad luck. "It's all cool, though. Word in the joint is you and Kanesha kickin' it now." Byron unexpectedly turned the conversation serious.

"Kanesha's a good girl. I'm just trying to treat her the way my momma taught me to treat a lady." Wilson looked Byron in the eyes as he spoke.

"It's all good, Playboy. She's cool. I ain't trippin'. I just stopped by to see if she'll let me go up to the spot and grab some stuff I left there. She's working, right?"

"You know she is, but you know the routine; assume the position," instructed Wilson before patting Byron down. Wilson was not going to jeopardize his job by assuming Byron was not carrying a weapon.

The club had a good size crowd for it to be so early in the evening. Byron had no problem scanning the room and checking out the females. He stopped his gaze halfway around the room and locked eyes with Percy. Byron could feel his temperature rising with each passing second.

Percy was the first to break the stare and flinch at the hint of physical harm. He swallowed the last of his warm beer and headed for the exit. He took in the hateful look Wilson was giving him once his feet hit the sidewalk and he started his foot journey away from the bar.

Kanesha didn't know how to feel, or respond when she looked up from the cash register to find Byron standing before her with a stupid smile plastered to his face. He looked so silly that she had no choice but to crack a smile.

"I haven't seen you in a minute. Where's your flavor of the month? Oops, I mean of the week?" Kanesha asked snidely.

"Ah, don't even start with all that. Look, I'm sorry

about what went down. You didn't deserve to be hurt like that. I hope you don't hold it against me," pleaded Byron.

"The old Kanesha would have cracked you upside the head with one of these bottles by now, but the new Kanesha accepts your apology," Kanesha said with sincerity, after hearing God whisper in her ear, *'Judge not less you be judged.'* She was trying her best to let go of the past and that included all the hurt she endured by the fathers of her children. "So what really brings you in here tonight? I know you didn't drive all the way across town just to say you're sorry."

"I know Moms told you about my recent stay at the steel motel," joked Byron. "I left a few things at ya crib and I need to get them. You didn't throw anything out, did you?"

"No, it's all packed in a box. I put it in the back of Malisha and Jordan's closet. Are you going to chill here until I get off?"

"Naw, I got to get back on the grind fo' sho. Can you trust me enough to let me get the key and I'll bring it right back to you. I promise to lock up behind myself, and I won't even raid the refrigerator," said Byron jokingly.

Kanesha thought about the request before answering Byron. *Shoot, what is he going to do? I don't have much and what I do have ain't worth catching a case over,* thought Kanesha. After taking her house key off the key ring, Kanesha put it in Byron's extended, open palm.

"Make sure you don't forget to bring my key back; I mean it."

"Right back; I promise."

An hour later, Miss Yolanda and Kanesha were busy keeping the customer's glasses filled. The bar patrons were having a good time dancing, drinking and socializing. The bar was standing room only, and by the time last call for alcohol was announced, Kanesha's tip jar was overflowing with money.

"Tonight was crazy busy, but I ain't complaining. Look at all this money," said Kanesha. She sat counting her tips after closing down her cash register and helping Miss Yolanda wipe down the bar.

"It looks like you made enough money to go on a nice little shopping spree," Miss Yolanda yawned.

"I'm putting this money up for emergencies and unexpected necessities the kids might have. Maybe I'll treat them to a day at Chuckie Cheese or skating one day soon. They will love that."

"I'm sure they will."

"And they'll be even more days like that to come." Kanesha smiled as though she was keeping a secret.

"Oh, yeah, and how is that so?" Miss Yolanda put her hands on her hips, waiting for Kanesha to spill the beans.

"Miss Yolanda, I've wanted to share some great news with you. Now seems as good as any," Kanesha smiled and continued. "I applied for a home health aide position. I have an interview this Tuesday. I figure it will be my first step into the medical field. The surgical tech class starts in a couple of weeks, so if I'm offered the position, it will be on a part-time basis."

"Kanesha, I am so proud of you. Come, give me another hug, girl." Miss Yolanda beamed with pride at Kanesha's great news. She was happy to see the positive changes the young girl was making in her life.

Kanesha wanted to be a positive role model for her children and decided to take the steps toward that goal. There was one major aspect of her children's lives that Kanesha felt she had failed them; she had not introduced them to the Lord. Unless one of their grandmother's had attended church services, there had been no consistent routine in showing her kids just how great God was.

Miss Yolanda finished up her paperwork and had Wilson follow her into the office to put the night's money into the safe. While her two co-workers were in the back, Kanesha tried to reach Byron on his cell phone because he had not returned with her house key.

"Where ya dude at, Kanesha?" asked Wilson. "He didn't make it back with your key yet?"

"He's probably on his way if he's not out in the parking lot already," Kanesha responded.

"Naw, I was just out there breaking up a fight. After all that commotion died down, the parking lot cleared out," explained Wilson. "The guy who started it is drunk off his feet, so I took his car keys. He's aware enough to tell me where he lives, so I'm going to drive him home."

"Maybe Byron got caught up with something. Did you try his cell phone?" inquired Miss Yolanda, catching the tail end of their conversation.

"Yes, ma'am, but it's going straight to voicemail. I even called the house, but he's not there either."

"Well, don't worry. He's probably somewhere playing cards or something and just forgot to bring it back," Miss Yolanda stated matter-of-factly. "I have your extra key in the safe. "Let me get it for you."

"You're probably right. Let me try him one more time."

Kanesha got a strange feeling as Byron's voicemail picked up again. She feared Byron may have gotten arrested again while out on the grind.

"Miss Yolanda, will you drive me home tonight? Wilson has to drive that drunk patron home so he won't get behind the wheel and kill somebody. I don't feel like riding with them. I'm tired and just want to go home and fall out," explained Kanesha.

"Of course, honey," replied Miss Yolanda.

"Do you want me to follow you up the street before I take dude home?" asked Wilson.

"Thanks, Wilson, but I'm sure everything is okay. Like Miss Yolanda said, Byron is probably somewhere playin' cards or rollin' dice. I'll be fine." Kanesha tried to convince herself there was a simple explanation for Byron's disappearance, but she had a bad feeling in the pit of her stomach. "Just call me after you drop the guy off. I'll wait up for your call."

After closing down shop, the three exited the bar and headed their ways.

Kanesha asked God to make everything be as it should be as she opened the door of Miss Yolanda's car and got in. The closer Miss Yolanda drove to her duplex, the more her stomach hurt. Byron's car was parked outside of her place, so Kanesha relaxed a little.

"He might have just made a run or something first before coming here to collect his things," reasoned Miss Yolanda. "Don't be too hard on him; at least you're not locked out."

Kanesha thanked Miss Yolanda for the ride as she exited the car. She walked up the rickety stairs and thought she heard weird noises coming from the other side of her front door. *It's probably just the television,* Kanesha tried to convince herself. Kanesha took in a deep breath and unlocked the door. Nothing on God's green earth could have prepared her for the sight before her.

Chapter Nine
Dis Youngstown, Partner, You Ain't Know?

"Oh, my God! What are you doing?" screamed Kanesha.

The sight of blood pooled on the floor was the least shocking thing before Kanesha. Byron lay on his side with his arms and legs hog tied behind him and duct tape covering his mouth.

"Byron!" Kanesha screamed and ran to him. Tears drained from her eyes like an open water faucet. She ripped the tape from his mouth.

Byron opened his mouth to warn Kanesha of the impending danger behind her just as the blow landed on the back of her head. Kanesha saw darkness as she fell to the floor.

When Kanesha opened her eyes, she prayed it had all been a nightmare. The piercing headache, mixed with her inability to move her limbs and the sight of Byron hog tied next to her, let Kanesha know she was actually living the nightmare.

"Why are you doing this to us?" demanded Kanesha.

"Did you think it would be that easy to get rid of me? Y'all two witches thinkin' y'all betta 'den me," snarled Percy. "Naw, y'all ain't nothin'." Percy stood over his two victims and kicked Byron in his side.

Kanesha had paid no attention to Percy leaving the bar but even if she had, nothing like this would have crossed her mind. There was no telling how long Byron had been in the midst of this horrible situation.

"Percy, we ain't done nothing to you. Why are you doing this?" Kanesha tried the best she could to speak to Percy in a calm voice. She thought that by hiding her fear, Percy would be more receptive to her pleas.

"You threw me out like a piece of trash. And this punk laying here treated me like I was less than nothing," Percy growled.

"I don't owe you anything, Percy. While we were together, all you did was use me, take from my kids and hit on me like I wasn't nothing!" Kanesha was so upset she didn't realize she was screaming at her attacker. She was angry and frightened for both her life and Byron's. Kanesha was so upset that her body shook and her teeth chattered.

"Shut up! I ain't tryna hear all that. You always tryna' talk down to me like you my mama." Percy bent down on one knee and punched Kanesha in her face. Blood shot out from her nose. She screamed out in pain. Byron lay helpless on the floor next to Kanesha, struggling to free himself.

Wanting to prevent Kanesha from screaming out for help, Percy decided it was time to shut her up. He tore Kanesha's shirt and stuffed it in her mouth before slapping duct tape on her lips.

"Since you and that man are so in love, why don't I make y'all suffer together?" He was obviously unaware of Kanesha and Byron's break-up. Percy applied the duct tape to her mouth with so much force; Kanesha thought her front teeth may have chipped. "Come on Byron, protect this piece of trash now," taunted Percy. "Now, Kanesha, I've planned an eventful night for da three of us." Percy's voice sounded demonic and threatening.

Kanesha's eyes grew as wide as saucers when Percy crept closer to her with a knife in hand. She began to squirm in vain as Percy cut what remained of her shirt. He then cut her laced bra. His eyes grew dark as his lips curled into an evil smirk as he concentrated on cutting all of Kanesha's clothes from her body.

Kanesha cried and tried hard to free herself with each cut of her clothes. Byron's rage seemed to reach a boiling point as he watched what Percy was doing to the mother of his child. Kanesha watched Byron struggle to come to her aid, but it was all in vain. She took her eyes off Percy and looked into Byron's eyes, pleading for him to do something. She knew Byron was in no position to save her this time. The subdued couple mumbled and swarmed around on the floor, to no avail.

After cutting off Kanesha's white laced panties, Percy began his reign of torment on her. "Look at you now. Laying there with no choice, but to spread ya legs for me," smirked Percy. "You would never be a freak for me when I wanted you to," Percy looked from Kanesha over to Byron and let out a toe curling laugh, "but it looks like you don't have a choice tonight."

"Man, Byron, would you look at this," said Percy while he stared into Byron's eyes, enjoying the tormented look on his face. "For a broad as young as her, don't you think her body is sickening? I've never seen a woman with so many stretch marks," teased Percy. Kanesha would only have sex with Percy with the lights off because of the toll having babies had taken on her body. Kanesha never thought that Percy would use such personal information to hurt her. Byron would always tell her that her body was designed by the wisdom of time and she had nothing to be self-conscious about.

Listening to the things Percy was saying made her more embarrassed than she already was. She had heard hateful things about her body come out of Percy's mouth before, but with another man in the room hearing his evil tirade, Kanesha wanted to bury her head in the ground.

"Call on me and I shall answer," God's voice echoed in Kanesha's head. She searched for strength to survive each passing minute.

"Let's get started," announced Percy.

Kanesha shook her head from side to side as her eyes begged Percy not to hurt her. Percy stood over Kanesha and slowly unzipped his pants. Byron continued to move about in hopes of loosening his restraints.

The room filled with an odor of rotten eggs and spoiled fish when Percy lowered his pants. Kanesha thought she would choke on her own vomit from the offensive smell. Percy held the six inch knife in his left hand and began massaging his muscle with his right. *"Pray for strength, child. Call out to me and I will hear your cries,"* instructed the strong, dominate voice. For the last few months, Kanesha was hearing the teachings from her mother speaking to her but as she lay on the floor, terrified of what might happen to her, she knew the only voice ringing in her ear was that of a higher being. Kanesha's heart and soul told her that the Lord was talking to her.

Kanesha tried to regain composure when she realized her fear empowered Percy. She was able to find enough strength inside of her to stop the tears from seeping from her eyes. Her ability to do so was not overlooked by Percy.

"Oh, you ain't scared no more?"

Percy released himself and grabbed Kanesha by the hair. He chopped off a handful and threw it on Byron. Kanesha refused to cry out, even when Percy banged her head onto the floor. All of the will power in the world is what Kanesha needed to keep herself from giving her attacker the satisfaction he was after.

"What? You think you bad now? That's okay because I got something for ya stupid behind."

Percy lay on top of Kanesha and rammed himself inside of her. Kanesha screamed on the inside, but refused to allow Percy to see any more fear from her. She focused her eyes on the chipped paint hanging from the ceiling. Each thrust caused an out of shape Percy to lose his breathe.

"You, stupid broad! I'll teach you to treat me like I'm some piece of trash you have to step over to get to where you going." Percy raped Kanesha and called her defiling names. Byron lay next to them with his eyes closed tightly. The lack of reaction from Kanesha and Byron infuriated Percy even more.

Kanesha listened to the voice in her head reminding her to never give an enemy power over her. *'Fear is the most powerful emotion we have. Being fearful of an enemy gives them complete and total control over you. Call upon me child, I will never forsake thee.'* Kanesha could feel the Holy Spirit hovering over her giving her strength.

Percy thrust in and out of Kanesha for what felt like forever. Unwilling to scream, cry or beg, Kanesha prayed for help and strength.

"You ignorant broad," spat Percy, "ya so stupid you don't even know to cry while having ya dignity took."

Kanesha continued to stare straight up at the ceiling. Byron lay next to her squirming, trying to free himself.

Percy withdrew from inside Kanesha and snatched the duct tape from her lips. He pulled out the piece of material from inside her mouth and put the knife up to Kanesha's neck.

There was a sound just outside of the front door causing Percy to apply more pressure to the knife he held at Kanesha's neck. "If you say a word or try to scream for help, I'll cut your throat from ear to ear," Percy threatened.

Kanesha remained as quiet as a church mouse but Byron chose to use the situation to their advantage by moaning in agony as loud as he could.

"Shut up!" Percy yelled in anger as he kicked Byron in his ribs. "Ain't nobody here to save you."

All of the will power Kanesha used to remain quiet also gave her the courage to follow Byron's lead by making as much agonizing moaning and groaning as she could.

Percy began to panic and grabbed her by the hair again. He snatched her head to the side and forced her to sit up. One tear escaped her eye from the pain. Her instinct was to touch her head where it throbbed, but her hands remained tied behind her back.

Percy yanked Kanesha's head back and scraped the dull blade across her throat. Again, Kanesha screamed out in pain.

"Shut up! You ain't hurt."

"Please, Percy, I'm beggin' you. Please stop," cried Kanesha.

"Oh, you still think I'm playin' wit you," Percy snarled. "Let's see how you like this." Percy reached over and rammed the knife into Byron's leg. Byron threw his head back in agony as Percy twisted the blade before pulling it out.

Kanesha's cries grew louder as she witnessed Percy's cruelty.

"Shut up, witch. Why you cryin' anyway, this is ya fault!"

"Please, Percy, don't hurt him anymore. I'll do whatever you want me to, just don't hurt Byron."

"Don't act like you got a choice. I know you gonna do what I tell you to."

Kanesha fell back onto the floor in tears wondering what was taking help so long to rescue them. The sight of Byron in agony and the thought of never seeing her kids again was more than Kanesha could take. Her mind raced, trying to find a way to get Percy to stop what he was doing. At that moment, Byron's well being was more important than that of her own.

"Byron, Byron, please be strong. Just think about Brianna and your boys, this will all be over soon. All of your kids need they daddy, so be strong," cried Kanesha. She thought Byron may go into shock by the amount of blood seeping from his leg.

"Naw, forget that mess. Dis ain't gon' be over 'til I get tired, and trust when I say, it won't be no time soon," promised a glassy eyed Percy.

Percy plunged the knife into Byron's leg again, this time pulling it out slow and twisting it from side to side.

Byron passed out.

Kanesha screamed for help in hopes that her neighbor would hear.

Percy punched her, forcing blood from her mouth.

"Shut up!" screamed Percy.

Kanesha screamed for help again.

Percy sat Kanesha up against the wall and stood over her, planting his legs on each side of her. "I got something to shut ya tail up." Percy continued his verbal tirade as he rammed himself inside of Kanesha's mouth, forcing her to perform oral sex on him.

"You never knew when to shut ya mouth. Always runnin' dat smart mouth of yours into da ground."

The smell of Percy made Kanesha sick to the stomach and vomit forced its way into her mouth." Kanesha began to choke. She silently recited a prayer to God, begging for help. *Dear Lord, if I've ever needed you before, it does not compare to how much I need you now. Please help me, please help us get us out of this situation alive. Lord, please forgive me of all my sins and receive this prayer,* cried Kanesha inwardly.

"What da-?" Percy was enraged by what he saw. Blood from Kanesha's neck trickled down her chest, causing her to panic.

Kanesha's life ran through her mind along with the faces of her four children. She was determined to see them again, hold them, and teach them about the sacrifices Jesus made for them. *I will carry you when you are too weak to walk on your own,* spoke the Spirit to Kanesha's heart. Kanesha knew God would see her through as long as she didn't give up. It was at that moment, Kanesha felt empowered to fight for her life, for her family's future and Byron's well being.

"I'm gonna die, Percy. Please, stop this. Just tell me what you want from us," begged Kanesha.

"Shut up, witch! You ain't got nothing! Do you hear me? There is nothing I want from you besides your life."

Kanesha had to think fast. She knew time was running out for her and Byron. Looking over at Byron, she saw all the blood gushing out of the knife wounds on his leg. Byron looked back at Kanesha, trying to say something to her with his eyes. Kanesha wasn't sure what it was he wanted to say, but she whispered to him, "Stay strong, God will see us through." Byron blinked his eyes rapidly and shook his head up and down. Percy was now pacing the floor, never taking his eyes off Kanesha.

"You stupid, witch! I should kill you right now, but that would be too easy. You deserve to suffer for throwing me out on the streets like I was trash."

"Stop for a minute. Think about my kids." Kanesha's voice was desperate and pleading, but her cries were exactly what Percy wanted.

"I ain't tryna hear that mess. You think I care about dem bastard kids of yours?"

"Please, Percy, I'm all they got," Kanesha continued to plead.

"I said, shut up!"

The knife cut Kanesha across her chest, and again, Percy punched her, forcing her to scream out in pain. Percy punched her again. Kanesha lay in excruciating pain, believing her jaw to be broken. She didn't move when Percy drew his fist back to punch her again. Kanesha closed her eyes in an attempt to brace herself for the blow.

The binding on Byron's wrist had loosened up from the blood that had soaked into it. Percy had all of his focus on Kanesha and he made the mistake of leaving his back turned on Byron too long.

"You, bastard!"

Byron grabbed Percy's arm, preventing it from finding its mark a second time, and body slammed him. Losing his footing in the pool of blood, tears and vomit, Byron fell along side Percy. The two men struggled, both trying to dominate the other with strength and power. Byron was in a battle for their lives. The two stab wounds in his leg handicapped him from subduing his attacker the way he had wanted to.

Percy was taken by surprise. He was totally unprepared for the physical battle before him. With Byron falling, and not as strong as he had been the day Kanesha threw him out of the apartment, Percy felt he could overtake Byron.

Byron glanced at Kanesha, who lay still on the floor, and he thought she was dead. He tried desperately to overpower his attacker.

Percy noticed Byron hesitate to get back on his feet and took advantage of the situation. He kicked Byron in his leg, making him scream out for help.

"Shut up, boy. Ain't nobody coming to your aid," Percy spat.

Percy tried to kick Byron again when he slipped in the blood and fell face down. Byron threw himself on Percy and fought for his life. Again, Percy overpowered his opponent. Percy straddled Byron and wrapped his hands around the weaker man's neck.

Byron tried effortlessly to pry Percy's hands from his neck.

"It's over, partner. Who da witch now? Who's da witch now?"

Byron struggled to breathe.

Kanesha's eyes opened. She lifted herself from the floor, struggling to sit up without falling over. Percy continued to choke Byron who was slowly losing consciousness, when all of a sudden-

Boom!

The front door was kicked in and forced off its hinges.

"Freeze!

"Police!"

Percy released his grip on Byron's neck and grabbed the knife next to him.

"Don't move," instructed a young police officer.

"Get down," yelled another officer with S.W.A.T. across his bullet proof vest.

"Drop the knife!"

Percy ignored the orders being barked at him by the numerous police officers inside the living room and lunged toward the officer standing the closest to him. "I ain't goin' back to prison."

"Stop!" ordered the officers in unison.

"Drop your weapon!" warned the sergeant.

Percy took three steps toward Kanesha as the police continued to yell orders at him.

"I'm not dying alone," vowed Percy as he lunged toward Kanesha.

Bang! Bang! Bang!

Three taps of the trigger from a policeman's gun stopped Percy in his tracks. The room was quiet, except for the rustled sounds of footsteps by the police.

"Ma'am, the ambulance is on its way. We're gonna get you help," promised a twenty-something looking officer who covered her with a blanket.

Kanesha looked into the police officer's eyes, unable to verbally respond due to the pain in her jaw. She took a deep breath and thanked God for ending the horrible ordeal. The officer covered Kanesha's body with a blanket before turning his attention to his partner who was tightening a belt around Byron's leg to stop the blood flow.

Byron looked over at Kanesha and reached out to touch her. Kanesha found Byron's hand, giving it a squeeze to let him know she was okay.

"It's over girl; we're going to be all right. It's over," said Byron after one of the police officers removed the tape from his mouth.

'When we are in our most vulnerable state, finding that inner strength that we all possess, is what will get us through.'

Kanesha tightened her grip on Byron's hand and closed her eyes to say another prayer, thanking God for allowing her and Byron to survive the horrible ordeal. When she opened her eyes, Kanesha looked over at Byron. With tears streaming down her face, she whispered, *"I get it, Mommy. I finally get it. Thank you, Lord, for seeing us through the darkness and into the light. I am nothing without you heavenly Father, thank you."*

The paramedics rushed in and immediately began tending to Kanesha and Byron. Less than ten minutes after their arrival, the E.M.T.'s had stabilized both their patients enough to transport them to the nearest hospital.

"She needs me, let me go! Kanesha, I'm here, baby! Please, let me go with her." Wilson pleaded with the police officer who had been restraining him from entering the duplex.

After dropping off the drunken patron, Wilson called Kanesha to let her know he was on his way home. It was not like Kanesha to ignore a ringing phone, especially when her children were not home. Wilson tried repeatedly to reach Kanesha. With each unanswered call; his heart sank a little more. He was worried that Byron may have lied about not feeling resentful about their relationship and had, in some way, harmed Kanesha. Wilson drove back to the south side to make sure Kanesha was tucked safely in bed, and for whatever reason, just didn't hear her phone ringing. He would not be able to get a good night rest until he was sure Kanesha's welfare was as it should be.

Upon arrival, Wilson wondered why Byron's car was still parked outside of Kanesha's duplex. He trusted Kanesha and thought maybe Byron's car had broken down or some other reasonable explanation. He stood outside of Kanesha's door, fighting with himself for showing up on her door step at four in the morning unannounced. Just when he was about to turn and leave, Wilson heard a strange noise come from the living room area of Kanesha's home. He tried to be quiet as he backed away from the door. He quickly pulled out his cell phone and dialed 911.

In the midst of everything, Denise Ramsey was awaken by the weird noises coming from her neighbor and rushed to call for help. Fearing that her and her kids might have been in danger as well, Denise gathered them up and decided to wait for the police in her car. She swung her door open and was startled by Wilson. He grabbed Denise's daughter from her left arm and led them out to his car and away from danger.

Wilson and Denise watched as the police approached and secured the building before kicking in Kanesha's front door. Wilson jumped from his car when an officer rushed out to retrieve blankets and first aid kits from his police cruiser. He stepped aside when fire trucks and ambulance workers rushed the door.

After the officials granted him permission to join Kanesha in the ambulance, Wilson was frightened by the sight before him. Kanesha was covered in her own blood and both her eyes were black and swelling shut. Wilson reached out to touch Kanesha but quickly pulled his hand back in fear of hurting her.

"Kanesha, it's Wilson. Everything is going to be all right. You're safe now. I promise you, I'll not leave your side," whispered Wilson through teary eyes.

Unable to move her jaw or open her eyes, Kanesha held out her hand and found Wilson's knee. Wilson gently placed his hand on top of Kanesha's and smiled when he felt her squeeze. It was her signal to him that she was grateful to have him with her. The simple gesture spoke so much between the two sinners whose individual walks with God would soon become one.

Wilson bowed his head and prayed out loud. "Our Father who art in heaven, please forgive us of our sins and please receive this prayer. Though we have both fallen short of your will, you did not give up on us and for that we are forever grateful. Thank you for delivering Kanesha and Byron from the evil that lived inside of Percy. Please continue to be with them both as their earthly bodies heal. Kanesha and I thank you for hearing and answering this prayer. For this and all things, we thank you dear Lord, Amen."

Wilson laid a gentle kiss on the back of Kanesha's hand and allowed the tears to fall from the back of his eyes and his heart. "Thank you, Lord, we thank you."

On this day, their belief in Jesus, patience with Christ and acceptance of the Holy Spirit proved that *Even Sinners Have Souls Too*...souls worth saving.

Shana's Smile
By
Victor L. Martin

Chapter One

Twenty-six year old Celisha Rae could sense an upcoming argument with her deeply religious aunt as they left the Sunday church services.

"Do you have to see that secular boss of yours today? One would assume he would give you the Lord's day off," her Aunt Faye questioned.

"He's not just some secular thing, Aunt Faye. And I wish you would stop referring to him as my boss. His name is Vincent. You won't go to hell for saying his name, Auntie." Celisha chuckled as she drove through a busy intersection in her metallic, Nile green Buick Enclave SUV. A Vickie Winans song was flowing easily through the speakers.

"Well those books he puts out are surely secular. Although I wouldn't dare read them with my own eyes, I've heard gals talking about them up in the beauty shop." She turned her nose up. "Just worldly."

"Why do you say that?" Celisha kept her eyes on the road.

Aunt Faye took off her cream colored extravagant hat, her thin lips pursed tightly. "I've seen the covers of his books," she said bitterly. "What man of God will write a book about a hood legend, and all those bad words; the cursing and the sex. It's secular, Celisha; just worldly and you know it. I'm surprised that you'd have anything to do with it. I mean, how can you be a child of God and work for the devil?"

"That's uncalled for, Aunt Faye. How can you sit there and call someone the devil having never even met him before? And you've said it yourself that you haven't read not one page of his books, but yet you've judged him. That's not right...or should I say, 'that's not Christ like.'" Celisha used the term her aunt had so often used on her to describe some of her actions.

"Oh really?" Aunt Faye replied. "So, are you suggesting that those ghetto, street lit, urban, hood books, or whatever they are referred to these days, can be a topic at Sunday school next week?" She raised her pencil drawn eyebrows.

"No, Aunt Faye." Celisha sounded upset. "Of course not. And stop being so sarcastic about it."

"I'm not being sarcastic, I'm being honest. There are plenty of Christian authors that you can work for and we both know it. As for why you continue to work for that-"

"Let's drop the issue," Celisha said and then added, "Please."

Aunt Faye reluctantly bit her tongue on this one by turning to stare out at the passing scenery. She didn't mean her niece any harm. She was only trying to protect her. She felt that Celisha's boss was a man of his words...his written words. Secular words that he pulled from his heart to write in his books. After all, authors always said that they write what they know or that they are what they write. In her opinion, that meant that her niece's boss was the devil. It was simple to Aunt Faye. If it was not dealing with God, then it wasn't good for the soul. The only bestseller in her opinion was the Bible. End of discussion.

"I still love your hard-headed behind," Aunt Faye muttered, giving Celisha a pat on the knee.

Celisha smiled. "I know you do, Auntie."

They rode listening to the music the rest of the short trip. After dropping her aunt off, Celisha elected to head for Coral Gables instead of going home. It was time for her to, as her aunt put it, go work for the devil.

Chapter Two

Author Vincent L. Manor was in his driveway washing his customized four door convertible Chrysler 300c SRT-8. His two German Shepherds, Rocky D and Rex, were laid out in the shade under a palm tree. The sky was cloudless, with the beaming sun poking its chest out. Both dogs came to their feet when Celisha pulled up to the nickel plated, wrought-iron gate.

Vincent used a remote attached to his key chain to open the gate. He was shirtless, wearing a pair of long shorts and Nike slip-ons. His bald head and torso was covered with a heavy sheen of sweat and he looked much younger than a man reaching his mid-thirties. His brown eyes were hidden behind his tinted designer prescription frames. He continued to wash his vehicle as Celisha was welcomed by two wagging tails.

"Dina Blain called me last night," he said, with the water hose aimed at the front, left 22-inch chrome rim, after he closed the gate again.

"Good news or bad news?" Celisha stood behind him squinting and shielding her eyes from the glare of his ride. She then took a few steps back when he started spraying the sparkling rim.

"Good. Said I will have a chance to write a full-length novel for her imprint if I'm open to it. I told her, fo' sho. Gotta return the love you know. Dina was one of the few authors that came to see me when I was in prison." He glanced over his sweaty shoulder for a second at Celisha in her Sunday best. "How was church?" he asked, changing the subject.

"Uplifting," was Celisha's reply. "I took my aunt with me. She's not one of your fans, you should know." Celisha chuckled.

He turned to look at her while spraying off the hood. "Has she even read any of my books?"

"No, but according to her, all the women at the shop where she gets her hair done have. Let's just say that my aunt is not a part of your target audience." She smiled briefly at Vincent.

He shrugged his broad shoulders, turning back to his work at hand. "I gave you the day off." He moved around, spraying the roof. "I hope you don't think I can't handle this speaking engagement alone today?"

"Yes...I know...of all people, I fully know what you're capable of doing alone." She was fiddling with the diamond engagement ring on her finger.

He looked over the cloth roof of his car, smiling. "So I assume you want to put in some overtime then?"

She nodded. "Yeah. I just stopped by to make sure that it was cool. I need to go change though," she said. "I'll be back in an hour."

Vincent nodded, and opened the gate as she backed out moments later. "Holler," was all he said as he finished up, glad that Celisha had decided, in spite of him giving her the day off, to have his back.

Let Vincent tell it, he owed his success around his career to his dependable personal assistant. Celisha was always on top of her job. If he was doing any type of public appearances as an author, she wanted to be by his side. In the author community, the two were quite a pair and had endured the false allegations that they were secretly sexually involved.

Celisha was a stunning, black, highly attractive woman with the warming looks close to Elise Neal. She was a devoted Christian Monday through Sunday. She didn't have any kids and could speak French and Spanish. She was also engaged to be married to a man named Aaron. She dispelled the allegations of an affair with her superior with grace and prayers. As for Vincent, he was viewed as handsome, and the title of being a bestselling author only added to his influencing attractiveness.

Minutes later, after Celisha was gone, Vincent's young, bubbly soul mate appeared in one of the open Dutch doors. She was wearing one of his linen button down shirts fully open, revealing her olive tanned body. "Brunch is ready," she said. The small yellow diamond stud in her belly button twinkled briefly when it caught the sun. It was no way near as bright as the twinkle in her hazel eyes and pouty smile she gave him before going back inside.

Vincent had left the streets, living the life of just another hustler, over a decade ago. But now, after putting the life he had once lived on paper, he was a famous author and his adjustment had not been easy. His readers wanted to know so much about him and he felt it was right to open up to them. Without his readers and their support, there would be no bestselling author, Vincent Manor. Yes, he was humble, but there was one aspect of his life that he managed to keep private-his love life.

He had met the outgoing twenty-two year old model only ten months ago at a huge book conference that was held in California known as BEA, short for Book Expo of America, but lovingly nicknamed by authors in the industry as the Book Zoo. Micki was bi-racial; black and Argentina. She was the book cover model on a popular urban trilogy, plus she had over ten music videos to her credit. She was also a die-hard fan of Vincent's books. Micki had approached Vincent at the BEA seeking his autograph, which led to a brief conversation, leaving both interested in the other.

After BEA, the two headed their separate ways across the map. With miles between them, the two started up contact via the Internet. After they traded a few friendly emails, Vincent later reached her through her manager to see when she would have some free time. To his surprise, two days later, Micki called him back personally. Vincent invited her to spend the weekend hanging out in his neck of the woods, and she boldly told him that she could be on the next flight out of New York, where she was currently living, to see him. Once she got off the airplane, their chemistry was too strong to ignore. Her weekend visit turned into her moving in with him; something they both wanted.

"Have you made up your mind yet?" Micki asked as Vincent entered the kitchen and sat down. She was seated across from him at the glass and bamboo table. She maintained her stunning looks miraculously twenty-four seven as if every day was a photo session. For her effort, he made it a point to tell her how beautiful she was twenty-four seven.

"Not really," he said, cutting into the stack of buttered and maple syrup covered pancakes.

"Baby, I'm going to New York next week. Why haven't you made up your mind?" Micki asked. "I know how you feel about keeping our private life, well...private. But I wanna tell the world that you're my man. You know the people, I mean, the ones that will do the interview, will ask if I'm dating anyone. They ask all the models they feature in their magazine that question." She pushed back from the table and stood with her hands on her inviting hips. She now had on a pair of tight, lacey boy shorts gripping her tiny, twenty-five inch waist line. "I need an answer, Mr. Manor!" She pouted her glossy lips. "Now."

Hearing his last name, he knew she was getting upset. He calmly laid the fork and butter knife down. "Who are you yelling at?"

"You! And I'm not yelling...not yet." She folded her arms. She stood a short and spirited five feet four inches tall with long, soft, curly, brown hair framing her exotic face.

"C'mere for a second," he said, pushing back from the table.

Micki continued to pout as she made her way around the table and onto his lap. Her arms eased around his neck.

"Can we speak on this tonight?" He kissed her softly.

"I knew it," she said as she attempted to get up.

Vincent pulled her back to him. "No, really, this time I'm not brushing you off. We really will talk about it, okay?"

Micki hesitated. "Promise?" she murmured.

"Promise," he said, kissing her on the nose.

"Fine," she said, managing to get up from his lap.

Vincent acted like a spoiled baby when she pulled herself free from his caress. He could have sat there and held her forever, but he had plans. "I need to go take a shower anyway and get dressed. If I'm late for that speaking engagement, I'll never hear the end of it from Celisha." He took a couple more bites of food, then jumped in the shower. About a half hour after that, Celisha showed up as promised, ready to take him to his engagement.

In the passenger side of Celisha's car, Vincent opened the laptop that sat on his lap as Celisha backed out of his driveway. He was checking his My Space page since Celisha was behind the wheel. Normally she checked it for him.

"How's Micki doing?" Celisha asked. She now had on a pair of white, ankle-length pants with a white chiffon blouse and some open-toed heels. Even when she tried to hide her curves, her effort was lost.

"Still bugging me about letting her put our relationship on blast in the interview she has with that magazine in New York."

"I don't think it's such a bad idea, Vincent. That's major pub; pub you can't buy," Celisha reasoned. "Did she find out if she's getting the cover?"

"Yeah. The editor called her last night. They picked her over Ester Baxter. She's going to get the cover plus a ten-page spread inside." He glanced up from the laptop. "Can you open the sunroof?"

She nodded as she touched the button to open the sunroof.

"Thanks." He returned his attention to his laptop.

"So, why the big deal about going public with the relationship? It's not like you have a woman on the side," she kidded.

"And how would you know?" he smiled, closing his laptop as a plane flew overhead.

"Please, Vincent," she laughed. "Not only am I your faithful, and might I add, trusting personal assistant, but I also happen to be your friend." She turned to smile at him. "You love Micki and she loves you as well, so why hide it? And as for you having a woman on the side, you're not crazy. But back to the original concern; it's really not a bad idea to go public. You write so hardcore and street. Your supporters will see that you're a man that's not afraid to love."

He shifted in the leather seat. "I just don't want it to come off as a publicity move."

"Have you shared your thoughts with Micki? I assume she would be upset for you to feel that way."

"Nah. We're going to discuss it fully tonight. I guess I'm just...you know...nervous about making it public; making it official." Vincent's voice trail faded.

"Making it official? Now we're getting somewhere," Celisha surmised. "Vincent, she's been living with you for almost a year now. I believe you two are past the point of being official. Let me be frank with you; I think you're acting silly about the entire issue. Micki loves you and I know this. Both of you have careers that are public to some degree. I know you also wanted to keep your love life private, but Micki isn't going anywhere and you know it."

Vincent took the glasses off he was wearing. "So, as my personal assistant, you're telling me it's okay to let her go public about our relationship?"

"No," she smiled, "as a friend I'm telling you that it's okay."

He slid his glasses back on. "Okay. I'll think about it."

"Thanks for having an open mind."

Their conversation switched to business as they rode up I-95 North. Celisha later changed lanes to make an exit on 62nd. Rolling past Edison High School, they made a left at the light.

Childhood memories inflated Vincent's mind as he entered his former stomping grounds. The familiar scent of diesel fuel from the city buses reminded him of the many miles he had traveled by public transportation. He would always take the city bus over the small, always crowded Jitney van. He was deep in thought as he went back to his past.

Being poor wasn't a big deal to him when he was a child. Standing in line at the corner store on 62nd and 12th, everyone carried food stamps. There was no embarrassment in that. Liberty City, a.k.a. Pork & Beans Projects was his home and playground. Back then, nights were filled with random gunshots, police helicopters, violence, crime, drugs and death. Today he was returning to Liberty City to speak to a small group of kids ages ten to sixteen at a recreation center.

Through a street campaign led by Celisha, Vincent's public image was put on blast as a positive role model from the inner city. He was received with love and support from the hood with his moniker, Mr. Hood Legend. He gave a kid with a faint dream a firm belief of hope. Vincent knew about the pain, the loss and the stigma of the streets. He knew about the suffering and oppression behind bars. He knew how to fight for what he believed in, and that was his right to write and to seek a positive change in his life. As for those Jim Crow prison rules that he defiantly broke to keep writing, his drive was unbroken with their worthless punishment.

At the Rec center, Celisha stood in the far corner watching Vincent with faultless respect and admiration as he spoke to the kids. She could see in his eyes that his heart was behind every word he spoke.

"In all my life, before I became an author, I would have never imagined to be where I stand now. I once played outside at the same park where some of you spend your time. I grew up and became lost at some point. I deeply regret screwing up in life, but I've been given a second chance, and I'm taking advantage of it. I'm saying this to prove that I was given a chance to become something. All of you before me have a chance."

Vincent looked out at the young faces and then continued. "A chance to succeed, and many chances to fail. I failed when I foolishly embraced a life of crime. I ruined my life; betting on my freedom as well as my life. I lost my freedom when I messed up bad and found myself in prison, where I came close to losing my life on more than one occasion. Sometimes you'll..." he paused when a young girl raised her hand. She looked to be no more than twelve . Her name tag indicated that her name was Shana. "Yes, Shana." Vincent nodded toward her.

"Ummm...should we go to church every Sunday, Mr. Manor?"

That question came out of left field for Vincent. He stole a furtive glance at Celisha, wishing she could step up and help him. She would always have the right words whenever it came to stuff about God, church or religion. Typically, she would have stepped in at an opportunity to "share the good news," but not today. Vincent was on his own. He didn't know what to say. This was supposed to be a discussion about positive thinking, not religion.

"Do you think it's good to go to church, Shana?" Vincent decided to turn the question back on her.

"Yes, sir," she nodded.

"Do you enjoy going to church?"

She nodded again.

"Then I guess as long as you enjoy going, then it's good to go."

"Then can you and your..." she looked over at Celisha, "your girlfriend come to church with me next week? You two can be my guest for Friends and Family Day."

Vincent looked at Celisha. She was smiling and deeply embarrassed.

"Shana." Vincent cleared his throat and then grinned. "That beautiful woman is my personal assistant, not my girlfriend."

"Oh," Shana giggled. "I'm sorry."

"It's okay," Vincent told her.

"So, will you and your assistant be my guest next week?"

Vincent stammered out the words, "I...we...will be honored to be your guests." He looked over at Celisha once again. "Wouldn't we?" Celisha confirmed with a head nod and a smile.

Shana gasped in excitement. "Really?"

"Really," Vincent replied and then continued with his speech.

"Do you promise," Shana said for security purposes.

"I promise," Vincent said. "And not only will I visit your church, but I'll come pick you up so we can ride together."

The smile on that little girl's face lit up the room.

Celisha hoped Vincent would keep his promise; that he wasn't just accepting the little girl's invitation because she'd put him on the spot and he didn't want to appear as though he was Satan himself.

The rest of the event went by smoothly with Vincent receiving a standing ovation from his audience. He hung around and willingly took pictures with anyone that had a camera. Three members of the Rec staff pulled out his latest novel to get his autograph. Each staff member was pleased with the time Vincent had spent with them talking about his books and writing career. He thanked them all for their support and asked that they tell a friend about him and his books.

Celisha was in a different part of the building finishing up a phone call when someone tapped her on her arm. She turned to find the young girl, Shana, standing there.

"How may I help you, young lady?" Celisha closed her cell phone.

"What is an...umm...personal assistant?" she asked.

Celisha smiled at her. "You're interested, huh?"

Shana nodded. "Yes, ma'am."

Celisha bent down to get eye level with the girl. "How old are you?"

"Eleven," Shana replied, "and I like to write poems," she added. "So, I was just wondering that since Mr. Vincent writes and has a personal assistant, if I needed one too."

Celisha stood back up. "That's wonderful that you write too, Shana. Well, as a personal assistant for Vincent, I help to keep him organized and up to date on everything. For example, I need to get the name of your church, as well as your address and phone number." Celisha nodded to a bench that sat in the hallway. "Let's go sit down and I'll tell you more about what I do and why I enjoy it so much while you give me the information I need to pass on to Mr. Vincent." Celisha reached for Shana's hand and led her toward the bench.

Celisha and Shana chatted before Celisha saw that Vincent had wrapped up with the staff and was ready to go. Nearly a half hour later, Vincent and Celisha were back on the road. Vincent sat behind the wheel this time.

"I should be upset with you, Vincent." Celisha turned slightly in the seat facing Vincent.

He glanced her way. "Why? What did I do, or forget to do, this time?"

"I've asked you on several occasions to visit my church, and each time you gave me some lame excuse as to why you couldn't. So tell me, why did you grant that little girl's request? Don't get me wrong; I'm glad you said yes, and I hope you won't find a reason to back out. That girl is excited about you going to church with her. But are you going because you want to, or because you didn't have the heart to tell the child, no? I mean, I saw that girl's smile. She probably gets anything she wants out of her daddy with a smile like that."

Vincent shrugged his shoulders.

"That's not an acceptable answer, Vincent. That's a response I'd expect from a child, and you are far from being a child."

"You calling me old?" he smiled.

She folded her arms. "Don't turn this into a joke. I'm serious."

"I know, I know. You're always serious. Too serious sometimes," Vincent said. "You know I can fire you and then this topic would be over."

"Please," she smiled. "You wouldn't fire me if I paid you to." They both smiled at each other.

"If I said my reasons for accepting her invitation were both of those you suggested, would that be acceptable?" he asked.

"No," she replied, shaking her head.

"I knew you were going to say that." He slowed for a yellow light that was about to turn red. "I just don't understand a lot of things, Celisha."

"About what?"

"About the man above." He nodded up through the open sunroof.

"Vincent." She unfolded her arms, reaching over to touch his shoulders." You can't find the answer you seek in the streets. You have to read the Bible and go to church to learn. You have to seek Him. You have to make that first step." Celisha paused momentarily and then continued. "I feel your passion through your books. I mean, look at how you had your character, Ménage, seeking a link with God. Something inside you is yearning. Don't go to church because you have to; go because you need to and want to." She removed her hand from his shoulder.

Just as the light turned green, a booming Range Rover blasting Kanye West's "Jesus Walks" pulled up behind them.

"How's that for a coincidence?" Vincent asked.

"I don't believe in coincidences," Celisha replied. "But what I do believe is that God is trying to tell you something, my friend."

On that note, Vincent sped off, hoping that if God was in fact trying to tell him something, that he could slow down long enough to hear exactly what it was God had to say.

Chapter Three

"Micki!" Vincent shouted, stepping through the front door. His two dogs matched his every step. He had two large shopping bags in his grip. "Micki!" he called out again when he didn't receive a response the first time.

"I'm out at the pool, baby," Micki shouted back.

Vincent was pulling out a Gucci shoe box when Micki entered the living room wearing a green two piece string bikini. Her hair was bone straight and wet.

"How did your speaking thing go?" She came up behind him, wrapping her arms around his waist.

"It was perfect." He turned around to face her. "Here." He handed her one of the size six Gucci Stilettos. She immediately released him, taking the stiletto from his grip.

"Ooooo, baby. Thank you, thank you, thank you. These are sooo hot!" She stood up on her toes to kiss him on his lips. "I got to call Celisha. These are hot."

"Call Celisha for what?" He pulled out the *American Gangster* DVD he had purchased when he and Celisha stopped off at the mall after the speaking engagement.

"Because I know she picked these shoes out. I'll wear these for my photo session in New York." She reached for the other pair.

"How do you know I didn't pick them out? You act like my taste in fashion is a zero or something."

"Vincent, baby, I know your taste is bad," she giggled. "What about those tiger striped stilettos that you did pick out; the ones you paid too much for? The ones that I keep in a locked box? And those zebra ones." She turned her nose up. "What is it with you and animal prints?" she laughed.

"You wore them a few days ago," he reminded her with a wink.

"Yes, I did," she said in a soft, seductive voice. "And that was all I had on too. Speak on that." She slid her pedicured feet into the new stilettos. "Let's break these in." Micki returned the wink as she led him to the bedroom.

A couple hours later, Micki woke up in the dark bedroom, still wearing her new stilettos. She forced her eyes to look at the time on the digital clock while Vincent was asleep, spooned behind her.

"Baby," she whispered, "it's going on nine o'clock." She rubbed his arm, repeating herself. He murmured something into her scented hair. "Baby," she whined. "Look at what time it is."

"So." His voice was hoarse.

"So? It's late. I haven't even..." she yawned, "started washing clothes yet. And I'm hungry too." She turned and twisted in his embrace until she was facing him. "Wake up, sleepy head." Unable to resist his soft lips, she began to kiss him. He returned her kiss. Micki loved her man inside and out, but that didn't stop the world from revolving. She had to get up and get a move on.

They managed to leave the bed before ten o'clock. Vincent took the chore of doing the laundry while Micki cooked some steaks. By five minutes pass midnight, they were fed and relaxing in the Jacuzzi. Micki sat behind him on the padded edge, giving her man a relaxing massage.

"How is the new book you're writing coming along?" she asked, raking her nails lightly up his muscular chest. "I Can't Stop Loving You" by Kem was playing softly in the background.

"It's a short story," he corrected her with his eyes shut. "I'm almost done with it," he added. "I got about thirty more pages to write," he moaned when she started kneading his shoulders. "No explicit sex scenes, no bad words...it's a challenge."

"I read the guidelines in that email you printed out. So, it's sort of a religious theme?"

He nodded.

"What if your story is good?" Vincent looked at her like she was crazy. "I mean...what if your readers want you to start writing more of that kind of stuff?"

Vincent thought for a minute. "Shouldn't I be versatile?"

"Yes, I suppose, but didn't you once tell me that you would only write about things you believed in? For example, I know you will never write a gang related novel because you don't understand their mind-set. You haven't lived that life. So, how can you write about something religious based if you...you know...aren't really into religion?"

"Have you read what I've written so far, by any chance?"

Micki was known, whenever she had a minute, to open Vincent's latest work on his computer and read it.

"No. For some reason I want to wait until you're completely done with this one," she replied.

"So, how do you know I'm not writing about something I believe in?"

"Well, I've never seen or heard you say a prayer or go to church. So what, if any, form of religion do you believe in, baby?" After a brief moment of silence, he tilted his head back into Micki's lap without giving her a reply. "I asked you a question, Vincent." She looked directly into his brown eyes.

"It doesn't bother you that I don't pray or go to church?"

She looked away. Releasing a deep sigh, she gave a, "no." It wasn't like she went to church. She prayed sometimes, but it wasn't a daily habit like real Christians do. Religion wasn't something she was big on. Micki had always been taught not to get into religious or political discussions.

"You know what?" she said as if she suddenly

remembered something. "We were suppose to finish our conversation from this morning." She stood up.

"We both forgot, so chill. I made up my mind anyway."

"Which is it?"

"Go ahead and tell the world about us."

She squealed, bouncing up and down. "Thank you, Vincent! I love you so much, and now the whole world will know too."

"I love you too, Micki." In the back of his mind, he was disappointed behind Micki not caring about his lack of religion. He could say the same things about her that she said about him. Vincent believed in God, but he didn't know God. He believed in a heaven as well as a hell, but that was about the extent of it.

As Micki basked in excitement, Vincent looked at the woman he loved. He'd go to the ends of the earth for her. He'd die for her and protect her against anything that might try to come up against her, but that was only physically. What about her soul? How could he even think about protecting her soul when the fate of his own soul was in question?

Chapter Four

Monday mornings were becoming a routine for Vincent. Micki forced him out of bed at eight o'clock in the morning and had him fed and sitting in front of his computer by nine twenty a.m. He had a ton of emails from his supporters that needed to be answered. By eleven-thirty, he left his computer to feed his dogs. By noon, he was ready for The Room, which was the name he had given to his personal writing area. Every author had their very own vibe to turn on their creative writing switch. It was kind of like how Christian's have their prayer closets. Vincent's space was personal to him.

The window remained covered with black Venetian blinds. The bare walls were painted a dull sand color. On the left side of the room was a cheap desk covered with a cup full of pens, a two and a half inch stack of blank writing paper, a flip dictionary and two regular dictionaries. There was no chair, no computer and no phone. Vincent always wrote his first draft in long hand. On the carpeted floor was a single mattress covered with two sheets.

Lying down on his stomach, Vincent would write on the wooden board at the left corner of the mattress. He found much comfort in doing this. He explained to Micki how he had written his books in prison while laying his mattress on the floor. He never had a sore back or neck to interrupt his flow. Micki knew not to disturb him when he was in the The Room. Since The Room had a bathroom, Vincent didn't have to come out until he was good and ready. Micki knew when Vincent was emotionally attached to a story; The Room became his prison.

The longest Vincent had held himself incarcerated in The Room had been four days straight. Micki had cooked his meals and left the food at the door. It excited her in an odd way when he was deep into his writing. He did it without any physical contact with Micki and she never fussed. She knew it was his life and his passion; a part of him that she loved.

Inside The Room, Vincent picked up his pen and briefly closed his eyes. He pushed the real world from his mind while pulling in the life of his characters that awaited movement through his pen. His mind released reality and gripped fiction. He opened his eyes and began to write-straight from his spirit-things he never knew was there.

Meanwhile, in the living room, Micki was stretched out on the sofa watching television. Within reach was a glass of rum and coke. Rex, the smallest of the two dogs, was in the corner asleep under the huge aquarium. It was now 8:38 p.m. and Vincent was still in The Room. If he wasn't out by nine p.m., she was going to heat up a plate of spaghetti for him and set it outside the door.

She finished her rum and coke, and then closed her eyes, counting to twenty. She felt the urge to go and lock herself in the bathroom and do what she often did sometimes lately. This was the only thing she did in secret behind Vincent's back. She would always go into the bathroom feeling stressed or miserable, but come out feeling rejuvenated.

Right now, something was heavy on her mind; she didn't know if an escape to the bathroom would do the trick this time. Tears slowly began filling her eyes as she stood up, sobbing softly. Without thinking, she headed straight to where she knew was off limits.

Micki burst through the door of The Room crying, startling Vincent, who was deep into his writing. He was unable to come to his feet before she crashed into him. Rex and Rocky D stood at the door with their legs stiff. Even the two dogs understood that The Room was off limits.

Vincent managed to stand Micki up and escort her back into the living room so they could talk. It took a few minutes for Vincent to calm her down, and for the third time he asked her what was wrong.

Through tears, Micki looked up at him. "Vincent," she sobbed, clinging to him. "What...what's wrong with me? Why won't you marry me? Why won't you make an honest woman out of me; like Aaron is doing with Celisha?"

Vincent was thrown off guard. He wondered if Celisha had been pushing her religious beliefs on Micki. But that wasn't Celisha's style. But if not, then why all of a sudden was Micki trippin'? Maybe for the same reasons he'd all of a sudden been trippin', too, inside. Only Micki was no longer able to hide her thoughts.

Without answering Micki's question, Vincent told her to go get dressed. From his tone and demeanor, she knew it was best to just do as he asked. So, twenty minutes later, she was sitting beside him in the passenger side of his car, cruising down Douglas Road.

Mary J. Blige's song, "We Ride", filled the car. Vincent hadn't spoken a word since they had gotten in the car. Micki didn't have the slightest idea where the two were heading. When Vincent reached the East-West Expressway, he merged into the thick traffic, heading east. He later exited off the Expressway and hit I-95 North. To his left was the flat landscape of Miami. Tiny lights were stretched out as far as the eye could see. Miami at night was always a special sight to him. When he crossed into Broward County, he turned the music off, then reached for Micki's hand. She held his hand with both of her hands.

"The sun isn't out, Micki. You can take those crazy looking stunna shades off."

She removed the shades, tossing them carelessly over her shoulder. She had a gloomy look on her still beautiful face. "Are you mad at me for disturbing you while you were writing?"

"Of course not." He switched lanes then accelerated pass a tow truck. "I'm not thinking about my writing right now. My story will be there when I get back. Let's talk about us."

She squeezed his hand while looking into his face. There was no doubt in her mind; she was in love. "Okay," she replied.

"Let me start by saying that nothing is wrong with you. You asked me that, along with why I wouldn't marry you, if I'm correct." He glanced at her.

She nodded, blinking away tears.

"Micki, it's like this, baby. When I did those ten years in prison, I forced myself to do it alone. I had a little mantra that I drilled into my mind, which found a way to my heart. I told myself I couldn't deal with matters of my heart behind bars. When I became an author, I met a few women that wanted to cross that line; the line of being a supporter to being my woman." He released a deep sigh. "I was lonely, Micki. I hated when Valentine's Day rolled around because I never had that special someone to share it with. I held back from this one woman I met through my books. I just couldn't open up. My reasons were selfish and childish now that I look back on it. I was afraid that I would get hurt. Afraid that another man would be with the woman I loved while I was behind bars. I held faith in a woman staying true to me." Vincent squeezed Micki's hand. "Micki, in my books I control the life of my characters. They come alive inside of me. In my writing, my world, I can create the faithful girlfriend, the perfect wife, and the perfect life. Hardships are even under my control. Will you think less of me when I can admit that I'm afraid of reality? I can't control life in reality. I can't create or control your mind. Micki, not that I want to, but it...it's hard for me."

"Baby," Micki said, wiping her eyes, "you are a very special man in my life, and I love everything about you. No, I would never think less of you for what you just told me. Life with me will not be perfect, Vincent. We'll have our bad days and our good days. You got to face that.

We're not perfect, but what I feel for you is not fiction. I'm in love with you." She wiped her eyes again. "Life is what we make of it. And you can control reality. I've been faithful to you because I love you. Love isn't built on control. It's built on trust. I said what I said about you marrying me because it's been on my mind. I need to know how much you really love me. I want to be a bigger part of your life. More than a girlfriend. I want to be with you forever."

Vincent held no doubt in Micki's words. He knew her well enough to understand where she was coming from. She said what she had in her heart. He was more than happy with her. Not once had he dwelled on second thoughts of allowing her to move in with him.

"Micki?" Vincent's tone was soft.

"Yes, baby?"

"I will only get one run at this life, and you know what?"

"What?" she said while squeezing his hand gently and rubbing it with her thumb.

"I want to spend it with you," he smiled. "Micki, will you be my wife?"

Without hesitation, she replied, "Yes! Yes, baby, I'll marry you." She exploded with joy and fresh tears. She squeezed him so tight and held him for what seemed like forever.

Once Micki finally released Vincent from her love grip he looked at her. "What do we do now?" he inquired.

She leaned across the leather console and kissed him. "Shut up and drive," she giggled. "We've got some wedding ring shopping to do."

Chapter Five

"Celisha," Micki said into her cell phone. "Guess what?"

Celisha took a guess. She figured that Micki was happy about being able to go public with her relationship with Vincent, especially after the last conversation she had with him about it. But Micki was quick to tell her how wrong she was.

Micki took a deep breath before saying, "Celisha, Vincent asked me to marry him last night and I said, yes."

"Really? That's fantastic, Micki. You must let Aaron and I take you two out to celebrate. This is a special moment and calls for a celebration. I'm so happy for you, girl."

"Thanks. I'm sure Vincent will accept your offer when we get back."

"Get back?" Celisha was confused. "If you two love birds done went and eloped without me, I will be so mad."

"No, we haven't eloped." Micki giggled. "We're in Orlando at the MGM studios. We drove up here on a spur of the moment thing. This is like our private celebration. I'm having the time of my life and I've never been more happy with Vincent. Instead of going back to the house last night, after shopping for rings, we went shopping for clothes too and decided to get a hotel and spend the night . The next morning, we woke up and decided to have a little fun."

Cclisha could hear the excitement in Micki's voice while at the same time her voice began to break.

"Don't start crying on me, Micki. I can hear it in your voice. Where is the lucky man?"

"I'm not gon' cry," Micki assured her before clearing her throat and gaining her composure. "Vincent is gone on that ride where that jaws thing jumps out. It looked too real to me, so I passed on that one."

Celisha laughed. "Girl, you are something else. But look, what time are you two expecting to be back?"

"We should be back home by eight tonight, if not earlier. We can't stay too long or Rex and Rocky D will destroy the place." They hadn't thought to let the dogs out before they left. "I don't know how I'll act when he slides an engagement ring on my finger." Her voice began to quiver again. "We went looking last night, but not too many places were open."

"Keep it together, girl. Now, do me a favor and try to keep your stomach empty for tonight. I'll see if I can pull a few strings to get us a table at the Tantra Restaurant. Micki, I'm really happy for you, and I mean it."

"Thank you, Celisha. You've been such a true friend since day one." Micki wiped her eyes. "I never knew being in love would feel this good."

"It only gets better," Celisha told her. "It only gets better."

Micki was on the phone the entire trip back to Coral Gables. Spreading the news about her engagement to Vincent was a special moment to her. As for Vincent, he made only a few calls. His longest was with Celisha. His friends greatly outnumbered his family members that he called. They only included his cousin Erica, and his aunt, Diane. He was estranged from the rest of his family since getting locked up. Although nobody had hollered for him when he was down, the minute they saw his name on the *Essence Magazine* bestseller's list, they started claiming him as their peoples. Vincent was straight on that.

"Vincent, I've been thinking about something," Micki said. "Now that we're engaged, and about to do this thing under God's eyes, I think we should abstain from sex until our honeymoon."

Vincent looked at her, only to see that she was serious. "Fine," he said as the Welcome to West Palm Beach sign came into view. "We'll get married tomorrow."

"I'm serious," she pouted.

"Okay. It's April. How long do you want to put the wedding off?"

She leaned over, rubbing his hard bicep as he drove with one hand. "I don't know yet. How long has Celisha been engaged to Aaron?"

"Going on a year, I think. That's too long. Micki, I hope you-"

"Uh uh," she interrupted. "I wouldn't even dream of stringing our engagement on that long. Baby, I've never done anything like this before, so let's just enjoy it, okay? There's no need for us to make this stressful."

"I second that idea." He leaned over to give her a quick peck on her lips.

"What about us abstaining from sex? Will it be an issue?"

"Nope," he replied truthfully. "What I feel for you isn't built on sex. I know we are two freaks," he smiled, "but straight up, I love you for your mind...and your behind."

"Aww," she smiled. "My man, the romantic freak." She slid her hand up his arm to play with his ear.

"You know that's my spot, baby."

"Ooops." She stopped.

Changing the subject, Vincent asked, "What did your family down in Buenos Aires say?" He checked his speed, then switched on the radar cruise control.

"They were all elated. Everyone said how happy my mother would have been if she were still alive." Micki suddenly lost the glow that had been prevalent on her face.

Vincent reached for her hand in a comforting gesture.

Before Micki had moved in with Vincent, she told him about her mother being killed in a car crash. Micki was thirteen at the time. A year later, she left Argentina to stay with her brother, Sierra, in the United States. Sierra was a Master Sergeant in the U.S. Marines, a soon to be brother-in-law that Vincent looked forward to bonding with.

"Did you reach your father?" Vincent asked.

"No. I have to try again later." She leaned back into the seat and closed her eyes. "Turn on some music." Micki hit the recline button on the side of her seat and relaxed.

Seconds later, they were riding down I-95 South with BBD, "When Will I See You Smile Again" flowing through the speakers. This was another quality she loved about her future husband. His taste in music was unrivaled. Later on that night, Micki stood in front of the mirror in a satin, royal blue, chiffon dress. She had her hair piled up on top of her head with a few strands hanging. This hairstyle showed off her flawless neck that sported a thin, diamond choker. She knew she was filling out the Oscar De La Renta dress like nobody's business. She was spraying on Rosamor perfume when Vincent walked into the bedroom.

"Micki, you look good!" He walked toward her.

"I'm your woman; of course I look good," she smiled.

He stood behind her, softly rubbing her hips. "Why did you have the bathroom door locked when you took a shower? I told you about doing that. What if you slip and fall or something?"

Vincent's inquiry had caught her off guard. She'd meant to unlock the door after she finished doing what she had to do, but obviously she had forgotten. "Baby, relax. I guess I locked it by mistake," she lied. "Take that shirt off, 'cause it's so not related to those slacks." She pointed to his slacks. "Put on that dark brown Salvatore Ferragamo shirt I got you from New York. And you're wearing your glasses too. I hate seeing you squint to see things far off." She turned to face him. "You should just go on and have laser surgery to correct your vision."

Vincent smiled. "You like bossing me around, huh?"

"I'm good at it, right?" she giggled, rubbing his face. "I'm the boss."

"You can boss me around all you like." He kissed her then walked toward the lit walk-in closet. "But come the time when we become parents, I ain't changing no funky diapers. I'll be in The Room chilling. Besides, I let you boss me around because it's cute."

Micki whopped Vincent upside his head with a pillow. He turned around, picking up the pillow while she laughed.

"Oh, we throwing pillows now?" he said, grinning. You're safe right now. Since you're all dressed up, I'ma let you get off for now." He tossed the pillow back on the bed, then turned back into the closet.

"Baby," she giggled, You're talking crazy if you think you're not changing any diapers. You deserved to get hit in the head."

"First things first," Vincent told her. "Let's get down the aisle first, then we'll argue about who's gonna change our son's diapers later." On that note, Vincent felt the pillow bop him upside the head again.

"You mean daughter," Micki smiled as the two finished getting dressed. The two would have to argue about that later as well.

Chapter Six

"Welcome to the society of being an engaged brother," Aaron joked with his raised glass of Scotch in a toast. The two couples sat inside the Tantra Restaurant and Lounge located in Miami Beach, Florida.

"Did you enjoy those steaks, Vincent?" Aaron asked.

"Bruh, it was almost as good as Micki's cooking." Vincent had a glass of Henny in front of him.

Micki smiled and winked at Celisha.

Aaron cleared his throat. "Excuse me," he muttered. "Vincent, as a Christian, it's my obligation to share a few things with you and Micki. As you all know, I had my doubts about you when Celisha mentioned working for you. Yes, I was guilty of judging you on your past and I spoke to you up front about my feelings. Your very words were, 'A man would be careless and naïve not to be concerned about his woman working for an ex-convict.'" Aaron smiled. "That statement changed my view of you. And I am pleased that you have confessed your love for Micki, and it will please the man up above when you two tie the knot."

"Thanks, man," Vincent said.

"Celisha tells me you'll be going to church this Sunday," Aaron said.

"Church?" Micki looked at Vincent in surprise.

"Why am I not surprised that it slipped your mind to tell Micki about church?" Celisha said, shooting Vincent a look.

He shrugged his shoulders, grinning as Celisha proceeded to tell Micki just exactly how it came about that Vincent was to be at church on Sunday.

"Awww, that's so sweet." Micki rubbed Vincent's back after hearing how he had accepted Shana's request for him to visit her church. "I wish I could go too, but I have to leave for New York Friday night."

"When will you get back?" Celisha asked.

"Umm...Monday. My brother will be on leave and he's going to meet me in New York. We're coming back together."

"There's always next Sunday," Aaron replied. "Sorry, I take that back. I know this is a very special moment for you two. But no one is promised tomorrow, so we can't assume there will be a next Sunday."

Under the table, Celisha slightly tapped Aaron's foot before he started preaching. Not that she had anything against it, it's just that she didn't know how seriously he would be taken after downing that glass of Scotch. He got the hint and smoothly changed the subject.

Vincent enjoyed the positive friendship he had with Aaron. Aaron was younger at the age of twenty-nine. He was a Christian and proud that life did not have to be dull and bland. Aaron was a high end real estate agent, closing deals from low six figure homes to high eight figure luxury estates throughout South Florida.

Vincent believed his past life of crime was simply that; his past. He would never forget his past or where he came from. That statement was well known to others that rose from the hood. People in poverty were working and struggling to leave the ghetto, not stay in it. No one was poor by choice. Vincent knew his background shaped him into the man he was today. Through trial and error, he had learned about life. For him, at times, his life was an everyday struggle.

"Baby." Micki lowered her glass of Strawberry daiquiri onto the table after taking a sip. "I'll be right back. I need to use the ladies room." She kissed Vincent on his cheek.

"I'll join you as well." Celisha stood up.

When the two men were alone, they started grinning as the ladies disappeared around the corner.

"How do you suggest we pull this off? Aaron asked in a mischievous tone.

"Do you have it now?" Vincent asked.

"In my jacket. Want to see?"

"Nah." Vincent glanced over his shoulder for a second. "I've been thinking. I want to do it in a private setting."

"I can understand that. But what about the element of surprise?"

Vincent nodded with a sly grin. "You'll find out soon enough."

As planned, Vincent was later walking barefoot down the peaceful moon lit beach, hand in hand with Micki. His leather loafers were in his free hand. He and Micki were walking in one direction while Aaron, per Vincent's request, had led Celisha in the opposite direction.

"Do you miss being a flight attendant?" Vincent asked Micki.

"Not really," she shrugged. "I only did it for a year and a half. It was fun though. I didn't have much of a personal life because I was always in the air. And living out of a suitcase in different hotels got dull. Honestly, Vincent, if I hadn't met that modeling agent, I believe I would still be a flight attendant." She leaned her head on his shoulder. "I was lonely too," she whispered.

"I knew all about being lonely when I was in prison. Some nights I felt as if I would never get out. After I tried to escape, I..." he paused, looking out toward the dark ocean.

Micki stopped walking, then moved in front of him. "Talk to me, Vincent," she said, looking up into his face.

He released her hand, reaching up to caress the side of her face. She was real. Not a character in his book. He could not read her mind.

"Let's walk some more." She took his hand again.

After a few slow steps, he released her hand to slip his arm around her slender waist. He wanted her closer. "Like I was saying, about that night I tried to escape from prison. They took me to seg after I came back from the hospital. From all my cuts from the razor, it took thirty-eight staples to close all the cuts. Adrenalin is powerful, Micki. I don't even remember feeling any pain when I cut myself. I just wanted to escape the only way I knew how. Anyway, when I was placed in seg, I was at my end mentally. Failure ate me up from the inside. Well, there was this older guy I knew from the yard that was on some heart meds. Long story short, I managed to get a bunch from him." He relieved a deep sigh. "I took them, Micki. I took every single pill with the hope of never waking up. I even wrote a letter to my mom and sister and left it on the desk. I had nothing to live for, so I thought. "I woke up the next morning. I wasn't even sick, Micki. After two attempts, I couldn't even leave this earth." He chuckled. "Talk about being a failure." He shook his head at the irony and then continued. "That entire day I was silent, thinking about my life. Past, present and future. I realized that I was failing in life because I was focused on being negative. At one point of my life, I was proud to claim how I could chop cars with ease or how I could be in a new whip like the average man would buy some new shoes." Vincent thought back to how stealing cars was what landed him in prison in the first place. "Negative things don't last long. Well, I made up my mind to turn my life around. Under the bed was my rough draft of *A Hood Legend*. I now had a reason to go on...something positive."

"So you threw all your energy into your writing?" Micki asked. She had taken in each word with a bit of pain.

"Yep. I felt I needed a change in my life. And a challenge. Baby, if I didn't have my books, my time in prison would have been hard."

They walked the next few yards in silence. Their closeness spoke loudly with unheard words of their love for each other. Micki cared for his past because it was a part of him. But most importantly, she loved him for today. A man who she respected and adored. Their serene moment was broken when Vincent's cell phone started ringing.

"Hello," he answered. "Oh...okay. Peace," he ended

the call. "Baby, that was Aaron. Let's head back. He said they're heading back as well."

She handed him her wrap-up sandals then jumped up on his back. She was tempted to suck on his ear. Instead, she whispered how much she loved him and how proud she was of the man he was now, in spite of his past.

After dropping Vincent and Micki off back home, Celisha had driven back to her apartment with Aaron. Celisha knew that things between herself and Aaron was at odds end. How could she explain why she felt uncomfortable around her soon to be husband?

"I think I might need to spend the night," he said, sitting on the sofa. "I don't want to catch a DWI."

"I thought you said you would go easy on the drinking, Aaron," Celisha reminded him.

He loosened his tie. "I'm happy for Vincent and Micki," he said, ignoring her remark.

Celisha stood at the sink in the dimly lit kitchen. "So am I," she said softly as she reached for a glass in the cabinet above the sink so that she could get her some water. She had her back turned toward Aaron so she didn't see him walking up behind her.

"You look so good tonight," he whispered against her ear. His body was pressed firmly against hers. "You know how much I love you, right?"

Fidgeting with discomfort, Celisha nodded.

"You mean so much to me, Celisha." He rubbed his hands up and down her arms.

"Aaron-" Celisha started as she tried to pull away.

"Shhh," Aaron stopped her with his words. "I just wanna be close to you right now."

Celisha closed her eyes as Aaron began to touch her intimately.

"Aaron, we can't do this. It's not-"

Aaron suddenly spun her around, then placed his lips against hers. Celisha gave in to his slow and tender kisses as his hands roamed up and down her hips. Celisha fought to gain control of her urges. She knew how things would end if she kept going.

"I love you, Celisha," Aaron moaned against her neck, bound and determined to tell Celisha what she wanted to hear in order for him to get what he wanted. This was a hidden talent of his he had learned at an early age from his father who had been a pimp.

Vincent wasn't the only one who knew of the streets. Aaron had knowledge of how slick the street game could be as well. This was why he sometimes tripped on Vincent and Celisha's relationship. He knew that where there was a will there was a way, and deep inside he felt that if the day came that Vincent wanted his way with Celisha, he'd use his street mentality to get it. But for right now, it wasn't about Vincent getting what he wanted; it was about Aaron getting his.

For an instant, the thought of enticing the woman he loved into the sin of fornication crossed his mind, but in an instant it was gone.

"Aaron," Celisha whispered as she continued to fight inside her mind.

"I love you so much, Celisha," was his only reply.

"I love you too, but we shouldn't be doing this." After a few more moans, Celisha finally gained control of herself. She pushed Aaron away. "No, I can't!" Celisha was stern in her tone

"What?" he suddenly shouted in an equally stern tone that startled Celisha. "What is it? You're not attracted to me anymore or something?"

"No, it's not that, it's just that I can't."

"You wasn't saying that last month," Aaron sarcastically reminded her. What's the difference between then and now?"

"We both backslid, but I repented and asked God to forgive me. I can't turn around and keep doing the same thing over and over."

Aaron wasn't trying to hear nothing about God right

about now. The so-called Christian in him had lost the battle with his flesh. "So you're just a tease, huh?" The insulting words escaped his mouth.

"Aaron, what's wrong with you? Why are you acting this way?" Celisha had never seen Aaron carry on this way before.

"Ain't nothing wrong with me. Maybe except for the fact that I ain't Vincent. Because you know it's all about Vincent. I bet if it was him standing here you would-"

"How can you even think that, let alone say it?" Celisha shouted on the verge of tears. "Look, I think maybe you've had too much to drink."

"No, I think I've had too much of you and your games." Aaron snatched up his car keys. "I'm out!"

Before Celisha could even find the words to speak to her fiancé, he was out the door, slamming it behind him. Celisha looked down at her engagement ring wondering, if now, a wedding band would ever follow.

Chapter Seven

Micki stood at the dresser putting her jewelry away. Vincent was behind her in bed reading a *Faithful Sister Magazine.* Micki was surprised to see him reading the magazine, reason being, it had a small religious concept. It was her magazine that she had left out in the open. Just as she turned around to ask if he was enjoying the magazine, her attention was halted. At the foot of the bed was the tiger print shoe box. The only time they broke them out was when they were going to get intimate. Vincent had a foot fetish indeed.

"Um, Vincent," she pointed at the box. "Why do you have that box out? You know we're not doing anything until our honeymoon, remember?" She placed a hand on her hip and moved one foot forward.

He slowly lowered the magazine until only his eyes showed. "Yeah, I know. I just want to see you in them tonight." He closed the magazine, placing it by the lamp next to the digital picture frame.

"Vincent, I'm going to bed. I'm not messing with your butt tonight, and plus..." She paused, folded her arms and frowned. She remembered that he was going to get her back for throwing the pillow at him. Sure they were grown, but their little games were a part of their love. She knew he was up to something. She could see it in his eyes.

"Are you going to put them on or not?" He did his best to keep a serious face.

"No, I'm not." She unfolded her arms, walking toward the bed. "We're going to bed, Vincent." She picked up the shoe box. "So you might as well..." Her words trailed off as she looked at the box curiously.

"This box is empty. It's too light." She shook the box and heard a faint rattle. "Okay, I know you're up to something." She moved the shoe box to cradle it in her arm. She took the top off. No shoes, just the white paper that lined the shoe box. When she moved, something slid in the box under the bunched up paper. She looked at him suspiciously.

"What?" he grinned. "Why are you looking at me all crazy?"

"Where are my shoes and what's in the box?"

Vincent reached for the remote. First he dimmed the lights to a real low setting, then filled the bedroom with some music. Maxwell's "Fortunate" filled their ears.

"Vincent," she reached inside the box. "Don't make me act a fool up in here so-"

She gasped, dropping the shoe box. In her hands was a small, black, Tiffany box. She stood motionless with a shocked look on her face. The Tiffany box was clutched against her heart.

Vincent propped up on the pillow. "Open it, baby."

"Wha...what is this?" She was still in shock.

"Open the box and find out." She shook her head side to side. "Open the box, Micki,"

Again, she shook her head. Vincent didn't have his glasses on, and plus the lighting was low and red. He squinted briefly and saw that she had tears sliding down her beautiful face. She was shaken up. This was not the reaction he had expected. Again, he told her to open the box and again she shook her head. He started to get out of the bed, but then she moved. She crawled in the bed, clutching the box with a tight grip. He sat up hugging and rocking her slowly. She cried softly. Slowly he pried her grip from the box. She was hugging him tightly as she watched him open the box.

"I love you, Micki," he said intimately. "I'm fortunate to have you in my life." Through tears, she watched him remove the two carat rhombus diamond set in a platinum band. Her sobs turned heavy as he slid the engagement ring on her left hand.

"You're all the woman I need, baby," he spoke softly against her ear. "There's no me without you, Micki."

She cried into his chest, clinging to him. "It's beautiful, Vincent. It's…"

"Yours, baby." He ran his fingers through her hair.

"I love you," she sobbed, wiping her tear streaked face on his chest.

There was a brief two seconds of silence when the song ended. Next, Jodeci's, "Cry For You" began to play. Caught up in the moment, Vincent looked into Micki's eyes and could tell what was on her mind; what she wanted to happen next.

"But what about waiting?" he asked her.

She thought for a moment and then replied, "We'll start tomorrow."

Micki was leaving for New York today. Her trip would be the longest she would be away from Vincent since moving in with him. She managed to hold her tears when she left on the first class flight to New York. She was missing him before the plane even left the airport.

Without her knowing, Vincent had slipped three scented handwritten love letters into her tote bag. She would open one for each night that she was away. Each day he was learning he was good at a new subject…loving his woman and not just making love to her.

Vincent's weekend was filled with work. Two hours after leaving Micki at the airport, he was on I-95 North with Celisha. He had a mini book tour at a bookstore in West Palm Beach where he patiently signed sixty-eight copies of his book. After leaving the bookstore, they headed for a trip to Tallahassee. He was scheduled for a book signing at two black owned bookstores that would take up much of the day.

Vincent drove nonstop, only stopping for gas. Reaching Tallahassee, they checked into their reserved rooms at the Hilton. Vincent ordered a pizza and shared it with Celisha in her room. She made sure he knew what time he needed to get up the next day and urged him to go to his room to get some sleep. It wasn't even nine o'clock when Vincent had taken a shower then crashed out on the bed.

Saturday came too quickly for Vincent. Proving her worth, Celisha had him dressed and alert at the first book signing near the campus of Florida State University. The majority of his supporters that showed up were young, college women. He stopped counting after signing the sixtieth copy of his latest novel.

The second book signing ranged from supporters young to old. Pictures were taken and hugs were given, but most importantly, books were sold.

By 10:40 p.m., Vincent was back home. Celisha informed him that the visit to Shana's church was all set. She planned to go as well, bringing along her aunt and Aaron, who she invited as a make-up gesture. Vincent assured her that he would be up and ready. He'd promised the little girl, and this was a promise he planned to keep.

His crib felt empty without Micki's presence. Even with Rex and Rocky D, he still felt alone. He was unable to fall asleep after restlessly tossing and turning. For the last couple of times he'd tried to enter the bathroom while Micki was in there, he'd found the door locked. Although he didn't make a big deal about it, for some reason he now couldn't get it off of his mind. Micki's funny actions of locking the bathroom door had him feeling uneasy.

Jumping from the bed, he later found himself in the lit bathroom. He avoided looking into the mirror at himself. He felt stupid for what he was about to do. For what he was about to look for. *Micki is not on drugs*, he told himself. That thought held no weight when he started searching through her cosmetics. He went through everything with guilt pressing down on him. He found nothing. No drugs, no pills, no type of drug paraphernalia. He was wrong. For the first time in his life, he was glad to be wrong. He felt bad about going through Micki's things, but reasoned that his actions proved that he cared about her?

While putting things back in place under the sink, he knocked a pack of toilet paper over. Behind it, tucked in the corner, was a leather Bible. He pulled it out. It belonged to his Aunt Diane. She had come to visit him last year for a week, with her nine year old son. Vincent recalled how his little cousin fell in love with Rex and Rocky D. It came second to how he enjoyed hiding things that didn't belong to him. The missing Bible was a big issue before his aunt had left. Now it was found. He would have to remember to call or email her tomorrow to inform her of the discovery.

The next morning, Vincent was up before sunrise. He managed to shower, eat and get dressed an hour before Celisha showed up to pick him up for church. Once she did arrive, she stood at his door wearing what he sensed was a forced smile. Once they made it outside, he spoke briefly to Aaron, thanking him for feeding his dogs while he was on the road.

He'd decided that morning that he'd just follow Celisha to Shana's in his Benz CL600 since she had map quested the directions. He wanted to make sure there was plenty of room for all to ride in just the two cars, and more importantly, he knew riding in his own car would avoid an interrogation by Celisha's aunt...for now anyway.

Chapter Eight

Shana stayed with her mother and cousin in a three bedroom home near Brownsville Middle School. Shana's mother was in her mid forties and favored the thinner version of Star Jones. Since Celisha had spoken to Shana's mother over the phone, she went forward with all the introductions. Shana's mother insisted that everyone call her Claudia. Everyone accepted her hospitality.

"Mr. Manor," Claudia admired closely.

"Please," Vincent smiled, "you may call me Vincent." Out of the corner of his eye, he saw Celisha's Aunt Faye nodding her head approvingly. Why did he feel she was waiting for him to say or do something wrong? She had already given his kitted up big-bodied coupe a stern disapproving look.

"Okay, Vincent," Claudia spoke. "My daughter will be downstairs in a few minutes. My niece is finishing her hair." She sat in a black cloth recliner facing her four guests who sat in the living room on the matching sofa. "Your personal assistant...whom I see is more of a friend," Claudia smiled as she nodded at Celisha, "has told me a few remarkable things about you, Vincent. I did the rest of my homework on you by going online. And, Vincent, I must say you have been blessed. I want to personally thank you for granting Shana's request. She has been talking about this day all week long. She's very happy today because of you, Vincent. I hope what you're doing for Shana hasn't caused any trouble with your book tour."

"No, ma'am, none at all," Vincent assured her.

Claudia smiled. "Before we leave, I need to share

something with you all. It's about Shana. You will have to understand that my baby is innocent. Her dilemma has not caused my faith to waver with God. I don't' mean to be rude," she paused, "but if you should feel different about my daughter after I tell you her issue, then I'm sure you can find your way out." Claudia took a breath before she continued. "My daughter has AIDS."

Sympathy covered Celisha's face while Aaron shifted nervously. Aunt Faye murmured a quick, silent prayer. Vincent was expressionless.

"Shana is fully aware of her sickness and it hasn't been easy for her. She was exposed to the disease by-"

"Momma, I'm ready!" Shana appeared at the top of the stairs in her Sunday best. Her smile conquered any pity that was held by anyone in the room.

Vincent came to his feet abruptly. "Your chariot awaits you, Princess Shana."

"See, Momma! I knew he would come." Shana's smile and voice was working on everyone's emotions.

Vincent noticed how thin she was. It was hard not to feel saddened. To ignore the hurt, he focused in on her smile. A smile she wore because of him. He took the honor of introducing Shana to Celisha's aunt and Aaron. They both greeted her without an ounce of stigma.

"Did you put your clothes up, Shana?" her mother asked her.

"Yes, ma'am." She was still smiling ear to ear, acting shy.

When Shana's cousin came down, another round of introductions were made. Her name was Takeitha. She was tall and slender, with her hair braided in a hip, up-to-date style. She held a brief conversation with Vincent and thanked him for what he was doing. She mentioned that she was a student at Miami Dade Community College taking classes to become a registered nurse. After the brief chit-chat, it was time to go to church.

Claudia elected to sit in the back seat with her niece

while Shana rode shotgun. Her daughter was acting like it was Christmas Day as Vincent started up the vehicle. He allowed Shana to press the button to open the sunroof. Along the way, he explained every function inside his car and answered all of her questions.

"How fast can this car go?" Shana asked.

Vincent grinned. "I'm not sure of the top speed. But one time I hit one-eighty nine."

"Whoa! That's fast! I like this car. It's pretty."

"Just like you," Vincent replied.

In Celisha's SUV, Aunt Faye and Aaron voiced how surprised they were by Vincent's actions toward Shana. Celisha wasn't. She knew Vincent was the last person to ever place judgment on anybody as he'd had to deal with it most of his life.

"Vincent's a nice young man," Aunt Faye admitted. She still had her doubts though.

"I wonder how Shana was exposed to AIDS," Aaron said.

No one wanted to assume anything, so no one even dared to vocalize their theory.

Twenty minutes later, they were all inside the packed church. Shana sat next to Vincent on his right, along with her mother and Celisha's aunt. Celisha and Aaron were to his left, along with Claudia's niece.

Five minutes later, the choir came marching in. They split in two and moved through the three aisles. The entire congregation was on their feet clapping as the joyful voices sang praises. Vincent was filled with pleasant memories. He remembered his days of being a member of the junior choir, singing as a tenor. He knew a white lie was told about his singing abilities after he once sung a solo. The deep embarrassment he felt when holding that microphone left him scarred for life. He would never again be encouraged to sing.

He used to enjoy choir rehearsal and being in church. It was fun. But unfortunately, he had no relationship with God. In eighth grade, he was drinking forty ounces of Old English beer before school, with his best friend. Friday and Saturday nights belonged to the clubs and promiscuous girls. He only thought of church when he was in church. Deep down, he knew he had lived a lie. He wondered how many people around him were lost. Living a lie.

He glanced down at Shana. She was singing at the top of her lungs with the choir. A beautiful, dying little girl. Why? Situations like Shana's had him questioning life and God. What was the reason for Shana to have AIDS? What purpose would it serve? His life was full of sin. Even now, with Micki. He thought of his younger days. Days of foolishly having unsafe sex with women, and yet he was STD free. He had many questions but was too shallow to sincerely read the Bible.

The choir marched into the lit retro choir stand behind the altar. They sung two more hymns before the congregation was asked to be seated. The services moved along smoothly. Announcements were made, followed by one of the deacons reminding the congregation of next month's revival. Another hymn was sung before the preacher moved up behind the glossy wooden podium. He smiled at his congregation of four hundred strong, as a deaconess handed him a glass of iced water. There was silence as he sipped the water and the choir sat down behind him.

"Let us bow our heads, saints," he began. "O' heavenly Father, we come before you today asking for peace and acceptance of our fallibility. We ask that you pull us in when we open the door for you. Welcome us into your grace and everlasting love. I pray that you work through me. Guide me. Use me, O', Lord. For none is greater nor higher than you. Through Jesus name I pray, let the church say, 'Amen'."

"Amen," the entire congregation replied.

"Good morning, brothers and sisters. And blessed are the little ones," the preacher said, scanning the familiar and unknown faces in front of him. "To those of you that are visitors, I welcome you to God's house. My name is Reverend Jenkins and I love the Lord," he smiled. "Church, before I get into the word today, I want each of you to ask yourself if you really understand the meaning of knowing God. See, I know some of you know of God. But do you know Him in your life?" He scanned the many faces, with his hands bracing the edges of the altar.

A chorus of "Amens" and "Preach ons!" sounded from the congregation.

"Let me clear it up for you," Reverend Jenkins said. "See, I know of the mayor of Miami. I know of the governor of this state. I know of T.D. Jakes. I know of Big Shaq on the basketball court. I know of them all. Some of you know your landlord, the bill collectors and you know the friends that sometimes let you down...or you might let them down." He smiled as a murmur rose from the congregation.

"Now stick with me, church. See, knowing of God is not the same as knowing and having Him in your life. I know my wife and kids. They are in my life. I have a bond with them and it's deep. You see my point? I know of T.D. Jakes but I don't know him. Sadly, some of you place God in that first stage. You know His name, but you know nothing about Him. You know nothing of His forgiving mercy. His love. His truth. His laws. His promise of forgiveness. You can't know these things without Him in your life. Just knowing of God will not get you in heaven. Just as my knowing of the mayor will not get me out of a speeding ticket." He laughed.

"See, our relationship with God needs to be deeper," he continued. "Don't have a limited knowledge of God. Have Him in your life completely. Some of you are lost. And I'll tell you today, this is the place to be found. We don't deal with lost and found cell phones and stuff like that up in God's house. We deal with lost and found souls! Having God in your life is not hard, people," he said sincerely. "We can reach this through Jesus.

Blessed are they which do hunger and thirst after right-
eousness for they shall be filled," he quoted St. Matthew
5:6. "The Lord pointed out the difference of one knowing
Him and those that had Him in his life." He looked down
at his Bible and read. "Not everyone that saith unto me,
Lord Lord, shall enter into the kingdom of heaven. But
he that doeth the will of my Father...which is...in heav-
en," he then went into his sermon, preaching from St.
Matthew chapter 7 verses 21-27.

Vincent absorbed every word. He feared that he was
lost, and now it had just been confirmed. His life was
not where he wanted it, mainly his soul. His issue with
his family took a hard toll on him. His estrangement
from them was a part of his life that he was not proud
of. It started while he was in prison. With no letters, no
visits, blocks on phones and ignored letters, he felt they
didn't care. In time, he gave up on reaching out to them.
His pain came from not knowing why he was ostracized
from his family.

"Forgiveness," that was a word that Vincent needed
to get an understanding of. It had been years since he
had spoken to, or seen, his mother. It was a bitter
falling-out that left him heartbroken and confused. All
he wanted was for her to admit she was wrong for how
she treated him; to seek his true forgiveness. Suddenly,
he realized he had a greater issue. God was waiting,
waiting for him to seek forgiveness and confess his sins.
He wondered if God was missing him and still loving
him as bad as he missed and loved his mother.

Vincent was beyond stubborn when it came to him
reaching out to his mother first. In his mind, he had
done no wrong and should stand his ground. She had
driven the fence between them. A tear rolled down his
face with thoughts of his mother. Could God fix it? He
wiped his eyes, thanking her for, but not accepting the
tissue Celisha offered him.

"I'm okay," he muttered. The choir stood up to sing
a soft, slow hymn. He looked at Shana. She had her

head down...tears streaking her face. "Why are you crying, Shana?" he asked her.

She looked up, lips quivering. "Because you're sad."

Her words touched Vincent. Reaching for the tissue that Celisha had offered, he used it to wipe Shana's tears away. "If me being sad makes you cry, then I won't be sad anymore."

"Promise, Vincent?" she sniffled.

"Promise."

Shana smiled.

After service, Celisha was starved. Vincent suggested Hardaway's House of Wings on Grand Avenue and asked Claudia if they'd all like to join them. The invitation was accepted and they headed for the restaurant.

Vincent had to nearly beg Claudia to allow him to pay for their meals. In the end, Claudia gave in. Everyone enjoyed the food, along with the sermon still on their minds.

Later, out in the parking lot of the restaurant, Aunt Faye exchanged numbers with Claudia. Aunt Faye wanted to invite her and Shana to her church in return. Aaron, Aunt Faye and Celisha said their goodbyes and headed off on their own.

"Do you need me to run you anywhere?" Vincent glanced at Claudia in the rearview mirror as he drove.

"I can't impose on you, Vincent," she said from the back seat.

"Today is Sunday. I don't have anything planned," he said. "Really, I'm free."

"Well, I do need to do some grocery shopping," Claudia confessed, and on that note, Vincent took her to the grocery store of her choice.

Vincent was enjoying his time with Shana. Walking with her down the aisles in the grocery store had him contemplating on being a father.

After all the shopping was done, Vincent returned to Shana's house and helped carry in the groceries.

"Vincent," Claudia said, "thank you for your kindness today."

Vincent was seated at the kitchen table with his tailored, single-breasted jacket on the back of the chair. Claudia had just put away the last of the groceries while Shana was watching television with Claudia's niece.

"In truth, Claudia," he smiled, "I feel I should be the one thanking you and Shana."

Claudia folded her hands, smiling at him. "You made my baby very happy today. I don't like to talk about her issue in front of her. It makes her uncomfortable. I'm sorry I was cut off before we left. So, I'll tell you what I was going to say." Claudia took a deep breath and then spoke. "My baby was in a car accident when she was only five. A piece of flying glass struck her leg and she lost a ton of blood before help arrived. At the hospital, she was given some blood to replace what she'd lost. We had no idea the blood was HIV positive." Claudia paused. "When she started getting sick, it was too deep into its stages. Vincent, it's been hard. She started coming home from school crying. Said the other kids were picking on her. Didn't want to sit near her or play with her. I tried to help. The teachers couldn't do much and my baby kept coming home in tears. One day I asked if she wanted a teacher to home school her. Vincent, her smile told me what I needed to do. So, yes, I took her out of school." She looked up to the ceiling, closing her eyes. "My baby will be leaving me soon."

"I'm sorry to hear that," Vincent consoled her. "Um, I assume her list of friends is to a minimum."

Claudia slowly nodded her head up and down. "My niece helps out a lot. If Shana goes out, it's with my niece."

Vincent thought for a minute. "Has Shana ever been to the zoo?"

Claudia pondered a few seconds. "No. She had a field trip planned with her class, but she was taken out of school before she had the chance to go."

"Well, if it's okay with you, I'd like to change that,"

he smiled warmly.

"Vincent, Shana will be attached to you if you spend another second with her. I know you are a very busy man. I don't want any new sorrow in her life. I hope you can understand that."

"Without a doubt, Claudia. I wouldn't dare tease Shana with my friendship. One that I offer for a lifetime. So, how about the zoo?"

Claudia nodded. She had prayed for an angel to give Shana a bit of peace. In her heart today, she felt as though her prayers were heard and answered. Claudia and Vincent turned at the sound of Shana running down the stairs. She came into the kitchen wearing a pink and white short set.

"You're still here?" She halted to a stop when she saw Vincent.

He smiled. "Yep. Hey, do you know what B.F.F. stands for, Shana?"

"Yes, sir," she nodded. "It means best friends forever," she smiled.

"Do you have one?"

She lowered her head, looking sad. "No, sir." She sounded heartbroken.

Vincent slid back from the table then walked toward Shana. He tenderly lifted up her face. "I made a promise to you in church, remember?"

"Yes, sir."

"Okay, if I can't be sad, then you can't be sad. And besides, why are you looking sad when you now have a B.F.F.?"

"Who?"

"Me." He held his arms out.

"Really?" she perked up instantly.

"Yep. And to start off our new friendship, I'm taking you to the zoo."

Shana jumped and hugged Vincent. "Thank you! Can my cousin Takeitha come too?" she asked, referring to Claudia's niece.

"I don't see why not," Vincent replied as they immediately made plans for a trip to the zoo, and that very next morning, before Micki and her brother were to return from New York, Vincent fulfilled yet another promise to the little girl.

Chapter Nine

"How was New York?" Celisha was out by the pool with Micki, lounging on the shaded alabaster white chaise lounge.

"Crowded, loud, hectic and stuffy," Micki answered. "Same as usual." The two chuckled. "I'm never moving back there." Micki was sitting up on the chaise lounge filing her fingernails. Both women were wearing two-piece designer bikinis. On the wicker table between them was a pitcher of lemonade.

"How long has Vincent been in The Room?" Celisha pushed her tinted shades up on her head.

"Since nine this morning." Micki paused to blow dust from her nails. "That short story he's writing for that anthology is really a challenge for him. It's like he would have felt defeated if he didn't write it." She went back to filing her nails. "I just hope he doesn't push himself too hard. What do you think?" She laid the file down, looking at Celisha.

"Don't underestimate your man, Micki. I'm sure he'll be fine. He takes writing like no other author I've ever dealt with and you see how serious he is about it. Have you read any of it yet?" Celisha reached for her glass of lemonade and sipped through the straw.

"Not yet," Micki said, adjusting her bikini top. "So, how did church go? I really haven't had the chance to talk to Vincent since I've gotten back."

"It was special, Micki. Vincent wore that nice Steve Harvey suit you bought him."

"The fedora too?" Micki asked smiling.

"No," Celisha grinned. "And yes he wore his glasses. Aaron and my aunt Faye went too." There was a sad tone in Celisha's voice." Celisha placed her drink back on the coaster.

"What?" Micki asked

Celisha told Micki about Shana having AIDS. A strange look appeared on Micki's face that went unnoticed by Celisha. It made Micki uneasy to hear Shana's issue. Right now she needed some alone time in the bathroom, in secret, behind a locked door. She snapped out of her mental uneasiness when Celisha asked about a wedding date.

"Oh, um..." Micki stammered, caught off guard. "I'm thinking about July. I haven't spoken to Vincent about it yet."

"Oh, when would he like to get married?"

"If it means us being intimate again, Yesterday," Micki laughed. "I have to admit myself, though, I miss making love to him," she said, unsmiling. "I admire how you and Aaron are holding out as well."

Celisha became pensive, sliding her shades down over her eyes. She crossed her arms. Her mind was back to last month. A late night visit from Aaron had turned into a deep regret. A long heavy wet kiss and intimate touching ended with regrets.

"Is something wrong, Celisha?" Micki asked, noticing Celisha's sudden change in behavior.

"Micki...I'm not perfect," Celisha said stoically.

"I didn't-"

Celisha held up her palm. "Please," she said, "let me explain." She sat up and faced Micki, taking her shades off. "Um, Micki, last month things went too far and Aaron and I had sex."

Micki was taken aback, unable to find anything to say. She had assumed that temptation was not an obstacle for Celisha, with her being a practicing Christian and all.

Celisha's ringing cell phone ended the awkward moment that came as a relief to both. The call was an excuse for Celisha to end both her chat and visit with

Micki altogether. She stood up tying a voila shamrock green sarong around her waist and shapely hips.

"Call me later, okay?" Micki said as Celisha left. To ease her mind, Micki slid out of her platform wedges and dove into the pool.

Hours later, Vincent was being fed by his woman. The smell of his favorite meal had pulled him from The Room; buttered yeast rolls, macaroni and cheese and fried pork chops. He was at the kitchen table with Micki sitting sideways in his lap. Literally feeding him. It was an intimate act she enjoyed doing.

"You're my big spoiled baby." She slid the fork from his mouth. "All mines."

He chewed while rubbing her jean covered thighs. "Where's your brother?"

"At the bowling alley. He wanted to drive your Benz and I said no." She slid another piece of pork chop into his mouth. "Are you going back into The Room tonight?"

"Nah," he said after chewing and swallowing. "Why, what's up?"

"Nothing." She broke off a piece of buttered roll and fed it to him. "Celisha told me what you did for that little girl. Taking her to the zoo. That was very thoughtful." She held a spoonful of macaroni and cheese in front of him.

He opened his mouth. After he swallowed she held the glass of cranberry juice to his lips. This was devoted love at its best.

"I can't wait for you to meet Shana. She's-" Vincent started.

"Here, baby." Micki cut him off as she fed him more macaroni and cheese. "Celisha told me all about her. How's the story going?" Any talk of his books would deaden any other topic. She knew her man.

"I think I really surprised myself this time."

"I can't wait to read it. Better yet, how about you read it to me? I know it's challenging since it's like a new genre for you."

Micki fed Vincent a couple more bites before he asked her, "Have you circled a date yet?"

She nodded yes as she continued feeding him a piece of roll. "How about early July? Yes, in the month of your birthday and before it." She waited for him to swallow.

"Why July, and why you say that?" He looked at her puzzled.

"Because, silly," she giggled." If you ever forget our anniversary, you can cancel any type of birthday party."

He kissed her neck. "I'll never forget our wedding date because I'll be reminded of it daily."

"How?"

Vincent grinned. "Because you're gonna get the date...and my name tattooed on you."

"Are you serious?" She smiled, slipping her arms around his neck.

He gave her a serious look.

"Well, since it's like that, I want my name on you too."

"Not a problem."

"And only my eyes will ever see it." She smacked him on the butt.

"Say what? Girl, I'm not getting no tattoo on my butt. That's suspect," he frowned.

"I'm not talking about your butt." She moved her lips to his ear and whispered where she wanted her name.

"Girl, that's crazy!"

She burst out laughing, clinging to his neck. "I'm just playing, boy. I know Mr. Masterpiece is too sensitive for a needle."

"That's not even close to being funny," he replied. "Might have to spank you for that."

"Anytime and anyplace." She paused, caressing his bald head. "Te quiero, Vincent."

"Te Quiero too."

"I'll stop my birth control pills if you want me to." Micki was snuggled up under Vincent in their bed. "I don't want no type of issues when we start on our family in July," she added.

"That's a good idea," he said, finger combing her hair. "This time next year, little Vincent Junior will be in our arms."

"We're having a girl. I don't know what you're talking about," she corrected him.

"Boy."

"Girl." She raised up on her side. "Wanna bet? Since you're so confident that your soldiers will produce a boy, why don't you make a bet?"

"Who you talking to?"

"That owl," she giggled. "What's up?" She laid her head on his pillow rubbing his chest.

"Okay...let me think of a good wager." He ran a few ideas through his mind. "Check this out; when my boy is born," he smiled, "I will be free of having to change any diapers for umm...a year."

"Boy!" She smacked his chest. "You done bumped your head. Talking about a year! No...I'll bet you six months." She raised back to her side.

"Seven."

"No, I said six, Vincent."

"...Six and a half."

"Five!"

"Okay, okay. I'll take six," Vincent laughed. "Now what's your bet?"

"I'll take the same. When, not if, but when your first born is a girl...Daddy will be on diaper duty."

"Bet locked," he said.

"You are going to lose," she lowered her lips to his.

"Vincent Manor never loses," he assured her, then sealed the deal with a kiss to her nose.

Chapter Ten

"Hello, Aaron." Celisha closed her door and Aaron stepped inside her apartment. "You're late." Her tone was neutral.

"I'm sorry." Aaron stood by the sofa. "I had a last minute deal that needed closing."

"You can sit down." Celisha gestured for him to sit on the couch.

Aaron sat down, avoiding eye contact with his fiancé.

"What's going on with us, Aaron?" Celisha sat down in the chair across from him.

"What are you talking about?" He attempted to act nonchalant, even though he, too, had noticed how awkward things had been between them since the night they slipped up.

"Aaron!" She raised her soft voice. "I'm sorry." She looked at him, lowering her tone. "I'm just tired of putting on a front for others that things are fine between us. I'm trying to love you, Aaron, but you-"

"I got needs, Celisha," he interrupted angrily.

She stared at him. She had seen this painful side of him before. She knew he had needs; needs that he had controlled until last month. Celisha had realized it was a mistake. But for Aaron, he wanted to keep making the mistake over and over. His frustration mounted as Celisha refused to give in.

"Aaron," she said, now speaking calmly again, "we made a mistake that night. We have to wait until we get married. So-"

"No!" He stood up. "You think your sex is...is based on our marriage, Celisha? I didn't want to wait. I got needs now, and you...you keep tripping." He threw his arms up in the air.

"Aaron!"

"Why the late night calls? Huh, you a tease now? You can't sit there and say you didn't enjoy what we did that night. We did it more than once, and you expected me not to want more? I'm a man. I'm your man; your man who has needs that-"

This time Celisha cut him off. "Aaron, I'm pregnant!"

Aaron's mouth fell open. "What did you say?"

"I'm pregnant," she repeated. "My doctor confirmed it today."

"Wait!" He started pacing in front of her. "How much?"

She stared at him. "I'm three weeks pregnant."

"No," he said. "How much will an abortion cost?"

Celisha stood up, facing him. "Are you serious?" She feigned a slight chuckle, thinking that he couldn't possibly be serious.

He sighed angrily. "Yes, I'm serious. You just said what we did was a mistake, so let's take care of this mistake."

"Get out!" Celisha yelled as she pointed to the door. Tears began to fill her eyes.

Aaron glared at her. "If I walk out that door, I'm never coming back."

"Get out!" she screamed again.

He picked up his car keys. "If you decide to have this...this baby, you can expect my lawyer to seek a blood test to deter-"

Aaron's words were ended with a slap from Celisha right across his face. He smiled at her as he rubbed his jaw.

"I swear to God, if you don't get out of my house now..."

He looked into Celisha's eyes and could tell she was hurting. "Maybe your ex jailbird of a boss should take a test too. But in the meantime, I'll be glad to leave."

Celisha sat in her dark living room in tears. "Why?" she cried out loud. "Why am I being punished?" Celisha shook her head as she thought about how she was supposed to be a Christian, yet she was about to have a baby without a husband. Did this cause her to be a sinner? A lie is a sin. No sin is greater than the other. But Celisha's night of sin would have a permanent reminder. Even through her tears and pain, she would view her baby as a blessing. Why shouldn't she?

Vincent was a light sleeper, so his eyes popped open when Micki slowly slid out of bed. It was now a few minutes past midnight. They had once again defeated temptation and refrained from having sex. Vincent waited a few seconds, then slid out of the bed himself. Out in the dark hallway he bumped into Rocky D. He paused when he reached the bathroom. He wondered why Micki hadn't used the bathroom in their bedroom? He placed his ear close to the door, heart pounding.

Vincent could hear Micki riffling under the sink. Apparently she didn't find what she was looking for when he heard her sigh with disappointment. He suddenly wondered if she would recognize anything out of place from his search. It didn't feel right to be snooping on her behind her back. No matter how hard he tried to justify his actions, Vincent knew he was wrong, but still, the unknown was getting the best of him, so when he heard the toilet flush, he stood his ground outside the bathroom door, in wait of Micki. He wasn't going to slip back into bed without getting answers.

Micki turned the bathroom light out as she opened the door.

"What were you looking for?" Vincent asked in a tone that demanded an answer.

Micki shrieked, jumping back into the dark bathroom. She immediately turned the light back on and looked at Vincent. "Boy!" she vented. "Why are you standing in the middle of the hall, in the dark? You scared the crap out of me." As she looked at him, she started frowning. "Wait. How do you know I was looking for something, Vincent?"

"'Cause I got ears." He refused to back down. "Now answer my question."

"I'm not answering nothing!" She turned to slam the door in his face but he stopped it with his opened hand.

Vincent pushed inside the bathroom. "Don't play with me, Micki!" He had her backed up against the wall. He was pleased to see anger in her eyes and not fear. If it had been the latter, he would have eased up. He never wanted Micki to think that he would ever hurt her.

"I'm not talking to you," she snapped, folding her arms, looking up at him.

"What are you hiding from me, Micki? You think I haven't been paying attention to this locked bathroom door thing you got going on?"

She turned her head.

"Look at me." He turned her chin tenderly. "Micki, I love you. No secrets should be between us, baby." He placed his hands on her shoulders. "Talk to me, baby. I'm not dropping this until you tell me what's been going on here...behind my back." His shoulders sagged. She closed her eyes, leaning her head back against the wall. "Talk to me. Don't force me to assume anything."

She opened her eyes. "Has anyone been in this house while I was in New York?"

"No, and what does it have to do with now?"

Micki reached up to rub his forearms. "Where's the Bible, Vincent? I left it behind the toilet paper and now it's not-"

"You hid that Bible?" he exclaimed.

She nodded. "Where is it?"

"You were looking for the Bible? Are you telling me that?"

"Yes, Vincent. I've been reading and praying. Now where is it?"

Vincent was dumbfounded. He released her shoulders and sat on the closed toilet lid. Micki stepped toward him, embracing his head into her stomach. He hugged her waist.

"I'll explain," she whispered while grabbing his hands and leading him back to their bedroom. And for the next half hour, she did just that; explain. She explained how lately she'd been drawn to the Bible and God's word and how she had been learning how to commune with God.

"Why did you hide this from me? I don't understand." Vincent was sitting up in the bed with Micki.

"Because I didn't want you to judge me."

"Baby," he took her hand in his, "why would you think that? Of all people, how can I judge anyone? You had me thinking you were on drugs or something, and the whole time you were talking to God."

"I'm sorry." Micki slid closer to him and came clean. She told him how the car accident had left her mother in a coma for six days before she died. "My family was deeply religious, Vincent. I was young and I loved my mother madly. I was at her side reading the Vulgate."

"Vulgate? What's that?"

"The Latin version of the Bible. Like I was saying...I turned into a young preacher. It was all for show. I never really had a real relationship with God. I did it for the wrong reasons. When my mother died, I turned my back on religion. Like many, I never read the entire Bible. When I found your aunt's Bible in the sunroom, I started reading it again. I wanted to know why...why my mother died."

Vincent got up and went and retrieved the Bible he had planned on sending back to his aunt. "Here's what you were looking for." He handed it to Micki as he sat back down on the bed.

She opened the Bible to St. Matthew chapter 6. "Read verse one through eight and you'll see why I pray in secret." She pointed as Vincent read. When he was done, he looked at her. She believed. She believed in God's word. "I've been praying for us, Vincent," she said softly.

"Baby, I don't know what to say. I don't know God

like I need to, but I know it's not wise to be ashamed to love Him." He flipped through the Bible. "Listen to this." He began to read. "Unto thee, O Lord, do I lift up my soul. O my God, I trust in thee, let me not be ashamed. Let not mine enemies triumph over me. Yea, let none that wait on thee be ashamed. Let them be ashamed which transgress without cause. Psalm chapter twenty-five, one through three." He looked at her.

"Do you believe in God? Do you believe in heaven?" she asked him.

Vincent chewed his lips briefly. "Let's go to church this Sunday."

"Really?" Micki wanted to be sure she'd heard him correctly.

"Really," he said.

"Okay." She hugged him. "I love you."

"I love you the same." Slipping his arms free, he slid from the bed. "But before we do that, can we do something else together first?"

Micki gave him a suspicious look.

"Not that." He shooed away her dirty thoughts with the wave of his hand. "I want us to pray. Let's pray together. We have a lot of things to repent and confess."

Micki got down on her knees, where she joined Vincent at the side of the bed, and the two did something they'd never ever done together...pray.

Chapter Eleven

It was Sunday afternoon. Micki stood outside, next to Vincent, by the sizzling grill. After church, he had invited new friends over; his two neighbors and the South Korean married couple from across the street. Celisha, Aunt Faye, Claudia and Shana were present as well.

"Okay, pour a bit of my secret sauce on the steaks." Vincent nodded toward the grill.

Micki rolled her eyes while adding the sauce to the steaks. "Mixing A-One steak sauce and ketchup isn't a secret sauce, Chef Manor. "

"Don't hate on the chef," Vincent laughed.

Micki looked at their guests. They were all enjoying the pleasant weather and the food. She hoped Vincent's choice of music wasn't offending anyone. At the moment, the sounds of Raheem Divine's, "Woman" , was playing. Walking around the pool was Shana, heading straight for her.

"Um...Ms-" Shana started.

"You can call me Micki."

"Okay," Shana smiled. "Um...thank you for coming to my church today." She looked toward Vincent. "And you too, Vincent."

Micki looked at Shana, feeling sorry for her. Micki knew how AIDS could kill. Her older sister had died from complications from the deadly disease. It was a family secret she had never shared with Vincent, or any one for that matter. Unlike Shana's unfortunate accident, her sister had contracted the viral syndrome from drug use and prostitution.

"You're welcome, Shana," Micki replied.

"I'm glad you and Vincent got saved today."

"Are you?"

"Yes, ma'am," Shana nodded. "Now I'll have more friends in heaven when I leave."

Micki was speechless.

"I'm not afraid to die," Shana said. "I don't want to, but I'm not afraid."

"You shouldn't be, Shana," Micki finally said. "But for now, I want you to be happy. Just like Vincent, I'm your B.F.F. now too. Let's let the chef do his thing." She reached for Shana's hand as Vincent looked at them both. "Let me show you a few new things we can do with your hair."

As the two walked off, Micki's brother walked up drinking a beer. Sierra was in his late thirties with a regulation military hair cut. "What's up, brother-in-law? I see that my sister is a happy woman."

"Look who she's in love with," Vincent joked. "Hey, Sierra, man, hand me that seasoning salt." "No problem," Sierra obliged. "Hey, on another note, I thought your personal assistant was engaged."

"She is," Vincent replied.

"Well, your news must be out of date, because I just heard different."

"From who?"

"She just told me. Said the engagement was called off." Sierra shrugged. "Wouldn't tell me why though. I know women...and she's stressed out. Look at her." Sierra nodded toward the far end of the pool where Celisha was sitting alone, eyes hidden behind her shades.

"Sierra," Vincent said, removing his apron, "take over for me. I need to talk to her."

"Thought you'd never ask." Sierra took the apron and Vincent's spot behind the grill.

Vincent headed straight over to Celisha, on a mission to get the truth about exactly what was going on between her and Aaron.

A few minutes after Vincent finished talking with

Celisha, Micki sat at the kitchen table with Shana. It was then Vincent came storming in. Micki immediately noticed the anger written on his face. "Baby, what's wrong?" she asked him with concern.

"I'll be back in a few," he said, snatching up his car keys.

"Vincent-"

"I'll explain everything when I get back."

Vincent was out the door before his fiancee could say another word. He sped directly to Aaron's spacious house in Miramar without calling first. His trip wasn't wasted when he rounded the corner seeing Aaron's two cars in the driveway. Parking behind the silver Audi A8L, he exited his car, making his way toward the front door. The front door was ajar behind the completely closed screen door.

"Yo, Aaron!" Vincent rang the doorbell. No answer. He waited, pressing the doorbell twice more. He looked over his shoulder across the street. Everything was quiet. Coming up the sidewalk was two Asian women speed walking. When he turned back around, Aaron was standing in the doorway.

"What's up, bruh?" Vincent was unable to hide his anger.

"Look, man..."Aaron rubbed his face. "I know why you're probably here, and the issue I have with Celisha is my business and not yours. Matter of fact, maybe you should just-"

Vincent exploded by roughly pulling open the screen door and stepping inside, causing Aaron to stumble. They started to tussle. Aaron's body was fit, but nowhere near the prison formed body that Vincent had.

"Have you lost your mind?" Aaron was on his back with a torn shirt and a bloody lip.

Vincent sat on his chest, ready to rain blow after blow toward his face.

Aaron knew he was defeated. He remained on his back even when Vincent got up.

"Celisha is like a sister to me, Aaron. And this lame-"

He halted himself from cursing. "What's up with you? Why you dissin' her? She told me what you said."

Aaron slowly sat up rubbing his jaw.

"You ain't got nothing to say?" Vincent shouted.

Aaron lowered his head. "What can I say?" he muttered.

Vincent's cell phone rang. By its chime, he knew it was Micki. She'd been calling him repeatedly since he'd left out the house. He didn't answer. He wanted to finish his conversation at hand. "It's not what you can say. It's what you can do. What can you do to fix things between you and Celisha. Do you still love her?"

Aaron looked up with blood lightly flowing from his lip. "I...messed up, bruh."

"Answer the question."

Aaron nodded. "I do love her. Of course I do, but it's too late."

"Is that what you think? See, this is what I think. You don't seem to understand how much Celisha loves you. And if you really loved her so much, why have you been dragging out the engagement?"

Aaron moved to his feet. "Because...I was jealous of you. I thought you two had something going on when those rumors started."

"Jealous of me?" Vincent exclaimed. He looked at Aaron closely. "Man, this is crazy. Look, Celisha is an attractive woman, but I'm not attracted to her."

"I see that now." Aaron flopped down in his recliner. "Guess I look real stupid, huh?"

Vincent sat down as well. "Aaron, during all this mess, did you ever once pick up the Bible you've so enjoyed telling me about whenever you got the chance? Celisha is going to have the baby with you or without you, and I hope it's not the latter. For what it's worth, she still loves you. I made her look into my eyes and tell me how she felt before I came over here. She's hurting real bad, man. She is willing to forgive, but you got to take that first step," Vincent explained.

Aaron thought for a minute and then looked at Vincent. "Why did you bring up the Bible?"

"Micki and I got saved today."

Aaron looked at Vincent with deeper respect. For so long, he had been playing the role of a Christian, a witness, always the first to suggest folks read the Bible, and here hadn't even followed his own advice when it came to his situation. He knew he was wrong for what he had said to Celisha, and the fact that she still loved him was powerful.

"Do you think she'll take me back?" Aaron asked Vincent.

Vincent stood up. "Aaron, she has never let you go."

Chapter Twelve

Micki was ticked when Vincent finally walked through the door an hour and a half after he'd left. "Where have you been, and I know you ignored my calls, Mr. Manor!" She blocked his path with her arms folded. Rocky D stood beside her, wagging his tail.

"I'm sorry, baby," he said, circling his arms around her waist, resting his chin on top of her head. "Celisha still here?" He had noticed that her SUV was still parked out front.

"She's in the guest room." Micki unfolded her arms. "She told me about that sorry Aaron."

"Don't judge him, Micki."

Micki smacked her lips. "I know you're not taking his side, Vincent," she vented. "Because he is not," she paused when someone entered the front door. She leaned over to find Aaron standing in the doorway holding a large bouquet of long stem, red roses.

"Shhh," Vincent said. "Let's let them talk." He reached for her hand and led her outside where he apologized to his guests for his disappearance.

Once Micki and Vincent were outside, Aaron made his way to the guest room where Celisha was laying in bed with a troubled heart. She looked up when someone knocked on the door. She figured it to be Micki. She wiped her eyes, sitting up. "It's open," she said.

Aaron entered the room and closed the door behind him. Celisha stood up from the bed and was standing there speechless.

Aaron got down on one knee. "Celisha, I want to prove that I'm sorry. I know I caused you a ton of pain with my words and my actions. I'm so sorry for hurting you. I beg of you to forgive me, and take me back, please. I promise-" He paused as she reached out to tenderly touch his bruised lip.

"What happened?" she asked.

"Uh, some sense got knocked into me." He tried to smile.

"I love you, Aaron." She caressed his face. "I forgive you."

Aaron laid the flowers on the bed, then stood up. They hugged each other and started to cry. He felt blessed to have her. She silently thanked God for answering her private prayers.

"House and riches are the inheritance of fathers and a prudent wife is from the Lord," he whispered, quoting Proverbs chapter 19 verse 14.

Two weeks later, they became husband and wife.

Vincent kept his promise to be a B.F.F. to Shana. It saddened him that she would not experience the simplest of life's pleasures, so he did something about it. He rented a helicopter for two hours and she rewarded him with an endless smile. He took her out on a jet ski and on an airboat ride in the Everglades. Although it was a first for him as well, he even took her fishing.

Shana was speechless when she fed and touched two playful dolphins at Sea World. Her greatest joy came when Vincent printed one of her poems in his book.

Celisha and Micki added smiles as well by having an all girls' pajama party with Shana.

With all the fun and activities outside of Vincent's busy career schedule, the summer moved in quickly. It was time for Vincent to make Micki his wife. He was still out of touch with his mother. The burden hadn't been helped by her, by any means. It wasn't as if Vincent hadn't taken the first step to reconciliation. After she ignored his countless emails, he had given up.

Micki was his life now; his wife, whom he cherished daily. She took his name and became Micki Nicole Manor. They continued their growth in knowing God and having Him in their life. Vincent's writing was on a new level. He found a way to keep his readers hooked and in the truth of life. With Micki and Celisha's encouragement, he reached a dream that he had once given up on. He started his own publishing company. He was now his own boss!

Chapter Thirteen

"Four more months," Vincent smiled as he and Micki laid in the bed on Christmas Eve, "and my baby boy will be here."

"You mean, your baby girl will be here," Micki corrected him.

Their private bet was still going. Vincent was learning about life and love. It was all based on trust and communication. He treated his wife with respect. He did not understand how some men seeked fear from their women. Their reasoning was sad.

"Yo, my woman won't cheat on me 'cause she knows I'll beat that behind," he had heard one time too many in the jail house.

Vincent's stance was this: "My wife loves and respects me."

Life was not perfect. Vincent certainly grew tired of Micki's mood swings, but he never ignored her. They focused on never going to bed upset with each other. Some nights he would rub her belly, or feet, until she fell asleep. She enjoyed it when he read the Bible to her. Her favorite was Proverbs chapter 31.

"You'll make a great father," Micki told her husband.

"You think so?"

"Yep. Look at how you act with Shana."

"In all honesty, at first I thought I'd make a good pops too. But since I never knew my father and the issue I have with my mom, I've been having doubts lately." He paused for a moment. "What would you have done if I had tripped on you like Aaron did when Celisha told him that she was pregnant?"

"Hmm...call the hospital to see what time I could

visit you." They both laughed. Vincent's iPhone started ringing. Micki was closest to it, so she picked it up and answered it. "Hello?...For Real?...Yes...Okay, thanks!" Micki laid the phone down. "Baby, that was Celisha's aunt. Celisha just went into labor. She's at Jackson Memorial Hospital."

Vincent and Micki hurried out of the bed, got dressed, and went to the hospital.

"Because of you, Vincent," Aaron said, holding his newborn baby girl, "I now have diaper duty for eight months."

Vincent laughed at how Aaron had presented the same bet he and Micki had to Celisha.

Celisha was in the hospital bed, looking drained. Micki sat next to her, rubbing her hand.

"Don't worry, Aaron," Micki told him, "Vincent is going to lose his bet too."

"Let me see my new niece." Aunt Faye had joyful tears in her eyes as she walked over to Aaron and took the baby from his arms.

Everyone was happy for Celisha and Aaron.

"What's her name?" Micki asked Celisha.

Celisha held out her arms for her baby. "Natabia," she answered.

Everyone stood around the bed as Celisha held Natabia to her bosom. Vincent was still the funny man by whispering in Micki's ear. "Hey, think your hair is gonna look that bad when you have my son?"

"It won't make a difference," she replied. "You'll still love me!"

The New Year came with Micki on her knees in church. Vincent was with her, along with Shana and her mom.

"I'm going to be a father this year," Vincent said later while driving Shana and her mom home.

"And changing diapers for half the year too," Micki added.

Shana was silent. She understood life and death. She was happy for Micki, even though she knew her own time was short. Shana hid her tears knowing she would miss her family and her two BFFs. "I love you, Vincent. And you too, Micki."

Vincent glanced in the rearview mirror at Shana. This was the first time she had spoken those words. Shana's life was not fair. Vincent believed that some assumed that being saved would amount to the perfect, carefree life. Didn't preachers get sick? Being saved too, Vincent was acknowledging that what he read in the Bible was true. And this meant the laws were a way to live by. Was he able to love everyone? No, that was an issue that he dealt with each day. His actions were changing slowly. He found peace of mind through knowledge and prayer. Life, Vincent's life, was a journey he would take day by day.

"We love you too, Shana," Micki said, reaching back for Shana's hand.

"Sure do," Vincent added. "And keep those eyes dry and your hcart casy."

EPILOGUE
Three years later

Vincent stood under the cloudy gray sky trying to keep his promise to Shana. He was looking down at her grave. His B.F.F. had left him. He missed her smile and heartwarming giggles. She had died in her sleep after being hospitalized for phenomena. Vincent had made a promise to her before she died that he had every intention on keeping. His promise was not to be sad.

His watered eyes blinked rapidly. Carefully he laid some flowers at the grave.

"Daddy, rain coming look!"

Vincent looked down at his daughter, Vincentia, as she held his finger. "I see it, baby."

"Daddy, why you sad?"

"Daddy is not sad. He's just upset. Come on, let's go home. Say bye-bye to Shana."

Vincentia released his finger and waved. "Bye-bye, Shana. We go home now." She turned and held up her tiny arms, wanting to get picked up.

Vincent carried his daughter to the car.

"Daddy, Mommy is crying." Vincentia pointed at her mother.

Micki sat in the passenger seat wiping her eyes. She missed Shana too.

"Mommy, I'm hungry." This came from Vincentia's fraternal twin brother.

Vincent and Micki's gender bet was a tie since she had fraternal twins, Vincentia and Michael. Since Micki was now seven months pregnant...all bets were on again.

Vincent drove away from the cemetery trying his best not to be sad. When he looked in his rearview mirror at the beautiful blessings from God, he realized he had so much to be happy about. Although he hadn't had a good relationship with his parents, he was going to be the best father God would have him to be to his own children.

Before putting his eyes back on the road, both his son and daughter locked eyes with him in the rearview mirror. Each shot him a huge smile.

"Thank you, God," he mumbled, returning his eyes on the road. It had been Shana's smile that had softened his heart and moved him to start going to church, but it would be his children's smiles that would move him to live the life God had for him all along.

The End

Personal Invitation

If you have never made a decision to accept Jesus Christ as your personal Lord and Savior, God Himself extends this invitation to you. If you have not trusted Him and believed Him to be the giver of eternal life, you can do so right now. We do not know the second, the minute, the hour, the moment or day that God will come to claim us. Will you be ready? The Word of God says, *"If you confess with your mouth, Jesus is Lord, and believe in your heart that God raised Jesus from the dead, you will be saved. For it is with your heart that you believe and are justified, and it is with your mouth that you confess and are SAVED." (Romans 10:9-10 NIV).* Being saved is just that easy. It's not some formal ceremony. It is simply being obedient to the scripture above by confessing with your mouth out loud that Jesus is Lord and that God raised Jesus from the dead to cleanse away your sins. Believe in your heart and confess with your mouth the following:

"I _____ believe in my heart that Jesus is Lord. That He died at Calvary for me-for the remission of my sins-and that God raised Him from the dead."

You, my friend, are now saved. You are not the same person you were before reading this book. To God Be the Glory!

Author Contact Information

Darrell King:
www.modirty.blogspot.com
www.myspace.com/dak1968
Email: darrellking@publishedauthors.net

Tysha:
www.NovelsByTysha.com
www.myspace.com/NovelsByTysha
www.myspace.com/TyshaMichelle
Email: Tysha@NovelsByTysha.com

Michele Moore:
www.msmichelmoore.com
My space: sayupromisebooks
Email: sayupromise@hotmail.com

K'Wan:
www.kwanfoye.com
www.myspace.com/kwanfoye
Email: asoldierstory@aol.com

Victor L. Martin:
www.leonjeanpublications.com
www.myspace.com/authorVincentlmartin
Vincentl.martin@yahoo.com

E.N. Joy:
www.enjoywrites.com
www.myspace.com/enjoywrites
Email: enjoywrites@aol.com

Even Sinners Still Have Souls
Coming Soon

Kiki Swinson

Karen Williams

Tammy Fournier

Brandi Johnson

Introducing new author, Redd

ORDER FORM

End of the Rainbow Projects
P.O. Box 298238
Columbus, OH 43229

Name _____
Street Address _____
City _____
State _____ ZIP _____
Phone _____ Email _____

Even Sinners Have Souls (Noire, Chunichi…)
$15 per copy (includes shipping and handling)

Even Sinners Have Souls Too
$15 per copy (includes shipping and handling)

NUMBER OF COPIES _____ (EVEN SINNERS HAVE SOULS)
NUMBER OF COPIES _____ (EVEN SINNERS HAVE SOULS TOO)

Total Price _____

Make check or money order payable to **End of the Rainbow Projects**